"A classy bit of storytelling that combines myth, dreams, and plot complications so wily they'll rattle your synapses and tweak your sense of humor." —*Kirkus Reviews*

DEAD SOUL

"Hillerman gets the most press, but Doss mixes an equally potent brew of crime and Native American spirituality."
—*Booklist*

"Lyrical, and he gets the sardonic, macho patter between men down cold. The finale is heartfelt and unexpected, and a final confrontation stuns with its violent and confessional precision." —*Providence Journal Bulletin*

THE SHAMAN LAUGHS

"Harrowing . . . suspenseful."
—*The New York Times Book Review*

"A mystery that combines the ancient and the modern, the sacred and the profane, with grace and suspense."
—*Publishers Weekly*

THE SHAMAN SINGS

"Stunning." —*Publishers Weekly*
(Starred Review; named Best Book of the Year)

"Doss mixes an equally potent brew of crime and Native American spirituality." —*Booklist*

"Magical and tantalizing." —*New York Times Book Review*

"Gripping . . . Doss successfully blends the cutting edge of modern physics with centuries-old mysticism."
—*Rocky Mountain News*

"Doss plots like a pro . . . an encore would be welcome."
—*Kirkus Reviews*

ALSO BY JAMES D. DOSS

THREE
SISTERS

JAMES D. DOSS

St. Martin's Paperbacks

This is a work of fiction. All of the characters, organizations, and events portrayed in this novel are either products of the author's imagination or are used fictitiously.

THREE SISTERS

Copyright © 2007 by James D. Doss.
Excerpt from *Snake Dreams* copyright © 2008 by James D. Doss.

Cover photo of sky © Getty Images. Cover photo of mountains © Photocorral.com. Cover photo of woman's face © Daniel Dos Santos.

For information address St. Martin's Press, 175 Fifth Avenue, New York, NY 10010.

Library of Congress Catalog Card Number: 2007027130

ISBN: 978-1-250-30587-9

St. Martin's Press hardcover edition / November 2007
St. Martin's Paperbacks edition / October 2008

St. Martin's Paperbacks are published by St. Martin's Press, 175 Fifth Avenue, New York, NY 10010.

This book is dedicated to Lyman Mark—
Book Sleuth, Colorado Springs,
to fond memories of his mother,
Helen Randal
and to another departed friend—
Shirley Beard,
former owner of Murder by the Book in Denver.

God bless them, every one.

ACKNOWLEDGMENTS

I wish to express my thanks to
Kirk W. Doss
for helpful technical consultations.

ONE

WEST-CENTRAL COLORADO——THE
COLUMBINE RANCH

In this grassy, glacier-sculpted valley sheltered by the shining mountains, one man celebrates Thanksgiving every day of the year. Around about midnight, when he pulls the covers up to his chin, Charlie Moon is reminded of the multitude of blessings that enrich his life. Mulling over a few favorites helps him smile his way to sleep. Consider this evening's excellent selection.

Crisp, high-country air that fairly crackles with energy.

Soaring granite peaks that drip with dawn's golden honey, blush rose and crimson at twilight.

Hardly a stone's throw from his bedroom window, the rushing, murmuring, sing-me-to-sleep river—rolling along on its journey to the salty sea.

Ah—the lullaby has accomplished its soporific task.

He'll sleep like a log all night, wake up with a lumberjack's appetite, jump on whatever job needs doing, and get it done *right now*. Before the sun sets on another day, he will shoe a fractious quarter horse, arc-weld a fractured windmill axle, install a new starting motor on a John Deere tractor. In addition to these workaday skills, the resourceful man has a few other talents that come in handy from time to time. Not entirely clear? Okay, let's put it this way: On those occasions when business gets deadly serious, Mr. Moon knows how to tend to it—and he does. By doing *whatever is necessary*.

You'd expect a man like this to have plenty of friends,

and you'd be right. There's no shortage of "Howdy Charlie!" backslappers and fair-weather sweet-talkers. But really *good* friends? You never know for sure till you hit bottom, but Moon reckons he can count the ones he can count on—on the fingers of one hand. His best buddy, Scott Parris (the thumb!), is right up there at Number One. Numbers Two and Three—on account of something bad that happened here last year—are an enigmatic hound dog and a man-killing horse.

As far as close family goes, they're all gone. Well, except Aunt Daisy—his "favorite living relative."

All things considered (even Daisy), Charlie Moon is an uncommonly fortunate man.

So, is he completely satisfied in his little slice of paradise? Afraid not. Close to his heart, there is an empty spot. What the lonely man hankers for is a special *someone*. Sad to say, the ardent angler's attempts at courting the ladies mirrors his experience at pursuing the wily trout. One way or another, the best one, the keeper—the *catch of the day*— she always gets away. But Moon has neither the time nor the inclination to dwell upon unhappy thoughts. So he doesn't. Flat-out *refuses* to.

MORNING

Awakened by a pale silver glow in his window, Charlie Moon rolls out of bed, soaps up under a hot shower, slips into a lined canvas shirt, pulls on heavy over-the-calf woolen socks, faded jeans, comfortable old cowboy boots—and stomps down the stairs to get some meat frying in the iron skillet, a batch of fresh-ground coffee perking in the pot. Doesn't that smell *good*? And listen to the radio— the announcer on the *Farm and Ranch Show* is predicting an upturn in beef prices. Encouraged by the hope of turning a good profit, the stockman fortifies himself with a thick slab of sugar-cured ham, three eggs scrambled in genuine butter, a half-dozen hot-from-the-oven biscuits and two mugs of sweet black coffee. Good news, stick-to-your-ribs grub, and a double shot of caffeine—his day is off to a dandy start.

Moon steps out onto the east porch to greet the rising sun. The Indian gives each dawn a name. He stands in awed silence. Calls this one *Glorious*.

Slipping across the river, a breeze approaches to whisper a tale of snow in his ear. Not a surprise, especially during a deceptive late-winter thaw that is luring vast pastures of wildflowers into early bloom. Here in the highlands between the Misery and Buckhorn Ranges, snow is never far away. Even on the Fourth of July there's generally a dab of frosting left on the top of Sugarloaf Mountain, and foreman Pete Bushman likes to tell about a mid-June blizzard in '82 that buried his pickup right up to the windshield. While considering the chilling rumor, Moon hears a startled cloud mumble about something that's amiss. He blinks at the sun. What is this—the amber orb is caught fast on the jagged teeth of Wolf-Jaw Peak! Not to worry; it is a stellar jest. From a distance of one astronomical unit (93 million miles), the heavenly body smiles warmly upon the mortal's face.

Moon returns the smile. *Thank you, God—for everything.*

From somewhere *up yonder* booms a thunderously joyful response.

He hears this as a hearty "You're welcome, Charlie."

No, he is not superstitious. Far from it. Charlie Moon is a practical, down-to-earth, well-educated man who understands that the thunder was produced by those white-hot lightning legs tap-dancing across the Buckhorn Ballroom. Even so, over the years he has become aware of a deeper Reality, of which this flint-hard world is but a fleeting shadow—an infinitely magnificent thought in the mind of the *I Am*.

But *talking thunder*?

Certainly. The Ute has come to expect such courtesies from the Father.

TWO OF THE WOMEN IN CHARLIE
MOON'S LIFE

Some miles to the south of the Columbine—on the Southern Ute reservation—the wind also huffs and puffs, but the breath exhaled from the mouth of *Cañón del Espíritu* is not so chilly, which is a good thing, because Daisy Perika (who has buried three husbands) is older than most of the towering, pink-barked ponderosas atop Three Sisters Mesa. In addition to those ailments common to the geriatric set, the damp cold makes every joint in her body ache. Plus her toe-nails. An exaggeration? Perhaps. But this is what the lady claims and so it must be reported.

Sarah Frank (who has a crush on Charlie Moon) cannot imagine Aunt Daisy as anything but what she sees—an ever-shrinking, bent-backed, black-eyed, wrinkled old husk of a woman with a tongue sharp as a sliver of obsidian. But what does this mere slip of a girl know? Not so many winters ago, Daisy was a cheerful, slender, pretty lass who danced to thrumming guitars, sang wistful love songs, and rode her black pony bareback, thrilling to the tug of the wind in her long, dark locks. Now she spends most of her time indoors, crouched close to the warm hearth, where during the entire circle of a year a piñon fire crack-les and pops. And there, just on the other side of the Ute shaman's window pane, the harsh wilderness remains—ready to freeze the flesh, bleach the bone. There is much more to tell about this cantankerous old soul, involving cunning, conniving, self-serving schemes that cause no end of trouble for her amiable nephew, the brewing of overpriced, often dangerous potions from flora gathered near her home, plus an unwholesome liaison with the *pitukupf,* that dwarf spirit who (allegedly) lives in an aban-doned badger hole in *Cañón del Espíritu.* If all this were not enough, there is also the tribal elder's alarming tendency to—No. For the moment, enough said. When Daisy is "of a mind to," she will make herself heard. Count on it.

THE THREE SISTERS

Towering up from the eternal twilight of *Cañón del Espíritu* to dominate the austere skyline above Daisy Perika's
remote home is a miles-long mesa whose summit (unlike
those tabletop structures depicted in glossy picture post-
cards) is not flat. It is, due to a peculiar geologic history,
quite the opposite of that. Residing on its crest is a trio of
humpity bumps, the smallest dwarfing the largest man-
made structure in La Plata County and Archuleta Co. to
boot. According to a tale told by older Utes, the origin of
these sandstone formations is rooted in violence. Once
upon a time, only a few hundreds of years ago, there was a
thriving Anasazi community in the vicinity. This is a fact,
verifiable by remnants of venerable cliff-clinging ruins
and thousands of distinctive black-on-white potsherds
scattered along the canyon floor. It is also true that Old
Ones' village was destroyed by a marauding band of
thieves and murderers, but these were not necessarily
Apaches—that is a lurid tale cooked up by the Utes. The
Apaches assert that the crime was committed by a roving
gang of Navajo, who in turn blame a rowdy band of West
Texas Comanche, who point accusing fingers at the
haughty Arapahos, who attribute the atrocity to those
shifty-eyed Shoshone, who claim the thing was done by
the Utes, and so the venomous slander-snake swallows its
tail. The truth is—none of these tribes was involved.

But back to those bumps on the mesa. Not surprisingly,
the few facts have become thoroughly mixed with myth,
and Daisy Perika will tell you that the only members of the
Anasazi village who escaped (if *escape* is an appropriate
term) were a trio of young sisters who climbed a precipitous path to the top of the mesa, which in those olden days
was smooth and level enough to shoot pool on. The terrified women hoped to hide among the piñon and scrub-oak
thickets until the brutal foreigners had departed, but before
reaching the summit they were detected by a keen-eyed
warrior who alerted his comrades. While the bloodthirsty

enemy with filed-to-a-point teeth and hideously tattooed faces ascended the mesa with exultant whoops and terrifying war cries, the sisters prayed to Man-in-the-Sky to protect them. He did. They were (so Daisy's story goes) instantly turned into stone by the merciful deity. Hence, we have Three Sisters Mesa.

• • •

It is hoped that this technical information on instantaneous petrification is appreciated—in spite of the fact that Three Sisters Mesa has nothing whatever to do with those particular Three Sisters with whom the following account is concerned. This being the case, let us leave the ancient stone women atop their mesa.

We now return to the twenty-first century, where we shall (in due course) encounter the relevant trio of female siblings—Astrid, Beatrice, and Cassandra Spencer.

But first we must pay a call on Daisy Perika.

• • •

TWO

What Cassandra Saw

Hunched like an old toad in her rocking chair, eyes half shut, hands folded in her lap, knees toasting before the stone fireplace, Daisy Perika appears to be asleep. Or dead. She is neither.

Since supper, the Ute tribal elder had hardly stirred, and was very close to dozing—when she heard the patter of feet.

These particular feet belonged to Sarah Frank, the fifteen-year-old Ute-Papago orphan who had lived with Daisy for almost a year, and loved Charlie Moon for as long as she could remember. Having completed her algebra and American-history homework assignments, Sarah switched on Daisy's television, inserted a blank disc into the DVD's thin mouth, and set the controls to begin recording at one minute before the hour. The devoted viewer had every single episode of *Cassandra Sees* in her collection.

Daisy did not spend many of her precious remaining hours purchasing what the medium had to offer. On a lonely weekday morning, while the girl was away at school in Ignacio, the Ute elder might watch a talk show for a few minutes before falling asleep, and on a Friday night she would tell Sarah it was "all right if you want to turn on that *Country Music Jamboree* you like so much and watch them silly hillbillies." Though she would pretend to have no particular interest in the energetic *matukach* entertainment, Daisy waited all week for the high-stepping, foot-stomping clog dancers, thunder-chested yodelers, nimble-fingered guitar pickers, and whoopin'-it-up hoedown fiddlers whose sounds and images traveled (at the speed of light!) all the way from gritty, spit-on-the-sawdusted-floor Texas honky-tonks, pine-studded Arkansas ridges, and mist-shrouded Kentucky hollers—into her cozy parlor. Their merry exuberance would curl Daisy's mouth into a little possum grin and set the old woman's shoe toe to tappity-tapping on the floor. But no matter how good the beginning and the middle were, the end was the best part. After all the crooning about Momma, railroad trains, prison, adultery, fornication, drunkenness, theft, lies, slander, and murder were finished, the closing was invariably an old-time gospel song. *Hidden deep in the heart of every sinner is a yearning for God.* Last week, when an ancient, snowy-capped black man had called upon those angels to Swing Low in that Sweet Chariot, tears had dripped from the old woman's eyes. Daisy was ready to hitch a ride and go arolling up yonder—last stop, that unspeakably lovely mansion her Lord was preparing in His Father's House. Home at last! It could not come too soon.

Daisy raised her chin, looked over the thin girl's shoulder. "What's coming on?"

"Cassandra." Sarah was clicking through the satellite channels.

"Oh." *That's pretty good.* She turned the rocking chair to face the expensive "entertainment center" Charlie Moon had contributed, along with other furnishings for her new home.

Sarah was perched on a footstool, her face close to the television screen. She would not miss a thing.

Mr. Zig-Zag (Sarah's spotted cat) padded in from the kitchen, stretched out on the floor beside her, yawned at the flickering picture.

The broadcast began with a sooty-black screen, and an eerie strain of organ music that was the psychic's trademark. Then, on the dark electronic velvet, a bloodred script was traced by invisible pen: Cassandra Sees.

"Yes!" The girl clapped her hands.

Having had its say, the title bled away. As the last crimson drop fell into an unseen reservoir, the psychic's all-seeing eye appeared, filling the screen. Iridescent it was, and opalescent—the platter-size iris mimicking a blooming cluster of multicolored petals, turquoise blue, twilight gray, spring-grass green!

That is so cool, Sarah whispered to herself. "But I don't know how she keeps from blinking."

The enormous eye faded, Cassandra Spencer's pale, masklike face appeared. The oval countenance, at once strikingly sinister and hypnotically attractive, was framed in long locks of raven hair, artfully tucked behind her ears. The psychic's eyes were aglow with terrible secrets, arcane knowledge. They seemed to say: *We not only See; we Know.*

"Oh," Sarah breathed. "Cassandra just gives me *goose pimples.*" As she held out a skinny arm so Daisy might see the proof of this claim, her frail little frame shuddered with a delicious fear. "I wonder if she'll talk to a dead person tonight."

The Ute shaman, who was certain she talked to more ghosts and spirits in a month than this uppity young white woman had encountered in her entire lifetime, offered a "Hmmpf." But Daisy was leaning ever-so-slightly forward in her chair.

Mr. Zig-Zag, who had his own visions to pursue, drifted off to sleep.

As the psychic uttered her usual greeting, Sarah silently mouthed the words: *Dear friends . . . welcome to my home.*

Her face faded off the screen. A camera panned the walnut-paneled parlor in the star's Granite Creek mansion, sharing with the audience a cherry cupboard housing delicate bisque figurines of ballerinas on tiptoe, a miniature flock of crystal swans, a cranberry vase that held a single, gold-plated rose. Then, as an unseen technician threw a switch, viewers were transported out of the parlor-studio to a scene in the host's dining room, where several enraptured guests were seated, smiling at images of themselves on a cluster of video monitors.

"What a bunch of dopey half-wits," Daisy muttered. *You'd never get me on a dumb show like that.*

The psychic's face appeared again, the lovely lips speaking: "This evening, we deal with the controversial subject of reincarnation. Our special guest is Raman Sajhi, a citizen of India, who is touring the United States to discuss his best-selling new book—*My Five Thousand Lives.*"

Five thousand lives my hind leg! Daisy snorted at such nonsense.

Camera 3 picked up the turbaned guest's pleasant face. He responded to his host with a polite, semiprayerful gesture—delicate fingers touched at the tips, a modest bowing of the head.

Daisy Perika eyed the bespectacled foreigner with no little suspicion. "Raymond Soggy don't look a day over a half-dozen lives to me."

Sarah giggled.

Mr. Zig-Zag, who still had eight to go, dozed on.

Mr. Sajhi commenced to pitch his book with thumbnail sketches of selected previous lives. In addition to his miserable stint as a convict on Devil's Island, the poor soul had also done time as a golden carp in a Shanghai pond, an Ethiopian dung beetle, a camel (of no particular ethnicity or distinction), a wealthy rajah's hunting elephant, and a ferocious female Bengal tiger who had devoured several citizens, including a British subaltern who was a close friend of Mr. Kipling. Though a combination of jet lag, TV appearances, and signings at mall bookstores may have been contributing factors, the author reported that he was tired-to-the-bone from the hard labors of his many incarnations, the current of which was, by his meticulous calculations, appearance number four thousand nine hundred and ninety-nine.

Mr. Zig-Zag abruptly awakened, gaped his toothy mouth to whine.

During a commercial break, Sarah Frank addressed Daisy Perika: "Do you think people can really come back to live more than one time?" The girl, who had once dreamed of returning as a butterfly, glanced at the cat. "Do you think we could come back as animals?" Before the Ute elder could respond, Sarah asked: "If we could, what kind of animal would you want to be?"

Three questions too many.

Resembling a ruffled old owl, Daisy scowled at the impertinent girl. Which settled the issue.

Cassandra appeared on the screen. "Now we will discuss a particularly fascinating category of spirits—those who return for the sole purpose of communicating an important message to the living."

Daisy and Sarah watched the psychic introduce a second guest, who provided a fascinating account of how her deceased grandfather had, once upon a certain snowy night in December "nineteen-and-eighty-two," appeared by her bed and told her where to find a Havana perfectos cigar box stuffed with rare and valuable nineteenth-century coins. The box was there, of course, under the loose floorboard in the smokehouse where the old fellow had stashed it, half full of coins. But that was not all. The mournful specter had also confessed several youthful misdeeds to his astonished granddaughter—including a colorful account of how he had dealt with a Tennessee sharpster who had made a pass at his first wife. Granddad had, so he said, used a scythe to remove the unfortunate fellow's head from his shoulders. The lady explained to a rapt television audience that this was "very unsettling to hear." No one in the family had the least notion that Grandpa had been married but once, to Grandma. The fact that he had "killed his man" was of little consequence. "Back in those days in the Ozarks, that was just the way things was." The guest was about enlarge on how things was back in those days in the Ozarks, when—

With an alarming suddenness, Cassandra dropped her chin.

The psychic's eyes seemed to be gazing blankly at her knees, which were modestly concealed under a black silk skirt—or, as the many viewers assumed, at something (other than her knees) that they were *not able to see.*

"Murder." This was what Cassandra saw, and what she said.

• • •

A hundred thousand viewers (more or less) are holding their breaths.

Let us leave them in that uncomfortable state while we visit another, more sensible Cassandra Sees *fan, who is breathing approximately twelve times per minute.*

We fly over the Cochetopa Hills, the northern neck of the San Luis Valley, skim the Sangre de Cristo Mountains—halt at a location 172 miles east-by-southeast of the TV psychic's home in Granite Creek. See, down there, that isolated spot glistening in the darkness beside Interstate 25? It is the Silver Dollar Truck Stop, which, in addition to dispensing diesel fuel, provides a large restaurant for hungry truckers—where we shall find our subject.

• • •

His rig (tagged by the DEA as the "I-25 Pharmacy") was parked among some two dozen other long-haulers. The driver, a heavyset ex-con known only as Smitty by his customers from Buffalo, Wyoming, to Las Cruces, New Mexico, was seated at the sixty-foot lunch counter. Having taken delivery of Dinner No. 39, he was applying fork and knife to a hearty supper of meat loaf, mashed potatoes (with brown gravy), and Great Northern beans. Smitty had planned the run from Casper down to Albuquerque so he would be here in the Silver Dollar Restaurant, astraddle his favorite stool, staring goggled-eyed at—as he had told a friendly trucker just this morning during a quick biscuit-and-gravy breakfast in Cheyenne—"the biggest doggone TV screen I've ever seen." Smitty's taste leaned toward football and *The Simpsons* reruns, but he was to be counted among those Cassandra fans who rarely missed one of the psychic's weekly appearances. Unbeknownst to Smitty, the "friendly trucker"—who had never driven anything bigger than an F-250—had tailed him south along the interstate, and was—at this very moment—outside. Looking in. Who might this be?

An undercover DEA agent, tailing the trucker in the course of an investigation?

Some kind of stalker-pervert, harmless or otherwise?

Or, try this on for size—a hired gun, employed by another distributor to rub out the competition.

Or even a—But let us dispense with pointless speculations. Soon enough, the sinister presence on the dark side of the window will play out his hand. In the meantime, back to television land.

• • •

Cassandra's lips are moving, and those viewers who choose to may breathe again. "He's a middle-aged man," she murmurs. A long, thoughtful pause. "Reddish brown hair. Overweight."

• • •

As he chewed a mouthful of the dinner special, Smitty muttered: "Effs bess. At cuff be amos hemmygobby." *Including me.* What our amateur TV critic was attempting to say, and would have, had not the mastication of ground beef and beans impeded his enunciation, was: "Hell's bells. That could be almost anybody." *Including me.*

Which illustrates why well-mannered diners do not attempt to talk whilst eating.

• • •

The pale face on the television screen continued to describe what Cassandra Sees: "I see a man who drives a truck."

• • •

Smitty, who liked to talk back to the tube, snickered. "Well, that sure narrows it down a whole lot." From the clarity of his speech, it was apparent that he had swallowed his food, for which we may all be grateful. Moreover, he had forgotten the meat loaf, mashed potatoes, Great Northerns, et cetera that remained on his plate. Cassandra, who was hitting on all eight cylinders, had gotten the trucker's entire attention.

• • •

"There is a tattoo on his arm." The psychic breathed a heavy sigh. "A knife of some sort. And a snake." She shuddered. "And a horrible *spider.*"

• • •

This is not meant as criticism, but Smitty was one of those persons who could not do two things at once. First, his jaw dropped. Then, he glanced down at his hairy left forearm, squinted at the art form the Tenderloin-district artist had adorned it with: a medieval Italian dagger with a spotted viper wrapped around the blade, a hairy-legged tarantula crouched on the hilt. Marveling at this coincidence, he returned his attention to the television image.

• • •

Cassandra's face was frozen, except for the pretty red lips, which moved: "I see a murderer—a brutal, cold-blooded killer!"

• • •

The drug pusher shook his head. "I ain't never killed nobody!" The almost-mute remnant of his conscience begged to disagree. In his defense, he murmured: "That ol' woman I run over at that railroad crossing don't count as no murder—I didn't do that on purpose."

• • •

"I cannot make out the killer's face," the psychic whispered. "I can see only the back of his head . . . and his shoulders." She caught her breath, stiffened. "But he is about to pull the trigger!"

• • •

Smitty, who was not the brightest of his mother's three sons, still did not get it. "I ain't about to pull no trigger." *I couldn't even if I wanted to. My .45 is locked in the truck, inside the backpack with my Buck knife and brass knuckles and the forty kilos of Mexican crack. So either she's way off this time or she's talkin' about some other guy with a tattoo like mine.* The marked man slapped a ten-dollar bill on the counter and was about to get up when—

In the outer darkness . . . the hammer fell.

The slug was expelled from a six-inch, stainless steel barrel.

The plump missile drilled a neat round hole through the plate glass window, punched a larger one between Smitty's shoulder blades, and opened a fist-size wound where it erupted from his shattered sternum. The "biggest doggone TV screen he had ever seen" was shattered into too many fragments to count.

• • •

It is clear that the shooter is not your run-of-the-mill stalker-pervert. And we may safely rule out DEA agent; while initiative and spontaneity are valued in that U.S. government service—summary executions are not condoned. Not *officially*. Which narrows it down some.

• • •

Cassandra's hypnotic eyes looked *through* the camera, *out of* the television sets, *into* the souls of a hundred thousand viewers, more or less. Well, certainly *one* less.

"He is dead." She frowned, shook her head, appeared to address the deceased man's loved ones from the depths of her heart: "I am so *terribly* sorry."

Fade to black.

• • •

"Oh!" Sarah Frank said (more to herself than to Mr. Zig-Zag, more to her cat than to the wrinkled old woman). "How did Cassandra know about the shooting?"

Unaware of her status as one notch below a spotted cat, Daisy Perika pointed out an indisputable factoid: "We don't know that anybody got shot."

But they did, of course. Daisy knew and Sarah knew and thousands upon thousands of other viewers knew—Cassandra was *never* wrong.

It would be reported on early-morning news broadcasts all over the state, then in newspapers, and by tomorrow evening the major television networks, radio talk shows, and Internet news sites would be buzzing with accounts of the Colorado woman's amazingly accurate vision of a drive-by shooting at a truckers' restaurant on the interstate. As the authorities conducted a thorough investigation, Cassandra would be questioned by the Huerfano County sheriff, Granite Creek Chief of Police Scott Parris, several state-police detectives, agents of the United States Department of Transportation, and an attorney representing the National Truckers Association. What they got out of the psychic, which wasn't much, can be summed up by Cassandra's remark to Parris: "I see what I see; it's as simple as that." Which was true. More or less. Well, less. There was nothing *simple* about it.

Oh, by the way: The ratings on the quirky television program increased nine points following the lady's uncanny, real-time vision of the trucker's shooting. When Nicholas "Nicky" Moxon (Cassandra Spencer's enthusiastic business manager) saw the numbers, he whistled, shook his shiny bald head. "This is dynamite, Cassie. Absolute *dynamite.*"

• • •

THREE
GRANITE CREEK, COLORADO

Since November, the unseasonable weather has confused man and beast alike. Following a hard winter, the approach of springtime has produced a series of balmy, shirtsleeve days suitable for roof repairs, softball games, and leisurely strolls in the park. Robins are afoot in search of earthworms. Bears have left cozy dens to break a winter-long fast. The chirp of the hungry chipmunk is heard in picnic grounds.

On this Monday in mid-March, as the solar system's gigantic thermonuclear furnace sinks to its nightly rest in the west, silent pools of twilight seep into valleys, a soothing coolness envelopes granite mountain, pine forest, the soon-to-be-sleeping town. For many, the pleasant end of a perfect day. But for one unsuspecting soul, the ultimate misfortune is only a few hours away.

• • •

After the calamity, Cassandra Spencer, the eldest of the sisters, would declare to Nicholas Moxon that she had been caught quite off guard—such a violent event had not been "in the stars." (Among her several esoteric pursuits, which include spirit photography and Persian numerology, the television psychic also dabbles in astrology.)

Beatrice Spencer (by age, the middle sister) was more reserved than her psychic sibling, and kept a tight lip about an act of violence so utterly excessive as to be considered an obscenity.

The third, and lastborn, of the Spencer sisters?

Patience. Nothing shall be withheld. Momentarily, Astrid Spencer-Turner shall make her appearance—in a manner of speaking. The antithesis of that ideal child of yesteryear, Astrid will be heard but not seen. Listen for the telephone to ring.

Brrriiiinnnng!

The sound is made by the instrument that Andrew Turner usually carries in an inside jacket pocket. Usually. At the moment, which is late in the evening, the communications device is in his leather briefcase, which is in his hotel room, which is on the fourth floor of the Brown Palace, which is where it has been since 1888—on Seventeenth Street in downtown Denver. As it happens, Mr. Turner, husband of Astrid Spencer-Turner, is not in his hotel room with his briefcase, wherein the telephone resides. He may be found in the Brown's famous Palace Arms Restaurant. Having finished his lobster enchiladas, the diner has his attention focused on the dessert menu. Ah, so many delectable delicacies to titillate the tongue—but too little time to taste each one.

This is why he does not hear his cell phone ring. Nine times.

• • •

The agitated caller, Astrid Spencer-Turner, his wedded wife of barely one year, is in their home on the so-called Yellow Pines Ranch, which is situated approximately ten miles northwest of Granite Creek, Colorado. The family homestead is a five-hour-and-twenty-minute drive from downtown Denver, which is precisely how long it took Andrew Turner to get to the Brown Palace after he kissed his wife goodbye at 10:00 A.M. on the dot. Turner, who has a master's degree in computer science from Georgia Tech (the clever fellow graduated in the top 10 percent of his class), is one of those types who does everything by the clock. Precision is his *thing*. Somewhere, there must be women who appreciate these qualities in a man. Astrid is not one of them. What she appreciates is a husband who remembers to keep his telephone in his pocket and turned on—and answers it when she calls.

On the ninth ring, Astrid slams her telephone into the cradle hard enough to rattle other items on her bedside table. "Dammit!" *Now what should I do?* "I'll call the front desk." (The young woman has developed the endearing habit of talking to herself. Especially when she is alone in the ancestral family home.)

• • •

"Excuse me, Mr. Andrew Turner?"

The owner of Granite Creek Electronics and Computers looked up from a four-thousand-calorie slab of cherry cheesecake, flashed a smile at the young man who had addressed him. "That's me."

"I apologize for disturbing you, sir." The hotel employee offered a cordless telephone to the guest. "You have a call from Mrs. Turner." He lowered his voice, added discretely: "Urgent."

"Thank you." Turner held his hand over the mouthpiece. "She's probably just lonely. Or there's a problem with the plumbing."

The young man, who also had a wife, smiled. Excused himself.

Turner pressed the electronic appliance to his ear. "Hello, dear. What's up—well pump on the fritz again?"

"No. Nothing like that."

"Ah, you're lonely then."

"I always am when you're away."

"You should have invited one of your splendid sisters over to spend the night." He smiled. *I'd be glad to spend the night with either one of 'em.*

"I called Bea and Cassie just minutes before I rang your cell phone. But neither one answered." *Which is odd, because they're usually at home on a Monday evening.* "Andy, I hate being here all by myself. Especially at night."

"Tell you what, babe—next time I come to Denver, I'll

bring you with me. And I'll take you to the telecommunications show in Vegas. We'll take in some great floor shows, donate a few dollars to the casinos."

"I'll take you up on that." Her shudder reverberated along the telephone line. "It feels awfully spooky in this big house."

"Spooky? Really, now—Cassie is the one who talks to ghosts of long-dead Egyptians and such."

Astrid sniffed and said, "I don't mean like ghosts and goblins. It's a *different* kind of spooky."

"Different how?"

"For one thing, there's this peculiar odor."

The smile slipped off Turner's perfectly tanned face. "Probably the septic tank. I'll have someone take a look at it."

"It's not that kind of odor, it's more like—" She paused to listen. "And I hear strange noises."

"Define 'strange noises.'" This is the sort of response one learned to expect from the Andrew Turners of this world. "Creaks and squeaks, chains rattling in the attic?"

"Please don't be flippant, Andrew."

"Uh—sorry, dear. I didn't mean to seem—"

"I hear it at our bedroom window—like something shuffling around outside. And just a few minutes ago, I heard a snuffing-snorting sound."

"Probably a wandering porcupine looking for some bark to chew on."

"I certainly hope so. But I've made certain that all the downstairs doors and windows are securely closed and locked. Except for the French window in our bedroom—I can't shut it. It's stuck. So there's nothing between me and whatever's out there on the patio but the screen—" This remark was interrupted by a shriek, a thump as the telephone slipped from her hand, struck the floor.

Turner spoke loudly enough to startle other guests in the restaurant: "Astrid—what's wrong?" His wife's pitiable, pleading screams were intermixed with guttural growls. Abruptly—the screaming ceased. The absence of sound was so utterly complete that he assumed the line had been broken. The dead silence was suddenly interrupted by gruesome sounds that Andrew Turner would never be able to speak about—not to Astrid's sisters, not even to the police. But the haunting memory would never, ever leave him. In his darkest nightmares, he would hear it again and again— the ripping of flesh, crunching of bone, gluttonous, snarling grunts—and finally, as the meal progressed—*the smacking of the satisfied diner's lips.*

Despite the mind-numbing circumstances, there were things to be done. Turner proceeded to do them with a relentless, some would say *cold,* efficiency. Astrid's husband broke the connection, removed a card from his wallet, scanned a list of telephone numbers, and dialed one that was underlined.

The police dispatcher responded on the first ring: "Granite Creek Police."

"Clara, is that you?"

"Yes, it is. Who's this?"

"Andy Turner. I'm in Denver, at the Brown Palace." His words had the effect of a hammer striking nails. "I was just speaking to my wife on the telephone. I am *certain* that she has been attacked in our home. Please get someone there as soon as you can. I'm going to have my car brought around; I'll call you on the way home."

Flinching at the decisive *click* in her ear, Clara Tavishuts alerted the nearest unit, which was dealing with a bar fight on Second Street. The officer who took the call agreed to check out the possible assault at the Yellow Pines Ranch, gave her an ETA of forty minutes. At best. The second unit was responding to a domestic dispute, where the wife was threatening to decapitate her mate with a seven-hundred-year-old samurai sword. Clara knew exactly what to do— pass the buck up to the boss. An effective dispatcher always knows where all the cops are, including the chief of police. On this particular evening, Scott Parris was a guest at Charlie Moon's ranch, and the Columbine headquarters was not all that far from Yellow Pines. Clara steeled herself. *Whenever*

*I call him on his poker night, the chief always grumbles. But
if I don't contact him, he'll get all red in the face and tell me
I should have alerted him to the emergency call.*

• • •

Scott Parris was holding a pair of fives and some trash. After asking for three cards, the player was holding a pair of fives and some trash. He looked over his hand, across the table at Charlie Moon's world-class poker face. "How's your aunt Daisy getting along?"

"About the same."

"And that orphan girl that's staying with her—what's her name?"

Moon pretended to be shocked. "You don't remember?"

Parris pretended to be offended. "If I did, would I be asking you what her name was?"

"Sarah Frank," Moon said. "First the memory goes and then the hearing. . . ."

Parris leaned forward. "What?"

Moon repeated the statement at full volume.

"Charlie, nobody likes a big smart aleck."

"That's not so, pardner. *I* like you."

Parris snorted, pushed a pair of shiny Tennessee quarters to the center of the table. "There's not a thing wrong with my memory."

"Okay, then what's Sarah's cat's name?"

"That's not fair. Nobody should have to remember the name of a cat."

"Don't let Sarah hear you say that." Moon glanced at his hand, then: "I'll see you." He sweetened the pot with a crisp new dollar bill. "And raise you four bits."

Parris folded, glumly watched the Ute rake in his winnings. "Charlie, how come we never get to play any big-time high-stakes poker like them high rollers on TV?"

"Because we ain't got the ante."

" 'Ain't' ain't good grammar," Parris muttered. The cop, who had been dating an English major, was attempting to improve himself.

"Okay, we *isn't* got the ante, and even if we did—" The

Indian's response was interrupted by the rude warble of his guest's cell phone.

"Who'd be calling me this time of night?" *Maybe it's Sweet Thing.* The chief of police glanced at the caller ID. "It's dispatch." The middle-aged man pressed the instrument against a once presentable ear that now sprouted unsightly tufts of reddish brown hair. "Why're you buggin' me on my poker night, Clara?" He listened to the dispatcher's terse report. "Okay, I'm practically on my way." Aiming a sly grin at his best friend, he added, "No, I won't need any backup—I'll be taking Charlie Moon along." *I'd rather have the Ute with me than a battalion of National Guard.* He thumbed the End button.

Moon shed his poker face, which enabled him to assume a mildly inquisitive expression. "Taking me where?"

"Old man Spencer's Yellow Pines Ranch."

"I thought the place had been vacant since Mr. Spencer died."

"Not since Astrid—his youngest daughter, who inherited all six thousand acres of Daddy's ranch—moved in with her new husband."

Moon searched his memory. Came up with "Andrew Turner."

"That's right. And Turner, who's in Denver tonight, just called in a report, claimed that while he was talking to his wife on the phone she was assaulted. It'll probably turn out to be a false alarm, but I've got to go check it out and I might need some backup." Parris had pulled on a jacket, was jamming a decades-old felt hat down to his hair-sprouting ears. "So don't give me no static about how a big-shot tribal investigator like you ain't—hasn't got any jurisdiction offa the Southern Ute reservation." The broad-shouldered man lumbered down the hallway to the parlor. "Grab your revolver, Charlie—and consider yourself duly deputized!"

Moon was unlocking the gun cabinet. "What's the compensation?"

"Twelve fifty an hour and the pleasure of my company."

Strapping on a heavy pistol belt, the brand-new deputy grinned. "Make it ten bucks per and I'll take the call by myself."

• • •

Six miles north of Castle Rock, Andrew Turner made the second call to GCPD, interrupted the dispatcher's standard greeting: "Clara—it's me. Andy Turner. What've you found out about my wife?"

"Nothing yet. But Chief Parris is on his way to your home."

"The moment you hear from him, call me."

"Will do. What's your cell number?"

The husband recited the requested digits. Twice.

As he sped south along the interstate, Turner attempted to gain control of his emotions. *I have alerted the police. Now, I must call Astrid's sisters.* He entered the preprogrammed number for Beatrice Spencer. No answer. *Bea is out rather late.* He tried Cassandra. Seven rings of the TV celebrity's unlisted number got him Cassie's answering machine. *I'll call them again another hour down the road.* He took a deep breath. Another. *Whatever has happened, I must be prepared to deal with it—and in as rational a manner as humanly possible.*

A cool customer? It would seem so.

But from that electric instant when Astrid's scream had seared a wound in his soul, Andrew Turner had moved like one suspended in a horrific dream. He would awaken, of course, to live for a few hours in the sunshine—only to fall asleep when darkness came around—and dream again. And so would the cycle go. As this long nightmare rolled toward a veiled finale, the *rational* man would discover that logic and reason are applicable only to a certain limit . . . take one step beyond that invisible boundary, the unwary pilgrim falls into the Deep, twists and flows in dark currents—never to surface again.

• • •

FOUR
THE GATHERING STORM

Most of the graveled road between the Columbine headquarters and the state highway was sufficiently well graded
that a motor vehicle could roll along at a reasonable clip,
but a two-mile stretch of tooth-rattling "washboard" spiked
Scott Parris's blood pressure, flushing his beefy face a
ruddy hue. Because his countenance was illuminated by
greenish dashboard lights, this crimson display went unap-
preciated by Charlie Moon, who was riding shotgun, so to
speak, in the passenger seat. The moment the GCPD unit's
wheels got traction on the paved road, Parris switched on
the emergency lights and siren, heavy-booted his almost-
new black-and-white into a hair-raising sideways skid,
straightened it, grinned while he watched the speedometer
climb. Tranquil as a man of his temperament can ever be,
his BP gradually drifted down toward normal, which in this
instance was 138 over 93.

As Charlie Moon checked his revolver, counted the shiny
brass cartridges in the cylinder—he caught a definite whiff
of gun smoke. *Now where did that come from?* The Ute was
overwhelmed by a sudden suspicion that the cartridges
were empty—that someone had fired all six shots from his
gun and not reloaded. To make sure the ammo wasn't
spent, he removed the bullets for careful inspection. All
was well.

Up yonder, a moon glistening with reflected sunlight
was about to be gobbled up by a hungry thundercloud. A

great horned owl circled overhead, dragged a winged shadow across the highway. As the automobile roared past a clump of galleta grass, a startled cottontail bolted. In the wake of the black-and-white, hungry Ms. *Bubo Virginianus* blinked her bulbous eyes, made the practiced dive. Though he would not see another sunrise, Mr. Rabbit was, for the moment, intensely alive.

But back to the chase.

Along the stretched-out miles between the Columbine gate and the entrance to the Yellow Pines Ranch, the two-lane highway was mostly straight, except for a three-mile section where it snaked over a cluster of undulating ridges that, even at the posted speed limit, produced a stomach-floating roller-coaster effect in which children and well-adjusted grown-ups took childish delight. At a steady ninety-five miles per hour, the low-slung Chevrolet hugged the highway in the dips, went almost airborne on the peaks. After the road leveled, the speedometer ticked its way up to 110.

Having checked his sidearm, Citizen Moon, the more intellectual of the pair, was pursuing the pleasant pastime of musing about this and that. By way of example: how responding to a trouble call was a small parable of life. Nine times out of ten, when the cop showed up at the other end, things would be okay. The prowler would be gone, the lost child found, the frightened lady unharmed. But then, there was always the possibility of—Number Ten.

As they neared the turnoff, the chief of police shut down the high-pitched siren. When he could see the gate in the high beams, he switched off the emergency lights. If the assailant (assuming that there actually was an assailant) was still lurking on the property Astrid Spencer had inherited from her father, Scott Parris did not want to scare him away. *I'll trap the bastard.* There was one narrow lane connecting the Yellow Pines Ranch to the highway, and Granite Creek's top copper was about to plug that jug with his black-and-white stopper.

As Parris jammed on the brakes, did a stomach-turning,

skid-sliding turn under the massive sandstone arch and onto the darkened mile-long ranch road the deceased millionaire had spent a fortune to blacktop, the Chevrolet sedan seemed, by some uncanny automotive instinct, to sense the driver's sense of urgency. It kicked out a few extra horsepower, the all-terrain tread grabbed on to the roadway. As they slipped swiftly along, passing through isolated congregations of dark evergreens, the warm rubber tires hummed a thrumming whine, while in the darkened forest, melancholy woodwinds mourned and pined for a first glimpse of morning sunshine. It was to be a long, long night.

The blacktop, which was never intended to approach too close to old man Spencer's semirustic abode, terminated abruptly at the outer arc of a long, elliptical driveway. Parris braked again, stopping a few yards from the extensively remodeled home that had once been the headquarters of a working ranch.

Before the hot V-8 engine had stuttered to a stop, two pairs of boots hit the ground.

Parris and his recently deputized Ute sidekick did what sensible lawmen always do before they rush to the rescue: For a half-dozen heartbeats, they stood as still as the trunks of trees. Looked. Listened. And employed other, more primitive senses.

Aside from the yip-yipping of a distant coyote and the discontented rumble of thunder over Spencer Mountain, there was not a sound. Aside from dusty-winged moths batting about the wrought-iron lantern at the center of the porch, there was no movement. The slate roof of the century-old, two-story log house glimmered in cloud-filtered moonlight.

It seemed a scene of perfect peace—a serene night, made for restful sleep.

The lawmen knew better. Neither man could have explained *how* he knew, but this holding-its-breath quiet, this anemic, lifeless light—it did not *feel* right. Whoever slept here would awaken nevermore. Not in this world.

Exchanging nods that conveyed what words cannot, the lawmen split up, Parris to the left, Moon took the direction that was left, which was right, and so the man-shadows melted into the night. Slowly, warily, guns in hand—the hard, silent men began to close the circle around the still dwelling.

God have mercy on any two-legged scoundrel they might encounter.

But whoever had been there was long gone. Which was lucky for him. Or her. Or them. Or *it*.

It was the Ute whose nostrils first picked up the unmistakable scent of fresh blood, his dark eyes that perceived the glint of broken glass on the sandstone patio, a crumpled door screen, and—with the aid of a hazy shaft of moonlight—caught a glimpse of mangled flesh. What he presumed to be the remains—the *what-was-left-behind* of Astrid Spencer-Turner—was beyond all human help.

The lawmen spent a long, long three minutes peering about the wrecked, blood-soaked bedroom. Much of what they saw was the ordinary stuff of life. A battery-operated clock on the wall, second hand clicking away precious seconds. On a shelf above the clock, an antique china doll with shy, painted eyes that, no matter where you were, never looked at you. Flung into a far corner, a hardcover novel, crocheted bookmark still in place. The book leaned against a dusty pair of hand-tooled horsehide cowboy boots that were small enough for a girl to wear. In contrast to the overturned bed, the torn quilt, the ripped, blood-splattered sheets—the hideously mutilated corpse—the personal belongings were so normal, so shockingly commonplace. And though it is not always the case, there is often something odd at the scene of a homicide, something queerly out of place—an object or feature that grabs the eye. It might be a hole in the heel of a rich woman's stocking. A box of crayons and a Peter Rabbit coloring book in a house where there are no children. A "lucky" rabbit's foot on the victim's key chain. Astrid Spencer-Turner's bedroom was not to prove the exception. Almost lost among broken furniture, fractured glass, and torn bedclothes, at the edge of a slightly dusty rectangle of carpet that defined the place where the overturned bed had stood—there was something else. Something that simply did not belong; something a passerby might have left behind.

A single, lusciously plump, red-ripe *strawberry*.

Though riveting, such details rarely have anything to do with the crime.

The first order of business was to call in whatever help Scott Parris could muster from his understaffed department—which would require waking every officer who was not already on night duty. The harder part would be notifying the deceased's nearest of kin.

• • •

Approaching an exit to the Air Force Academy, Andrew Turner could see the glow of Colorado Springs. He was about to place another call to the police station in Granite Creek when his cell phone vibrated in his hand. "Yes?"

"Andy, this is Scott Parris. GCPD."

Astrid Spencer's husband listened to a slight electronic buzz that hung over the dark silence. "What is it, Scott?"

"I'm awfully sorry to have to tell you this on the telephone, but I didn't want you to show up and—" Parris cleared his throat, tried again: "I'm afraid it's *very* bad news." He inhaled deeply. "I'm sorry."

"Then Astrid is . . ."

"Yes. Yes, sir. She is."

• • •

Trailed by the pair of German shepherds, Beatrice was entering the mud room from the garage when she heard the telephone in the hallway ringing. The lady of the house picked it up, checked the caller ID. "Hello, Andy." She listened to the monotonic voice. "I'm sorry you've been having trouble reaching us. Cassie must have her telephone

turned off. I've been outside, exercising Ike and Spike."
She referred to the dogs.

Andrew Turner broke the bad news.

"Are you absolutely certain?"

He was.

Starting with her hands and feet, Beatrice felt a dull
chill begin to creep over her entire body. "I'll leave immediately for Yellow Pines, pick up Cassie on the way." She
hung up, looked at herself in the mirror. No, *immediately*
was not an option. *I'll take a quick shower. Change
clothes.*

• • •

It was a blessing (which Scott Parris would later thank God
for) that he and Charlie Moon had arrived before Beatrice
and Cassandra—the *surviving* Spencer sisters.

When Parris saw the headlights approaching, he was
in his unit, verifying that Clara Tavishuts had dispatched
the requested uniformed officers and the county medical
examiner. Almost as an afterthought, he asked her to no-
tify the state police. Diplomacy was part of the job. Next
time, the state cops might get the hot call, and the chief
of the Granite Creek PD did not intend to provide the
troopers any reason to leave his department out in the
cold.

Beatrice steered her Mercedes around the sleek black-
and-white, which once again pulsated with red and blue
lights. The sisters seemed to hit the ground running.

Parris yelled, was ignored by the women, who were
sprinting toward the house.

Charlie Moon had stationed himself on the brick walk
that led to the porch. The recently conscripted deputy
raised both hands, boomed, "Stop!"

They stopped.

Though Cassandra had a mouthful of questions, it was
Beatrice who addressed this exceptionally tall, lean man
they had occasionally seen on the streets of Granite Creek.
"We're Astrid's sisters—what has happened?"

Moon's voice was deep, somber. "I'm sorry." And he meant it.

Beatrice heard herself say, "Get out of our way—we're going inside." And she meant it.

The Ute shook his head. "Nobody's going in."

"We most certainly are." Beatrice took her older sister firmly by the hand. "And you are *not* going to prevent us."

"Yes I am." His words were like thunder on the mountain.

The presumably unstoppable sisters took a tentative, testing step toward the certainly immovable Ute.

He spoke oh-so-softly: "Don't make me do it."

Beatrice's query carried a slight tremor: "Do what?"

Moon's response was blunt: "Pick both of you up, one under each arm. Stuff you into the back of Chief Parris's unit. Lock you inside."

They knew he could. And would.

Beatrice's voice regained some of its edge. "Tell us what has happened."

Charlie Moon hesitated. "We're not sure."

"Hi, Bea. Cassie." Scott Parris had materialized. "This is my friend Charlie Moon. He's my deputy—whatever he says goes." Having made his point, he took a deep breath. "Ladies, I'm awfully sorry, but you can't do anything here but get in the way of an official police investigation. So the best thing is for you to go home. I'll call you as soon as—"

"We are not leaving!" Beatrice stamped a spotless white slipper on the worn brick walk. "Not before you tell us what has happened to Astrid."

"Okay." The suddenly weary policeman pointed at the dwelling. "Here's the deal. It looks like an intruder entered her bedroom through the French windows. Astrid is dead." *Dead. There, it's been said.* Now it was official.

These were not ordinary women. These were the Spencer sisters, who had been raised by parents only two generations removed from those hard-bitten pioneers who had arrived in wagons, on horseback, fought

Apaches, Navajos, and Utes, endured sudden mid-May blizzards that froze small children who got caught in a far pasture, suffered through summers hot enough to fry eggs on black basalt boulders. There were no shrieks or wails. No wringing of hands. Only a cold, stony silence before Beatrice said, "You are absolutely certain that our sister is dead?"

"Yes." *I'm sure* somebody's *dead.* The chief of police, who had suffered through his minutes in the wrecked bedroom, waved his hand in a sweeping gesture. "Until further notice, the area will be treated as a crime scene. Aside from police and the ME, no one goes inside, or off the driveway. Soon as the sun comes up, the dwelling and grounds will be examined for evidence." *Like footprints.* "We can't afford to miss a thing—we've got to find out who's responsible for what happened here." A flash of white-hot sheet lightning split the sky asunder, then a heavy rumble of thunder. Parris cringed at the threat. *Oh no, Not rain. Please don't let it rain and wash any tracks away. . . .*

Big fat drops plop-plopped onto the brim of his hat.

More thunder.

And then the waters came. Oh, how it did *rain.*

Faced with the pair of determined men and a deluge that was soaking them to the skin, the sisters retreated to Bea's automobile, where they would remain until Andrew Turner arrived.

By then, the place was crawling with lawmen of every stripe.

The loamy Yellow Pines soil was ankle-deep mud. The deluge was a great blessing to desperate farmers and ranchers. A serious piece of hard luck for lawmen who would have given a month's pay for a single footprint.

• • •

As the cloud-filtered rays of a gunmetal-gray dawn announced the beginning of a new day, Chief of Police Scott Parris felt oddly alone in the crowd of cops. What he sensed was a certain emptiness. His deputy was nowhere to be seen. His eyes attempted to penetrate the morning mist.

Ol' Charlie's out there somewhere . . . looking. I hope he gets lucky.

• • •

Charlie Moon had begun by walking an ever-widening spiral around the dead woman's home. But, despite a hopeful search for a tuft of hair on a piñon branch, a deep paw print that the torrent of rain had not completely obliterated, luck was not walking with him. Now, within the fringed hem of Spencer Mountain's forested skirt, he was particularly alert. The Ute sensed a *presence.*

It was as if all the feathered and furry creatures who lived here were—like the stilled breeze—holding their collective breaths. Aside from the slow drumming of his heart, not a sound. Nothing moved. Moon melted into the undergrowth, became one with his unseen companions. Indeed, the petrified man seemed caught in a single frame of time—every leaf of aspen or fern, every blade of grass, a still life painted on glass.

But something did not quite fit the picture. Which was why he noticed it. The thing near the toe of his boot might have been a red pebble. Or a crimson-tinted mushroom. It was neither. Charlie Moon picked it up. What he held in this palm was a large, plump strawberry. *Now how'd this get here?* The answer, when it came, was obvious. Astrid Spencer not only ate strawberries in bed . . . the careless lady carried her favorite snacks on walks into the woods. Which would explain how bears had picked up the scent, followed it back to her bedroom, and—He looked up the mountainside. Again, the distinct sense that something was up there. A man-killing bear?

By instinct, the Ute's right hand found the handle of his holstered revolver. The ghost of gun smoke returned to haunt his nostrils. And again, that absurd certainty that every cartridge was spent.

• • •

Atop a crumbling granite crag, cloaked by the morning's misty gray shroud, lurked a hairy, foul-smelling creature. Blood representing a variety of species was caked on its swarthy, unwashed skin. A pair of hard, unblinking eyes looked down upon the Ute. What went through its mind is beyond knowing, and does not invite speculation. But the mouth, after a manner of speaking, said something—so softly that the Indian's sharp ear did not hear: "Hhhnnngh."

A brooding, bestial threat? Perhaps.

Or was it something quite different—an expression of affection . . . of *endearment*?

• • •

FIVE
THE PUBLIC SERVANT

When District Attorney Bill "Pug" Bullett got the 9:00 A.M. telephone call from Beatrice, he immediately acquiesced to her semipolite "request" for a meeting. The subjects for discussion, she told him, were:

(A) The violent death of her sister.

(B) What was being done about it.

The DA said that he would invite the chief of police, the medical examiner, and—of course—the deceased woman's husband.

Beatrice advised him not to trouble Andrew Turner. He was in seclusion. Accepting no invitations, taking no calls.

(The grieving widower was, at that very moment, relaxing with a favorite book—B. P. Lathi's *Linear Systems and Signals,* chapter 7, "Continuous-Time Signal Analysis: The Fourier Transform." A real page-turner. What is that old saying? Right. *To each his own.*)

Pug advised the lady that though he was busy with several pending cases, he had an opening in the middle of next week. Actually, "middle" was as far as he got.

"Today," Beatrice informed him. Curtly. At precisely 11:10 A.M. Although she did not bother to explain it to this doltish graduate of a second-rate law school, after she enjoyed her midmorning honeyed tea and imported *bisquitos,* this schedule would allow her sufficient time for a leisurely drive into town, where she would pick up Cassie at her three-story nine-gabled Victorian mansion, which was, by general consensus, a major architectural blight on the corner of Copper and Second.

"Ah," the bullied DA muttered, shuffling some papers on his desk. "I think I can fit that in. I'll call Scott Parris and Walter Simpson and see if they can break away from whatever—" There was a sharp click in his ear.

Beatrice and Cassandra Spencer arrived at nine minutes and forty-five seconds past eleven, were courteously greeted by the district attorney's smiling receptionist, who said, "Good morning, ladies. I believe he is ready to see you, so you may go right—"

They swept imperiously past the hapless gatekeeper, charged into the inner sanctum. What they saw was the district attorney getting up from behind his desk. Pug was flanked on either side (protectively, it seemed) by the broad-shouldered chief of police and the elfin medical examiner. As Pug offered a few hopeful homilies about how mild the weather was for March and how pleasant it was to see the ladies and how terribly sorry he was for their "recent loss," the sisters responded with appropriate nods and murmurs, ignored the proffered seats.

Now that the polite little waltz was over and done with, Beatrice Spencer looked the DA straight in the eye. "Well?"

The bull-necked politician tugged at his starched collar, which had instantly shrunk by two sizes. He jerked his chin to indicate the cherubic little man with the halo of white hair. "Doc Simpson has kindly agreed to give us a summary of his examination of the—uh . . ." His ugly bulldog face grimaced. "The remains."

The medical examiner seated himself in a padded armchair. His little feet dangled, barely touching the floor. The longtime friend of the Spencer family addressed the sisters in a stern, grandfatherly tone: "Sit down, girls."

They sat.

Ignoring the THANK YOU FOR NOT SMOKING plaque on the DA's wall, the elderly physician fished a slender black cigar from his coat pocket, bit off a plug, spat it in Pug's wastebasket, lit it, took a puff. Exhaling, he said to the ladies, "Astrid was attacked by a carnivore. From a first look at the remains, could be a mountain lion, maybe even one of those wolves the government has turned loose. But during the process of a more careful examination, I discovered several animal hairs." The medical sleuth added, with an air of satisfaction, "Probably left behind by a bear."

Beatrice responded in a dull monotone: "That would seem to settle it, then."

Cassie hugged herself, shuddered. "Poor Astrid—killed by a *bear!*"

The ME's little face had a distinctly foxy look. "Well, not necessarily."

The DA squinted at the aged physician. "What's that mean?"

Doc Simpson revealed a choice piece of intelligence that he had been keeping to himself. "Back in nineteen seventy-eight, your father killed a black bear on Yellow Pines Ranch. The cheeky creature was practically in his backyard, stealing peaches from the orchard. Joe kept the pelt in a ground-floor bedroom." He removed the cigar, pointed it at Beatrice. "The same bedroom where Astrid was attacked. As time passed, it got pretty tattered—and was *shedding hair.* Joe threw it out years ago."

Beatrice glanced at her sister. "I had forgotten all about that old bearskin."

Cassandra nodded. *So had I.*

"It does complicate matters." The ME smiled at the Spencer beauties, who were preserved in his memory as disarmingly charming little cuties. "But I've sent some tissue samples to FBI forensics. I've no doubt they'll find traces of saliva, which will contain a few mammalian cells. And those cells will identify the species of animal that killed your sister."

Cassandra's big eyes popped. "They can tell all that—just from some *spit?*"

Doc Simpson's chuckle jiggled the cigar, popping off miniature smoke signals. "You bet your boots, Cassie—that and lots more. If we happen to get our hands on a suspect animal, the forensics techs can do a cross-check on the DNA and determine whether that specific bear or cougar or whatnot is responsible for the mauling." Wolf was a long shot. Simpson had an afterthought. "It might've even been that vicious dog pack that's been running wild, pulling down sheep and—" Seeing Beatrice pale, he clamped his mouth shut.

Cassandra sighed. "Poor Astrid. How horrible, to have a bloodthirsty animal break into your bedroom and—and . . ." Her eyes seemed to glaze over.

Doc Simpson was observing the elder sister with intense clinical interest. *I hope she doesn't have one of her seizures, right here in Pug's office.* "It happens more often than you might think, Cassie. The bear—if it *was* a bear— probably smelled something good to eat in the house. A bear'll eat anything from roadkill to roast pheasant, but what really turns 'em on is something sweet. Like candy. Or fruit."

Parris and the DA exchanged quick glances. The ME did not know that Charlie Moon had discovered a lone strawberry in Astrid Spencer's bedroom, and another a mile away at the foot of Spencer Mountain. But every GCPD cop knew about it, plus the state police, so it was only a matter of time before that information appeared in the newspaper.

Beatrice seemed almost relieved by this tentative conclusion. "A hungry bear attracted by the scent of food." A sniff. "Yes, I suppose that must have been what happened."

Pleased at this convergence toward consensus, the DA chimed in, "Happens all the time with campers. Last year— it was on Labor Day weekend down at Raccoon Creek Campgrounds—there was an attack on some twelve-year-old scouts that had a stash of candy bars in their tent." *Dumb kids.* "But all they got were some scratches and a bad scare."

Pointedly ignoring Pug, Beatrice smiled at Doc Simpson. "Cassie and I appreciate your lucid explanation of what you have determined so far." A glance at the clock on the wall. "Now, we must be going." As if they were coupled together by some invisible sister-mechanism, Beatrice and Cassandra simultaneously got up from their chairs.

The DA raised his palms in a gesture that suggested boundless generosity. "You have any more questions or concerns, ladies—feel free to call my office."

Beatrice nodded at the assembly of solemn men. "Good day, then." With this, the Spencer sisters departed.

District Attorney Bill "Pug" Bullett sighed to vent his pent-up anxieties, shot a scowl at Scott Parris. "Now, all we need to do is find that killer bear and destroy it."

Walter Simpson got out of his chair, drew himself up to his full height of five feet three inches. "Let's not go slaughtering any forest creatures before I get the forensics report back from the FBI."

The DA cocked his head. "How long could that take?"

"At least six weeks. Probably a lot longer." The ME took a long pull on his cigar. "They've got a huge backlog of work. And as you know, Pug"—*as you ought to know*—"when a citizen is mauled by a wild animal"—*if it was a wild animal*—"there's no crime involved. So the Bureau won't give a high priority to analyzing the samples I submitted."

The DA grunted, scratched himself in a spot where he could not when the women were present. "I can't very well prosecute a bear for killing somebody." He turned his head toward the chief of police and whispered, "But we can sure as hell *shoot* the fuzzy bastard."

Scott Parris didn't know whether to roll his eyes or grin. He exercised both options.

THE DOGS

Late that evening, as Beatrice and Cassandra were having a telephone chat, the former sister mentioned something odd that, she said, had occurred around dusk. "I was outside, working in the garden when Ike and Spike seemed to sense something up on the mountain."

The spookily gifted sister was intrigued. "Sensed—what do you mean?"

"It was odd. They didn't bark—they growled, and skulked around. Then, Ike stalked off into the forest and Spike tagged along. That was hours ago. They have not returned."

"Peculiar," Cassandra murmured.

"Yes." Beatrice nodded at her distant sister. "Very peculiar, indeed."

Following a silence pregnant with forebodings, Cassandra murmured, "I see . . . dark vibrations."

A wry smile curled the sensible sister's lips. *I thought you might.*

The psychic: "I have a bad feeling about this." Heavy sigh. "I don't think Ike and Spike will be coming home."

Bea's eyes were hard. Cold. Two blue Saturnian ice moons.

• • •

SIX

SCORE ONE FOR THE CLAIRVOYANT

As so often happened, Cassandra's psychic dart had hit the bull's-eye.

The German shepherds did not return home. Nor would they ever. Never again would the energetic canines romp exuberantly on the lawn, chase a Frisbee thrown by Beatrice, or—for that matter—pursue an unseen creature into the forest on Spencer Mountain. Though she had been fond of her pets, Bea accepted the loss as one of those unfortunate events that are bound to happen from time to time, and comforted herself with the observation that having dogs around the house was not all wine and roses. Animals could be such a bother. No sentimentalists, these Spencer women. Like Daddy, they were made of tough stuff. But was it the *right* stuff?

• • •

A few days after the meeting in the DA's office, the sisters marched into the Sugar Bowl Restaurant, nodded curtly at a middle-aged waitress whose feet ached from too many years on concrete floors; knotty varicose veins traced circuitous backcountry road maps on her parchment-pale legs. In hope of a generous tip, Mandy smiled through the pain and led the wealthy women to a booth that was partially concealed behind a walnut-paneled partition.

They waved away the proffered menus.

"Sun tea," said Beatrice with a flippant cheerfulness. "Lightly iced, with a slice of lemon."

Cassandra ordered a carafe of New Mexico Piñon coffee. "Freshly ground beans, if you please."

The weary waitress yes-ma'amed her customers, turned her back, allowed the smile to fall away.

Beatrice and Cassandra exchanged a few bright comments about the new spring outfits at Felicia's Fashions on Main Street. When Mandy had delivered the beverages and departed, Beatrice looked past her sister. "Well, guess who has surfaced."

Behind her, Cassandra heard footsteps on the tile floor. "Is it *him*?"

The older sister smiled. "Good morning, Andy."

Andrew Turner approached the booth, gazed at the attractive women. "Morning, Bea. Cassie." The melancholy expression added just the right touch of gravitas to his boyish features. "I came in for some coffee."

"You may share mine." Cassandra patted the seat beside her hip. "Please sit with us."

"Well . . . I wouldn't want to disturb you." Uncertainty clouded his brow. "Are you sure?"

"Of course." Beatrice was tempted to wink at her sister, who'd had a crush on Turner since he'd hit town two years ago and bought the ailing Granite Creek Electronics and Computers.

"Very well, then." Turner slid into the booth. Beside Beatrice.

Cassandra's mouth went thin. Hard.

Oblivious to the tension, Turner released a mere spark of the dynamite smile—that dazzling flash of charm that had disarmed so many of their tender gender. "How are you two getting along? Under the grim circumstances, I mean."

Beatrice put on a brave face. "We are managing." She arched an elegant eyebrow. "And yourself?"

"The days are barely tolerable." A manly set of the jaw, a shrug. "It's at night when I . . ." His voice cracked, choked to a stop.

Bea reached around his shoulders, gave him a hug. Also a little peck on the cheek.

The best Cassandra could do was reach across the table and pat his hand. Hardly an effective follow-up to a kiss, the affectionate gesture went unnoticed. The dark-haired beauty felt cheated by her sister. If only the psychic could have foreseen the treachery that was just around the corner. . . .

Having lost interest in coffee, Turner waved away the approaching waitress, said to the sisters, "There's something I must talk to you ladies about."

The sisters waited.

He tap-tapped a finger on the table as if transmitting Morse code, decided on a preamble: "As you can well imagine, this has been a terribly traumatic time for me. I find it difficult to concentrate on practical matters, which nevertheless must be attended to."

The golden-haired sister took his hand in hers. This affectionate gesture was definitely noticed. Andrew returned Bea's little squeeze.

The star of *Cassandra Sees* displayed a brittle smile. Unseen, under the table, the psychic bent a spoon into the shape of a horseshoe. No. Not by *that* means. With her hand.

Had her jealous sister vanished in a puff of sulfurous smoke, Beatrice might not have noticed. "It has been terrible for us all, Andy—but you and Astrid were practically newlyweds." As they disengaged hands, she added quickly, "I do hope you're not thinking of hiring a manager for your store and going away on some long trip. Cassie and I would miss you so."

Relieved at having his revelation made easier, Turner smiled across the table at Cassandra. "It would appear that you are not the only mind reader in the Spencer family."

The psychic blushed to her toes. Vainly attempted to straighten the unseen spoon.

Evidently weary of telegraphy, he drummed all four fingers on the table. "I'm thinking about putting my business up for sale." Granite Creek Electronics and Computers would bring a pretty price. "And travel is definitely in the picture."

There were quite audible gasps from the sisters.

Beatrice frowned. "But where will you go—and how long will you be away?"

"As to the first part, I've not quite made up my mind. But I'm thinking about France. Toulon, perhaps. And Nice. Then off to Italy. I've always wanted to visit Rome. And Naples. As to the 'how long' . . ." The fingers kept on drumming. Like a spirited horse running. "I might not return at all."

Beatrice felt almost faint. "Oh, dear—you can't really mean that!"

"But I do. With Astrid gone, I don't have any reason to remain in Granite Creek." He concentrated his gaze on a heavy glass ashtray. "I'll be putting the Yellow Pines Ranch up for sale. I thought I ought to tell you ladies immediately—offer you right of first refusal."

The sisters were struck dumb.

Sensing that this was turning into an awkward situation, Turner promised he would telephone them within a day or two, said a hurried goodbye, got up, and strode away.

"Well," Cassandra said. And again: "Well."

"Indeed," her sister murmured. And after taking thought, she added, "Poor, dear Andrew—he believes he is going to inherit Yellow Pines."

Cassandra nodded. "Evidently, Astrid neglected to tell him about Daddy's will. Andrew doesn't realize that in the event of any of our deaths, our share of the Spencer real estate passes on to the surviving sisters."

"Cassie, I hate to sound catty—especially under the circumstances. But I would not have put it past Astrid to have *purposely* led Andy to believe that he was marrying into her lion's share of the Spencer land holdings." Beatrice added, somewhat acidly, "A woman who has her heart set on a man will stop at nothing." She bared her teeth, suggesting a shark about to attack. "And I do not exclude myself. Or you."

Cassandra pretended to be shocked. "Bea, you are really *terrible.*"

The terrible sister took no offense. "Do you know what Andy is lacking?" This was one of those pesky rhetorical questions that Cassie detested. Beatrice clarified: "The poor baby needs a wife."

Unable to think of a word to say, Cassandra kept her mouth shut.

Neither sister was aware of the fact that their waitress was just on the other side of the panel, wiping a damp cloth on the immaculately clean salad bar. And being a sponge for gossip, Mandy was soaking up every word.

Beatrice continued to provide the desired product: "Andy will be terribly shocked to discover that he is not going to inherit an acre of real estate." She had an odd glint in her eye. The left one. "Which shall provide us with an unprecedented opportunity."

Sensing that her sister was about to suggest something outrageous, possibly even dangerous, Cassandra's asked, "What sort of opportunity?"

Beatrice flashed a beatific smile at her sister. "To add a measure of happiness to our lonely lives."

"Oh." *I don't get it.*

She doesn't get it. "Cassie—one of us must marry Mr. Turner."

"Did you say *marry* him?"

"I did."

"Oh." Now she got it. But the solution to one problem often raises another thorny conundrum. Cassandra's brow furrowed. "But whom will it be—me or you?"

"I can think of only one solution." The calculating sister removed two wooden toothpicks from a glass dispenser. She broke one in half, tossed the unwanted splinter into a potted palm, pinched the remnants between a pair of perfectly manicured digits, and tapped the sharp tips until they were precisely even. She offered her younger sister the choice.

Cassandra stared at the pointy little objects. "What?"

"Think of it as drawing straws."

Never one for games, the brunette was looking askance. "Straws?"

"It is a simple process. She who draws the short straw loses." Regretting the necessity for redundancy, Beatrice added, "And the sister holding the long straw wins." When explaining such matters to Cassie, one must not presume too much. "But as there are no straws readily available, we shall use toothpicks. One whole one, one half."

Cassandra frowned at the little spikes of wood. "I don't know." The psychic sibling felt an odd chill ripple along her spine. "Resorting to a game of chance to see who vamps our poor dead sister's husband . . ." She seemed about to cringe. "Under the circumstances, it all seems rather *icky*."

"Icky?"

"*Triple*-icky."

"Dear Cassie—I did not realize you had such scruples."

"It's not only icky. It's crazy." She raised the most serious objection: "And it could be embarrassing. I mean— what if he's not interested?"

"If you have what men want—and both of us do—they are always interested."

Cassandra's face burned. "Oh, Bea, you are absolutely *shameless*!"

Beatrice arched a brow. "My reference was to valuable real estate, with which—in light of Astrid's untimely demise—we are both rather well endowed." She effected a coquettish pose. "And as to physical attraction, I daresay neither of us resembles a mud fence."

Cassandra stared at her sister. *You were always the prettiest.*

"But if you are suffering an attack of conscience, you may leave the snaring of Andy Turner entirely to me." Beatrice, a natural actress, raised her chin in an impudent gesture. "I'll show you how easy it is to trap yourself a man."

"Perhaps that is just what I should do. Leave him to you, I mean." To demonstrate her contempt for Sister's brazen plan, Cassandra tossed her raven mane. Came very close to snorting. But she could not tear her gaze from the toothpick ends that protruded between Bea's finger and thumb.

As she had during all their years of growing up together, Beatrice waited for the inevitable. She had not the least doubt that Cassie would reach out and select the toothpick that would seal her fate.

Which she did.

Beatrice threw back her head, laughed. *Games are such great fun. Especially when you win.*

• • •

Mandy was distressed to be called away from her eavesdropping to attend to a famished couple at table 5 who desired to see a menu.

• • •

Cassandra stared at the offending splinter. *Bea was always the lucky one. Dammit—dammit—dammit!* She dropped her puny little half toothpick into the ashtray, announced, "I'm *glad* that I got the short one."

"No you're not." The winner of the pot pointed a long-stemmed teaspoon at her forked-tongue sister. "And don't let me catch you cheating on the deal. If I so much as see you batting those big eyelashes at Andy—why, there's no telling what I might do."

• • •

Shortly after the Spencer sisters had departed, Mandy, wincing at a stinging shin-splint pain, came to clean the table. *Just imagine them two rich young women, drawing toothpicks for who'll marry that poor widow-man.* Beatrice had left a five-dollar bill, which covered the coffee and tea . . . *and twenty-five cents for me. Big whoopee. I'll go see a movie and buy me a queen-size popcorn. With six squirts of hot butter.*

A sense of humor is a great blessing.

Going about her monotonous duties, Mandy removed Cassie's discarded half toothpick from the ashtray. Noticing a metallic gleam under the table, she squatted with a painful grunt, found a spoon bent into a U. *Now why would anybody do a thing like that?* As she was retrieving this piece of damaged flatware, the meticulous cleaner-upper noticed a second, smaller object on the floor—on Bea's side of the booth. Another *half* toothpick. Curious. Suspicion that she was "on to something" led to an extended search. In the potted palm, our Sherlock discovered the whole toothpick. As she examined these artifacts of the game, the sordid truth became apparent: *Bea was holding two broken pieces—so Cassie would be bound to draw a short one.* Mandy smiled, shook her head. *Well, don't that just beat all, how rich folks will cheat each other—and blood sisters at that!* The happy woman dropped the souvenirs into her apron pocket.

SEVEN
SOUTHERN UTE RESERVATION

Daisy Perika had heard only a few tantalizing words on the tribal radio about the white woman up by Granite Creek who had been killed in her bedroom. Rumor had it that an animal was responsible—probably a bear. During the lunch she had prepared for herself and Charlie Moon (Sarah Frank was away at school), Daisy had kept on pressing her closemouthed relative who had been *right on the spot*. But, as was his habit, the tribal investigator was keeping whatever he knew to himself. She watched the tall man get up from his seat across the kitchen table and head for the propane range. Daisy spoke to the back of his head: "The announcer on KSUT said the bear must've smelled food in the house."

"He did, did he?" Moon picked up Daisy's sooty coffeepot.

"I can't imagine a grown-up person doing a messy thing like that."

"Like what?" He began to pour a dark, viscous stream into his cup. *That looks strong enough to grow hair on a doorknob.*

Daisy was watching Moon intently, to gauge his response: "Eating strawberries in bed."

"Ow!"

Aha! Innocently, she asked, "What'd you do?"

"Poured coffee on my thumb."

Big dummy. "Put it under the cold-water faucet."

He preferred to suffer. "It was on the radio about the strawberries?"

"No." It was *so* much fun to put one over on Charlie. "I heard *that* from Willow Bignight." Willow's husband, Danny, was a tribal cop; he picked up all sorts of juicy rumors at the Southern Ute police station. Daisy grinned at her nephew. "But it's true, ain't it?"

Moon scowled. *Danny Bignight talks too much.*

Daisy cackled a crackly laugh. "You don't have to tell me—I can see the truth all over your face."

"You see whatever you want to see." He seated himself at the kitchen table, spooned six measures of highly refined, granulated cane sugar into the acidic beverage. Tasted it. *Not all that bad.*

The old woman shuddered at the thought of being ripped apart by a ravenous beast. "I'll have to remember to keep my windows closed at night."

"That'd be a smart thing to do." A merry light twinkled in his eyes. "Especially if you've just baked a couple of pies and put 'em on the windowsill to cool."

"Well, I haven't baked no pies and I don't intend to, so you might as well stop dropping hints." She reached for the sewing basket on the chair beside her, put it in her lap.

Moon reached a long, lean arm across the table, selected an apple from a cedar bowl, polished it on his shirtsleeve.

Daisy began sewing tiny blue and white and yellow glass beads onto a miniature, soft-as-morning-mist goatskin vest. The garment was a birthday present for Myra Cornstone's year-old baby, who, if Charlie Moon had married that nice Ute girl, would have been *his* baby boy instead of a white man's son, which annoyed the tribal elder no end. "That Spencer woman who was killed by the bear—was she any kin to old Joe Spencer?"

"She was one of his three daughters."

"Ouch!" The old woman had poked the wickedly sharp needle past the rim of her brass thimble, where it plunged deep into her finger, right to the bone. She pulled the thimble off, sucked at a drop of blood, and glared at Charlie Moon as if he were responsible for her injury. "Oh, sure—Astrid. And Cassandra, she's the one on TV. But who's the third one?"

"Beatrice." Moon smiled at his aunt. "I didn't know you were acquainted with that rich man's family."

"Well, there are lots and lots of things you don't know—enough to fill a five-story library full of books." Daisy shot her nephew a smug look. "Joe Spencer and his wife used to visit the reservation every summer. When that pale-skinned man got too much sun, he used to get sores on his head and neck. More'n once, I let him have some of my Ute medicine for skin cancers." The fact that the "Ute" medication was Navajo *Hisiiyáaníí* oil and that Daisy had sold the pungent yellow salve to the wealthy man for a five-hundred-percent markup was a trifling detail that she did not bother to trouble her memory for. "I used to see them two or three times every year. And even after his wife died, every once in a while ol' Joe would bring his pretty little daughters to a powwow or bear dance or rodeo. And once or twice I saw them at a sun dance."

He took a sip of coffee. "I don't recall ever meeting any of the Spencers on the res."

"That's because you spent so much time hanging out with riffraff." Daisy puckered her lips, sucked another drop of blood from the needle puncture before saying, "A person don't meet high-class people like the Spencers in stinky poolrooms and dirt-floor bars." Having sucked her fingertip bloodless, Daisy commenced with her sewing. "Those girls was just like stair steps—must've been about two or three years between 'em. This Astrid that got killed—was she the littlest one?"

"I expect so. She was the youngest." Moon twisted a tablespoon in a jar of honey, dunked the sweetener into his coffee.

Daisy held the unfinished baby vest up to the sunlight shining through the east window. *Something don't look quite right. I think it needs more white beads in with the blue ones. But not so many yellow ones.* "Sometimes I can't remember what I had for supper last night, but I remember them little girls all right. And I recall something that happened to them—just as clear as day—even though it must've been almost thirty years ago." In an attempt to conjure up the long-lost scene, the aged shaman stared intently at the beadwork thunderbird. "I believe it happened at a rodeo." A slow shake of the old gray head. "Or maybe a powwow." She scowled at the blank space in front of her face. "No, it was a big *matukach* to-do."

He tasted the honeyed coffee. "So what happened at this combination rodeo-powwow-big-*matukach* to-do?"

Big smart aleck. But Auntie smiled. "One of the bigger girls won a prize of some kind. The one with the yellow hair."

"That'd be Beatrice."

"And Astrid, the littlest sister, got awfully sick." Daisy closed her eyes to concentrate. Soon, the scenes from that memorable summer day were coming back to her. "Ol' Joe Spencer was holding little Astrid up in his arms; him and her both was white as a bleached bedsheet, and the bigger sisters was crying, and wringing their hands, and reaching out to pat Little Sister and tell their daddy that she'd be all right." As the memory faded, the old woman opened her eyes. "Sisters don't always get along as good as they should. And if they're mad about something, they can be lots meaner to each other than brothers would. That's what they say."

Charlie Moon assumed a solemn, philosophical expression that would have impressed Plato. Possibly even Socrates. "Don't pay too much attention to what *they* say." He pointed the apple core at his aunt. "Half the time, *they* are just blowing smoke."

Daisy Perika stared at her nephew as one might regard a backward child. *Every once in a while, Charlie says the strangest things, like his brain was about half baked.* The tribal elder, who was not a devotee of dead Greek sages, pursued her own philosophical persuasions, which included pseudogenetic hypotheses such as "blood will tell" and "insanity is passed on by the males." *I think he gets that craziness from his daddy's side of the family.*

• • •

Hours after her nephew had left for the drive north to the Columbine, and Sarah was home from school and asleep in bed, and Mr. Zig-Zag had extended his after-supper nap into a long night of mysterious feline dreams, Daisy was under the quilts. But not asleep. The aged woman stared at the ceiling, sighed at a parade of sorrowful memories. Young loves. Missed opportunities. Old friends gone. Her parents, of course—and baby brother. Uncle Blue Hummingbird. Charlie Moon's mother, a sweet woman and a good Catholic who had done her best to raise Charlie up right. Most of all, though Daisy would not have admitted it to a living soul, she missed Father Raes Delfino—in spite of the fact that the Jesuit priest was a tough, no-nonsense fellow who had never hesitated to warn Daisy that she should have nothing to do with the dwarf spirit who lived in *Cañón del Espíritu.* Unlike most whites, Father Raes (probably because of his strange experiences as a missionary in the South American jungles) accepted the Ute shaman's "power spirit" as a reality. A *dangerous* reality.

Daisy was surprised to realize that she also missed seeing the dwarf, who, though he would occasionally provide her with useful information in exchange for a modest gift of food or tobacco, could be an annoying fellow to deal with. But it had been well over a year since their last encounter. *I guess it's because I don't get up into Spirit Canyon much anymore.* Not that the shaman had always met the *pitukupf* at his badger-hole home. Once, the impudent little imp had shown up in church! Daisy had been horrified at the creature's brazen intrusion into St. Ignatius, and had the uneasy feeling that Father Raes had spotted the uninvited visitor there on the pew beside her. On a few occasions, the dwarf had visited Daisy at her home. She half wished he would show up now. *Maybe he could tell me something about those Spencer sisters. I'm still not sure where it was that I saw them. Or what it was that made little Astrid get so sick.*

The clock ticktocked away the minutes. Almost an hour's worth.

The *pitukupf* did not make an appearance.

Having worried about everything else, Daisy began to fret about the little man. *Maybe he's like me—too old and feeble to get out and go anywhere without help. Yes, that must be it. He's probably layin' in that dirty hole in the ground, thinking back about old folks that are gone—like his momma and daddy.* Which suggested a startling possibility that she had never considered. *I wonder if he ever had himself a little half-pint wife. If he did, the poor thing was probably every bit as homely as he is.* This might be why no one had ever reported seeing a baby *pitukupf*. *Maybe, a long time ago, the Little People were fairly good-looking.* But if they were, something bad must have happened to the *pitukupf* clan. *An ugly-curse, I bet—put on 'em by a Navajo or 'Pache witch they got crosswise of.* Since then, she conjectured, the tribe of tiny folk had been dying off.

Late at night, when the mind tends to drift off into silly thoughts, is not the best time to develop startling new theories intended to reshape the very foundations of human knowledge. Nobel Prize winners know this.

The weary woman's yawn was interrupted at half-gape when she spotted a dime-size spider eight-footing it across the windowpane. It had not been all that long ago when another such pest had taken a hike across her bedroom ceiling—and fallen onto Daisy's face. The startled woman had slapped her forehead so hard that her fingers still ached at breakfast time. Well aware of the taboo against killing Spider People (the murdered member's kin, bent on revenge, will come and find you!), she had searched for the tiny corpse so she could draw an imaginary circle around it and mumble, "I didn't kill you—it was one of them uppity Navajos. Tell your relatives to go and bite the Navajo." But she had not found the remains. Now, as Daisy eyed the creature on the window, it occurred to her that the spider's ghost probably knew who'd stopped his clock. If so, the avenging relatives might be camped close-by, and this one could be a scout sent to locate the Ute spider killer.

The guilty party jutted her chin, scowled at the intruder. *You even* think *about putting the bite on me, you nasty little bugger, I'll smack you flat as a flapjack—just like I did your ugly cousin!*

The leggy critter took off like a shot, boppity-bopping it back the way he had come from.

Daisy witnessed the retreat with the taste of gratification sweet on her tongue: *Hah—look at that lily-livered little backpeddler trot!* Satisfied with this modest victory, the feisty old warrior took up the yawn where she had left off. Cleared her throat of whatever it needed clearing. Shifted her stiff legs to find a more comfortable position. Sighed. Closed her eyes—one at a time, right then left, because this is the way shamans do it.

Blackness was what she saw, like a mile underground in the bowels of a coal mine. But gradually, as if the Cosmic Artist were dabbing silver paint, the dark canvas became studded with innumerable little pearls of light that bloomed, faded, tried ever so hard to look like stars. Just as she drifted off, Father Raes's kind face appeared among those uncertain constellations, smiled down upon Daisy Perika.

Nice touch.

• • •

EIGHT
THE COURTSHIP

Cassandra Spencer was astonished at how easily (and quickly!) Beatrice snagged her man. The psychic wondered whether her pretty sister might have bought a spell from one of those Mexican *brujas,* because she seemed to be doing nothing at all. As if by magic, Andrew began to drop by Bea's home. Call her on the phone. Within a week, the blooming romance was the talk of the town. There were quiet dinners in fine restaurants. Hand-in-hand walks in the park.

The shortest engagement in the recent history of Granite Creek was announced at a gathering of close family and friends. The date was set for the same day in April, forty-one years ago, when Beatrice's parents had exchanged solemn vows—and not quite a month after Astrid's death. It was quite a scandal, of course, which set tongues-a-clucking, eyes-a-rolling. For those who were not invited to the wedding, the fascinating details (with a splash of color photographs) were published in the Granite Creek weekly.

THE COLORADO SPRINGS AIRPORT

Cassandra Spencer lifted her dark glasses, leaning until her nose almost touched the plate-glass window. The aircraft the newlyweds had boarded just minutes earlier roared down the runway, lifted off the asphalt like a silver missile catapulted from little David's sling. The elder sister watched the sleek aircraft downsize to blackbird size, shrink to a mere speck in the sky, vanish into the southern mists. The thought that her ecstatic sister and drop-dead-handsome Andrew Turner were on their way to Costa Rica for a blissful honeymoon was irksome. *If I had pulled the whole toothpick, the bride clinging to Andy's arm right this minute would be me instead of Sister Bea. And she would be standing here, watching our plane leave.* But moping over bad luck was for losers. *I must drive back to Granite Creek, concentrate on my career. Think things out.* There was plenty to think about. Like how to come up with something really creepy that would grab the TV audience by their collective throats, give them a good dose of the shiver-shudders. That would take something more than your ordinary, run-of-the-mill spirit. Ghosts from ancient times were old hat. And so she would put on a brand-new thinking cap.

Thus resolved to come up with some really nifty notion—something that would make even Nicky Moxon sit up and listen—the psychic installed the blue shades over her luminous eyes, turned, and listened to the click-click of her high heels on the floor as she headed for the atrium. She was unaware of the eruption of human cargo currently being disgorged by the flight from Albuquerque. But soon enough, it would catch up with her.

A HAZARD OF THE PROFESSION

Cassandra Spencer was approaching the exit side of the security portal when she heard the shout behind her.

"Hey, you—hold on there!"

She stopped abruptly, turned.

A spry, snowy-haired old lady in a black dress spotted with tiny white polka dots was fairly tripping along, attempting to wave, which was a difficult maneuver with a heavy purse in one hand, a black canvas bag in the other. "I thought so—you're Cassandra. The spooky lady on TV!"

Oh, no. A fan. Which was, Bea had once informed her, an abbreviation for *fanatic.* The television personality was about to deny her identity when the enthusiast laughed and said: "And don't say you ain't, because I watch you practically every week!"

Trapped, Cassandra decided to make the best of it. *I'll autograph something for her, make an excuse about an urgent appointment, then hurry away.* She forced a smile, and was about to say that she was always pleased to meet a viewer, when the fanatical fan cornered her victim, gushed, "I flew in from the Duke City just to see you and tell you about poor April. I'd planned to ride a bus all the way over to Granite Creek and rent a motel room that'd probably cost me at least eighty-five dollars a night and me trying to live on Social Security and what little money my daughters—the two who are still alive—send me every once in a while—" She paused to gasp a breath. "But the very *minute* I get off the airplane, who do I see—just like she was meant to be here waiting for me?"

"Myself?"

"Well of course. Which means I don't have to pay for all that extra transportation, or a big motel bill, and what it'd cost to eat three times a day in the coffee shop—" Another breath. "Well, you know how much it costs; I expect you travel a lot."

The psychic's full, sensuous lips had gone thin. "I'm in quite a hurry at the moment, so—"

"Well of course you are, dearie—big TV star like you must have oodles of things to do. So I'll get right to the point." She lowered her voice. "My name is Florence Valentine."

She's probably sent me e-mails. Or letters. "Do I know you?"

"Oh, no, honey, we've never met before right now—and this is my first time in Colorado. I've only been in New Mexico for about a year. It was after poor April's death that I come out here to live with my first cousin, who has a cute little adobe house in Taos. Well, it's actually in El Prado, but that's just north of—"

"I'm *really* in quite a hurry." Cassandra made a point of glancing at her wristwatch.

"Don't fret, this'll just take a minute. But I've got to sit down—I've got arthritis in my hips and knees and my old feet are just killing me." Collapsing onto a cushioned seat, she patted the vacant one beside her. "Now you sit down too, and I'll tell you what this is all about."

Her other options being limited, Cassandra sat.

Florence Valentine explained that she knew that Cassandra had lost a sister because she had read "everything I could get my hands on about how poor Astrid had been attacked by bears—" gasp for breath, "and right there in her own bedroom. Well, I say!"

The psychic listened with increasing tension. *Somehow, I must disentangle myself from this goofball.*

But as is so often the case, there was considerably more to this dotty old lady than one might expect. As the words fairly poured from her mouth, what she had to say became more interesting.

Florence Valentine's finger tapped Cassandra on the arm. "Lately, poor April has been coming to me in my dreams and telling me I should contact you and tell you all about how she died."

Cassandra was pulled in opposite directions. The weary sister of the bride wanted to go home. The TV psychic, who loved to hear about such stuff as was her stock in trade, was inclined to stay—if only for another minute.

"The sheriff back in Clay County, North Carolina, said it was an accident. Said April must've slipped in the mud when she was slopping her prize hogs, and fell into the pen with 'em and she must've hit her head on the hollowed-out-log feed trough and got knocked out and then the pigs et her!"

Cassandra heard herself saying, "The pigs . . . actually *ate* your daughter?" *That is really icky. Triple icky.* She would have gone further, but *quadruple* was not in her vocabulary.

"Oh, they et poor April all right. Pigs'll swaller anything." The black eyes were flashing with anger. "But it wasn't no accident."

"It wasn't?"

"Shoot no. April's bastard of a husband knocked her on the head and pitched her into the pigpen."

"And how do you know this?"

Florence stared at the psychic. *She seems a lot more clever on the TV.* "Why, because April told me, of course."

"Oh. When she appeared in your dreams."

"That's right. And I told the sheriff what she told me, but Poke Unthank—that's the sheriff's name—Poke's as dumb as a poplar stump." She paused, calling to mind a long list of Mr. Unthank's shortcomings. "When I think about him, I almost wish I was still back in North Carolina, so's I could vote against the big tub of lard!"

"Mrs. Valentine, that is quite an interesting story." Another glance at the wristwatch. "But I really must run, so—"

"I understand, honey." She patted Cassandra's pale hand. "And I guess it would take way too long to tell you the whole, sorry tale." The woman in the polka-dot dress got a firm grip on her black canvas shopping bag and plopped it into the psychic's lap. "So you take this home with you—it's alla my re-search. There's some newspaper stories about poor April's death. Read it when you get a chance and you'll see why—out of all the spooky ladies in the whole U.S. of A.—my daughter picked *you* to help her." The tired traveler got to her feet. "After you've read it, I'm sure you'll be able to make contact with poor April, who's just bustin' a gut to tell you lots of stuff." Florence V. found a small notebook in her purse, wrote down a telephone number and her cousin's address in El Prado. "And if you want to talk to me again, here's how you can get in touch." She shot an anxious glance at the departure schedule on the monitors. "Now, I guess I'd best see if I can get myself on a plane back to Albuquerque."

As she lugged the heavy canvas bag to her black 1957 Cadillac Eldorado Brougham sedan, Cassandra Spencer considered tossing it into a trash can. She decided against this course of action, for two reasons. First, such an act in an airport might have appeared suspicious, and she did not wish to be taken aside, questioned by one of those hard-eyed Homeland Security types who might conclude that she was a disgruntled Arab in disguise. Second, the psychic had *that feeling*—which conveyed the strong impression that it would be unwise to discard the daffy old woman's "re-search." And so she carried it to her car, carted it all the way home, and dropped it in the hallway between Daddy's ancient grandfather clock and Momma's hideous elephant-foot umbrella stand. And there the shopping bag might have remained until cobwebs covered it. Except for the fact that Cassandra was an occasional insomniac.

Let us skip quickly past what happened between *then* and *now*. Watch the big hand on the granddaddy clock spin full circle—151 times.

Six days and seven hours later, long after she had gone to bed, Cassandra was not even slightly drowsy. When the hopeful sleeper would attempt to shut her eyes, they would pop open again. She tried reclining on her right side. Her left. Also flat on her back. After considering such time-honored remedies as sleeping pills, a glass of warm milk, a hot soak in the tub, counting stupid sheep jumping a rail fence, reading the history of Plano, Texas, or last month's article in PSYCHICAL REVIEW about how death by violence affects the personalities of recently disembodied spirits—Aha—"Recently Disembodied Spirits!" This reminded her of that odd encounter at the airport with the talkative old lady from somewhere or other whose daughter had been dined upon by a herd of famished swine. The wide-awake lady switched on the light, found Florence Valentine's black canvas bag between the tall, ticktocking timepiece and the deceased elephant's foot, took it back to her bedroom, and began to examine the contents.

This was not the solution for insomnia.

Indeed, on this night, Cassandra would not get a wink of sleep. Not one.

A long, hot soak in the tub—*that* would have been the very cure for what ailed her.

• • •

Oh. Another thing. On the following morning, when Cassandra Spencer stepped onto her front porch to pick up the weekly newspaper, she noticed a letter-size manila envelope in the mailbox. No stamp, no address, no return address. Only a printed READ THIS on both sides. She opened it with a long, pointy fingernail, removed a single sheet of paper. The message was also printed:

> I KNOW IT'S NONE OF MY BUSINESS BUT I
> THOUGHT YOU OUGHT TO KNOW THAT YOUR
> SISTER CHEATED YOU. SHE WAS HOLDING TWO
> HALF-TOOTHPICKS IN HER HAND.

Mandy the waitress was across the street in the Corner Bar, watching the darker of the Spencer sisters through a dusty window. She was unable to see the expression on the psychic's face as Cassandra learned The Truth. No matter— merely knowing that her note had been received was enough. In fact, Mandy was so excited that she— No. It is too indelicate to mention.

But one might go so far as to observe that the wielder of the poisoned pen had, while waiting for the climactic moment, polished off three beers. Without visiting the ladies' room.

• • •

NINE

THE HONEYMOON

This was their final night in Costa Rica, at the small but well-appointed beach cottage on the Golfo de Nicoya. How sweet it was, here on the flower-scented veranda. A light mist of rain drip-dripping off the thatched roof, tap-tapping onto shiny pebbles and pearly fragments of seashells. Hardly a stone's throw away, a gentle surf whispered of lost histories, ancient mysteries. A short walk inland, beyond yon cluster of coconut palms, within the lantern-lighted hotel ballroom, a rhythmic steel-drumming, a vibrant guitar thrumming, a woman's throaty voice calling for her lost lover.

Barefooted Beatrice Spencer-Turner, seated on a wicker couch beside her husband, was pleasantly cool in the cotton dress Andrew had purchased from a street vendor in Puntarenas. An embroidered vine twisted and twined around her hip; blue and red roses blossomed from the stubby little stems. As she dipped a silver spoon into a crystal bowl of pineapple-mango-coconut ice cream, allowed the ambrosia to melt on her tongue, the bride filled her eyes with a sunset of blue and gold wisps, murmured to her mate, "The moment is absolutely perfect."

The man nodded his agreement, raised a frothy glass, and responded in authentic beer-commercial fashion: "It doesn't get any better than this."

The bride indulged in another spoonful of the exotic dessert. "This stuff is simply scrumptious."

"It's also about a hundred calories per bite."

The slender woman cast her man a look. "Are you afraid I'll get fat?"

"Uh . . . no. Not unless you start eating sweets in between meals." Turner stared at a horizon that was swathed in shadows. *Or taking them to bed for nighttime snacks.* He blinked. *Now why did I think that?*

The dead sister had invaded the absolutely perfect moment. Ghosts have a way of doing that.

Beatrice recalled that within a few weeks after Sis had married Andy Turner, she had put on a few pounds. The eldest sister had become somewhat—there was only one word for it. *Chubby.* She frowned. "Andy . . ."

"Yes?"

"I want to ask you something."

"Ask away."

"I hope you won't mind—it's about poor Astrid."

Since the wealthy sister's tragic death, it was as if her first name had been legally changed to Poor.

The groom turned to regard his new sweetheart. "What is it?"

"Did Astrid indulge in bedtime snacks?"

Andrew Turner stared at the fading sunset. Sighed. "Yes. She developed a craving for sweets."

"Such as?" Bea dipped her spoon into the ice cream.

He shrugged. "Bonbons. Also coconut macaroons." Turner watched a gull skim the beach, snatch up a hapless land crab. "And strawberries."

With the spoon at her lips, Bea paused. "Strawberries?"

Turner smiled. "She dipped them in powdered sugar." A shadow wiped the smile away. "Whenever I was in Denver, I used to drop by a little mom-and-pop candy shop. I'd buy Astrid a box of chocolate-covered strawberries. Or a pound of apricot bonbons." He turned to gaze at his new wife. "Does that surprise you?"

"Yes." She put the bowl of ice cream on a small metal table.

"Before Astrid and I were married, she would never

touch a dessert. Always worried about gaining weight." He paused, listened for a moment to what the sea had to say. It said *Shhhhhhhhhh.* . . . "But people change."

"Yes," she said. In the hotel ballroom, the long, melancholy song ended. There was a muted murmur of applause that might have been a faint echo from the surf. "Even those persons nearest and dearest to us—I suppose we never really know them as well as we would like to imagine." It dawned on the bride that the honeymoon was over. From now on her life would be filled with new, unanticipated responsibilities. And Beatrice was determined to be a perfect wife. Discipline, that was what was called for. She made herself a solemn promise to lose five pounds. And keep them off. She squinted at the sunset, which display was now blemished by a long, purple bruise. *Poor, dear Astrid. You loved Andrew so very much. But now you are dead. And Andrew is mine. . . . To have and to hold. Till death do us part.*

• • •

A few minutes past midnight, when her husband was deep in a dreamless sleep, Beatrice padded silently from their bedroom, removed a satellite telephone from her carry-on, and placed a ridiculously expensive call to her sibling.

Cassandra answered on the second ring. "Bea—oh, I'm so glad you called. I've been dying to talk to you but had no idea which hotel you were—"

"Well of course you didn't. A blissful bride does not wish to have her honeymoon disturbed by frivolous calls from her silly sister. Andrew and I will be arriving in Colorado Springs tomorrow, and I wondered whether we should rent a car at the airport, or would you like to pick us up in your snazzy Caddy?"

"I'll meet you, of course. But let me tell you what was in today's newspaper. The police haven't verified it, but the word is that they found strawberries in Astrid's bedroom, which was what attracted the bears—"

"The story is undoubtedly accurate, Cassie. Just today, Andrew told me that our sister ate strawberries in bed."

"He did?"

"Yes."

"Well then . . . that would seem to settle things."

"As you say."

Count eleven heartbeats. Four for Bea, seven for Cassie.

As if someone might overhear, the TV psychic lowered her voice. "There is something else. Just minutes after you and Andrew left for Costa Rica, I was cornered by this eccentric old woman whose daughter had died in the most *horrible* manner and she wanted me to—"

"Save it, Cassie."

"But—"

"Your story will keep till I get back."

"But—"

"No buts. I mean it. Not another word."

A tense silence.

"Cassie, are you still there?"

"Yes." Her tone was awash with sulk.

Beatrice smiled. *Oh, my, I've hurt her feelings.* "Dear— I'm sure that what you want to tell me about is absolutely fascinating. We shall have many things to discuss. But *not over the telephone.*" She inhaled a breath of tropical flower scents. "See you at the airport?"

"Same flight as on your original itinerary?"

"That's right."

The response was icy: "I'll be there."

Cassie is having a major pout. "Okay, Sis. See you—"

CLICK!

"—then."

• • •

TEN
TWO SISTERS

As she had promised, Cassandra was at the airport to meet Beatrice and her recently acquired husband. Customary greetings were exchanged, not excluding the obligatory hugs, but the embraces were lacking in enthusiasm, and even the perfunctory pecks on cheeks were replaced with air kisses. Being unaware of Bea and Cassie's brief, tense telephone conversation last night, Andrew was puzzled. But due to his limitations, which included not understanding the least thing about the other gender, he observed their odd behavior with aloof, male bemusement.

On the drive to Granite Creek, conversation was limited to snippets about how warm and humid it had been in Costa Rica and how cool and dry it had been in central Colorado and Cassie's stated hope that they were not suffering from jet lag and Beatrice's explanation of the difference in longitude and latitude and Cassie's resultant tight-lipped attitude. And so it went as the Cadillac ran a losing race with the setting sun.

That evening, while Andrew was at Granite Creek Electronics and Computers, checking on how his assistant manager had been handling the prosperous business, the ladies closeted themselves in Beatrice's bedroom and engaged in sister talk. Bea listened with intense interest to Cassie's tale about Florence Valentine and her unfortunate daughter's gruesome demise, and how the psychic proposed to exploit the lurid details. Cassie heard her sister's honeymoon report, which included such details as how loudly her new husband snored, the heart-shaped mole between his shoulder blades, and further details of Andrew's shocking revelation that Astrid had taken up the habit of eating sweets in bed. Well, that alone was enough to give one pause. But sugar-dipped and chocolate-coated strawberries—how absolutely extraordinary!

Toothpicks? The subject never came up. Evidently, Cassie had forgiven her treacherous sister.

Henceforth, it would be reasonable to presume that they would be loving, caring, sharing sisters—nothing could come between them. Not even a perfectly tanned, brown-eyed handsome man.

And so it seemed.

Beatrice, who had won a multitude of ribbons and medals for her paintings, began to plan her masterpiece. It would be a gift for Andrew.

Coincidentally (or perhaps not), Cassandra began to pursue plans of her own, which centered on her career. It seemed that her star was on the rise. The darkly attractive woman was, in a word, charismatic. And in two more, a hot property. Ever since her on-air, real-time vision of the cold-blooded shooting of the truck driver, the audience of her television broadcast had continued to increase.

Whispered speculations had begun to circulate and take on weight and—as those young Turks of the TV business say whilst sipping five-dollar paper cups of caffé latte—the buzz-bug grew legs and took off in a brisk trot. *Clippity-clop*. Insiders in the local broadcast industry winked and whispered that they had the "inside word"—*Cassandra Sees* was going to be picked up by one of the big networks. ABC. Or Fox.

Unaware that her crafty business manager, Nicholas Moxon, was both providing feedstock and turning the crank on the rumor mill, Cassandra was quite excited about her potential future as a coast-to-coast psychic celebrity. She realized that the road ahead would be difficult. Pitfalls, potholes, gridlock—all that sort of thing. But being the trooper that she was, the star of *Cassandra Sees* stiffened her upper lip and called upon another proverb that has long provided steely-eyed Americans with a stiff dose of get-up and go: *Where There's a Will, There's a Way*. The lady had oodles and gobs of Will. More important, she had come up with a Way. The solution had occurred to the psychic on that sleepless night while she was reading the pile of newspaper clippings about April Valentine's death. Cassandra's devious plot—if carried out *just so*—would accomplish two very important objectives. One professional, the other personal.

Moxon was surprised and delighted with his formerly languid client's newfound energy. It was, as he had often pointed out to the TV psychic, much easier to promote a public figure who wanted to go somewhere with her career.

But Miss Spencer, like others of her gender, was a mysterious creature whose dark, roiling depths Mr. Moxon could not plumb.

Cassandra's *motive* in concentrating on fame and fortune would have astonished her business manager. Her frenetic activity, both physical and mental, served to keep the lady's thoughts from being overwhelmed by her primary objective.

Which, as it happened, was a man.

A man who was . . . but what adjectives could do him justice? Only a few days ago, Cassandra would have gone with "devilishly clever, drop-dead handsome." But that was then. By now, her obsession had taken a sinister twist and turn. The mere *thought* of her sister's husband engendered raw, animal lusts that were beyond desire— even jealousy. These were dark, sinful cravings that the oldest Spencer sister had never believed herself capable of. The mania that threatened to consume her was at once repellant and thrilling—and might drive a passionate woman to do anything. *Anything.*

To divert her fragile psyche from leaping off the precipitous cliff, the psychic focused all her pent-up emotional energies on the career. She was, for the most part, successful.

There were those evenings when she would lie flat on her back in the queen-size four-poster, dark eyes wide open, heart pounding, thinking about *that man*. Imagining that Andrew was there . . . within her reach. On such nights as these, she could not sleep.

What she did was plot. And plan.

For what? Why, *to get her man*.

• • •

ELEVEN

A FEW DAYS AFTER THE HONEYMOON

Having finished a breakfast of bran muffins and orange juice, jogged on the treadmill for a sweaty half hour, and enjoyed a brisk three minutes in the shower, Andrew Turner donned blue cotton underwear and socks, a white silk shirt, ash-gray trousers and vest, and a pale blue tie with an ebony clip to match the studs in his cuffs. He slipped on an immaculate pair of black cowboy boots, did a stiff-backed West Point–cadet pose before the mirror in the master bedroom, admired the image.

Industrious Beatrice Spencer was already at work in her spacious upstairs studio, where a half-dozen mullioned windows admitted that soft northern light that would not cast stark shadows, or create vulgar glares on an artist's delicate composition of form and color. Wearing a paint-splattered canvas smock, she was putting the final touches on her "masterpiece." As Bea dabbed and daubed and cocked her head and held her mouth "just right," she absorbed heavenly strains of Chopin's *Fantaisie* in F Minor, Opus 49. What unadulterated bliss. But, like tumbleweeds riding on the wind, such moments pass all to quickly. This particular reverie was interrupted by the sharp clicks of Andrew's boot heels coming up the stairway. Thus forewarned, the creative lady hurriedly cast a cast-off cotton bedsheet over the work in progress and turned her attention to an earlier creation that could do with a few brushstrokes.

The man of the house barged in like the captain of a

shoot-'em-dead SWAT team about to confront a terrorist with bomb in hand, boomed out, "What're you up to, my little Sweet Bea?"

Grimacing at this crude horticultural pun, Beatrice made a deft brushstroke. "I am touching up *Wild Burros Grazing in Sage.*"

"Burros?" The husband came closer to the canvas, picking his teeth with a spruce toothpick. (Oh, but had he known how the sisters had played at pull-the-toothpick—and what the winner had gotten for fixing the game!) Try as he might, the prize did not see anything that resembled a four-legged creature. Neither could he discover any sage being grazed upon. He canted his head sideways, tried to think of something complimentary to say. "That gizmo on the left looks like a flamingo. With a monkey on its back."

Now, despite her few faults (and none of us is perfect), Beatrice was as good a wife as Andrew had any right to expect, and the soul of patience with her secondhand husband. Since the brief honeymoon, she had endured a number of his oafish remarks on the subject of her Art, and had passed them off as symptoms of a combination of afflictions—which included a deplorable ignorance and a deprived upbringing in a family where the only visual art in the home was on a calendar from Chuck's Corner Hardware. But one can take only so much. She turned on her husband, cast the blue-eyed, icy glare. "Andrew, do not think me unkind—but someone must tell you this: You are a Neanderthal."

"Maybe I am." He pointed his chin at *Wild Burros Grazing in Sage.* "But I could paint a helluva lot better horse on a cave wall than that."

"I assume that you refer to the ancient sketches in the caverns of France." She aimed the paintbrush at his pale blue tie. "That ageless art was created by Cro-Magnon man, no doubt while your slope-browed cousins stood by grunting, scratching themselves in unseemly places, and generally making sport of their intellectual superiors."

His happy laugh twanged at her nerve strings. "You are *so* cute when you're mad!" He grabbed her, inflicted the woman with a suffocating kiss, and was gone.

Beatrice managed to catch her breath. *Andrew is such a brute! I don't know why I married him.* But she did know, of course. Almost every day, the bride would remind herself that when a person weds another person without a lengthy getting-to-know-you engagement, there are bound to be a few unpleasant surprises. Ever the confident one, Beatrice assured herself that she was capable of managing difficult situations. With all his faults, Andrew was merely a man. It was largely a matter of facing the facts of his shortcomings, and working out a corrective plan.

And she had. By and by, things would be just fine.

THAT EVENING

When Andrew Turner returned to hearth and home after a busy day at Granite Creek Electronics and Computers, his wife was neither adding split pine to the flames crackling in the hearth nor preparing dinner in the kitchen. He found her in the wine cellar.

Beatrice was on a small stepladder, replacing a dusty bottle that did not quite meet the requirements for tonight's meal.

Hubby crept up with admirable stealth, slapped her on the behind.

Not stealthily enough. She had heard the door at the top of the stairs creak open, seen his slender, sinister shadow creeping ever closer. This was why the lady did not flinch at the stinging smackimus on her gluteus maximus.

Understandably disappointed by this unenthusiastic response, Andrew scowled, fell back on his witty repartee: "So what're you up to, Sweet Bea?"

"I am attempting to locate an appropriate vintage."

"For fish or fowl?"

"We shall feast on what Madison Avenue refers to as the Other White Meat."

"Ah—oinker flesh."

"Grade-A pork, Andrew. Which, in this instance, has been genetically engineered to produce copious quantities of omega-3." *Or is it omega-5? I can never remember.*

"The mere mention of high-tech biology gives me a horrendous appetite." The computer expert licked his lips. "Ham, I presume?"

"Ix-nay on am-hay. For dinner, we are having butter-flied chops. With baby green peas." She looked down to smile at the handsome man. "And homemade applesauce, with just a touch of cinnamon."

"That sounds good enough to eat."

And it was.

As the man of the house was carving off a triangular chunk from an inch-thick pork chop, the missus advised, "Don't forget that Cassie's TV show is on tomorrow night at nine."

"Has another week already come and gone?" Andrew Turner interrupted the meat-cutting task, gazed across the mahogany dining table at his elegant wife. "The pleasant days in between your sister's whiz-bang public performances seem to slip by so quickly." His smile barely lifted the sparse growth of mustache he had been cultivating since returning from the Costa Rican honeymoon. "It seems only last night that the Dark Lady was predicting spectacular disasters and communing with various spooks."

"You should not make sport of dear Cassie."

"Very well, I will attempt to restrain myself." He got back to work on the pork chop. "But you must admit, she is a bit of a . . ." He searched for the word. It had something to do with dessert. *Aha.* "Fruitcake." *Good-looking fruit-cake, though.*

"That is unkind, Andrew. Cassie is—shall we say—*gifted.*"

"That is too generous, Bea. She is—shall we say—creepy."

"I suggest a compromise. My gifted sister is mildly eccentric."

"Agreed. But only for the sake of keeping peace in the family." He hefted a succulent morsel of roasted pig flesh to his mouth. Chewed. This supper grub was downright tasty. As was a spoonful of infant butter-soaked peas, another of cinnamon-sprinkled applesauce.

Beatrice, who had only pecked at her food, picked up a bone-china teacup, took a dainty sip of Darjeeling. "If you will make a pretense of being interested, I will pass on some inside information about Cassie's next show."

"Very well, I will pretend as best I can." A gulp of black, cold-brewed coffee. "What is Miss Mildly Eccentric serving up tomorrow evening—another conversation with a long-dead celebrity?"

Beatrice shook her head.

"Oh, *pack rats.*" To his credit, and to please his wife, Mr. Turner was attempting to clean up his language. "I was looking forward to a chat with Professor Einstein. Or Thomas Edison."

Bea regarded him over the teacup. "Much better than that."

"I doubt it." He winked at his wife. "But give me a hint."

"Very well—Cassie is communing with a new spirit. But not a celebrity."

"Animal, mineral, or vegetable?"

"Minerals and vegetables do not have spirits."

"And animals do?"

Beatrice had a sudden sensation that the ghosts of Ike and Spike were watching from a darkened hallway. The German shepherds were presumably eager to hear her response to this weighty theological question. "Of course animals have spirits. But the communicant in question is a *human* spirit." She put the teacup aside. "Cassie is in touch with a soul who died a horrible, violent death."

Andrew Turner felt his hands go cold. "Bea, please tell me that Cassandra isn't pretending to talk to Astrid!"

"Oh no. Nothing like that."

"Color me thankful."

"And she is not *pretending*. Cassie has been communicating with a perfect stranger."

"Then advise her to proceed with caution." Andrew put knife to pork chop. "There is no such thing."

"Please explain."

"Tell your gullible sister, and you may quote me: 'If strangers were not an inferior lot, we would already be acquainted with them. It follows, then, that there can be no perfect ones.'" He inserted his fork into the succulent swine morsel.

"Andrew—you are so terribly droll!" Beatrice put a napkin to her lips. "Shall I tell you more about Cassie's most recent contact from the spirit world?"

"If it will make you incandescently happy." He raised the fork.

"Her name is April Something."

The sterling silver instrument stalled just below Andrew's chin. "What?"

"It's a funny last name." Beatrice waved the napkin, as if this gesture would help her summon the memory. Evidently, it did. "Oh—now I remember. The spirit identifies herself as April Valentine. Sounds like a showgirl's name." Expressing just the merest hint of disapproval, Bea arched a brow. "And when I tell you how this distraught spirit claims she died, you will not believe it."

Andrew Turner stared at his wife.

"April Valentine told Cassie that she had been eaten by hogs."

The distraught diner returned the fork, pork and all, to his plate.

• • •

TWELVE
HIS HOBBY

According to St. Augustine, what every man desires is *peace*. And you can bet your boots and saddle too—the Bishop of Hippo knew what he was talking about.

Whether or not sweet, inner tranquility was what Andrew Turner was seeking, the man was definitely in need of solitude. He wished to withdraw to a secluded spot where a fellow—if he was a mind to—could gnaw on a ten-dollar pork chop without having to put up with the wife's incessant chatter. Happily for Mr. Turner, he was the sort of far-sighted individual who had already prepared just such a refuge for himself. After dinner with Beatrice, he mumbled something about needing to attend to a couple of things, and retreated quickly. Along the hallway he marched, boot heels saying *clickety-click*. Sudden left turn, through the door, down the narrow stairway, into the musty-cool wine cellar.

No, an alcoholic beverage was not what the man was after. He made a beeline to the sealed-off corner that had once served a similar purpose for Bea's father, when the old man felt that occasional need to deprive himself of the wholesome company of his attentive wife, who was always offering excellent advice upon such weighty issues as how her mate might lose a few unsightly inches around his middle by substituting crispy celery for fried potatoes and unsweetened tea for pale German ale.

Unlike his hale and hearty bear-shooting predecessor,

Turner was not overly fond of either greasy potatoes or imported beer. He was of that peculiar segment of society that has a taste for overpriced coffees flavored with cocoa and spices, Chopin as interpreted by Evgeny Kissin, and a yen for things electronic and digital. Bea's recently acquired husband was, it is fair to say, an electronics and computer *genius*. Also fair to say—a geek. This is honestly meant to be a compliment. (Really.)

Shortly after moving in with his new wife, Mr. Turner had assumed squatter's rights to old Joe H. Spencer's basement hideaway, which included a full bath, a comfortable leather couch, a modern kitchenette, which the usurper had stocked with a selection of foods and beverages, including coffees that would have made Mr. Starbucks roast with envy, and also the most remarkable assembly of—No. Rather than tell (so it is said by those who know), it is better to show. So let the show begin.

Andrew Turner unlocked the door to his sanctuary, entered the darkened space (there were no windows in this crypt), and locked the door behind him. He took four measured steps across the carpet, paused, addressed a concealed microphone: "It begins."

This code phrase was promptly amplified, filtered, digitized. The result was compared to a 90-kilobyte digital file of Andrew's voice (also saying, "It begins"), which was stored in a SanDisk flash memory stick that was plugged into a USB port on his Dell computer. Within about four hundred milliseconds, the result was determined to be "within parameter," which enabled the interface between computer and external-control circuitry to do its stuff. Which was to switch on an overhead spotlight that illuminated the man, and activated a ten-second digital recording of a Carnegie Hall audience applauding a sterling performance of Dvorak's Symphony no. 8.

Andrew Turner bowed, murmured a modest "thank you." As the clapping of thousands of pairs of enthusiastic hands continued, he smiled (condescendingly) at the invisible crowd, waited as the appreciative sounds gradually faded.

The moment having arrived to get down to serious business, the performer flipped back the imaginary tails of an imaginary tux and seated himself on a varnished oak bench at a magnificent grand piano. For about three heartbeats—no. That is incorrect. There was no bench. One gets carried away. He was perched on a quite ordinary, padded black office chair. But where were we? Oh, yes.

For about three heartbeats—while he imagined the expectant audience sitting raptly on the edges of their expensive seats (tickets ranged from fifty to five hundred dollars!)—the maestro's thin, pale hands were poised above the ivories. No. Not above the ivories. As there was no bench, there was also no piano, grand or otherwise.

The maestro's thin, pale hands were poised above a QWERTY keyboard.

His nimble fingers began to dance across the keys.

Rapture!

Not quite at the speed of light, a command was sent over the modem, along the telephone lines, to awaken a computer in another home and provide him with access to the hard disk. Which is what Andrew Turner—who might be likened to a digital Peeping Tom—often did merely for the joy of voyeurism. But this particular entry was one from which he expected to profit. After downloading 2,641 files from the unsuspecting computer and disconnecting from that machine, he applied himself to the tedious process of analyzing data. Turner began with word-processing files. Nothing of great interest. He moved on to e-mails sent and received. Almost at once, he discovered that some dozens of incoming messages were encrypted—which made them immensely interesting. It required only about fifteen minutes for Turner to locate the password in the stolen files. After this, the process was mere child's play. One by one, he began to read the secret e-mails. On the very first one, he knew he had hit (as the crusty old silver miners used to say) "color." Pay dirt. Andrew had the dirt, all right. The question was—what to do with it? The answer, when it came to him, was: Hmm. How best to put it? After due consideration, one concludes that there are only two descriptors sufficient to the task. One of them is "perfect." The other is "just what the doctor ordered."

The computer expert was feeling measurably better. He had found a kind of peace.

But not that *peace which passeth all understanding.* What Andrew Turner had settled for was that ersatz variety offered by this world, which *doth not satisfy,* and *quickly fadeth away.* . . .

Even a brief encounter with St. Augustine might have helped him immensely.

THIRTEEN
SOUTHERN UTE RESERVATION

Red Shoes

Sarah Frank moved expertly about Daisy Perika's kitchen, flipping fatty beef patties in a blackened cast-iron skillet, taking plates and bowls to the table, hurrying back to the propane range to add a quarter cup of chopped onions and three tablespoons of brown sugar to the bubbling saucepan of beans, all the while promising her mewing black-and-white cat that his portion would be ready before long. Judging by his expression, Mr. Zig-Zag doubted this promise.

Daisy was at the dining table, hunched motionless in a cushioned maple chair. Her form suggested a long-deceased toad whose husk had mummified in the dry, high-country air. But she was definitely alive. For the time being.

Her dark eyes watched the lively girl, who had already packed their bags for tomorrow's trip to Charlie Moon's Columbine Ranch, as she prepared a supper of cheeseburgers, garlic-flavored potato chips, and beans from a can. The old woman would have preferred a steaming bowl of homemade green-chili posole and a hot flour tortilla (rolled up tight with butter melting inside), but the fifteen-year-old had, one baby step at a time, taken charge of the household chores. Grateful to have a home where she was welcome, the orphan was showing her gratitude by taking care of "Aunt Daisy." The tribal elder was aunt only to Charlie Moon, and Charlie was old enough to be Sarah's father—which did not deter the girl from the notion that, one way or another, even if it took the rest of her life, she would be Charlie's wedded wife.

Bone-weary from an accumulation of hard winters, Daisy did not object to Sarah doing all the work. But the *realization* that she did not mind was bothersome. For all her life as an adult, which had begun at the age of nine (when her mother succumbed to overwork, underappreciation, and tuberculosis), Daisy had been an independent soul. For almost as long as she could remember, she had made and mended most of her clothing on a pedal-operated Singer sewing machine, cooked squash and pinto beans from her small garden, roasted cottontail rabbit, wild turkey, and mule deer, which—when there wasn't a man handy—she hunted and killed with her father's Winchester rifle, or the double-barrel 12-gauge that she kept in the closet by the front door. Now, during the space of only a few months, and largely by her own choice, she had become dependent upon this girl, who was only half Ute.

Sarah brought the aged "aunt" a glass of cold milk and a plastic bowl of potato chips, then a platter with a generous helping of beans and onions and a burger capped with two melted slices of Velveeta cheese. "You'll like this." She beamed at the doubtful diner, added in a motherly tone, "And it'll be good for you."

"Yes, I hear cheeseburgers does some really special things for the heart." When this sarcasm washed over the girl without effect, Daisy added, "Beans give me gas and make me—"

Sarah interrupted quickly, "Do you want a dill pickle?"

"No, I'm sour enough already." Having forgotten what she was about to say about the consequences of gastric gas, Daisy consumed a small helping of the delicious beans, then got to work on the greasy cheeseburger.

While the old woman ate in moody silence, the girl fed her cat and fixed a plate for herself, all the while filling the kitchen with a torrent of words. She hoped Daisy's cousin (Gorman Sweetwater) would arrive right on time at nine tomorrow morning, that he wouldn't mind Mr. Zig-Zag riding in the pickup cab—her aged pet would get very lonely in the back, and not only that, he'd try to get into the box of pecan cookies and the two rhubarb pies Sarah had made with her very own hands and was taking to Charlie and how long did Aunt Daisy think it would take Gorman to drive to the Columbine and did Charlie ever mention that pretty white woman (what was her name?) who worked for the FBI—was she still out in California and did they ever talk on the phone and did Charlie have any other girlfriends and do you like your cheeseburger?

From time to time, Daisy would shake her head and sigh. *I don't know how that girl can talk so much and eat at the same time and I never see her take a breath.*

After supper, while Sarah washed the dishes, Daisy hobbled off to her cozy parlor, seated herself close to the fireplace. As flame tongues licked hungrily at tasty morsels of split piñon, the old woman watched the curling swirls of smoke, thought her melancholy thoughts. *My bones hurt. Every one of them! Back when I was in my seventies, I could work all day. Now I sleep half my life away. I'm too old and tired to do anything useful—I can't even take care of myself.* A long, self-pitying sigh. *Nobody needs an old woman like me.* Unaware that Mr. Zig-Zag had curled up beside her rocking chair because he liked being near her, and that Sarah adored her, and that Charlie Moon's world would have been much less appetizing without the presence of his salty old aunt, Daisy nodded to agree with what she thought was a ruthlessly honest analysis. *I'm just a burden to Sarah and Charlie Moon.* And what was worse—*I don't have much fun anymore.* Noticing Mr. Zig-Zag, she made a halfhearted attempt to step on the cat's tail, but the canny animal always managed to be just out of reach. This failure to accomplish such a simple task did nothing for Daisy's morale. She scowled at the animal. *It's time for me to move on down the road, let the young ones run things. Or ruin things, more likely. But that's none of my business.* Business. The word brought to mind a troublesome detail. *I need to get a will made out, so Sarah gets my house. Charlie Moon don't need anything I've got, but I'll put him a few things in a box, like that old Barlow pocket knife that belonged to my second husband. And I need to write Charlie a note so he'll remember that I want to be buried in my nice purple dress.* Which reminded her: *But I need to get me some brand-new underwear and a nice pair of white cotton stockings.* Daisy looked at her feet. *And some pretty shoes.* She pictured herself in the coffin. *Red shoes.*

Knowing ahead of time that she would soon "cross that River" had one compensation: A person could look forward to some prefuneral shopping. But what she looked forward to at the moment was a good night's sleep. And so off to her bedroom she went.

On the way, she stepped on a spider. No, this was not an accident. The deed was done *on purpose,* and with some relish.

To quote Chief Washakie: "Young men sometimes do foolish things."

What does this Shoshone proverb have to do with an aged Ute woman? Merely this: From time to time, even old women do foolish things. By way of illustration, consider Daisy's recent encounters with eight-legged creatures. It is one thing to smack a careless spider that falls onto your face—one can hardly be held responsible for a reflex action. However, it is quite another matter to commit deliberate, premeditated arachnicide. Of the first degree. And not even bother to draw the circle, mumble the appropriate lie about how a Navajo was responsible, et cetera. Such behavior reeks of arrogance.

It may be that what followed so closely on the heels of her callous crime was the revenge of the Spider People. Or perhaps it was the cheeseburger.

THE WEE HOURS

After Sundown, many senior citizens sleep away the dark hours, and are thereby refreshed. Not Daisy Perika. Seven days a week, and all around the clock, she has what could rightly be called "an interesting life." For one hair-raising example, take tonight.

• • •

Miss Daisy was precisely where she wanted to be—on her bed by the window, bathed in the silver radiance of a full moon, adrift on a sea of deep, restful sleep, immersed in a blissful self-told tale wherein things were definitely going her way. Any card-carrying member of the Pessimists' Club will tell you that such a happy state cannot last for long.

Her dream was interrupted.

Daisy felt something. Something close-by. *In the bed with her*—snuggled up against her side!

Was it Sarah, who'd had a nightmare and come to climb in bed beside Auntie?

No, the teenage girl was larger than whatever this was.

It's just a bad dream. I've got to make myself wake up so it'll go away.

Hardly daring to breathe, the sleeper opened her eyes.

Nice try.

The thing was still there, a quivering coldness pressed against her ribs. Yes, quivering. Or was it purring?

Must be that damn cat. Along with a flood of relief, Daisy enjoyed a surge of righteous anger. *I'll grab that old fleabag by the tail and swing him around a few times and pitch him against the wall so hard he'll*—But wait a minute.

It occurred to her that there was another, more alarming possibility. *Maybe I forgot to latch the back door. It might be a raccoon that got cold and come inside looking for a warm spot.* Or worse, a skunk. Or worse still, a rabid pack rat. But wait another minute.

Her unwelcome bedmate could not be any of those varmints. Raccoons, skunks, and rabid pack rats are warm, furry mammals. The intruder in bed beside her was cold and clammy as a piece of dead meat. Also hard and lumpy as a bag of brass doorknobs. And now that she thought about it, the whatever-it-was was not exactly quivering—it was shivering.

Discretion was called for. *Maybe if I just lay real still, it'll go away.* Taut as a banjo string, the plucky woman avoided the least movement. Counted off thirty-six of the clock's clickety-tickety tocks. Prayed for this nightmare to end. It did not.

But, as she waited, the shivering gradually subsided. And every few heartbeats, the tribal elder fancied that she could hear the creature breathe. *What in the world has gotten into bed with me?* Additional scary possibilities were blooming in Daisy's fertile imagination when—

Her companion began to snore. But not at all like a skunk or pack rat snores. Like a *man* snores. The evidence was in, there could be only one conclusion: *Some drunk has wandered into my house, crawled into bed with me.* Well, that flat *did* it. *I'll strangle him with my bare hands!*

Daisy raised herself on an elbow, jerked back the covers—stared in astonishment at what she saw in the moon's vaporous glow. Her companion, curled into a fetal position, was outfitted in a tattered black hat, a faded green cotton shirt, beaded buckskin breeches, and moccasins. And though he was about the size of a five-year-old boy, this was not a child. The intruder was the Little Man, who lived in the badger hole. *So what's he doing here in my house—in bed with me?* A fair question.

The dwarfish creature shuddered, blinked, fixed pale, yellowish eyes on the shaman. His poisonous expression said it all: How dare she disturb his rest!

Now the *pitukupf* was not the only person who had been awakened. And old folks are apt to be a mite grumpy when their slumbers have been disturbed. Especially by a pushy outsider. The aged woman ground her remaining teeth. Ready—nay, *eager* to commit a violent act, Daisy went with her initial impulse. Strangulation—that was just the ticket. This furious woman—whose Christian mother had named her tiny girl-child after a delicate wildflower— flexed her fingers, anticipated the satisfying feel of his scrawny little neck, the ensuing desperate struggle, her victim's last gurgling gasps, saliva bubbling from between his lips— But enough of mayhem and violent death.

There are several reasons why it is not possible to provide a precise and accurate account of what happened next. First, the dwarf speaks an archaic version of the Ute language that even Daisy Perika has trouble understanding. Second, the shaman is reticent to share every detail concerning her dealings with the *pitukupf*. Third, there is a strict taboo against revealing certain . . . Forget third. First and second are sufficient.

A brief summary is called for.

The upshot of the encounter was that Daisy, who recalled the "Thou Shalt Not Murder" commandment, cooled off somewhat. After which, the little man explained the reason for his visit:

(A) The juniper fire on his hearth had gone out.

(B) In the ensuing darkness he could not locate the leather pouch where he kept his flint-and-steel fire starter.

(C) He had come to borrow some matches. Also a candle or two.

(D) He would help himself to these items on the way out.

At the moment, his paramount desire was to go back to sleep, which he could not do with the moonlight blinding him. Imperiously, the cheeky fellow pointed a finger at the window, directing the tribal elder to pull the shade.

Daisy's pithy response would be unsuitable for a family audience. It would also shock and scandalize drunken Bulgarian sailors, Denver pimps, Juárez drug pushers, and several senior members of the New Mexico State Legislature.

The tribal elder's verbal assault did not faze the *pitukupf*.

Either the little man was as thick-skinned as a Yucatán pineapple or he possessed one of those rare, blessed souls that do not take offense. Take your pick. He proposed a deal: If Daisy would give him time for a few winks and provide the means for making a fire on his underground hearth, he promised to depart before first light. Without waiting to see how she would respond to the carrot, he brandished the Big Stick. (Diplomacy was not the dwarf's long suit.) If she forced him out into the cold, he would burn down her barn and kill all her horses, sheep, and goats.

Daisy informed him that she possessed neither out-buildings nor livestock.

This statement seemed to confuse the little man, who was hundreds of years old and could not be expected to remember every detail about his neighbor's holdings. But no matter. One way or another, he would get even for any act of inhospitality on her part.

Knowing that this was no idle threat, Daisy told him where she kept a brand-new box of Fire Chief "Strike Anywhere" kitchen matches. He could take no more than a dozen, and she would know if he did. But sleep in her bed? That was unthinkable. No way. She would not even consider such a brazen proposal. Unless her diminutive guest would provide her with something of comparable value in return.

He suggested a turquoise pendant (shaped like a raven's gizzard) that would cure nosebleed, diarrhea, and excessive verbosity.

No, thanks. The shaman already had a half-dozen such charms. What she needed at the moment was a mere trifle— a minor piece of historical information. Before he could object, she got right to the point: Did the dwarf happen to know who Old Joe Spencer was?

Well of course he did. Knowing such stuff was his business.

Good. She proceeded: When the three Spencer sisters were little girls, one day at a big to-do where hundreds of people were present, one of them had gotten sick. What had been the occasion? And what was it that had made the little girl sick?

The first question was evidently not a challenge to the little know-it-all's powers. The dwarf immediately mumbled his response. But as far as what had caused the little girl to become ill, the sly fellow either did not know or would not say. He yawned, began to shiver again, complained that the moonlight was making his eyes ache, and pulled the covers over his head. He advised Daisy to be quiet. And, as she slept, not to roll over onto him.

The rightful owner of the bed settled down onto her pillow, began to recall that singular day, decades ago at the Durango Arts and Crafts Fair. As usual, the *pitukupf* had hit the nail square on the head—that was definitely where it had happened. But she still did not know *what* had made little Astrid sick. Her eyes closed, one at a time. *Sooner or later it'll come to me.*

As she yawned, it occurred to Daisy that she was now quite at ease with the strange little creature sleeping by her side. And that wasn't all. For the first time since her third husband had died, she had a man in her bed. Well, a *sort* of man. An ugly, odorous, mean-spirited little snip of a man. Even so, it was a comfort. *Which, if you think about it, is pathetic.* This realization, which might have been deeply depressing to a more sensitive soul, struck the Ute woman as hilarious. Not wanting to awaken her grumpy bedmate, Daisy Perika managed to keep from laughing out loud. But she snickered.

FOURTEEN
DAISY'S REMARKABLE BREAKFAST ADVENTURE

It might have been last night's greasy cheeseburger, the murder of one too many spiders, or the startling appearance of the dwarf in her bed. Or some combination of the three. Whatever the reason, Daisy Perika did not sleep soundly. On the contrary, the shaman shuffled along through dismal dreams where she waded through icy streams, was plagued by the *pitukupf*'s malicious schemes—was terrified by Astrid Spencer's dying screams! On those occasions when she floated up to semiconsciousness, only to feel the chill presence of the dwarf's knobby little body pressed against her—Daisy wondered what he might do to get revenge if she happened to roll over and smother him. And what would happen if the elfin creature failed to depart before first light, and Sarah Frank came into the bedroom to say "good morning," noticed the suspicious lump under the covers, and (with eyebrow arched in prim disapproval) asked, "What is *that*, Aunt Daisy—an ugly little man in bed with you?"

Well, the strain of it all was almost too much. But, as is so often the case, her worries turned out to be wasted. She did not roll over in her sleep and crush the dwarf. And well before the first hint of dawn, the little man had vanished from her bed. Indeed, she could almost have been convinced that *he* was one of her bad dreams. Daisy got herself out of bed with the usual grunts and groans, toddled off to the kitchen to check the fire sticks. She was pleased to find the box of 250 Fire Chief matches almost full. *At least that little thief didn't take 'em all.*

The rosy glow of sunrise found Daisy seated at her kitchen table, about to enjoy the day's first taste of bubbling-hot, black-as-soot coffee. It was a pleasant experience, with the warm mug clasped in her hands, a vaporous mist of steam rising off the perfectly smooth surface, the delicious scent of . . .

Hold on. Rewind to "perfectly smooth surface."

Look at that. The surface was not. (Not smooth.) What should have been a flat, mirrored pool was blemished by an unsavory something. But what was this splotchy little blot? To better focus upon the minuscule object, which was *wriggling* in her beverage, Daisy held the cup close to her left eye, squinted. Aha!

This was truly disgusting—a creature even uglier than the *pitukupf.*

The upside-down beastie doing a panicky backstroke in her coffee was a fuzzy spider. Precisely like the one she had stepped on last night. Not a word-class swimmer, this one appeared to be drowning. *Well it serves you right for—* But her righteous rebuke was interrupted by a sudden chill of realization: The shaman could not see them, but she *knew—*

The Spider People were gathered close at hand!

The evil clan had come to carry out their vengeful plan.

When I'm not paying attention, they'll swarm across the floor, crawl up my legs, and bite me all over and I'd swell up like a prize pumpkin and die in terrible pain!

The situation was serious. Vigilance was called for. Also strategy and tactics.

Pretending to be causally examining the furniture and appliances, Daisy cast her gaze about the kitchen, searching for some sign of the hidden battalions: a stray scrap of web; a tattering of teensy spider tracks; a scout, peeking from behind a broom. There was nothing sinister to be seen—which only proved how clever the little fiends had planned their invasion and assault. But wait. Daisy had spotted something.

Over there, sitting on the countertop, between the red Folgers coffee can and the Quaker Oats box, brazen as a brass monkey and glaring at the rightful occupant as if *she* had no right to be there—the creature she most despised. A plump, round, deadly black widow—the biggest one she had ever seen. *That'll be their war chief.*

After her heart had skipped a few beats, Daisy managed to get hold of herself. The Ute elder put on her stern warrior-woman expression, addressed her adversary thusly: "I ain't afraid of you." Making fists of her trembling hands, she drew in a deep breath. "Or your whole Spider People tribe."

Apparently unmoved by this bold assertion, Ms. Chief Black Widow stared back. Presumably, with all six eyes.

Never mind. Daisy Perika's mouth twisted into a wicked little grin. "Matter of fact, I *like* spiders."

No, this was not a ploy to curry favor with the enemy.

To demonstrate her point, Daisy raised her cup. Drank deeply thereof. This was a *very* foolish thing to do. But she was fortunate; and correct in her belief that the spider in her coffee was of the nonpoisonous variety. Even so, the experience was unpleasant—the bothersome creature got caught between her teeth. And though she had an overwhelming urge to spit the horrid thing out, there could be no backing down—not under the hard gaze of the enemy. Steeling herself, the Ute elder ground the corpse between ancient molars, swallowed against a latent gag, licked her lips. "Mmmm—that was tasty." She raised her chin, addressed the leader of the Spider Clan. "Would you like to come swim in my cup?"

As was her taciturn way, Black Widow said neither yea nor nay.

Tickety-tock clicked the kitchen clock.

For the longest, time, the plump intruder did not blink.

Tickety-tock.

For an equally lengthy interval, Daisy stared back.

Tickety-tock.

She recalled the tale about how Chief Washakie had dispatched the Crow war party. *If I was to kill the chief, maybe the rest of 'em would go away.*

Tickety-tock.

Or maybe that'd just make the Spider People mad.

Tickety-tock.

Who knows how long this standoff might have continued, had not Sarah Frank appeared on the scene. Rubbing her eyes, the pajama-clad girl said, "Good morning, Aunt Daisy." *What's she staring at?*

Daisy was feeling feisty. And boastful. *Wait'll I tell her what I swallowed on purpose.* But before the old woman could make her brag, some serious business must be taken care of. She whispered, "Kill it."

"What?"

Ah, how errors do muddle up our day.

The intent of Sarah's abbreviated question was: "What did you say?"

Daisy's interpretation was: "Kill what?" She pointed at the awful thing.

The girl saw it. Without hesitation, she walked over to the counter, picked up the stray grape, popped it into her mouth, chewed. Sarah turned to smile at the tribal elder, swallowed.

The aged shaman was stunned. Stupefied. Horrified. *Silly girl—she'll fall down dead!*

But of course our youthful heroine would suffer no ill effect. Indeed, the nutritious snack seemed to perk her up. Impressing Daisy right down to the marrow, the girl smacked her lips, said "Are there any more?"

Unable to utter a word, the tribal elder shook her head. *The whole bunch of 'em are probably in the next county by now.*

From Sarah's expression, it was apparent that she was mildly disappointed. And on top of that, the heroine did not boast of her accomplishment. The very soul of modesty, she changed the subject. "It won't be long before Mr. Sweetwater shows up. You want me to make you some oatmeal?"

This was like meeting a U.S. Marine who didn't

remember where he'd put his Congressional Medal of Honor. Maybe in the drawer with his socks? Still incapable of speech, Daisy shrugged off the offer of food. The eccentric gourmet, who had a *spider insider,* was feeling a mite nauseous. But the arachnid-eater did accept a second cup of coffee. As Daisy observed the spunky youth, she realized that there was much more to this orphan girl than met the eye. *All this time, I've been trying to teach her stuff, like how to cure warts and bring the rain—but she could teach me a thing or two.* After Daisy had taken a sip or two of brackish brew, in that peculiar way that jarring experiences often do, the staggering sight of Sarah popping a hideous black widow into her mouth shook something loose from the residue of the old woman's murky memory, which promptly bubbled up to the top. *Now I remember what made that little Spencer girl sick at the arts-and-crafts fair—it was something she swallowed.* Daisy screwed her face into an intense grimace. Was it food or drink? Or something else entirely. *A bug?*

Isn't that always the way—as soon as one vexing lodger is evicted from the premises, another just-as-annoying tenant slips in to occupy the vacancy.

FIFTEEN
NORTH TO THE COLUMBINE

Having been warned by Daisy Perika that she did not oper-
ate on "Indian time," Gorman Sweetwater made sure that
he showed up in his snazzy pickup promptly at 9:00 A.M.
Right on the dot. Which was 9:24.

During the drive from Daisy's secluded home at the
mouth of *Cañón del Espíritu* to her nephew's equally remote ranch in the high valley between the snow-capped
Misery and Buckhorn Ranges, Sarah Frank—with Mr. Zig-
Zag napping in her lap—was seated between Daisy and the
tribal elder's cousin. The happy girl chattered incessantly
about subjects of cosmic importance: Would Charlie Moon
remember his solemn promise to provide her with a horse
to ride? Was Aunt Daisy sure that Charlie liked rhubarb
pie? Maybe she should have baked apple pies instead. Or
one peach and one apple. She hoped he wouldn't be working *all* the time, so maybe they could go horseback riding
together. Was Charlie's big lake really full of pretty-colored
fish? (Here, Gorman—who had caught several fine trout in
said body of water—assured her that a man could walk
across Lake Jesse on the back of five-pound rainbows and
cutthroats. Without getting his feet wet.) Sarah giggled,
which—to Daisy's disgust—encouraged her lying cousin to
tell more tales about his astonishing experiences as an
angler, such as when he caught a nine-foot Nile crocodile in
Navajo Lake. Using an eight-pound ham as bait. And a
barbed hook that a one-eyed Mormon blacksmith had

fashioned from a length of three-quarter-inch-diameter re-bar. On and on it went, until Gorman bumpity-bumped his pickup over the Too Late Creek bridge, braked it to a halt under one of the gigantic cottonwoods that shaded the two-story log headquarters—where the full-time rancher, part-time tribal investigator, hung his black Stetson. The teenager was fairly quivering with excitement. To no one in particular, she whispered, "Oh—oh—I hope Charlie's here to meet us."

The man had said he would be, so of course he was.

As Charlie was helping his aunt out of the pickup—Daisy's dismount was painfully slow—Sarah tumbled out on the driver's side behind Gorman Sweetwater and ran around the front of the truck, wanting with all her heart to enfold the tall Ute in a rapturous embrace. But as she encountered the flesh-and-blood version of her girlish dreams, Sarah slowed—succumbed to a numbing shyness.

As soon as his aged aunt was properly stabilized on Columbine soil, Moon greeted Gorman, then turned to the Ute-Papago girl, flashed a smile that almost stopped her heart. "So how're you doing, kid?"

Kid? She dropped her gaze to his boots, shrugged. "Okay."

"Well, 'okay' ain't nearly good enough." He assumed a stern, fatherly look. "Young lady, now that you're on Columbine territory, we'll see to it that you work your way all the way up to 'fine and dandy.' "

Young lady? This was the way grown-ups spoke to children. *He just doesn't understand.* Sarah Frank clenched her teeth, kicked at a pebble.

The rancher eyed the girl with the uncanny insight of a cowboy who could spot a sick heifer at fifty yards and make an instant verdict on the malady. *The kid looks like she's kinda off her feed. Probably something she ate for breakfast.* But, noting the pouty expression, he considered another possibility: *Could be she's ticked off about something or other. Probably going through one of those teenage phases you hear so much about.* But Moon knew his limitations. Compared to cud-chewing bovine creatures and spirited quarter horses, human beings—especially the females of the species—were an unfathomable mystery.

But his diagnosis had been close enough. Sarah was ticked off. *Maybe Aunt Daisy's right. Maybe Charlie Moon is a big gourd head!*

A half hour later, when Mr. Moon introduced Miss Frank to a bright-eyed pinto pony outfitted with a Mexican leather saddle studded with coin-silver conchos, all was forgiven.

• • •

That evening, Scott Parris showed up in response to an invitation to supper. The broad-shouldered, sandy-haired chief of Granite Creek PD was determined to make a hit with the Ute-Papago girl, whom he had not seen since her parents had died a decade earlier. Upon his arrival, Parris presented Sarah with an expensive gift he'd had shipped in from a specialty shop in Denver. Expressing his surprise at "how you've grown up," the clueless fellow watched with happy expectation as the big-eyed teenager opened the rib-boned package, was puzzled when the look of eager anticipation was replaced by a glazed expression of humiliation.

To Sarah's credit, she recovered quickly, managed a sweet little smile, said, "Thank you, Mr. Parris. It's very pretty."

The bemused white man shrugged it off. *I guess some girls don't like dolls all that much.*

During the evening meal, both Sarah and Daisy were silent, the girl picking at her food, the tribal elder exhibiting a similar lack of appetite. Sarah had almost forgotten her contribution to the feast, but as the men cleaned the last morsels from their plates, she was reminded by a look and a nod from the old woman. Excusing herself, Sarah hurried away to her downstairs bedroom, opened a cardboard box, and returned with a quite attractive pie.

Moon and Parris greeted the homemade dessert with whoops of delight. Gorman Sweetwater's mouth watered in sweet anticipation. "What kind is it?" Daisy's cousin inquired. "Apple?"

Sarah shook her head. "No, it's—"

"Blueberry," Gorman guessed. He turned to Daisy, who was seated beside him. "They say blueberries is good for you. They're loaded with vitums and annyoxants and whatnot."

Daisy corrected him: "Vitamins and antioxidants."

"That's what I said." *That knot-headed old woman is losing her hearing.* He repeated himself, louder this time: "Vitums!"

Daisy glared at her relative. "Don't yell in my ear!"

"It's rhubarb," Sarah mumbled. She was close to tears.

"Great," Moon said. "Rhubarb's my favorite kind of pie."

"Mine too," Parris rubbed his hands together. "And from what I read last month in *Reader's Digest,* rhubarb has ten times more vitums—uh—vitamins than the best blueberry you ever come across."

The girl offered the gift of food to her favorite man in the whole world. "I made it myself." *For you, and nobody else.*

Charlie Moon accepted the gift, patted his admirer on the shoulder. "Thank you, Sarah."

She was thrilled from head to toe. *Charlie called me by my name!* Add that courtesy to the ride on the pretty pinto pony and you get—heavenly bliss.

Moon turned to Granite Creek's top cop. "Seeing as how you and me are best buddies, and Daisy and Gorman are my favorite relatives, I guess you can all have a piece."

Parris affected a look of deep disappointment. "Only one?"

Though suspect of the *matukach* lawman's praise of rhubarb and its abundant content of vitums, Gorman allowed as how he could do with a taste of pie.

On the girl's account, Daisy said she would have a piece.

Sarah, too nervous to eat a bite, demurred.

The head of the household used a bone-handled Arkansas Toothpick to quarter the pie, plopped a slab on Daisy's plate, Gorman's, Parris's, reserved the last section for himself.

In almost ceremonial fashion, the three men and the elderly lady each tasted the rhubarb concoction at the same moment. The silent judgment was unanimous. Horrible.

Daisy pursed her lips. *Sarah didn't put in two cups of sugar like I told her—she must've got hold of the canister with the big "S" on it and poured in salt instead!* The old woman knew she could count on her nephew and the white man. But—*If Gorman says something to hurt that girl's feelings, I'll ball up a fist and knock him right off his chair.* She meant this quite literally. The prone-to-physical-violence woman gave her cousin a warning look, to which he was oblivious.

In his entire life, Gorman Sweetwater had never tasted rhubarb pie, homemade or otherwise, so, having no preconceived expectations, he was not bitterly disappointed. *Them rhubarbs sure is salty.* But there was no getting around the truth: *This tastes worse than a warm cow pie. Not that I ever actually tasted fresh manure. Or partic'ly want to.*

Moon's satisfied smile was a class act. "That is the best rhubarb pie I ever got past my lips." He immediately regretted the choice of words, and added, "First rate!"

Parris chimed in, "It's fantastic!" *God, please don't let me puke right here at the table.*

Cousin Gorman, who blamed the rhubarb, and had far more wisdom than Daisy gave him credit for, added this high praise: "That little girl is some fine cook!" He beamed at Sarah. "It'll be a lucky man that gets *you* for a wife."

Being of the opinion that a grueling task should be completed speedily, Moon took another big bite, winked at the delighted girl. "Now that's a fact."

Parris, who fancied himself a gourmet of sorts, managed a satisfied burp. "You bet." He grinned at the teenager. "If I was about thirty-five years younger, why, I'd be camping on your doorstep."

Sarah was so caught up in rapture that she could not speak.

Daisy, who had not gotten past the first bite, reached

over to pat the girl's thin little arm. "This pie is really something special." The old woman was enormously proud of the men in her presence. Even Cousin Gorman was a hero in her eyes.

The valiant fellows finished their dessert at about the same moment.

Sarah's face glowed with pride. "You really liked it?"

Nods all around.

A thumbs-up from Moon: "Absolutely top-notch."

Gorman: "Best rhubarb pie I've ever had."

Parris put on a hangdog look. "Too bad it's all gone."

Sarah got up, ran from the dining room.

Moon frowned. "Where's she off to?"

Daisy sighed. "You'll find out soon enough."

And they did.

Sarah Frank appeared, big smile splitting her face, carrying the second rhubarb pie.

As his Ute friend would put it later, Parris's chin dropped into his collar.

Mr. Sweetwater got distinctly green about the gills.

Something had to be done.

Grabbing the pie, Charlie Moon scowled at his guests. "Don't be begging for seconds—you've all had your fill. I'm saving this one all for myself."

Tears misted Sarah's eyes.

The others present were similarly grateful. Scott Parris, Gorman Sweetwater, Daisy Perika—they God-blessed him, every one. And his crotchety aunt decided that maybe she'd been a little too hard on him all these years. Maybe Charlie Moon was not such a big gourd head after all.

Eager to build upon her stunning culinary success, Sarah was already planning a future surprise. *Cherry* pies.

• • •

SIXTEEN
AFTER FOOD, ENTERTAINMENT

Charlie Moon entered the parlor expecting to find his
guests sitting in front of a crackling split-pine fire, Gorman
Sweetwater nodding off to sleep, Scott Parris entertaining
Aunt Daisy and Sarah Frank with highly enhanced tales of
his adventures as a Chicago cop. He did not expect them to
be on the far side of the room, backs to a dying fire, talking
in hushed tones, their entire attention fixed on his dusty
television set.

Scott Parris, Daisy, and her cousin Gorman were seated
in a small semicircle around the appliance.

Sarah Frank was slipping a thin, shiny disk into the
DVD slot to record the latest installment for her collection.

Moon hitched his thumbs under his belt. *What's this all
about?*

The girl's agile fingers danced over the remote control.

A Hungarian basketball game filled the screen. Score
48–46.

Moon grinned at his aunt. "You a big sports fan?"

Sarah glanced over her shoulder. "Cassandra's coming
on in a couple of minutes."

Daisy snorted. "Charlie don't watch TV. He listens to
the radio. And he *reads books*."

The alleged scholar defended himself: "I watch television every now and then."

Parris grinned. "When?"

"Well, sometimes when I go to the barbershop." *And the*

TV's right there in front of me and it's either watch them soaps and talk shows or close my eyes. Mostly, he closed his eyes.

Parris cocked his head, made a critical examination of the Ute's bountiful crop of hair. "Looks to me like you don't get to the barbershop all that often."

Moon was about to make an observation that a local chief of police he was acquainted with did not have all that much hair left to cut, when Sarah Frank intervened. "*Cassandra Sees* is a weekly TV show from Granite Creek."

The Ute nodded. "I've heard about that."

"You ought to remember Cassandra Spencer and her sister Beatrice." Parris gave Moon the eye, attempted to mentally transmit this addendum: *That night their sister was mauled to death in her bedroom, you threatened to pick both of 'em up and stuff 'em in the back of my unit.*

The deputy had not forgotten. *You still owe me for a good ten hours of deputy work. At twelve-fifty per. Which would fill my gas tank.*

Unaware of this attempt at nonverbal communication between the best friends, Sarah murmured, "Cassandra is also Astrid Spencer's sister. Astrid was that poor lady who got killed by the bear."

Moon thought it best to steer the teenager toward a more suitable subject for discussion. "So tell me—what does Cassandra see?"

"Spooky stuff," Sarah said.

He pretended to be surprised. "Spooky?"

She clarified: "It could be something that's happening *right now,* a hundred miles away. Like that truck driver who got shot while he was watching her on TV."

Moon was well aware of that sensational event.

"Or she might have a vision about a bad car wreck," Daisy mumbled.

Gorman felt obliged to comment. "Or a house on fire."

The Granite Creek chief of police had returned his gaze to the television. "Her audience is getting bigger every week. From what I hear, she's likely to be picked up by one of the big networks. NBC, maybe. Or CBS." Word does get around.

Sarah was switching through channels. "Cassandra also talks to ghosts." She found the right spot. "Oh—it's about to start." She pressed the Record button, watched the big eye appear. As the orb faded, the girl consoled herself that she would see it several times again before this evening's program was over. After every commercial break, minuscule details of Cassandra's pupil, iris, and cornea would be displayed—not to mention eyelashes that looked as large as soda straws, and pores in her skin big enough to throw a brick into. And every time, the huge eye looked right at her. *I wonder how she keeps from blinking?*

Moon smiled at the girl. *So Cassandra Spencer talks to ghosts—that explains why Aunt Daisy's hooked on this program.* Kids always liked spooky stuff, of course, and Gorman would stare at anything on the tube, including a test pattern. *I wonder if they still have those on late at night.* But why was Scott Parris so interested in Cassandra's weekly extravaganza? *Maybe he likes spooky stuff too.*

It was true. Parris liked books with titles like *True Tales of Civil War Ghosts* and *The Haunt of Kettle Mountain.* But there was more to it than that. Quite a lot more.

Aside from Charlie Moon and his guests, there were, of course, many other viewers. According to estimates that would become available an hour after tonight's show went off the air, seven thousand more than the count for last week's broadcast. Give or take a couple of hundred.

They watched Cassie's special guest (all her guests were special) guess eleven out of twelve items that a local Methodist pastor had sealed inside a coffee can. The ten-year-old boy could (so it seemed) clearly sense the presence of everything from a pickup truck ignition key to an 1851 half-dime, but he was unable to discern the presence of a black Brazilian beetle entrapped in amber. None of us is perfect.

Immediately after the half-hour commercial break, Cassandra had a vision wherein she received information from her most reliable source, who went by the moniker White Raven. With a shudder, she reported another drive-by shooting. This one in Denver. The victim was a short-order cook on his way home from work. She provided the name of the café on South Broadway, and the wounded man's license plate number—which would have been entirely correct had White Raven not substituted a *J* for a *K*. None of us is perfect.

ANDREW AND BEA

"Well," Andrew Turner said.

Beatrice arched an exquisitely shaped eyebrow. This was her way of saying quite a number of things, such as: "What are you talking about?" but in this instance: "What do you mean by 'well'?"

By now an expert on the shades of meanings of his wife's facial expressions, Mr. Turner explained, "That new spirit must have forgotten to put in an appearance."

This time she did not bother to exercise the eyebrow. "What are you talking about?"

He clasped the fingers of both hands tightly around a coffee cup. "Your hot tip from Cassie."

"Oh, you mean about April Something?"

He nodded.

Bea pointed at the quartz clock over the TV, which never lied by more than ten seconds per month. There were six minutes left.

Andrew, who had never liked the uppity clock, gave it a dirty look.

Immune to human ill-will, the 112-year-old mechanism kept right on ticking.

Bea's pained expression suggested that she was trying to remember something. Then, it seemed to come to her. She smiled at the commercial for a bestselling Mexican beer. "April *Valentine*. I still think it sounds like a dancer's name." She turned the smile on Andrew. "Don't you?"

He shrugged.

"I'm sure Cassie will say something about her."

Wives are almost always right. Husbands find this trait immensely annoying.

At two minutes before the hour, Cassie looked directly into camera one. "I have, quite recently, been contacted by the spirit of a young woman who died in a most horrible manner. I shall not mention her name at this time—"

"April Valentine," Bea muttered.

"—but over the next few weeks, I hope to reveal previously unreported information about the nature of her passing." A sly smile. Behind the smile: *If I can make contact.*

Fade to black.

Final commercial break.

Ratings for tonight's performance would be up 4 percent from last week.

• • •

At fifty-six minutes past 11:00 P.M., Cassandra Spencer was alone in her parlor. Wrapped in a black silk Japanese night robe, her small feet clad in matching black silk slippers, she was perched on a cushioned, three-legged stool near the fireplace. Dying pine embers provided a dull orange glow that illuminated her oval face. That ivory mask, framed in the dark locks, seemed to float in the midnight space.

Cassandra desperately wanted to talk to someone. No, the attractive woman was not lonely. She wished to converse with a *very specific* person. A lady who would tell her—But wait. She who Sees also speaks: "April . . . April Valentine . . . are you there?"

The heavy silence pressed hard on her chest.

Cassandra inhaled. Exhaled. Breathed in again. She smelled something sweet. Lilac? "I've been trying to communicate with you ever since I read the material your mother left with me. But I don't know enough. If you would provide me with a few details, I believe I could help you."

She waited.

In the hallway, the brass mechanism in Daddy's venerable grandfather clock ticked. And tocked.

"I've tried every night for weeks. But I cannot see you. I cannot *hear* you."

Against the windowpane, fat drops of rain. *Plop. Plop-plop.*

"April, if you can hear me—please *say* something."

April, she say not a word.

Grandfather Chronometer, he say, *Tickety-tock. Tickety-tock. Tickety-tock.*

Grandmother Rain, she say, *Ploppity-plop. Ploppity-plop. Ploppity-plop.*

Bearing only a mocking resemblance to the pretty celebrity, the face assumed a severe expression. "Miss Valentine—if you cannot communicate verbally, at least show me some sign that you are present."

She could barely hear the clock in the hallway.

The rain had ceased.

The psychic clenched her hands, bared her teeth. "Dammit, do *something*—I don't care what it is!"

Uh-oh.

At precisely one second before midnight, the tall hallway clock, which had, for all these years since Daddy's death, kept perfect time—began to gong the hour. *Bong . . . bong . . . bong . . .* Count them. Twelve, of course—

BONG!

Make that thirteen.

And the curious display was not yet over. Watch the mantelpiece.

Nothing yet? Patience. Count three more heartbeats . . . One. Two. Thr—

Aha!

From between the pair of black wax tapers, a silver-framed photo of Cassandra's dead sister tumbles, strikes the yellow firebricks with a shattering clatter, scatters a dragon puff of wood ash and red-hot ember sparks—the fractured glazing sprays a glittering array of pseudodiamonds onto the psychic's dark garment. From the hearth, Astrid's dead face stares at her startled sister. Smiles.

Dramatic, certainly. But a message from Over There? One hesitates to speculate.

• • •

SEVENTEEN
DAISY'S BEST DAY EVER

Last night, when she had pulled the Columbine blankets and quilts up to her chin, Daisy Perika had been feeling less pessimistic about her prospects. A good night's sleep might have washed away the conviction that she was of no more use in this world, and the morbid certainty that Death was practically breathing down her neck. Which would have persuaded her to go on living for another year, or even two or three. But the weary woman did not enjoy a restful slumber. On the contrary, the dreamer's fitful night naps were plagued by a snarling wolf whose long, hairy face peered hungrily from dark, forested places, as if (she would think between these unsettling dreams) *I was little Red Riding Hood all covered with bacon grease and he was pretending to be Granny in her bed, who hadn't had a square meal in a week. Or like I was a jackrabbit on a spit and he was turning the crank.* During these semiawake interludes, she could not quite make up her mind. And all too soon, she would drift off again, find herself walking the forest path—Mr. Wolf padding along behind.

It was hardly surprising that Daisy, aka Little Red Riding Hood, aka Roasted Jackrabbit Carcass (who had been sleeping under one quilt too many) awakened feeling rather well done. Also in a somber, reflective mood. *I should've died years ago, got it over with.*

The time had come for making the necessary preparations, and it was better to get the job done while Cousin

Gorman Sweetwater was still at the Columbine with his pickup truck. For the serious business she must attend to, Daisy would not think of involving Charlie Moon. Her nephew would smile, insist that she had years and years to live. These assurances would be extremely annoying. Neither would she enlist one of his hired hands to provide transportation to town; those smelly cowboys were nothing but spies for the boss. So it was settled. *Right after breakfast, when Charlie and Sarah have gone out to ride horses, I'll tell Gorman to take me into Granite Creek. If he asks what do you want to go to town for, I'll tell him it's so I can do a little bit of shopping.*

MR. SWEETWATER MAKES A DELIVERY

"Drop me off over there." Daisy Perika pointed with a jut of her chin. "Between that black iron bench and the maple tree."

As Gorman eased his pickup to the curb, he smirked at a twisting red-and-white spiral mounted beside a shop door. "You gonna get yourself a haircut?"

Daisy was about to say, "Don't be such a silly jackass," but that would be like telling an ape not to be ugly. The aged woman opened the truck door and, using her oak staff as a sturdy third leg, cautiously eased her frame onto the sidewalk. "I'm going into the Dollar Store." *They have nice things there, like white cotton stockings and underwear.*

Recalling his late wife's unhurried manner when shopping (and being of the opinion that all women are cast in more or less the same mold), Gorman frowned at his cousin's hunched back. "While you go up one aisle and down another, turning every knickknack and doodad over in your hands, what am I supposed to do—sit here and twiddle my thumbs?"

Though sorely tempted to tell him exactly what he could do with *one* of his thumbs, Daisy—who expected to encounter St. Peter before very long—prudently resisted the urge. "I don't care what you do, as long as you don't dog along behind me, looking at your pocket watch and mumbling, 'How much longer is this gonna take?' "

Gorman scratched his skinny neck. "Well, I guess I could drive around Granite Creek some and see the sights." *I'll drop in at the Red Owl Cantina, throw back a couple of cold Buds. If Three-Fingers Chico is there, maybe I'll shoot a few rounds of pool with him . . . at two bits a game. One of these days, I'm gonna get even with that slicker.* These pleasant thoughts were interrupted by Daisy's voice.

"You be back here at four o'clock sharp." For all the good it might do, she added the standard warning: "And I'm not talking Indian time." Daisy gave the driver a stern look and, as if she had read his so-called mind, added, "Don't you even think about any beer guzzling or gambling." Suggesting a Grandma Moses about to part the waters, Daisy raised the wooden staff at her errant cousin. "If you're not on time and sober, I won't fill your gas tank like I promised to." She slammed the pickup door—*bam!*

AN UNEXPECTED OPPORTUNITY

After watching Gorman's truck disappear down the tree-lined avenue, Daisy Perika was about to head for the Dollar Store—when a seemingly trivial distraction occurred. The sort that drastically alters the course of a life. In this instance, several lives. What happened was that she glanced across the street, saw a redbrick building at the end of a spacious, well-kept lawn bordered by a meticulously pruned hedge. At the entrance to the grounds, a tasteful sign suspended above a wrought-iron arch advised potential clients of the category of commerce conducted therein.

MARTINEZ & SONS
FUNERAL HOME
AND
COMMUNITY CREMATORY

Entranced by the fateful link between this instance of free-market enterprise and her urgent concerns, Daisy forgot all about burial stockings and underwear. Even red shoes. Oblivious to honking horns, squealing brakes, and shouted oaths, the old woman jaywalked though a jumble of traffic to the opposite sidewalk, trod along the bricked walk, up the concrete porch steps—paused at the door. *This looks like an awfully expensive place.* Doubts assailed her. *What I need is the Dollar Mortuary.* Curiosity trumped doubt. *But as long as I'm here, I might as well go in.* Daisy imagined that when she opened the door, she would be met by a haughty Hispanic. She could already see him. A middle-aged fellow with slicked-back black hair, who would look down his nose at her. Under that nose, just above the curl of his lip, would be a bushy mustache. *If some big-shot Martinez in a pinstripe suit asks, "What do you want?" what'll I tell him?* To help herself think, the Ute elder clicked her teeth together. *I'll just say I'm browsing.*

She need not have been concerned. Mr. Martinez Sr. (a kindly, big-hearted gentleman) was in Denver, attending the annual convention of the Rocky Mountain Funeral Home Directors. His estimable son Paulo was in the cellar, occupied with a cadaverous matter. The sales manager, a plump, well-done-up brunette with a white rose affixed over her left ear, was occupied in a corner office with prospective customers. Aided by colorful brochures and a slick PowerPoint presentation, she was explaining the Ten Significant Advantages of Funeral Insurance.

With the stealth of a sly coyote creeping into Farmer Martinez's henhouse, Daisy eased her way through the front door, found herself in a small, blue-carpeted atrium furnished with overstuffed chairs and a Tiffany floor lamp that looked to be the real McCoy. Off to her left, Daisy heard a woman's voice describing various "bereavement plans" to equally unseen persons whom the sales manager referred to as Mr. and Mrs. Murple. A boy's voice said, "Mom, can I go to the bathroom?" Mom responded, "Not right now, Ronny."

Imagining Ronny squirming, Daisy grinned. Straight ahead were a massive pair of closed oak doors. *That's probably where they have the funerals.* On her right was a more modest door, this one open just a crack. Peeking in, she saw an array of caskets on display. *That's just what I need to look at.* Our browser stuck her head inside. *Good—there's nobody here.*

Daisy padded across the plush, cranberry-red carpet, mouth agape, eyes agog. The magnificent caskets displayed on knee-level oak stands included burnished bronzes, gleaming blacks, pale ivories. They had names. Imperial. Hopewell. Shenandoah. And the insides—well, talk about lavish. *Oh my—it almost makes a person want to hurry up and die.* She paused at Sunrise and caught her breath. The pillow was pink satin, which matched the plush, quilted lining. It was smaller than the rest, and closer to the floor.

The shopper reached inside to stroke her fingers across the voluptuous pillow. *That looks so comfortable.* Her gaze darted around the silent room. *Old man Martinez would probably bust a gut if I was to . . .* Daisy's wrinkled face produced a wicked little grin. *But what he don't know won't hurt him.* She placed her purse on a lamp stand, leaned her oak staff in a corner. It took quite a few grunts and groans for the tribal elder to insert herself into the casket. She scooted this way and that until everything was just so. *Ahhh. That pillow's soft as peach fuzz.* Caught up in the magic of the moment, the would-be corpse folded her hands across her chest. *And it's so warm and cozy in here.*

No one in her right mind would do such a thing? That is a bit harsh. True, the old woman is not the soul of prudence. But a worthwhile life cannot be lived without some level of risk. It is admitted that our aged adventurer does have a way of creating trouble. On occasion, full-blown Calamity with Red-Hot Spurs On. But, in Daisy's defense—the disastrous outcome is not always her fault. Not entirely. And in this instance, everything might have turned out quite all right—except for that overhead light. The one up there. Directly above her resting place. The blasted thing was shining in her eyes.

Daisy closed them. *Just for a moment,* she told herself.

• • •

Taking pity on Squirming Ronny, the sales manager suggested that Mrs. Murple might wish to escort her son to the gender-neutral facility, and offered detailed verbal directions. Ronald's mother, who still harbored a childhood fear of cemeteries and funeral parlors, was not eager to leave her husband's side. At a stern look from Mr. Murple, his wife took their son by the hand and proceeded to go in search of the restroom.

No, do not leap to conclusions. After only a few false turns, mother and son found the his and/or hers toilet. Ronny relieved his bladder and, feeling immeasurably better, rejoined his mom—ready to create some mischief. If she wanted to go *this* way, he would insist on going *that* way.

Now, you may leap, jump, rush, et cetera.

Right. They ended up in the display room.

"Oh," Mrs. Murple whispered, her hand moving to her throat, "it's full of *coffins.*"

Ronny might have been at Disneyland. "Yeah. Ain't it neat!" The range of morbid possibilities boggled his little mind. *I wonder if there's any dead people in 'em.*

Mrs. Murple was looking for the nearest exit. *Should we go back the way we came—or . . .* She could not remember by which door they had entered, and was suddenly gripped with a cold horror that *one* of these portals might be the entrance into a cold, gray space with a chemical smell and row upon row of granite slabs, each with a nude corpse sprouting tubes of greenish fluid that was being pumped into cold, rubbery veins.

"Hey, Mom." Ronny was halfway across the room. "Come look at this one."

Long experience made her suspicious of the offspring. "Why should I?"

She was startled by his frank reply: "Because it's got a dead person in it."

He is such a mischievous little boy. "You should not take me for a fool, Ronny." She presented a thin, superior smile. "And you should not lie to your mother."

"I'm not lyin'—honest!"

When I get close, he'll yell "Boo!" and grab my arm and I'll scream and then he'll laugh. Well, I'll not play his childish little game. But curiosity overwhelmed her. Like a small child in footie pajamas approaching a dark closet where the hideous night monster is concealed—waiting to pounce—Mrs. Murple came closer. (It may help to know that she did so in mincing little steps.)

And then—she saw it.

Her hand, knowing what to do in situations like this, covered her mouth. The hoarse whisper slipped out between her fingers: "Oh my *goodness!*"

"See—I told you." The boy's manner could only be described as smug.

Momma continued to whisper: "What a dreadful thing—leaving the remains in plain view." Her narrow face hardened. "We shall certainly not do any business with an establishment which follows such shoddy practices." *Wait . . . did I see it breathe?* Recalling horrid tales of unfortunates who, though merely unconscious, were diagnosed as completely 100 percent deceased and taken to the embalming room to be pumped full of noxious preservative liquids, she leaned closer to the wrinkled "corpse."

It might have been the Murple's mutterings and whisperings, or perhaps some unconscious sense of the nearness of another human being. Or perhaps her brief nap in the comfortable coffin had simply run its course. But it was none of these. It was the hungry wolf in her blood-chilling dream, chasing the Ute elder through a dark forest, fairly nipping at her heels! In a desperate effort to escape, Daisy was rapidly surfacing from the depths of the nightmare.

Ronny's mother murmured to herself, "No, the poor old

thing isn't breathing. It must have been my imagination. I suppose we should just leave her be and go tell—"

The corpse's eyes opened wide, a gnarled hand reached up, grabbed Mrs. Murple by the wrist, the aged voice cracked, "Look out for the wolf!"

"Yeeeeeeeaaaaa!" Yes, this was Momma Murple.

"Yiiiieeee!" Ronny M., of course.

In the blink of an eye, Daisy realized that she was wide awake, in the funeral home, and that the wolf had been left behind. She snapped at the screamers, "You two yell loud enough to wake the dead!"

By the time the last word was out of her mouth, Daisy was speaking to empty air.

• • •

For rest of his happy life, Ronny would swear that in her wild panic, his mother had knocked him aside with her purse, and run over him. "One of her feet landed right on my face!" Whether or not this account was precisely accurate, it is a fact that the startled youth ended up on the floor and when he got up, his mother was nowhere in sight, which caused him to open the door to a closet full of brooms, mops, and so on, which slowed him only a few heartbeats before he exited the closet, and saw the supposed corpse struggling to get out of the coffin. *I don't think she's dead.* Very astute little fellow.

"Hey!" Daisy said.

"Who, me?"

"No, Shorty—I'm talking to the wall."

Maybe she's one of the Undead. Like the Zombie Who Eats Living Flesh. With due caution, the youthful horror-movie enthusiast approached. "What do you want?"

"Hand me my walking stick. And help me get out of this box."

If a zombie bites you, do you turn into one and start howling at the moon? No, that applied to werewolves. "What's in it for me?"

Daisy Perika was struggling. "I'll give you a brand-new, crispy dollar bill."

She's not a zombie—just an old weirdo. "Make it two old wrinkled dollar bills."

Little matukach *thief.* But the Ute elder was in a tight spot. "Okay."

• • •

Mrs. Murple found her husband and the sales manager, who was winding up for her final pitch on the Family Bereavement Plan, and startled them with wild-eyed babbling about a "hideous old dead woman in a coffin" who "reached out and grabbed me by the throat." In spite of the fact that she had substituted "throat" for "wrist," and that "hideous" was somewhat over the top, and the fact that Daisy was not dead, it would be unconscionable nit-picking to describe the rattled woman's report as grossly inaccurate. The purveyor of burial insurance, who did not deal with the cadaver side of the business, hurried off to locate a member of the Martinez clan.

When Mr. Murple arrived in the display room with his hyperventilating wife trailing three paces behind—you know what they found. The small Sunrise casket was empty, the alleged corpse nowhere to be seen. The husband eyed his mate. Sternly.

"But she was right there—in that coffin!" As if she thought it would add weight to her claim, Mrs. Murple pointed, repeated, "In that coffin!"

At this moment, Ronny, who had two dollars in his pocket and a certain knack for dramatic timing, reappeared at the scene of the crime, entering stage left.

The distraught woman seized her child with near-hysterical joy, shook him hard enough to rattle his teeth. "Tell Daddy, darling—tell him about the horrible old dead woman in the coffin who grabbed me by the throat!"

Oozing innocence from every pore, the lad glanced at the coffin, at his father, settled a bewildered gaze on his mother. "*What* dead woman, Mom?"

Oh, that Ronny. Such a little scamp.

• • •

EIGHTEEN
AT THE SUGAR BOWL RESTAURANT

Unaware of the lasting impact she'd had on the Murple family—Momma Murple in particular—Daisy Perika's thoughts were concentrated on her favorite subject. Herself.

I wonder how many people will come to my funeral. More than came to Sally Sweetwater's, I bet. She should've been kinder to the neighborhood children. It was just awful [Daisy barely kept the smile inside] *how Sally would load up her slingshot with rocks, and pepper those nice little Girl Scouts who was selling cookies.* A self-pitying sigh. *But there won't be nearly so many mourners show up for me as came to weep and wail for Nahum Yaciiti. Some people say Nahum was a saint, and I guess he was.* Which suggested that a certain mending of her ways might be in order. *Starting right now, I'm going to be a lot nicer to people. And that goes for every single person I know. Even the ones that ain't worth a thimble full of spit. No matter what those bone heads do to make me mad, I won't have a mean word to say about one of 'em.* These uplifting thoughts were interrupted by the tired-faced waitress who brought coffee and pastry on a tray. The Ute woman reached for her purse, asked, "How much?"

Mandy eyed the wrinkled woman. "You want your check now?"

"No, I don't need no bill—just say out loud how much I'm gonna get ripped off for this greasy coffee and stale doughnut, and I'll settle with you."

Well aren't you the sweet one. She scribbled on her order pad. "That'll be two-fifty for the stale doughnut, two dollars for the greasy coffee, which with tax comes to four dollars and eighty cents."

On account of having only a few more days to live, and knowing she would not have any need of cash money after she crossed over that deep, wide river, Daisy Perika thought she might as well be generous. It was the sort of thing God approved of, and the closer you got to the Almighty, the more you wanted to please him. She gave the young woman a five-dollar bill. "Keep the change, toots."

Toots? "Uh—thank you." Mandy accepted the currency, hurried away to deal with a fat man who wanted his Diet Pepsi refilled. And another piece of coconut crème pie.

In 1939, at the picture show in Pueblo, Daisy had watched a good-looking white man on the silver screen say those very words to a platinum blond hussy with eyelashes big as hummingbird wings and a little, pointy nose. Daisy had particularly admired the thin mustache. (No, the man had the mustache.) Liking the taste of the phrase, Daisy rolled it over her tongue again: "Keep the change, toots." She shook her head at the novelty of it. "I guess that's the very first time in my life I've ever said 'keep the change.'" The experience was surprisingly satisfying. So much so that she could not help smiling. "There goes Ol' Daisy Perika," they'll say, "the big spender from the Southern Ute reservation. From what I hear, she lights her pipe with ten-dollar bills!" It had been a fine morning for someone who was planning her funeral. And the day was far from over, the best yet to come.

• • •

Not quite a mile away, a sleek Cadillac sedan was transporting its occupants along a course that would intersect with the tribal elder's crooked path. Woe be unto them.

• • •

As she sipped the coffee and nibbled at the chocolate doughnut, Daisy ignored the other diners, preferring instead to peer through the window and watch the external world go by. *Hurry by* was more like it. Seen by a typical viewer, this would have been ordinary, everyday traffic. For the rugged old recluse who spent most of her days in the silent, canyon-country wilderness, a visit to town was fascinating entertainment. Daisy gawked at shiny automobiles, muddy pickups, transport of every size and description, heading this way and that, some with out-of-state license plates, a low-rider Chevy with no plate at all.

But more than the jumble of motor vehicles, it was the human beings who galvanized her attention.

Such as the cute little black boy running ahead of his harried mother, stopping to pick up a penny and put it in his mouth. *I bet he'll swallow it.* He did. *What he needs is a good whack on the butt.* The child's mother evidently agreed with this sentiment. *Hah! Serves the little bugger right!*

Such as that tall, flabby fellow in yellow knee-length shorts and a sweat-soaked white Cattleman's Bank T-shirt, jogging along the sidewalk with a pained look on his red face. *Poor man looks like he's hurting worse than I am. What he needs is a glass of cold lemonade, a hot bath, and a two-hour nap.*

As the jogger vanished from view, a box-shaped UPS van double-parked, and the uniformed driver rushed away with parcels under both arms. This brought back sweet memories of many delightful things (mostly gifts from Charlie Moon) that had been delivered to her remote home by the big, boxy trucks. *I remember the Christmas Charlie sent me that big box of fancy cheeses and them canned hams, and my birthday in 1992 when he bought me the brand-new rocking chair and*—Before Daisy (who believed it was more blessed to receive than give) had time to recall even a fraction of her nephew's love offerings, the UPS vehicle was gone.

Distracted by the approach of that category of vehicle she had always wanted to ride, Daisy leaned forward. *Oh, my, look at that—here comes a big black motorcycle.* And indeed, here it came—chug-chugging along, engine buggity-bugging, rusty exhaust pipes vibrating like they might fall off in the street. The lean, mean, flat-black machine, without a glint of chrome to be seen, reminded the elderly woman of those motorcycles back in the 1950s, like Charlie Moon's father used to ride around Ignacio, showing off his bulging muscles and big white-toothed smile and offering rides to all the pretty, giggling girls. By contrast, this pale rider would have had to get a lot healthier just to look like death warmed over, and his blank-eyed girlfriend—clad in brown leathers that might have been moleskin—clung to her sickly man like a persistent scab. Daisy noticed other interesting details, like how they didn't seem to be in a hurry. *Maybe these two don't have no place important to go.* As they came closer, she noticed that the man had a stubby black cigar clenched between a wide gap in his teeth, but the stogie produced no smoke. *Probably a couple of druggies.*

Then, Daisy realized that there was no exhaust coming from the throbbing twin pipes—and there was a long, jagged streak of scarlet running from the girl's hairline down to the corner of her lips. Looking right *through* them, the Ute shaman watched a mongrel dog trot by and give the riders a wary eye. Daisy was only mildly startled. She knew that there were more ghosts roaming about than people thought, and if you didn't look close you could mistake them for live people. She murmured, "Poor things—they must've been killed in a bad accident, and been riding around ever since—maybe for years and years." It occurred to her that the pair might not know they were dead.

Suddenly feeling Death's cold fingers clutching at her heart, his sour breath on her neck, Daisy prayed, "Please, Jesus—when my time comes, take me directly home to you."

In the fullness of time, her request would be granted.

• • •

The Cadillac slipped into the restaurant parking lot, stopped in a spot where, only minutes ago, the manager's assistant had placed a Reserved sign. The driver, a bald, almost muscle-bound man, got out to open the door for the lady in the passenger's seat. She emerged with the grace of a gazelle, eyes shaded behind tinted glasses, head covered in a droopy-brimmed black hat, slim body swathed in a black, beaded cape, and stepped smartly across the asphalt. Muscle-Man matched her stride for stride, opened the door, and they were inside.

• • •

Watching the pair arrive, and noticing the pale, big-eyed blond girl following a few paces behind, Daisy summoned the waitress, asked the question that she thought she knew half the answer to: "Who're they?"

Mandy half whispered, "That's Cassandra Spencer and—"

Daisy interrupted: "I thought so—I've seen her on TV." She murmured, "One of her sisters got killed by a bear." *At least that's what they say.*

Under the impression that she was still a party to this conversation, Mandy lowered her voice to a husky whisper. "It was Astrid who was mauled to death—poor thing—and then Beatrice—that's Cassandra's other sister—why, she married Astrid's husband." Mandy sighed. "And Andrew Turner is the best-looking fella that ever hit this town."

Daisy was watching the slim, pretty minicelebrity, who clung to the big man's arm. "Who's the bald-headed guy?"

Interrupting her Andrew Turner daydream, the waitress provided the requested information: "That's Nicky Moxon. He's Cassandra's agent or business manager or something like that." Determined to get back to the spicy stuff, Mandy leaned close to Daisy's face. "I'll tell you something about those two Spencer sisters—if you'll promise not to mention it to a soul." Without waiting a microsecond for Daisy's cross-my-heart assurance, she commenced to dish the dirt: "It happened right here in this restaurant, just a few days after Astrid's death." The compulsive gossip shot a furtive glance over her shoulder, then locked eyes with the old woman. "If I tell you what Bea and Cassie did, right over there at table number twelve—you won't believe a word of it!"

Daisy grinned. *I probably won't, but go ahead and give it your best shot.*

"Those brazen rich women actually *drew straws* to see which one of them would marry Mr. Turner!" Though Mandy attempted to project a kilowatt of big-eyed outrage, her semihonest face settled for a small measure of unadulterated pleasure.

Having compliant features that served her all too faithfully, Daisy had no trouble looking doubtful. "They really drew straws?"

"Well, toothpicks, actually."

"Oh, well—that's different then."

Lacking even a single sense-of-humor gene, Mandy did not realize that she was being ribbed. "Bea broke one of the toothpicks in half. One piece was supposed to be the short straw."

"Then the whole toothpick was the long straw." Daisy was having entirely too much fun for one day.

"It was *supposed* to be. But Bea got rid of the whole toothpick, and had the two broken pieces in her fingers." Another over-the-shoulder glance. "So Cassie was *bound* to draw herself a short one. And that's how Cassie got cheated and Bea got the man."

Daisy rolled this over in her mind. "I wonder."

Mandy arched a penciled brow. "Wonder what?"

"Uncle Blue Hummingbird knew lots of them old sayings. One of 'em was 'Cheaters cheat themselves.'" The Ute elder explained with an impish grin, "Maybe the sneaky sister ended up getting the short end of the stick." The woman who had survived three husbands explained to the puzzled waitress, "Not one man in ten is that much of a prize."

• • •

Unaware of the slanderous gossip being dispensed by his waitress, the manager of the restaurant greeted Ms. Cassandra Spencer and Mr. Nicholas Moxon with a genuine smile and a discreet "please follow me" nod. He had taken no notice of the skinny blond woman whose big eyes followed the psychic.

A moment later, the Spencer-Moxon party was seated in a private dining room with a single table. The privileged patrons would not have to suffer the attentions of Mandy. The most attractive, competent waitress in the establishment was already pouring Silver Springs mineral water into spotless crystal goblets.

The manager's crisply attired assistant appeared with a bottle of fine Belgian wine (1982), removed the cork with a pleasing pop, offered the aromatic stopper to the gentleman for his approval.

The lady's escort was no gentleman, but the fact that he preferred Budweiser beer and burgers to "candy-ass" wines and tasteless broiled fish garnished with tiny green weeds is not the reason for this observation. Decompose the descriptor, and it becomes clear that a gentleman is, of necessity, a gentle man. There was nothing gentle about this man. Though his tastes tended toward the more popular foods and beverages, Mr. Moxon understood what was expected of him. He sniffed the cork, nodded absently to the gratified assistant manager, who poured the appropriate amount of amber wine into elegant, long-stemmed glasses.

It took perhaps another two minutes to order, and then they were alone.

The bald man reached inside his jacket, where a hard-eyed fellow such as himself might carry a 9-mm Glock semiautomatic. Or, if he was on the far side of fifty, a .38-caliber revolver. This male person being of indeterminate age, it is difficult to predict what his choice might have been in matters of deadly weapons. Never mind; he removed a small, gift-wrapped parcel from the inner pocket and pushed it across the polished granite tabletop to the pretty lady.

Her hand went to her throat. "For me?"

He resisted the temptation to reply, "No, for the big snow owl sitting on your shoulder." What he said instead was: "I hope you like it."

Cassandra untied and untangled the red silk ribbons with exaggerated care, as if she might be preserving them to wear in her raven-black hair. This task accomplished, she removed the beige wrapping, opened the hinged Moroccan-leather box, and stared wide-eyed at what nestled inside, cushioned in comfy folds of snowy satin—a lovely antique brooch and matching earrings. "Oh, Nicky—you shouldn't have!"

He laughed. "Maybe you're right—these baubles set me back almost ten grand."

She slapped playfully at the cheeky man's hand, then removed the largest of the Italian cameos from the box. "It must be a hundred years old!"

"These babies go back closer to two centuries. And I had them mounted in platinum silver."

She pinned the brooch onto her dress. "It is *so* lovely."

"Try on the earrings."

Cassandra removed the pearl earrings from her pierced ears and clipped on the dime-size cameos. She tilted her chin. "How do they look?"

"Super, kid. But not half as good as you."

• • •

Daisy Perika was about to leave the restaurant for the Dollar Store when she noticed the forlorn figure. *Poor thing looks like she didn't know what to do next.* The Ute elder had seen her earlier, this yellow-haired woman who had arrived with the psychic and the bald man. The big-eyed creature was hovering near a door marked PRIVATE. Daisy hesitated. *The smart thing to do would be mind my own business.* There were street people all over town. Some were dangerous. Others were just down on their luck. *Maybe she's hungry.* The old woman approached the slender youth. "Hey—are you okay?"

The peculiar person seemed not to hear. Kept right on staring at the closed door.

Daisy raised her voice: "When I ask you a question, Blondie—I expect an answer!"

Slowly, the head turned. The huge gray eyes stared vacantly at the Ute woman. "Were you talkin' to me?"

Daisy cringed at the nasal drawl. *Oh, Lord help me—it's*

one of them hillbillies from Dogpatch or Grinder's Switch.
"I asked if you was okay."

A taut silence while the full lips thinned, then: "Tell me . . . what do I look like?"

She's a crazy hillbilly. "You look like you ain't had a bite to eat in days."

"I don't look . . . horrible?"

I ought to just turn around and walk away. But just in case St. Peter happened to be watching at this very moment, Daisy decided to do the right thing. She leaned on her sturdy walking stick, opened her purse. "Listen, Blondie—if you need something to eat, I've still got a couple of dollar bills I can spare." *A couple that the money-grubbing* matukach *midget at the funeral home didn't rip off.* "You could buy yourself a nice hot—"

"No."

Surprised, Daisy looked up. "You don't want the money?"

The pale face almost smiled. "No, thank you."

At least the hillbilly's got some manners. The crotchety old woman decided that this good-works thing wasn't half bad—especially when the intended object of the charity turned down hard cash. Which encouraged Daisy to give it another try. *I could take her down to that Salvation Army place on Copper Street, let them deal with her.* But something about the wistful stranger begged for personal attention. "If you're not hungry and you don't need money, is there something else I could do for you?"

• • •

NINETEEN
THE CRASHER

After taking a Dainty Nibble of aged Cheddar, a sip of wine, Cassandra Spencer was about to swallow. She choked, then: "Oh—oh—Nicky!"

About to punch a number into his cell phone, Nicholas Moxon blinked at the unpredictable woman. "What is it, Cassie?"

"Oh—" The psychic pointed at something behind him. "It must be the aura of these antique cameos, but I'm seeing an apparition—*really and truly!*"

Oh boy, here we go again. Not endowed with the psychic's gift, he did not bother to turn his head. "Who is it this time—John Lennon? General Stonewall Jackson?"

"No!" Cassandra was almost breathless. "I see an ancient old woman." From Nicky's perspective, one of her more annoying faults was the use of redundant adjectives. "She's all pruney-wrinkled—and hideous!"

"You ain't exactly no Marilyn Monroe yourself, toots." Daisy Perika said this with a sniff. "And I ain't no apparition."

The psychic's mouth drooped. "You're not dead?"

"I don't think so." Ignoring the only totally bald man she had ever seen, who had now turned to stare at her, Daisy stumped her way over to their table, plopped into a chair. "But at my age, I check my pulse every few minutes—just to make sure."

Mr. Nicholas Moxon had not lost his composure since

that day in the sixth grade when he broke "Pigeon" Nelson's jaw on account of how Pigeon had deliberately spit on Nicky's peanut butter and jelly sandwich. The psychic's business manager spoke softly to the peculiar, elderly person, whom he assumed was one of that endless population of gushing fans, borderline psychos, and certifiable lunatics who were constantly attempting to get some face time with his famous client. "Excuse me, ma'am—but this happens to be a private dining room. And it's reserved for me and my lady friend." He indicated the door with a jerk of his chin. "So why don't you toddle off and go bother somebody in the public dining—"

"Hush your mouth," Daisy barked, and banged her fist on the table. "I'm here to talk to this girl who talks to dead people—not you, Daddy Warbucks!"

Seeing her agent's eyes get that cold, smoldery look, Cassandra shook her head at Moxon. *Let me handle this.*

He responded with a shrug. *Okay. Granny Big-Mouth is all yours.* He took a gulp of wine.

Daisy leaned closer to the TV personality. "That's a pretty cameo pin, and your black dress really sets it off."

"Thank you." The lady nodded to indicate her male companion. "The brooch is a gift from Nicky." She touched an earlobe. "And the matching earrings."

"They're pretty too." Daisy was always ready to offer helpful advice. "But they're too small for ears as big as yours."

On his second gulp, Moxon choked on the expensive vintage.

Her face paling to the chalky white of an old plaster wall, Cassandra said, "It appears that you have the advantage over me."

The Ute elder frowned. *Why can't these white people talk in plain American, like us Indians.*

Cassandra explained, "You seem to know who I am." She raised a haughty chin, looked down the slender nose. "The question is—who are you?"

She must think everybody over eighty is stupid. "Oh, I know who I am too."

"Then perhaps you will share that information with us."

Why do these matukach *always use a dozen words when two or three would get the job done?* "I'm Daisy Perika."

The psychic pursed her pretty lips. "That name sounds vaguely familiar."

With a disarmingly earnest expression, Daisy nodded. "I know what you mean—every time I hear it, I think the same thing."

Nicholas Moxon threw back his shiny head, his laughter boomed off the rafters.

Daisy joined in.

Cassandra did not.

When the hilarity had subsided, Daisy addressed the sullen white woman: "I was sorry to hear about how your poor sister got chewed up by a bear."

The psychic had not seen that one coming. "My sister's tragic death is not a subject that I care to discuss—"

"I remember another time that little Astrid almost died," Daisy said. "And I was there when it happened."

Again, Cassandra was caught short. "Really?"

The Ute elder nodded. "It was about thirty years ago, at that art fair in Durango." Daisy watched the white woman's eyes.

The surviving sister's face had quick-frozen.

Moxon was watching both women.

Daisy continued. "You little sister passed out. Stopped breathing."

Cassandra stared past the Indian woman, as if she could see it all again. So plainly. "Yes. A nurse gave Astrid mouth-to-mouth."

Daisy recalled this detail. The aged woman's gaze penetrated deep inside the dark-haired woman, where all of Cassie's little-girl fears still lived. "Except for that, I expect your sister would've died there and then."

Determined to regain control of the rapidly deteriorating

situation, Cassandra glared at the intruder. "Tell me—did you interrupt our private lunch to dredge up unhappy family memories? And if not, for what purpose are you here?"

This rapid-fire assault rattled the old woman. *What did I come in here for?* A more sensitive soul would have been embarrassed by the failure of short-term memory. But, shrugging off the minor defect, the crafty old innovator invented a plausible reason for her presence: "I'm here to make you a business proposition." *But when she says "Then let's hear it?" what'll I say then?* Daisy lived in the moment.

Moxon addressed the peculiar visitor: "Then you want to talk to me."

She gave him the look reserved for sassy young smart alecks and week-old roadkill. "Why would I want to do a thing like that?"

"Because I am Cassandra's business manager." The ruggedly ugly face assumed a mock-serious expression. "She doesn't make a move without my okay."

"Okay, if that's how it works." Daisy tapped the table with a bony knuckle until the inspiration came. "I've been watching her TV show ever since it came on the air. And it's not all that bad. But the way I see it, the thing could use some improvement."

If she had tapped the psychic's face with that knuckle, the brittle mask might have fractured.

"Expert advice is always welcome." Moxon produced a leather-bound notebook from somewhere inside his jacket, pulled a platinum ballpoint from his shirt pocket, poised pen over paper. "Shoot." *Cassie looks like she's about to explode.* This was great fun.

Not accustomed to being taken so seriously, Daisy was all puffed up. "All this stuff about talking to spirits and ghosts—most of it's kind of . . . well—silly."

Cassandra's painted mouth gaped in the fashion of . . . Imagine a beached carp with scarlet lips. Not a pretty picture.

Moxon maintained a perfectly solemn demeanor. "You're a woman who says what's on her mind. I like that."

Daisy was beginning to like this hairless white man. She pointed a gnarled finger at the TV psychic. "What this lady needs is professional help."

Cassandra's business manager was biting his lower lip, which made it difficult to reply. But, being a resourceful fellow, he did. "Do you have a—er—particular medical professional in mind?"

As the psychic imagined herself beaning said business manager with the proverbial heavy, blunt object, Daisy frowned and shook her head. "You mean like a doctor? No—what she needs is a professional *consultant.*"

Moxon and his client stared. Taken aback is what they were. And perplexed.

The tribal elder was on a roll. "Miss Spencer needs help from somebody who knows everything there is to know about talking to dead people—a person who could tell her what's what and what's not and how to tell the difference."

The bald man nodded slowly, thoughtfully. "And you are applying for the job."

The Ute shaman grinned. "You're a little slow on the uptake, Daddy Warbucks—but give you enough time, you manage to figure things out."

Moxon reddened.

Cassandra shot him a now-you-see-how-it-feels smile.

Still addressing the male, Daisy aimed a thumb at the TV psychic. "She could drop by and see me from time to time—or call me on the phone." The old woman's face turned as hard as stone. "But I don't work for nothing."

Cassandra's business manager didn't blink. "What's your usual hourly rate?"

The Ute elder's answer was instantaneous: "Fifteen dollars."

The hairless one nodded. "A very reasonable price."

Daisy wanted to slap herself across the face. *I should have said twenty!*

Moxon exchanged glances with his client, then smiled benignly at the self-styled consultant. "Tell you what. Give me and Cassie some time to talk about it. We'll call you."

"Suits me." *Well, I talked my way out of that one pretty good.* Daisy was about to withdraw, when—right out of nowhere—she remembered why she had crashed this party. She spoke to the television personality: "Oh—I'd almost forgot. There's a young woman out there in the restaurant who'd like to have a word with you."

Cassandra cringed. *They follow me wherever I go. Why can't they leave me in peace—at least when I go out for lunch?* She shot Nicholas Moxon a look. *You handle this, Nicky. Earn your 30 percent plus expenses.*

Perhaps her business manager's receiver was out of tune. Whatever the case, he did not receive the psychic's message. *All these spooky groupies ought to be good for something.* His rubbery brow furrowed in not-so-deep thought. *Maybe I should get them talking to each other— start a fan club for Cassie.*

With no help forthcoming from the business-managing half of the team, Cassandra had to deal with the issue herself. "You say this person wants to speak to me—what about?"

Daisy shrugged. "She didn't say."

Cassandra regarded the wrinkled ancient. "Is she a friend of yours?"

"No, Blondie's nobody I know."

"Blondie?" *Egad.* Feeling the need for liquid refreshment, Cassandra lifted her wineglass.

"Blondie isn't her real name. It's April."

The long-stemmed glass slipped from Cassandra's fingers, was pulled by a warp in the space-time continuum into a crashing encounter with the tiled floor, where it shattered instantaneously into a thousand shards. More, if you count the teeny-tiny ones. Unlike the fractured glass ejected from Astrid's broken picture frame, these fragments did not stick to Cassandra's dress. But along with the spilled wine, they made a quite a mess. She uttered a single word: "What?"

Daisy frowned. "What do you mean 'what?' "

Ignoring the odd look she was getting from her business manager, Cassandra pressed her fingers against her temples, closed her eyes. "What did you say her name was?"

"April."

"April what?" The psychic held her breath.

The old woman studied about it.

Moxon: *What the hell is going on here?*

Still holding the breath, the oxygen-depleted psychic unconsciously leaned toward the enigmatic Indian woman. *Please please please. Let it be her.*

Daisy was straining to recollect. *It was a kinda funny last name, even for a* matukach. *Some kind of holiday.* She quickly eliminated Thanksgiving, the Fourth of July, Labor Day, and Chief Ouray's birthday. *Did she say she was April Halloween? No, that's not right. And it wasn't a big holy day like Christmas or Easter.* But wait a minute. *It was somewhere between Christmas and Easter. And had something to do with a saint.* Aha! "Now I remember." She grinned at the white woman. "It was Valentine. April Valentine!"

Cassandra's lips had turned blue under her scarlet lipstick; she exhaled. "Oooh!" *I knew it—April has found a sensitive—someone she's able to communicate with. And the clever spirit has sent her contact to me!*

Caught in a rut, Nicholas Moxon spun on the retread phrase: *What the hell is going on here?* It is commonly believed that Men of Business are not capable of creative thought. Bosh! Which is to say—do not be fooled; Mr. Moxon was, in his devious way, quite an inspired thinker.

Daisy also wondered what was going on. "D'you know this April?"

Having regained a measure of composure, the TV personality said quite truthfully, "I have heard of the young lady. But we have not actually met."

"Well, if you'd like to, she's waiting right outside the door. I can go get her for you."

Feeling the weight of her business manager's gaze,

Cassandra hesitated for only a moment. "Yes. Please do." *This should be interesting.*

Daisy got up from the chair, hobbled off to the door, opened it, poked her head into the hallway, turned her face this way and that. *Well, isn't that just like these young people nowadays. Ask you to do something for them, then wander off. The silly wart-head!* She turned, spoke to the psychic, whose alabaster skin shone exceedingly pale in the glow of fluorescent light. "She's gone." Daisy eyed the clock on the wall. "And so'm I."

Cassandra popped up from her chair. "Wait—how can I get in touch with you?"

Having forgotten about her "business proposition," the Ute elder regarded the TV psychic with wide eyes. "What for?"

Nicholas Moxon reminded her: "We might wish to discuss a consultant contract."

Daisy came very near blushing. "Oh, right."

Cassandra looked hopefully at the Ute woman. "Do you have a telephone?"

"Sure I do." Daisy chuckled. "And electricity and a well with an electric pump and a flush toilet and a septic tank with a leach field. When Charlie Moon built my new house, he put all those things in for me."

Cassandra's thinly penciled brows arched like black inchworms. "You are acquainted with Charlie Moon?"

"I'm his aunt." Daisy added, "His *favorite* aunt." *All the others are dead.*

The psychic was beginning to get a glimmer. *Of course. This is that old Ute woman I've heard so much about. The one who brews all kinds of herbal medicines—and talks to spirits.*

Nicholas Moxon was tiring of this dillydallying. "Daisy—may I have your telephone number?"

"Sure." The shaman recited the familiar digits. "And I'll give you Charlie Moon's number too." She did. "And while you're writing that down in your little book, I'll put some of these salty little crackers in my pocket and then I'll go out to the curb and meet Gorman Sweetwater, who's supposed to come pick me up in his shiny pickup truck."

Daisy did (pocketed crackers) and Moxon did (wrote down the phone numbers) and she did (went to the curb) and Gorman was there in his pickup, smelling sourly of beer—but right on time! Isn't it gratifying when things work out precisely as planned?

After the Indian woman had departed, and the assigned Sugar Bowl waitress had swept up the glass shards and replaced and refilled Cassandra's shattered wineglass and taken her leave, the burly, big-shouldered man asked the question that had been burning a hole in his brain: "Okay, Cassie—spill it. Who's this April Valentine?"

"The daughter of a middle-aged woman that I met at the airport." His client sniffed the alcoholic fumes, took a dainty sip of the volatile liquid. "But as I said, I have never met her."

"So what makes this young lady so interesting?"

"For one thing, she is dead."

"Oh." *Should've seen that one coming.*

"For another, she was—according to her mother— murdered in a most horrible manner by her fiendish husband." There was more, of course. Much more. But she did not share everything with Daddy Warbucks.

"Let me guess the rest." Moxon was just a tad smug. "April V's distraught momma wants you to talk to her dead daughter, find out how the husband did the dirty deed, and if the ghost can give you some hard proof—pin the rap on the lowlife wife killer."

"Yes. More or less." A listless sigh. "But, despite my best efforts, I have not been successful in making contact with April."

Moxon nodded his shiny head. "But now you figure this ghost's talking to the old Indian woman, and you might be able find out what you need to know from Daisy." *Which could boost the ratings another two points. Maybe three.*

"Nicky, your insight is absolutely awe-inspiring." Cassandra Spencer flashed her man-killer smile.

The return grin was toothily sharkish. "Hey—tell me about it!" Nicholas Moxon cocked his head. "Now, let me tell you what to do." He did.

His client agreed.

The business partners raised wineglasses, touched rims.

The musical *clink* would reverberate down through the years.

• • •

TWENTY
COLUMBINE RANCH HEADQUARTERS

At half past nine in the A.M., life was much the same for Daisy Perika as if she had been in her own home on the Southern Ute reservation.

For starters, Charlie Moon had already left the big log house to do whatever cowboys do. Punch some cows, the Ute elder assumed.

Sarah Frank was in the kitchen, putting away the washed and dried breakfast dishes.

Mr. Zig-Zag was asleep on the parlor floor by the fireside rocking chair that Daisy assumed squatter's rights to whenever she visited her nephew.

The tribal elder was sitting in "her" rocker, eyeing the spotted cat, reviewing her plan of assault. As has been revealed, this woman named for a flower harbored an overpowering desire to step on Mr. Zig-Zag's tail. We also know that by some finely tuned, prescient feline instinct, the intended victim always managed to locate his nap spot just out of reach of the enemy's foot. But Daisy was both clever and crafty—more than a match for any scruffy hair bag with mouse smell on his breath. Tactics, that was the thing. What she needed was extended range. This morning, she had a long-handled flyswatter in her lap.

Hearing the occasional clank of pots and dishes in the kitchen, our plotter was confident that she could get the job done before Sarah returned to catch her in the very act of cat whacking. The time had come. Zero hour.

The wrinkled warrior grasped the insect slayer in a firm grip, raised it high over her head. Adrenaline pumped out of her adrenofelinethumper gland, got the tired old pump to beating a war drum in her chest. *He'll never know what hit him.* She took careful aim, was about to give the cat such a thump—*But what if he lets out a big screech and Sarah comes running and says what's happened to my poor kitty cat?* The schemer was of the opinion that every problem has a solution. *If she does, I'll say why Mr. Rag-Bag must've had one of them cat nightmares you hear so much about on Oprah and them other educational TV shows.* Yes, that would cover her posterior. But there is always the worst-case scenario. *What if she sees me do it?* Hmmm. *I'll say there was this big ugly horsefly on Mr. Rag-Bag's hind leg and I thought I oughta swat it a good one before it sucked a pint of blood out of her precious pet.* Though these contingency plans fell somewhat short of perfection, they would have to do. General Perika took aim again, was about to lower the boom—when she was startled to hear the telephone ring. War is heck. The base station was mounted on the wall, but a cordless unit was on a small table, practically at her elbow. She peered at the caller ID, which informed her:

> *Caller Unknown*
> *Number Unknown*

I'll just let the thing keep right on jingling till the [expletives deleted] *get tired and call somebody else.*

The infernal invention went right on a-jingling.

Faced with this accumulating evidence that the (additional expletives deleted) evidently do not tire all that easily, she ground her stumpy teeth.

The nerve-jangling summons did not cease.

Nor did it awaken the cat, who continued to dream in that heavenly peace made perfect by innocence.

The realization that Mr. Zig-Zag was entirely comfortable did not escape Daisy's attention. She fumed all the more. *I won't pick it up!* One might speculate that if she had not answered the telephone, her life might have turned out very much different. But one would be mistaken. It did not matter. Why?

Because Sarah Frank, who had just returned from the kitchen, answered the telephone. "Hello, this is the Columbine Ranch." She listened. "Yes, she's here." The orphan turned to address her adopted aunt. "Aunt Daisy, it's for you."

"Who is it?"

Sarah cupped her hand over the mouthpiece. "I don't know, but her voice sounds familiar."

Her? Maybe it was Louise-Marie. *But she always calls me at night, right before I go to bed.* Daisy Perika snatched the telephone from the girl. "Who's this?"

The caller provided the information requested.

"Oh." Daisy's voice softened. "It's nice to hear from you." *And so soon.* "What can I do for you?"

The caller told her what she could do. Where she could do it, and when. And for how much.

The instrument almost slipped from Daisy's fingers, but she managed to sound almost nonchalant: "Yes, I guess I could find some time to do that." After a few essential details were discussed, the professional consultant said goodbye and hung up.

Sarah had been hanging on every single one of Daisy's single-syllable words. "Who was it?"

The elderly woman gave a careless shrug. "That woman who has the spooky TV program."

"Cassandra?" Sarah's eyes resembled poached eggs. Smallish, girl-sized poached eggs. "What did she want?"

Daisy took a moment to smooth a wrinkle from her skirt. "She asked me if I'd like to be a guest on her TV show." Another wrinkle needed smoothing. "A *special* guest."

The girl's delighted screech awakened her spotted cat from a deep sleep.

• • •

That evening, after hearing Daisy's big news and Sarah Frank's excited commentary, Charlie Moon went into his upstairs office, closed the door, and thought about it. Thinking didn't help. Just served to make him edgy. There were times when a man needed someone to talk to. Someone sensible, who was capable of offering sound advice. Knowing no such person, he placed a call to Scott Parris, told him all about it.

Sensing that his friend was worried, the chief of police attempted to console him: "That's great. Daisy'll liven up the show."

Moon frowned at his unseen comrade. "So would a shoebox full of tarantulas."

Parris chuckled. "Ah, you worry too much, Charlie. Daisy'll have a barrel of fun."

The Ute's response was terse: "I expect you're right about that." *She'd have fun starting World War Three.*

• • •

TWENTY-ONE
THE BIG EVENT

Beatrice Spencer was a highly organized soul. Every day began with a list of things to be done, with a priority assigned to each one. Now, with the mountain's evening shadow about to enshroud the family estate, she headed home from a brisk walk, gratified to mentally mark another task "completed." She shrugged off an Irish tweed coat, pulled off a pair sheepskin-lined boots, undressed down to the skin, and treated herself to a cleansing shower that was followed by a long, hot soak in the tub. Not quite an hour later, she entered the parlor looking quite chic in an ankle-length white silk dress (slit to the knee), a pink pearl necklace and matching earrings. On her feet, white goat-leather slippers adorned with pink pearl buttons. Mighty nice-looking was what she was, and then some. And she knew it.

Her spouse of a few weeks was suitably impressed, and yearned to say something that would convey his appreciation. But, being a run-of-the-mill husband when it came to praise, accolades, or even flattery, Andrew Turner was not up to generating a compliment that did justice to the lovely vision. And there was no shortage of eye candy. The frosting on the luscious lady-cake was a twirl of golden tresses, done up in a manner that he was at a loss to describe. But it reminded Andrew of something else he liked very much. Food. More particularly, dessert. He could practically taste it on the tip of his tongue—that sweet, fluffy stuff that floated atop Grandma Turner's coconut crème pies, that frothy sea of delectable waves, frozen stiff, yet toasted on the tips. He had watched Granny whip up egg whites with a fork, then stir in the sugar and whatnot. But name the topping, he could not. If he had been able to call the word *meringue* to mind, who knows what sort of memorable tribute the tongue-tied husband might have devised. But, not one to be defeated by his shortcomings, Andrew did what he could. He whistled.

Blushing at the compliment, Beatrice reminded him of the big event. "Now, don't forget, Cassie will be on at nine." She flashed the pearly whites at her mate. "And you promised to show up tonight—so please arrive on time."

"It's on my schedule." Mr. Turner glanced at his wristwatch. *Seven fifty-eight.*

The wife opened a white suede purse, found a platinum compact mirror, inspected her image, found a minuscule flaw that she thought needed touching up. "I must leave early. I promised Cassie I'd help look after her mystery guest this evening."

Mystery guest? "Who might that be?"

"I've no idea." *Sis has been rather tight-lipped of late.* She applied the pointy tip of a miniature lipstick. *There, that's better.*

Turner was ogling his shapely wife. "I wish I could leave early, drive to town with you." *But tonight is the night.*

She laughed. "Sure you do."

He put on a hurt expression. "I have a bit of work to catch up on." Quite true.

"Yes, you told me at breakfast."

From force of habit, he appended a lie: "I expect a call from an important client."

She snapped the compact shut, dropped the shiny disk and lipstick into her purse. "What is it this time—someone who needs a hugely expensive new telephone system installed?"

"Even better than that."

"Let me guess." She opened a walk-in closet that was

stuffed with exquisite gifts from Daddy Spencer, guessed, "A truckload of computers."

"Right on the button. But you forgot to mention the custom software—and that's where the serious profit is." He watched her select a magnificent Russian sable. *That little number must've set her old man back at least twenty grand.*

"I don't mean to nag, Andrew—but please, please try not to be late."

"Don't fret." He helped her slip into the cozy coat. "I'll show up before Cassie goes off the air."

"I shall hold you to that."

The antique marble mantel clock chimed. Eight times. One hour to . . . *show time!*

As if she did not completely trust that fine example of late-nineteenth-century French engineering, Beatrice checked her wristwatch. "I really *must* be going."

"Then say 'Goodbye, dear.' "

"As you wish." She exhaled a wisp of a sigh. "Goodbye, dear." Beatrice kissed her husband lightly on the cheek. "I hope you have an enjoyable evening chatting with your well-heeled client, and unload several dozen computers and tons of software on the unwary fellow."

"That is my intention. Have a good time."

• • •

Beatrice watched the garage door rise, eased her Mercedes off the concrete and onto the gravel driveway. By long habit, the mountain dweller lowered the front windows an inch to inhale a whiff of pine and cedar. The pungent aromas blended well with the scent of fine leather upholstery. The late afternoon had been pleasantly mild, but the night breeze carried a sage-scented promise of approaching dampness. A ominous crowd of billowing, roiling clouds was rising over the crest of Spencer Mountain. The artist perceived a ghostly company of Nez Percé cavalry, mounted on red-eyed, smoke-snorting ponies—hooves kicking fire off heaven's flint. What a delight it would be to paint that savage panorama! Even as she watched, the scene was transformed. An updraft of eagle plumes coalesced into a towering war bonnet, flashing with inner lights. Under the feathered helmet, a sober old face she recognized from a high school history book. *Hin-mah-too-yah-lat-kekt*— Thunder Rolling Down the Mountain. Oh, and did that thunder roll—a hundred huge drums adrumming like boulders come arumbling to obliterate whole forests of pine and spruce—along with the sleek Mercedes and its white-as-a-sheet driver!

Shaken by these loud, rowdy threats, Beatrice consulted that portion of the mind that deals with such issues as how to extract a cube root or an infected wisdom tooth, and the interpretation of meteorological data, and came to this conclusion: *Looks like we'll be getting some snow.* She closed the windows and proceeded down the long, twisting driveway, passing aspen saplings that were beginning to tremble in a suddenly chill wind. Rising above the passenger side of the motorcar, the shadowy mass of the mountain continued to grumble. Off to her left, unseen beyond a few yards of rocky ground, was that deep crack in the earth—the Devil's Mouth. The cruel grin split the mountain from the rugged, windswept domain of Broken-Tooth Mesa, where a scattering of basalt boulders did their level best to resemble cracked, black molars.

The barren mesa seemed benign enough, but even as a child Beatrice always trembled at the sight of the deep crevice. It was probably due to some peculiar congruence of prevailing winds and topography, but whatever the reason, nine-tenths of the snow that blew off the mesa or down the mountainside ended up in the fissure's dark recesses. On the bottom, unseen for millennia, was a pale blue bed of glaciated ice, where the well-preserved remains of giant ground sloths and single-hump camels were entombed with other Ice Age mammals—including a fine specimen of a shaggy-haired mammoth. Above this bizarre Pleistocene cemetery was a layer-cake accumulation of thousands of winters of snow, and as many strata of leaf, pollen, grit, dust, and other debris. On the top was a frothy, semiwhite frosting that would melt every few decades, but at the end of most winters it was at least thirty feet deep.

Why all this attention to such details? Why, because the Devil's Mouth swallows whatever falls into it. And never, ever spits anything out.

As Beatrice made her way down the long, winding driveway, the first big, fat flakes splattered on the Mercedes windshield. Still within sight of her home, she braked to a stop, exchanged the sable for a black raincoat, pulled big rubber galoshes over her delicate pink slippers, and got out to remove a football-size boulder that had rolled (along with the thunder?) down the mountain. From there on, *slow* was the name of the game. Before she reached the gate at the highway, the resolute woman encountered a fallen aspen limb, an emaciated coyote loping across the lane, and another rock in the road. Plus a few other minor obstructions and small distractions. Not a problem.

• • •

Andrew Turner posed in front of a full-length mirror, admired the splendid image that looked back with an equally approving expression. His wife's wish that he "have an enjoyable evening" still rang in his ears. *I would not be at all surprised if this turned out to be the best evening of my entire life. My finest hour.* As he straightened his pale blue tie, a glint of sly amusement sparkled in Andrew's eye. *If Bea knew what I'm up to, there's no telling what she might do.* But there was no way the spouse would ever figure it out. The Plan was absolutely first rate. No—scratch that understatement. It was a *masterpiece.* The man in the looking-glass exchanged a foxy grin with his flesh-and-blood twin. This evening's performance would create quite a sensation; people would be talking about it for years to come. It was, he thought, a great pity that the author of the piece must remain forever anonymous.

• • •

At the bottom of the driveway, Beatrice fumbled in her purse, found the remote-control device to open the heavy iron gate. The snow was mixed with rain at this lower altitude. Ten seconds after electronic detectors had verified that her automobile was clear, the gate banged shut behind her. She stopped long enough to shed the bulky boots and ugly raincoat, slip back into the sable. Ah, that was much better! Off she went, to spend a pleasant evening with Sister Cassie.

● ● ●

Even though he was quite alone in the house, Andrew Turner followed his habit of securing the door after entering his basement office. On this occasion, he would forgo the pleasure of the spotlight and the adoring applause from an unseen audience. As soon as he had turned away from the door, he said, "Low illumination."

In each corner, a daisy-shaped night-light bloomed to life.

Barely enough to see by.

He stepped smartly to the oak table. "Terminal Two."

The summoned hardware awakened, the hard disk yawned, began to hum, then to whine.

The maestro seated himself, placed his hands on the keyboard, deftly entered a twelve-character alphanumeric password, watched his custom e-mail software logo (a huge red AT) flash on the blue-green screen. To access the crucial item A. Turner entered a second password.

And in an instant, there it was—so innocent in appearance, so deadly in intent. Even in its deeply encrypted form, the file occupied a mere twelve kilobytes on the hard disk. It would be forwarded anonymously, through a series of untraceable foreign e-mail accounts that would be opened just long enough to transfer the data, then closed immediately following the transmission.

Well, here we are, Andy m'boy—time to start the ol' ball rolling.

This was one of those rare moments—a life-altering decision. Andrew Turner still had time to change his mind. But not much. Every segment of this evening's performance had been orchestrated down to the minute.

His index finger rested lightly on the optical mouse.

On the screen, the cursor blinked expectantly over the Send Now button.

The hacker chewed on his lower lip. Held his breath. Once the thing was done, there was no turning back. He felt an odd doomsday chill, as if he had a revolver to his temple, was about to pull the trigger. He hesitated. Cogitated.

There's no other way . . . I have to do it.

His finger pressed down, the mouse clicked.

There was an electronically generated whooshing sound, intended to suggest a supersonic mail plane outbound.

His future determined by this daring act, the man's face—bathed in sickly illumination from the computer screen—seemed to fluoresce bluish green. Seeing the identical glow on his hands, it occurred to Turner that he resembled a corpse. But this clever, ambitious fellow had no time for negative thinking. He voice-commanded the computer to erase the small file he had forwarded (which it did), to write a checkerboard of ones and zeros over the file location (which it also did), and to shut itself down (ditto). He departed from his office.

Once upstairs, Turner opened the door to the attached four-car garage, slipped into his Corvette, eased the low-slung automobile into the waiting night. The falling snow glittered in the headlight beams, coated the graveled drive with a frosty sheen.

As he headed down the steep driveway that wound its serpentine path between the edge of Spencer Mountain and the Devil's Mouth, the speedometer needle tarried in the neighborhood of thirty-five miles per hour. The wind moaned; naked aspen branches shivered as he passed. Rolling along in high spirits, he went over The Plan, ticking off each element in his mind. He considered the timing. Tried to spot the slightest flaw in the plot. Forty-four miles per hour. He assured himself that the scheme was perfection personified. It could not fail. Andrew Turner was a man with several strong character traits. Excessive humility was not to be counted among them. Forty-nine mph.

He laughed out loud. And, for reasons known only to himself, began to hum Abraham Lincoln's favorite song. It might well be that he wished he were in *de land ob cotton.* Did Mr. Turner feel the tug of that mythic realm where *old times am not forgotten*? One hesitates to hazard a guess. Whatever the case, as he rounded the tightest curve on the long descent to the paved highway, and the Corvette headlights swept impotently off into the darkness above the Devil's Mouth, he was well on his way. But to what destination? *To lib an' die in Dixie?*

It seems unlikely. But with such a man as he, who among us would categorically rule out such an eventuality?

Whatever he yenned or yearned for, by the time the low beams illuminated the gravel driveway again—the thing was as good as done.

TWENTY-TWO
PRELUDE TO THE PERFORMANCE

As Andrew Turner, tucked snugly in to his Corvette, rolled along the winding driveway, Beatrice was already far away, passing the familiar sign that welcomed her to Granite Creek—where a cold, chill rain pelted the dimly illuminated streets. She soon arrived at the corner of Copper and Vine, where her sister Cassandra's three-story Victorian brick ably played the role of seedy anachronism among a younger cluster of modern glass-and-steel office buildings. The familiar white TV-COM van was parked in the front driveway. She made a right into the paved alley, pulled into the graveled space behind the big, ugly house, parked in the soft, yellow glow of a 75-watt electric bulb concealed in a replica of an antique gas lantern. She was about to open the Mercedes door when a pair of headlights sliced through the night. *Who could that be?* Beatrice waited while the SUV pulled up beside her.

She watched a lean, tall man emerge from a Ford Expedition that had a wildflower logo on the driver's door—a Colorado columbine. The lanky fellow wore a gray Stetson, gray suede jacket, razor-crease gray slacks, and gleaming cowboy boots. *I'm sure I've seen him somewhere.* She got out of the Mercedes just as he opened a rear door and a thin little girl in a red coat practically leaped out. *That must be his daughter. His wife is probably in the front seat.* Beatrice called out, "Excuse me—this is a private parking space."

The man turned. "Soon as my aunt gets out, I'll be glad to move the car to the street." A friendly smile flashed across the dark face. "But the lady of the house said I could park here."

He's either lost or lying through his teeth. "And who would that lady be?"

"Miss Cassandra Spencer." The smile gleamed with a mischievous glint. "And if I'm not mistaken, the lady I'm speaking to is her sister."

Beatrice blinked. "And who might you be?"

The gentleman removed his pearl-gray Stetson, which was reserved for special occasions. "Charlie Moon."

Oh, now I remember. "You're the deputy who met Cassie and me when we arrived at Astrid's home that night. And refused us entry." *Even threatened to pick us up, one under each arm, and stuff us into the police car. And meant every word of it.* Her face burned. *What a man!*

Feeling, but misunderstanding, the heat, Moon hurriedly introduced the shy, thin teenager beside him. "This young lady is my friend Sarah Frank."

The Ute-Papago teenager cringed at the "my friend," but smiled and nodded at the pretty white woman.

Beatrice returned the smile. "Cassandra will be quite busy tonight. Perhaps you could tell me what your business is with my sister—"

There was an anxious squawk from the bowels of the Expedition. "Charlie, are you gonna help me outta this big car, or should I try to get out on my own and maybe fall flat on my face?"

He explained; "The sweet little lady in the front seat is my aunt Daisy."

Daisy? "Oh—is she the guest on tonight's show?"

"That's about the size of it." He jabbed a thumb at his chest. "And I'm her chauffeur."

For an instant, Beatrice disremembered that she was a married lady. And that she was a lady. *You could take me for a drive anytime.*

Hearing his aunt fumbling to open the car door, Moon

went to assist the elderly person. Upon exiting the car, Daisy's first words were, "This cold rain'll give me the double pneumonia."

Beatrice reached into her purse, found the key to Cassandra's door. "I'll take you inside."

In the kitchen, she introduced the Indians to a short, plump, balding, bespectacled man who needed no introduction. No, he was not famous. The name tag pinned to his shirt identified him as Gerald Sax, Assistant Director. The anxious AD nodded at Sarah and Daisy, gave Moon's extended hand a quick, perfunctory grasp, and murmured to Beatrice; "Cassie's still putting on her makeup. She should be on the set by now." *One of these times, she's gonna be late. I just know it. And when that happens, who'll get yelled at? The star of the show? Not a chance—me, that's who!*

After assuring the fidgety fellow that all would be well, Beatrice explained a Rule of the House to the newcomers: "My sister is a very private person. Mr. Sax is the only employee from the television production crew that Cassie allows into her home."

Sax barely allowed himself a momentary roll of the eyes. It was a running affront with the Denver/Salt Lake television company that the star of *Cassandra Sees* was so utterly independent of those experts who applied makeup, maintained the set, operated cameras and lights—all that professional expertise that would have added a definite touch of class to the plain-vanilla production. On the other hand, the fact that *C Sees* was a low-budget production certainly helped the profit margin.

The visitors from the Columbine followed the assistant director into the dining room, where a panel of switches, knobs, digital readouts, and four flat-screen monitors was mounted on a wheeled, stainless-steel cart. As he explained the hardware to the newcomers, Sax's countenance brightened. "On the day of the broadcast, I drive over from Denver, set up the cameras, microphones, and lights on the *Cassandra Sees* set—which is just on the other side of the wall. I take care of things from this remote-control console."

Beatrice addressed Daisy Perika: "The broadcast originates in Cassie's parlor. That's where she interviews her guests. And where she feels most comfortable."

Following the white woman's glance, Daisy looked toward the closed oak door.

Sax seated himself at the cart, pointed to each monitor in turn. "From here, I select the shot I want—camera one, two, or three, each of which you can see on the corresponding ten-inch monitors. The active camera shows up on the larger color screen. The video feed from that monitor is up-linked live, via satellite, to Denver."

Daisy leaned in to inspect the screens. Two of the cameras were showing different views of a beautifully upholstered high-backed chair. The third was focused on a smaller chair.

"Cameras one and two present Cassandra face-on and profile, respectively," Sax said to Daisy. "You'll be on camera three."

So, two pictures for her, one for me. Daisy's stomach was beginning to flutter. "How'll I know when to talk?"

"Not a problem." Sax patted the old woman's hunched back. "It'll be just like having a chat with one of your friends. To help things along, Cassie will ask you questions." His round face split in a grin. "Easy as falling off a log."

The image of falling off a log did nothing to bolster Daisy's courage. "But how does *she* know when to start talking—and when to stop?"

Daisy had inadvertently hit upon one of Sax's sore spots. He glowered at monitor one, as if he could see the woman who would be sitting in the star's chair. "Cassandra refuses to wear a miniature earphone. Says it distracts her. But I've rigged up a set of signal lights on the coffee table. The lights provide a countdown till she goes on the air—green for one minute, yellow for thirty seconds, red for five. Once she's on, the same lights signal the countdown till cameras-off. But Cassandra doesn't depend entirely on the lights—she has her own little television set stashed under the coffee table. It serves as a monitor to show her what's being broadcast. The sound is turned off, of course, but she can see when a commercial is ending—and her program logo comes on for three seconds before I take direct feed from the cameras to the satellite uplink."

Daisy frowned. "When the show's running, she can see herself on the TV under the table?"

"That's right." *And she loves seeing her mug on the silver screen.*

The mystery guest shuddered. "If I was trying to talk, and saw myself on the TV, that would make me nervous."

"Not an issue—you'll be on the other side of the coffee table, so you won't be able to see Cassie's television monitor."

The worrier had already thought of a new problem: "What if my voice gets scratchy?"

"There'll be a beverage of your choice on the coffee table. Coffee, tea, water—anything you want."

"Water will be okay." Her face screwed up with another worried look. "But what if I drink too much, and need to go pee?"

While Moon grinned and Sarah bit her lip to keep from smiling, Sax's pale face blushed. "Uh—when Denver runs commercials, you'll get a break. If you need to go to the bathroom, let Cassie know. It's just off the parlor, the door between the piano and the bookshelves."

Moon put his arm around the nervous elder. "You'll be fine."

Daisy Perika was not entirely convinced, but her nephew's encouragement did help. And despite being anxious about this unprecedented experience, she was also delighted at the prospect of appearing on television. Matter of fact, she was feeling quite young tonight. Not a day over seventy-five.

Sax disappeared into the parlor for a last-minute adjustment. Or perhaps to escape Daisy.

"As soon as Cassie is ready," Beatrice said to the Ute woman, "I'll introduce you to her."

"We've already met," Daisy said.

"Oh?"

"I happened to run into your sister and her boyfriend at a restaurant."

"Boyfriend?" *Well now—what has dear Cassie been hiding from me?* "What did he look like?"

"Great big fella," Daisy said. "Bald as a boiled potato, shoulders like a buffalo."

Beatrice laughed. "That has to be Nicholas Moxon. Nicky is Cassie's business manager."

Being on her best behavior, the old woman held back a derisive snort. *Call him whatever you want to, but in my day, when a man took a girl to a nice restaurant and bought her lunch, they was the same as engaged.* At the mention of lunch, Daisy's stomach responded with a peculiar, sickly feeling. Also started making odd little noises.

Cassandra chose this moment to make her entrance from the parlor. And quite an entrance it was. From the shining, raven-black locks that hung to her slim waist, to the perfectly tailored black silk dress that terminated just far enough above her knees to provide an eyeful of shapely legs sheathed in black net stockings, to the matching black heels—the star of the show was a fashion photo of self-assured elegance. The effect of her sudden appearance on those present varied somewhat.

Gerald Sax: *Spider-Woman looks like she's ready to go to work.*

Sarah Frank: *She is so beautiful—even better than on TV!*

Charlie Moon: *Wow!*

Charlie Moon's aunt: *She must have laid that lipstick on with a paintbrush. And look at them stockings!* Daisy arched an eyebrow. *She could pass for a Reno street-walker.*

Fortunately, the psychic was not a mind reader. After introductions were made, after her long lashes were fluttered at the flustered Indian cowboy *(He is so cute!)*, Cassandra turned her attention to tonight's mystery guest. "We have a few minutes before the show begins. Would you like to have a look at the parlor, see where you'll be sitting during the broadcast?"

"Not right now." Daisy's stomach made a sound like a pot of oatmeal about to boil over. "Take me to your toilet." *It must be that beef enchilada Charlie made for lunch. The big doofus put too much powdered red chili pepper in it.*

● ● ●

TWENTY-THREE
AT CASSANDRA'S DINING TABLE WITH
SISTER BEA

Beatrice Spencer poured fresh coffee into Charlie Moon's cup. "Cream or sweetener?"

"I like it black. But if you've got some handy, sugar would be dandy."

She passed him a silver bowl.

Moon helped himself to six heaping spoonfuls.

The psychic's sister beamed on the girl. "Would you like a soft drink, dear?"

Sarah Frank shook her head, tried so *very* hard to sound grown-up. "I'll have some coffee." Before the woman could ask, she added, "I don't use cream, but I'll have some sugar." *Just like Charlie drinks it.*

Moon gave Sarah a sideways glance. *I didn't know the kid liked coffee.* Daisy would have been glad to tell him that there were lots of things he didn't know. Much less, understand. The big gourd head.

Beatrice Spencer, who had once had a crush on a history professor old enough to be her father, understood perfectly. She poured a cup for the love-struck child, turned to ask Gerald Sax if he was in need of liquid refreshment.

Absorbed in his work at the control console, the assistant director shook his head, mumbled something about camera three's focus control.

IN THE PARLOR WITH SISTER CASSIE

Cassandra Spencer gazed across the coffee table at her elderly guest, who had just returned from the bathroom. "Do you feel quite all right?"

Daisy nodded in the halfhearted gesture of one who will die trying. But, following a healthy belch, she did indeed feel quite all right. *I should've asked for some baking soda in a glass of water. That was all I needed.*

Cassandra had planned to raise the critical issue after the show, but the moment seemed right. "Daisy—when we met in the Sugar Bowl, you mentioned a young lady who wanted to speak to me."

She must be talking about that hillbilly girl. "Sure. I remember. April Something."

"Valentine."

"Oh, right." Daisy smiled at the memory. "The Dixie belle."

"Why do you say that?"

"It was the way she talked. Like somebody from Georgia or Alabama. I bet she was raised on hog belly and grits."

The mention of "hog belly" caused the psychic's fingers to tingle. "April was . . . is from North Carolina." As if on the verge of prayer, she clasped her hands. "Have you spoken to her since that day in the restaurant?"

Surprised by this question, Daisy shook her head. "And it's not likely I will. The poor girl was just some drifter or runaway. Likely as not, she's in another state by now."

She doesn't know. Cassandra dropped the bomb: "Daisy—April is no longer with us."

The tribal elder stared. *She's a little bit slow on the uptake.* "That's what I just told you."

"I do not refer to earthly separation." How to put it? "When you spoke to April, she was not among the living."

The Ute elder blinked. Blinked again. "Are you dead-sure about that?"

A curt nod. "I've spoken with her mother. And I have a collection of news clippings about her death."

"With pictures of that hillbilly girl?"

"Certainly." Cassandra made her way over to a cluttered corner book shelf, opened a labeled stationery box, found the article that Daisy needed to see, and brought it to the coffee table.

The shaman examined a black-and-white reproduction of a photo under the headline LOCAL WOMAN DIES IN FARM ACCIDENT. "That's her, all right." *I must be losing my touch—I should've spotted this one for a dead person right off.* She was squinting to read the small print when her host snatched the article away, stuffed it into a magazine rack.

Cassandra locked eyes with her guest. "Daisy, it is terribly important that I communicate with April Valentine. I've been attempting to make contact with her spirit, but without success. There must be some kind of cosmic barrier between us. But I believe we could use you as a kind of go-between. So I would be enormously grateful if you would make some effort to—"

She was interrupted by Gerald Sax's voice barking from the intercom; "Heads up, Cassie—countdown!"

On a small black panel on the coffee table, a green light-emitting diode blinked on. One minute to show time.

The psychic glanced at the small television set under the coffee table. A Jeep commercial was running. About forty-five seconds. She produced a pocket mirror, performed a final inspection of her makeup.

Yellow light—thirty seconds.

As the unseen assistant director performed a final check of the instruments of his trade, camera-lens assemblies whirred in and out, tripod-mounted lights brightened and dimmed, and the boom microphone above the coffee table was lowered and raised by a hand's breadth. All was well at the remote-control console. At Gerald Sax's manual command, camera one zoomed in on the star's left eye, magnifying the orb to fill monitor one, automatically recorded sixteen shots over a period of 530 milliseconds, zoomed out to frame her semifamous face. None of this video information was broadcast . . . not yet.

Sarah murmured, "I don't know how she keeps from blinking."

Sax, over his shoulder: "Ah, Cassie blinks all right. What you see in the intro is a single frame from a close-up shot that I make a few seconds before she goes on the air." He turned in his chair to brag to the skinny little girl, "The eyeball shot was my idea."

"I really like it."

"Thanks." Sax swelled with pride. "Most directors would make just one shot at the beginning of the season and use it for months. But I take a new picture for every broadcast. And if I don't like what I got, I'll take another one—sometimes during a commercial break when our star doesn't know I'm doing it." He added, "Posed photos are okay if that's all you can get, but candid shots are always best."

Sarah reflected the man's infectious grin. *I bet it would be fun to work on TV.*

• • •

The Jeep commercial was replaced by the happy face of an up-and-coming Denver weather forecaster, who provided a rapid minireport: The late-spring snowstorm in western Colorado was building. Expect eight to twelve inches above seven thousand feet.

Red light—five seconds. Cassandra returned her attention to the small, on-the-air monitor. Four seconds. The screen went coal black. The lady's face was as calm as sculpted marble. Her pulse raced.

Three seconds. From Denver, bloodred script was painted on the black electronic canvas:

Casandra Sees

Two seconds: Bea's older sister put on her most alluring smile.

One-point-five seconds: Gerald Sax pressed a button to feed the on-site video stream to the satellite uplink.

One second: The psychic's magnified eye filled on the screen.

Zero seconds: Cassandra's face flashed over the air-waves.

IN THE DINING ROOM

Beatrice Spencer, Charlie Moon, and Sarah Frank were looking over Assistant Director Gerald Sax's shoulder. Though they uttered not a word, each of these four souls was occupied with a private thought.

Sister Bea, glancing at her wristwatch: *I wonder what has happened to Andrew.*

Charlie Moon: *Don't get nervous, Aunt Daisy—just be yourself.* He grinned. *On second thought . . .*

Sarah Frank: *Cassandra is so gorgeous!* A sideways glance at the grinning Ute. *I bet Charlie likes her.* Men were pushovers for a pretty face.

Gerald Sax: *Raise the ratings through the roof, Spider-Woman.*

• • •

Chief of Police Scott Parris, who was watching *Cassandra Sees* in the small but well-appointed living room of his girl-friend's condo, had momentarily lost interest in said girl-friend (who was fifteen years his junior, and quite a looker). He used the remote to turn up the volume. An-noyed by the commercials and distracted by the warble of his cell phone, he pulled the thing from his pocket. "Parris here."

The SUPD dispatcher said, "Hello, Chief," into his ear.

"Hello yourself. Whatcha got, Clara?"

What she had was a Wye-Star report of a vehicle acci-dent. Clara Tavishuts read the text. The gist of which was that Wye-Star Central had received an automated transmission of a motor vehicle's onboard-accelerometer trip, which indicated possible collision. The alarm signal from the vehicle was lost almost immediately, which could indicate serious damage. An operator had attempted to contact the driver via the vehicle's built-in cellular tele-phone. No response. GPS coordinates of the vehicle's last known location were referenced to the intersection of two state routes and the National Guard armory. The telephone number of the nearest residence was registered to one Beatrice Spencer. The registered owner of vehicle was one Andrew Bedford Turner.

Bedford? Parris was scribbling this information on a pink paper napkin. *I didn't know Andy Turner had a middle name.* "When did we get this alert?"

"About eight twenty-nine." Expecting an outburst, Clara hurried along: "I know that's a long time ago, Chief—but most of these reports turn out to be fender-benders, and both of our on-duty units have been occupied with serious business. Unit 240 is attending to a three-car accident out by the rodeo grounds, and car 260 has responded to a silent alarm at the Corner Drugstore. Corner Drug got hit last month by burglars who packed away a big haul of prescription painkillers."

"Yeah, I remember." Parris maintained an even tone. "When'll we have a car rolling?"

"Can't say, sir. But I'll dispatch one just as soon as—"

"How about an ambulance and some EMTs?"

"Negative on that. One team is with car 240 and the other ambulance is broke down—"

"See if you can put a call through to Andrew Turner's cell phone. If you can't get him, try to get in touch with Bea."

"I couldn't get access to Mr. Turner's cell number, but I should be able to contact his wife—she's usually at her sister's home for the TV show."

"Thanks, Clara." He hung up, pulled on his jacket, muttered an apology to his sweetheart.

Sweetheart was engrossed in the television program. "Cassandra looks really great tonight. And that little old Indian woman is so *cute.*" She tried to think of something to compare Daisy with, and did: "She reminds me of one of those little granny dolls that have dried-up apples for faces."

Imagining how Daisy Perika would respond to that innocent observation, Parris grinned. That little dried-apple face might look cute, but it had a mouthful of teeth. Sharp ones.

• • •

When the telephone on the dining-room wall rang, Beatrice picked it up. "Cassandra Spencer residence, this is her sister speaking." She listened to the police dispatcher's terse report. *What is she talking about?* "Clara, dear—what, exactly is a Wye-Star alert?"

The dispatcher explained that this was an electromechanical sensing system installed in some automobiles. If the car bumped into something, a signal was transmitted via cell phone (or, if that link failed, via satellite) to the Wye-Star headquarters in Kansas City, where it would alert an operator to a potential accident and provide a GPS location of the automobile. The operator's initial task was to contact the automobile and speak to the driver. If the driver did not respond, the next step was to contact the local police so that appropriate emergency vehicles could be dispatched to the scene.

Beatrice gripped the telephone tightly. "Clara, what's the bottom line?"

"I'm sorry, Bea—but the automobile is your husband's Corvette. And the GPS coordinates put the accident close to your home on the mountain." The dispatcher advised that as soon as she had a unit available, she would send it to check on Mr. Turner, but that Bea should not be overly concerned. The Wye-Star alert was probably a false alarm, or at worst, Mr. Turner had bumped into something along the driveway that triggered the collision sensor. The reason he had not responded to the Wye-Star operator's call was most likely because he had gotten out of the car to check the damage. By now he was probably walking back to the house. Miss Tavishuts would continue to ring the Spencer residence landline every few minutes.

"I've no doubt you're right, Clara." Beatrice's heart pounded. "But just to be on the safe side, I'll go home and find out what has happened." She hung up, grabbed her small purse and sable coat, murmured an "Excuse me, but I must run" to Charlie Moon and Sarah Frank, and hurried out of her sister's house.

The teenage girl turned big eyes on Moon. "What was that all about?"

"We'll have to wait and see." *I hope no one's hurt bad.*

Andrew Turner's distraught wife was behind the wheel of her Mercedes, rolling along the rain-slick streets of Granite Creek. On her way out of town, she ignored two Stop signs and three traffic lights and came very near to running down an elderly pedestrian, who shouted curses at the luxury automobile and the careless driver. The wobbly-legged citizen also threw a half-empty bottle of red wine at the rapidly receding taillights, watched it smash on the wet pavement, then wept and cursed himself for such a foolish waste of tasty hooch.

TWENTY-FOUR
ON THE TUBE

For the first few minutes, everything went according to plan. Cassandra began with the usual reading of selected e-mails and letters from those viewers who lavished her with praise and offered unsolicited testimony to the accuracy of her "readings." Quite a few provided descriptions of their own otherworldly experiences, some of which were highly interesting, even riveting. When this segment was finished, Cassandra introduced her "mystery guest," and by asking Daisy Perika a few simple questions about herself, managed to put the tense woman completely at ease.

Then, the psychic got down to the serious business of blatant flattery. "You have quite a reputation as a necromancer."

Startled, the Ute elder jutted her chin. "What do you mean by that?"

She is just precious. "You are rather well known in southern Colorado as a practitioner of the arcane arts." She laid it on thick: "Indeed, *famous* would be a more apt descriptor."

Startled was instantly replaced with *pleased. Me, famous?* Feigning modesty, Daisy shrugged off the praise.

Reading the shaman's self-centered thoughts required no paranormal powers. "It is said that you commonly talk to those who have passed."

Pleased gave way to *confused.* "Passed what?" *Kidney stones?* But that didn't make any sense.

Cassandra's turn to be startled. "Uh . . . passed over."

Daisy was getting downright annoyed. "Over *what*?"

The psychic's face flushed a pretty pink. "Why—to the other side."

The shaman cocked her head. "You talking about dead people?"

Relieved to have reestablished communication with her guest, the psychic nodded.

Unaware of the sensitivity of the tiny microphone pinned to her collar, Daisy muttered, not quite under her breath, "Well, why didn't you just say so."

Unlike the delighted audience (almost 9 percent of whom spat out their beverage of choice), the star of the show was unaware of this caustic suggestion. Cassandra flashed the engaging smile. "So, is it true that you commune with spirits of the departed?"

The Ute elder clarified: "I don't so much talk to dead people as they talk to me." *This is making me thirsty.* She reached for a water glass on the coffee table.

Cassandra waited with her rapt audience, who watched the old woman take a sip of atrociously expensive mineral water.

That sure hit the spot. The spot burped. "Like I was saying, the haunts are the ones who like to beat their gums." The aged shaman set the glass aside, scowled at memories of troublesome encounters. "Week in, week out—it never stops. Some old bag of bones slips up beside me when I go outside, pulls at my sleeve or nudges me with a pointy elbow. Start's telling me her life story. And if I stay inside for some peace and quiet, they'll come around my house, peck-pecking on the window"—she rapped her knuckles on the table—"or knocking on my door. Day or night, it don't make no difference." She fixed her pretty host with a gimlet stare. "Them dead ones never sleep."

The TV psychic had become one with the audience. "They don't?"

The expert on ghostology shook her head. "And they don't mind waking live people up in the middle of the night. And once they get to running off at the mouth—and all they want to talk about is themselves—you can bet your britches they have plenty to say!"

Cassandra had no britches to bet, but she had a question: "Do you actually *hear* the voices—or do you simply *sense* their words?"

"Oh, I hear 'em all right—just like I hear you right now." Daisy leaned forward, lowered her voice as if she was about to share a secret with this kindred soul: "Some dead people just whisper in my ear, others talk right out loud." The cranky old woman grimaced as she recalled one of her pet peeves. "And lots of 'em don't even speak English, or Ute, or even Mexican—just some foreign jibber-jabber. How am I supposed to know what they're saying?" From her sour expression, it was clear that Daisy generally found these uninvited guests to be a great nuisance. Which she did. Dead people—especially those who came prowling about at night—were a plague. "Sometimes," the shaman muttered, "they make me so damn mad I'd like to get my 12-gauge out of the closet and give 'em both barrels!" After a sigh, her mouth curled into a crooked little grin. "But it don't help to shoot somebody who's already dead."

According to carefully conducted scientific research on what draws and holds a TV audience, violence is right up there with sex. Low comedy occupies the third spot.

The delighted television-broadcast executives were giving the old Indian woman a solid two out of three, which wasn't bad. If Daisy got just a tad badder, it would be time to break out the pink champagne and party hats.

The star of *Cassandra Sees* sensed that she was on a roll. But what Daisy Perika definitely did not have was sex appeal, so Cassandra rolled with what she did have. Reaching for a blue-roses-on-ivory china teacup, the psychic said, "My goodness—it sounds like there are quite a few spirits residing in your neighborhood."

"They don't call it Spirit Canyon for nothing." Daisy watched the young woman take a sip of tea. "The place is practically crawling with dead folks."

The conversation might have continued more or less along this line, with Daisy stressing what awful pests ghosts tended to make of themselves, but the lady in charge decided to focus her guest on a specific experience. "Is there a particular spirit that you would like to tell us about?"

Daisy Perika, whose mood had tilted decidedly toward the positive side of the scale, considered telling a story or two about Nahum Yaciiti, her favorite of the lot. But somehow, it didn't seem *right*. Nahum was far too special to share with a bunch of strangers. And besides, he didn't hang around the canyon waiting for that Last Day, like those less fortunate spirits: The kindly old shepherd (who had been whisked away in a whirlwind!) had gone directly to that far, happy shore. She settled instead on another haunt: "Well, when I was a little girl, Uncle Blue Hummingbird was my favorite relative." She added, with perfect innocence, "Especially after he died."

Among the audience, more beverages were expelled from between the lips.

By now a seasoned pro, Cassandra Spencer managed to suppress even a hint of a smile. "Please tell us about him."

The aged woman obligingly described how, so many years ago (but it seemed like just last week), the spirit of recently deceased Uncle Blue Hummingbird had appeared with the dawn, riding through the morning mists on the finest pinto pony she had ever laid eyes on. The tribal elder surprised her host by raising the profound philosophical issue of whether Uncle's mount was the equine ghost of a once-living four-legged creature, or—and this was an interesting notion—was it a spirit pony that had never experienced the fleshly state? Daisy was about to state a firm opinion on the matter (firm opinions were the only kind she had) when she was interrupted by Cassandra's sudden yelp.

Yes, *yelp*.

This was not the sort of petite feminine squeak that might result from m'lady's sitting on a pointy thumbtack, or (with thighs bare) on a metal lawn chair that was uncomfortably hot. Certainly not. But neither was it that spine-riveting sort of screech that causes a long-comatose patient to sit up in bed and inquire, "What was that noise, nurse?" followed by, "Is Mr. Reagan still in the White House?"

No. None of the above.

It was more like that delighted shriek a four-year-old makes when she opens a gaily wrapped Christmas box, finds a fuzzy little puppy inside, and gets licked on the nose.

Daisy Perika's response fell somewhat short of delight (storytellers *detest* interruptions). But, audience-wise, Cassie's yelp did the trick.

Tens of thousands of television-land devotees who had been hanging on Daisy's every word were solidly jarred by Cassandra's unexpected exclamation. The psychic's head was half bowed, both hands clasping the teacup. "Oh—oh—one of the spirits is attempting to contact me!"

• • •

Far over the mountains and through the woods and down the east slope—in the city of Denver—the *Cassandra Sees* senior director muttered a colorful if sophomoric curse, grumbled, "Bet it'll be another warehouse fire." What he was hoping for was another cold-blooded murder. But not with some dope-pushing truck driver for a victim. *Maybe she'll see somebody take a pot shot at a blind nun who spends all her waking hours working with crippled children.* If there had been a local chapter of the Grumpy Old Men's Club, the TV executive would have been elected president by unanimous acclamation. But the old sourpuss was always pleased with the psychic's impromptu performances, even when a mere arson was the subject of her visions.

Away to the west, across the lofty snow-capped peaks, another old sourpuss was not the least bit pleased.

• • •

Back in Cassandra Spencer's Granite Creek home, within the dimly illuminated parlor that provided ample ambience for the spooky television broadcast, Daisy Perika observed her flighty host with a glare that could have curdled milk. Dairy-fresh, ice-cold, pasteurized, grade-A milk. What brought this on? Just this: When the tribal elder was retelling her favorite Uncle Blue Hummingbird ghost story for about the thousandth time—and to her largest audience ever—she did not appreciate a yelping female stepping on her lines. Daisy was way on the far side of irked. She was, to put it bluntly, chagrined. But sad to say, no one was particularly concerned about her feelings. Worse still, the Ute woman was no longer the center of attention; her flash-in-the-pan performance had been eclipsed by the star. A pathetic has-been, that's what Daisy was.

Camera one had zoomed in on Cassandra's face, which—if a viewer with modern high-resolution digital television had had the neurotic inclination—she (or he) could have counted every hair in the psychic's neatly plucked eyebrows. Not to mention no small number of— No. In the interests of good taste, we shall not dwell upon *that*. If one views the subject under sufficient magnification, there is no such thing as a physically attractive human being.

A boom microphone had been lowered, the better to pick up Cassandra's barely audible mumblings. Aware of this, she repeated what she had said, and louder: "At this very moment, someone is about to die. Someone who is very close to me." *I wonder who it could be?*

The only other person in the parlor did not wonder. *Uh-oh—my time has come!* Practically knee-to-knee with the visionary, Daisy withdrew, pressing her bent spine against the padded chair. Odd, what occurs to the doomed as they approach that final heartbeat. It dawned on the tribal elder that she was not prepared for her funeral. She had not purchased the new underwear and white cotton stockings. Or the pretty red shoes.

In the psychic's dwelling, yea, in homes across the state and well beyond Colorado's rectangular border, every viewer's voice was hushed, every gaze locked upon the dark-haired visionary.

Cassandra appeared to be staring at the teacup in her

trembling hands, but her devoted followers knew that she was looking into some unseen space *beyond* that mundane object. And they were quite right. "This is an extraordinarily talented, highly respected person—who is admired by everyone."

Daisy's face felt the heat of her self-conscious blush, which she countered with a humble thought: *Well, not everybody. There are maybe two or three mean people I can think of who won't miss me when I'm gone. For instance, there's—*

"Oooohhh!" Cassandra fleshed out this exclamation: "It is about to happen—Death has come to snatch the person's life away!"

The tribal elder's heart fluttered. She closed her eyes, tried to think of an appropriate prayer. *Dear God—please let me stay here just a little while longer.* This sounded selfish. *So I can help Charlie find himself a good wife.* Nice touch, but not enough. *And teach Sarah how to cure the sick.*

The psychic stared without blinking. "It is about to happen." Dramatic pause. "Within a few seconds—no more than that—this person is destined to die by terrible violence. I see pools of blood—flesh ripped to shreds—fractured bones!" Cassandra cringed. *How terribly icky.*

Daisy clenched her remaining teeth, steeled herself for the swift swing of the scythe. *Get ready, all you saints—here I come!*

"Oh . . . it has happened—the soul has been released!" That, she thought, was a nice expression. *I must remember to congratulate White Raven.* (The visionary refers to her favorite and most reliable informant.)

Just to make certain it was not her soul that had been released, Daisy pressed a finger to her neck, felt a steady pulse, expressed her relief with a sigh. *All this time, that silly white woman was jabbering about somebody else. I wonder who it was.*

The psychic responded to the unspoken question: "The identity of the recently deceased is coming to me . . . it is a man. This individual was very attractive, extremely intelligent and—" Cassandra's pale brow furrowed into a puzzled frown, "very dear to me and my sister Bea." *Who on earth could that be?* Cassie had always been a bit slow. "Wait . . . I'm receiving additional information. This man frequently has breakfast with my sister." That narrowed it down some. But more was coming to her. "And he sleeps . . . in Bea's *bed*?" *This is beginning to sound absolutely scandalous.* Determined to get to the bottom of the conundrum, the mystic-logician applied the process of elimination: The only person who had breakfast with Bea and slept in her bed was Andrew. And though Andrew Turner was quite attractive and fairly bright, he was not what one would consider *extremely* intelligent, and he certainly wasn't dead. . . .

When the truth hit her, it was not like being slapped with a slice of white bread. No. This was Mr. John Henry Truth, slamming a nine-pound sledge against her head.

Cassandra Spencer stared past camera one. Quite oblivious to her unseen audience, she said, "It must be Andrew . . . Andrew is dead!" She felt a sudden pain behind her eyes; in front of them danced a spray of multicolored dots. These fireworks were familiar, and frightening. She murmured, "Oh—something is wrong." *I must get control of myself.* The afflicted woman shut her eyes, lowered her head. *There, that's better.* She opened them, found herself looking at the small monitor under the coffee table, where her face was framed on the screen. From time to time, complex electronic circuitry fails. This was the wrong time. Inside the plastic box, the vertical oscillator lost synchronization with the demodulated video signal. As it did, Cassandra's image began to flip over, approximately four times each second. From time to time, in the presence of certain external stimuli, complex brain circuitry fails. Back came the field of multicolored dots—with a vengeance. The visual display was accompanied by the taste of garlic, an overpowering scent of ammonia, the familiar muscle cramp in her left leg. Cassandra turned her face toward the dining room, her enormous eyes stared *through* the wall, into the imagined space, where her mind painted a picture of her sister. "Bea." The teacup slipped from her numb hands. "Bea, please help me."

But unbeknownst to Cassie, the fair-haired sister was no longer among those present. Beatrice was already out of town, headed for the family estate on Spencer Mountain where, just possibly, a husband-in-distress required her immediate attention.

IN CASSANDRA'S DINING ROOM

Assistant Director Gerald Sax had cut the live audio/video feed immediately after Cassandra's "Something is wrong." He signaled Denver to run a string of commercials.

Without knowing what he might be called upon to do, Charlie Moon was on his feet, muscles tensed for action.

Standing by his side, Sarah Frank looked up at this man who, she believed, knew the answer to every question. "Charlie, what's happening?"

"I don't know." The tribal investigator frowned at the bank of video monitors. *But wherever she goes, trouble seems to follow Aunt Daisy.*

CRISIS IN THE PARLOR

Her brief moment in the limelight so rudely terminated, Daisy Perika seemed to have withdrawn inside herself. An onlooker might have concluded that she was sulking. Not so. The tribal elder had witnessed the unfolding of this drama with intense interest. She was watching the psychic, who was staring dumbly at what the Ute woman could not see—the silent shampoo commercial on the under-the-coffee-table monitor. Daisy was surprised to notice that Cassandra's lips were moving. *That white woman is talking to herself. And her eyes look funny. I think she's gonna pass out.*

Dr. Daisy's diagnosis was right on the mark.

Cassandra Spencer's vision suddenly shifted from sharply focused to fuzzy. She could no longer see the television monitor. Or the coffee table. Or her Native American guest. Or anything else in this physical world. Now, her visual experience consisted entirely of a bluish white pinwheel of twirling lights. Round and round the galaxy went. Faster. Faster. Her last conscious thought was: *Oh, no . . . it's happening!*

And so it was.

• • •

TWENTY-FIVE
HOW A STAR COLLAPSES INTO A BLACK HOLE

As Cassandra Spencer pitched forward, Daisy Perika reached out to catch her. If she had not, the lady's pretty face would have smashed onto the coffee table.

The assistant director came through the parlor door, clipboard in hand, stopped in midstride. "What happened?"

"She's passed out cold as ice." *And this little pipsqueak don't look strong enough to pick up a dime off the sidewalk.* "Tell my nephew to come in here."

Before all the words were out of her mouth, Charlie Moon appeared. Sarah Frank trailed after him.

Daisy addressed her favorite relative: "Charlie, take this woman to her bedroom." Her next order was directed to Mr. Sax: "Tell him where her bedroom is."

"Uh—two doors down the hallway on the right." Sax waved the clipboard. "What'll I tell my supervisor in Denver?"

Daisy shot him her barbed-arrow look. "Tell your boss she's had a seizure."

The frantic man was tapping his wristwatch. "But we've still got almost twenty minutes of air time left, and this is a live broadcast so we've got to do something—"

"Not with her, you won't."

The lanky Ute was gathering the limp form into his arms when Sax muttered, "What should I do?"

"Call 911," Moon said. "Tell 'em to send an ambulance."

"Uh—right."

Daisy issued further orders to her nephew: "When you find the lady's bed, lay her on her side—not on her back." To Sarah, she said, "I'll be there in a minute. Make sure she keeps breathing okay."

Gerald Sax watched the tall man and the girl disappear down the dark hallway, slipped back into the dining room, closed the door. Nibbling thoughtfully on a plastic ballpoint pen, he summed up the situation: *Star conks out during a live performance. This could kill the show. Which could lose me my job.* Deep breath. *Unless I can keep a lid on it. Which won't be possible if the EMTs show up and find Cassie unconscious.* Exhale. *I'll have to do the right thing.* Which was a matter of one's definition. *I'll wait a few minutes, see if she's all right.* Inhale. *If she's not better in a half hour or so, I'll check out the Yellow Pages. See if I can find a specialist.* His game plan made, Gerald Sax switched his headset to Denver. "Paul, Cassandra's . . . uh . . . feeling a little woozy. Run me a few more commercials."

The senior director's voice barked in his ear: "You got it, Jerry. How long d'you think it'll take to get her back up to speed?"

"Uh—problematic. Let me get back to you on that."

"Roger-dodger. Take a whole minute."

The assistant director switched his headset to Broadcast Audio, counted down to zero, crossed his fingers as the toothpaste commercial ended, breathed a huge sigh of relief when a Honda ad began.

HOW A STAR IS BORN

Glancing at an off-air monitor, the assistant director noticed that Daisy was hobbling in the direction of the hallway and Cassandra's bedroom. *She's leaving the set!* Sax opened the door, called out, "Mrs. Perika, I wonder if you would do something for me."

She turned to glare at the little man.

"It's nothing much." He made a delicate gesture, touching fingertip to thumb. "Just an itsy-bitsy, teensy-weensy little favor." The fellow had a moderate tendency toward extravagant and wordy understatement.

By contrast, the Ute elder was economical with her syllables. "What?"

"Oh, nothing all that difficult." He clasped his hands, and the little-boy face presented a wide-eyed innocent expression. "Just continue with your story about Green Jailbird."

"Blue *Humming*bird," Daisy snapped.

"Oh—right." His mouth cracked an apologetic grin. "When the commercial's over, I'll point at you." He demonstrated with his trusty pointing finger. "You tell us about Uncle Blue . . . uh . . ." *Mockingbird?*

She scowled at the assistant director. "I forget where I was in my story."

Salty beads of sweat were popping out all over the white man's forehead. "Look—you help me on this, the rest of this evening's show is yours." The agnostic prayed: *If there is a God, and I suppose there very well might be—I'd appreciate some help with this old crank.* He thought it prudent to offer something in return: *Do that for me and I'll see you in church tomorrow.* Having offered what he considered a reasonable deal to the Almighty, Sax directed his next remarks to the troublesome mortal: "Daisy, if you don't want to tell us any more about Cousin Blackbird, you can talk about some other stuff. Ghosts. Goblins. Big hairy monsters that bite the heads off innocent little children." Realizing that he was getting nowhere fast, the AD pleaded in an increasingly shrill tone, "Just do something spooky. Generate a hideous blob of ectoplasm—levitate the damn coffee table!" The obstinate old lady was not going for it. The Honda commercial in his headset faded, was replaced by another for Yamaha pianos, marked down 10 percent. One last, desperate attempt at enticement: "You'll get to sit in the star's chair." *That does it. I've shot my wad.*

His final round had hit the mark. Daisy's eyes goggled at the fancy chair. "I can?"

"Sure you can." He puffed up his chest. "I'm in charge here—whatever I say, goes!"

She shrugged. "Okay. I'll do it."

"Way to go!" The semiconvert closed his eyes. *Thank you, God. You'll see me in church on Sunday.* Which brought a conflict to mind: *But not tomorrow. I've got a golf date I can't break. But next Sunday, old Gerald will be right there in the front pew.* But wait a minute. Next Sunday was the big game. *Let's say Sunday after next. . . .*

Daisy Perika was ready to go *right now,* and did. For sixteen nail-biting minutes, *Cassandra Sees* would continue without Cassandra on the set.

Not that things didn't get off to a somewhat rocky start.

As Daisy Perika was settling herself into Queen Cassandra's throne, and the assistant director turned to check a camera mount, the stand-in was distracted by something annoying under the coffee table—a flashing light. The guilty party was the small television set that served as the psychic's on-the-air monitor. The picture was rolling over and over. Daisy made an expert diagnosis: *The stupid thing is out of whack.* And drew a sensible conclusion: *That flickering is most likely what started off her epileptic attack.* A personal observation: *And if it don't stop it'll give me a fit.* A genuine TV star would have called for someone to come adjust the annoying thing. Daisy, who had spent most of the past forty years alone, was accustomed to dealing with problems on her own. Without the slightest hesitation, she was out of the chair, on her knees, head and shoulders under the small table, arm reaching for the controls. She turned the sound up and down. *The flippity-flop button must be in the back.* She reached around the electronic appliance, found the controls, adjusted the brightness, the contrast, then—stopped the picture cold! This was a quite gratifying outcome. And there was more to come. In the steady light of the TV screen, Daisy noticed something on the carpet. The object was round and shiny, which suggested "coin" to the avaricial lobe of her brain, which sent an urgent command to her right hand: *That is cash money—pick it up and put it in your pocket!* Said hand received the message, acted reflexively, reached for the prize. It was not a coin.

The thinking portion of her brain kicked in: *It's probably just a dumb old button that fell off the TV set.*

Wrong again.

But as she got the item in her hand, and her eyes did a quick scan, Daisy realized what it was. She had seen it before. This was something better than a shiny dime. Considerably better. But Daisy, who was hardly ever satisfied, shook her head at having only half a pair and sighed. *Why couldn't there have been two of them?* Suddenly distracted by a colorful field-of-wildflowers deodorant commercial on the TV monitor, she raised her head to get a better look, bumped it on the sturdy coffee table. *Ouch.* Like a bonked-out cartoon character, she saw stars. And planets and meteors and comets and fireworks and flags awaving and banners apassing—but there is no need to go on and on about a thing. You get the picture.

IN CASSANDRA'S BEDROOM

After Charlie Moon gently placed the unconscious woman on an immense, canopied four-poster (on her side), Sarah slipped a silk-encased pillow under Cassandra's head.

Moon and the girl stood silently, stared at the lady, who seemed to be sleeping. Her breathing was steady. They waited. For what?

For Daisy Perika, who had been distracted by the assistant director's tempting offer.

For emergency medical technicians, whom the AD had not summoned.

Moon murmured, "Wonder what caused her to pass out."

Sarah whispered a reminder: "Aunt Daisy said she had a seizure." Which reminded the girl of a relative in Tonapah Flats, Utah. "I bet she's an epileptic, like my cousin Marilee."

Moon frowned at the prone figure. "That could be a serious problem for someone who does TV shows."

The girl nodded. "That's why we've got to keep it a secret."

The tribal investigator, who believed that an ambulance and EMTs were on the way, figured this business wouldn't be a secret for very long.

IN THE PARLOR WITH A HOSTILE INDIAN

After another conversation with Denver, a promise of more commercials, Assistant Director Gerald Sax turned to check on the Native American woman. His heart almost stopped. *Dammit, she slipped away when I wasn't looking!* But then he spotted the bottom half of her. The upper portion was under the coffee table. He slapped his forehead. *Great, now we'll start off with a shot of the old woman's butt in the air! What'll Denver say to that?* A worrisome question occurred to him: *What in hell is she doing on the floor?* And another: *Why isn't she moving?* Frozen by a nameless dread, the assistant director was not moving either.

But forget about G. Sax's immobility, which is of little importance.

Back to the tribal elder, and the AD's final question.

Daisy was not moving for this reason: She was experiencing an epiphany. Now there are all sorts of epiphanies. When it comes to these mind-expanding whatchamacallits, there are minor ones, a middle-size species, and a *very* rare few that deserve to begin with a capital *E,* but even the least of them have a way of commanding all of one's attention—focusing the entire faculties, as it were. And it were.

Having posed the questions about why the aged person was on the floor, on all fours, and not moving, Gerald Sax felt obliged to provide himself with something resembling a plausible answer. *She's probably had a heart attack or a stroke and fallen out of the chair.* The negative thinker felt a dull chill ripple up his spine, then down again. *Well, that's the icing on the cake. First the star of the show passes out, now our feeble old guest drops dead on the floor. What next?* He knew what next. Grim headlines on the front pages of the *Denver Post* and *Rocky Mountain News*:

AGED INDIAN WOMAN DROPS DEAD ON LIVE TV
YOOT TRIBE SUES NETWORK FOR TEN BILLION DOLLARS

Mr. Sax, who had never won a spelling bee, had no doubt that there would also be highly critical essays in the entertainment sections of these newspapers. And don't forget the tasteless jokes on late-night comedy shows. Plus demands for an immediate FCC investigation, and so on and et cetera. Not to mention humiliation and unemployment. He saw additional headlines:

ASSISTANT DIRECTOR HELD RESPONSIBLE
FOR TV GUEST'S DEATH
GERALD SAX GETS THE AX

And the abbreviated version:

SAX AXED

Assistant Director Gerald Sax might well suffer from overactive imagination, but he can be forgiven for not deducing that Daisy had discovered something important under the table, and how that discovery had led to her sudden enlightenment, which had yielded an instant solution to a significant mystery—after all, who among us could have done better than he?

But wait—now the presumed corpse was *moving*.

Almost sick with relief, the agnostic offered up a genuine prayer of thanks, promised again to attend some sort of religious service next month. Or perhaps the month after. If his busy scheduled allowed. Moreover, his joints suddenly unlocked, which enabled him to trot over to the star's chair and address the woman's posterior, which was practically all he could see of her. "Mrs. Perika—are you okay?"

Startled from her happy trance, she bumped her head on the coffee table again. *Ouch.* "I'm fine." And she was. Fine and dandy.

This isn't so serious after all. Maybe she dropped a contact lens. "Uh—what are you doing?"

"Watching TV."

She has got to be kidding. "You have got to be kidding." Mr. Sax tended to repeat himself. Especially when he was in a state of high agitation.

Mildly embarrassed at the position she found herself in, Daisy cackled a crackly "heh-heh."

The old woman is stark-raving bonkers insane!

But Daisy's explanation for her behavior was more mundane: "I'm trying to figure out how to turn off this little TV set." There was a quite audible *click.* "There—that did it." She began backing out rump-first, and as she made a groaning effort to get to her feet, she gladly accepted the assistant director's assistance, and provided an explanation for her behavior. "I was worried that if I saw myself looking back at me from that screen—" the elderly woman paused to catch her breath, "that I might get all fiddle-faddled."

"Well, we certainly wouldn't want *that* to happen." He liked to roll his eyes, and did so. Probably because he was rolling his eyes, possibly because he was assisting the geriatric guest by her left arm, Assistant Director Sax did not notice that Daisy's right hand was tightly clenched in a fist. Or that once she was comfortably deposited in Cassandra's chair, the sly old woman slipped something into her pocket. He restrained himself from shaking a finger in her face, but did assume an appropriately stern tone: "Mrs. Perika— please don't do anything like that again."

She smiled up at the nice young man. "Okay."

Startled by this mellow response, he blinked. "If you need something done, just ask me. That's what I'm here for."

"I'll try to remember that." Daisy, who was in a *very* good mood, reached out to pat his arm.

From the evidence in his headset, the final commercial was ending. The *Cassandra Sees* logo would hit the screen within a few palpitations of his racing heart. Sax spoke softly to the elderly lady: "Now keep your eye on camera one. When you're about to go on the air, I'll point at you."

Daisy nodded, waited. This was more fun than stepping on a cat's tail.

Sax counted down. Three. Two. One. He aimed his official assistant director's finger at the stand-in's forehead.

Daisy Perika looked directly into the camera displaying the tiny red light, smiled sweetly. "Well, we're back. At least I'm back—that white woman who runs things here has left for a while—I think she's upset because she thinks somebody she knows has died. I'm supposed to pick up with what I was saying before, but I can't remember exactly where I was in my story when I got interrupted. So I'll just start back at the beginning." She took a deep breath. "Blue Hummingbird was my favorite uncle. . . ."

• • •

Gerald Sax returned to the dining room, took his seat at the control console, checked monitor one, glanced at the meter on the audio panel. *I'm not picking her up clearly. Old lady's about two heads shorter than Cassandra. I'll get the mike a little closer.*

• • •

During the next commercial break, while Mr. Sax was busy with whatever tasks occupy the time of assistant directors, Daisy Perika noticed an old-fashioned telephone on a lamp stand. The instrument was near her elbow, and Cassandra Spencer's unlisted number was printed on the center of the circular dial. Mumbling them over and over and over, Daisy imprinted the seven digits in her memory. At the end of the broadcast, she would scribble the confidential number on a scrap of paper. One never knows when such information will prove useful. But Daisy did.

• • •

At precisely one minute before the end of the television broadcast, Cassandra Spencer opened her eyes. *Oh, I have such a stinking headache!* She rolled onto her back, looked up at Charlie Moon and Sarah Frank. *What are they doing here in my bedroom—gawking at me?* More to the point: *What am I doing here?* She blinked twice, said, "What happened?" The Ute, who was in one of his taciturn moods, let Sarah do the explaining.

• • •

When the eventful hour (which had seemed like a week to Gerald Sax) had ticktocked away its full allotment of thirty-six hundred seconds, the assistant director felt much like that proverbial drowning man who has gone down for the third and final time, only to be plucked from the raging waters by an unseen hand. He was, in his peculiar way, grateful to God. The AD was also much-obliged to the ancient Indian woman who had saved the show; he was ready to offer her several pints of his blood, the title to his brand-new Lexus RX 400h, and to name his first girl-child Daisy. As it happened, Daisy Perika was not in need of blood, and both the Lexus and the daughter were but fanciful gleams in Mr. Sax's eye. But what he did have for tonight's guest was the standard "special gift package"—a box of one dozen hand-made Cocotal Chocolates (which Daisy accepted with pleasure), and an up-to-date packet of *Cassandra Sees* DVDs which included off-air segments, which Sarah greatly lusted after (as a skilled and sensitive observer of teenage behavior might have deduced from subtle physiological indicators, such as the girl's clenched fists, hyperventilation, dilated pupils, and whispered, "Yes yes yes!"). Sadly, there was no such observer present. The Ute elder, who did not realize that a recording of *tonight's* show was included, idly passed the digitized disks to Charlie Moon, who dropped the parcel into his jacket pocket.

The girl was eyeing that pocket, framing the hint that she would drop to let Daisy know that these DVDs would be *such* a cool addition to her collection of *C Sees* videos, which were limited to what could be recorded from on-the-air broadcasts—when the assistant director presented Sarah Frank with a yard-long white paper cylinder, tied tightly in a red ribbon. Mr. Sax informed her that the mystery gift was ". . . a high-resolution full-color printout that I made *especially* for you." The subject: Cassandra's highly magnified eye! Well. She wanted to hug the sweet little munchkin man but could not bring herself to do such a thing. Not with her future husband looking on.

COMMERCIAL TELEVISION

In Denver, the senior director of *Cassandra Sees* was communicating with Assistant Director Gerald Sax, and shaking his head at revelations from his underling in Granite Creek. "I don't know how this'll fall out, Jerry—that was some pretty oddball stuff."

Consider the "stuff":

The quirky star of *Cassandra Sees* has a vision of her brother-in-law's death, then has to be carried off the set.

Cassandra's place in the sun is taken by an old Indian woman. This pinch-hitter, who allegedly communicates with dead people, retells a homespun yarn about (the senior director was not paying close attention) Uncle Redwing Blackbird. Well, what's in a name.

What matters in TV land are ratings.

As excited viewers had called family and friends to tune in, the surge in the *Cassandra Sees* audience broke records. The old Indian woman was a hoot!

For those who care about such matters, consider this statistic: It did not occur to 97.1 percent of the viewers that the psychic's clairvoyant powers had not yet been validated by an official police report of an actual death. Such was their faith in the up-and-coming celebrity. Cassandra was never wrong.

• • •

TWENTY-SIX
UP THE SLIPPERY SLOPE

As Beatrice Spencer approached the entrance to the long, winding driveway, she pressed the button on the remote-control unit. By the time she turned the Mercedes off the paved highway, the heavy gate was creaking open, pushing an arc through the wet snow. She braked to a crawl, pounded her fist on the steering wheel. "Hurry. Hurry!"

It would not hurry.

Moreover, the more she issued her urgent commands, the more slowly the massive thing moved. Barely half open, the wrought-iron structure ground to a halt in a pile of snow it was pushing. Bea eased the big automobile through the narrow opening, pressed the Close button on the remote control. No response from the stalled gate.

Never mind.

Lickety-splitting up the hill she went, kicking up a spray of snow.

• • •

Scott Parris's black-and-white slipped along the northbound highway though a frivolous, frolicsome could-not-make-its-mind-up snow or rain that would fade into the dark stillness, only to return again with a puff of wind. At mile marker 10, he switched the headlights to low beam, watched for a driveway unmarked by mailbox or sign. Going back a hundred years the Spencers had valued their privacy, and Beatrice carried on the family tradition. *Please, God—let the gate be open.* No. Withdraw that sissy prayer.

The hairy-chested fellow amended his petition, resubmitted: *MAKE it be open.*

And so it was. Well, half open. Even so . . . *Thank, you, Sir—and amen!*

As the chief of police passed through the constricted portal into the Spencer domain, he caught a glimpse of taillights. Parris switched on his emergency lights, flicked the siren switch on for a couple of heartbeats.

• • •

The siren's momentary howl, the sudden sight of red-and-blue lights flashing in the rearview mirror—these electrifying stimuli tend to engender strong emotions within the breast of the startled motorist, and surprising responses. Which can lead to unexpected consequences.

Beatrice Spencer had grown up in mountain country, where one either learned to drive on slippery roads or ended up as one of those sad statistics whose genes are removed from the motor pool. Precisely *why* the lady did what she did is, at the moment, unclear. Nerves, perhaps. Or perhaps . . . nerve.

Whatever the reason, she jammed the brakes like some forever-summer lass who had just passed her driver's test in Key West. But for superb German engineering, the vehicle would have probably skidded off the lane, stopping only to say howdy to a sturdy pine or surly boulder. As it happened, the Mercedes ended up broadside on the driveway, leaving about enough room for a Harley-Davidson (minus sidecar) to pass.

• • •

Scott Parris had not arrived on a motorcycle. But he was moving right along, "carrying the mail," as the old timers say. When he rounded one of the dozen curves in the Spencer driveway, there it was, the big automobile—lights off!—blocking his way. Instinctively, he shifted down to low, barely tapped the brakes with his boot toe, watched the blockading automobile get bigger and bigger. . . . *Please, God—please don't let me hit it.* He eased to a stop within a yard of the expensive motor car.

Another prayer answered. For which he was immensely grateful.

Ramming the Mercedes at full speed might have ended all his worldly troubles. Even at reduced velocity, the crunching encounter would have added considerably to his woes. It is difficult for a red-faced chief of police to explain to the mayor and the county council how he happened to drive an almost-new, forty-five-thousand-dollar police unit into a stationary vehicle that was "parked" in a prominent citizen's private driveway, totaling both cars, maiming or killing said prominent citizen.

This particular Christian was having a good night. And, he imagined, using up his quota of positive responses for the next several months. One might have expected a soul so blessed to behave accordingly, which is to say with the grace and generosity befitting one who has recently been the beneficiary of multiple heavenly favors. One might. But if one did, one would be jumping the gun, and expecting too much of a man whose temper can best be described as mercurial.

The beefy chief of police jammed the venerable fedora down to his ears, got out, stomped to the Mercedes driver's door, shone the beam of a five-cell flashlight into the plush interior, and roared at the woman behind the wheel, "What the hell are you trying to do, Bea—get us both killed?"

There was no response. Which was no great mystery.

There was no driver.

Scott Parris was yelling at an empty automobile.

Feeling the warmth of a blush, he aimed the flashlight uphill, was barely able to see fresh tracks that were already filling with snow. *Bea must've skidded, then decided to walk home.* A sigh. *Well, at least I didn't bung up her fancy car.* Which, being the cultured man that he was, brought to mind something someone famous had said about "all that ends well" was something-or-other. *But this is a helluva note. How am I supposed to investigate a possible vehicle accident if I can't drive up the mountain?* When it came, the answer seemed so obvious: *I bet I can drive her car out of the way.* He slipped inside. Bea had not left the keys in the ignition.

No matter.

Maybe I can push it just far enough so I can get my unit past it.

Our hero got out, set his cleated boots in the snow, put his hefty shoulder against the heavy Mercedes. Grunted. "Unnngh!" Grunted harder. No dice. Not an inch.

Granite Creek's top cop was no defeatist. *I'll call dispatch, get Clara to send me some help.* Parris found his cell phone in his jacket pocket, pressed the button, eyeballed the readout: LOW BATTERY. *Damn!* He was running out of options. Time for some serious thinking. Parris cogitated. Ruminated. Considered and rejected several plans.

Case in point: *I could back my unit all the way down the mountain in a blinding snowstorm.* No. *Even an oyster has more brains than to try a thing like that.*

Another case in point: *I could walk down the mountain, maybe flag somebody down for a ride back to down.* But in this weather, motorists would be few and far between.

Which left him with one viable option.

I'll hoof it up to Bea's house through this blizzard, which shouldn't take too long. The wind began to blow sleet in his face. *Unless I freeze my feet off and have to walk on bloody stumps, and when I get there I'll find Bea and Andrew Turner sitting by the fire, swigging hot toddies.* He could picture the cozy little domestic scene. *He'll be telling his wife how he bumped his fancy sports car against a stump.*

Scott Parris buttoned his jacket collar up to his chin, pushed the wet, droopy-brimmed hat down another notch, set his jaw, and began trudging up the driveway. And thinking profound philosophical thoughts. *Why does wind always blow snow in a person's face—just this once, why can't the wind be at my back?* He figured it was probably for the same reason as when you were casting your bait from the bank of the lake, the breeze *always* blew the line back at you. It was nature's way of having some fun. But the situation was getting less funny by the minute. As he made his way uphill, the white flakes were larger, wetter, more numerous. The powerful beam from his big flashlight penetrated less and less into the wind-driven snow. All ten toes were numbingly cold. Ditto the ten fingers. The miserable hiker muttered the same one-syllable comment, over and over. It was hard to hear over the roar of the wind, but the expletive might have been *shoot.* Or perhaps not.

Quite unexpectedly, something happened that got his attention.

The lawman thought he saw something lope across the driveway in front of him. Something big and hairy and—

But no. *That must've been a hallucination.* He hoped so. *Maybe I'm going hypothermic, losing my marbles.* He hoped not.

And then, just to his right, he saw something that was definitely *not* a hallucination.

A gnarled, knotty piñon tree. One among thousands. What made this particular gnarled, knotty piñon tree remarkable was that it had about a yard of bark knocked off a gnarly limb, and a sizable chunk of woody flesh was missing from the trunk. He half stumbled off the driveway, swept the flashlight beam back and forth across what he computed as the probable path that Andrew Turner's Corvette had taken after it bounced off the tree. The snow had long since covered any tire tracks, but about twenty paces from the damaged piñon, near the base of a snow-capped basalt boulder, he spotted something shiny, picked it up. A chunk of headlight glass.

Bad news.

The policeman was standing right on the lip of the Devil's Mouth, where Andrew Turner's GM sports car had, he deduced, gone over and down. Way down.

All business now, and oblivious to the cold, Parris followed his faint tracks back to the driveway, set his face uphill. Job number one was to tell Bea that her husband's automobile had gone into a skid, bounced off a tree and a boulder, fallen into the Devil's Mouth.

• • •

When the chief of police banged his numb fist on the front door, Beatrice Spencer opened on the second knock, stared wide-eyed at the broad-shouldered snowman. "Scott—Andrew's not here. And his Corvette isn't in the garage." She was trembling. "I can't imagine where he is!"

He told her.

• • •

His big Expedition humming along like Uncle Blue Hummingbird's feathery namesake, Charlie Moon kept his focus on the snow-packed road that would take them home. He spoke to his aunt: "After all the excitement, things turned out pretty good. When we left Miss Spencer, she seemed to be feeling a lot better."

Daisy Perika clutched the little prize in her pocket. "She'll be fine after she gets a good night's sleep."

He reached over to pat his aged relative on the shoulder. "And on top of that, you saved the show."

Daisy Perika snorted at this high praise. Following a triumph, skillfully faked modesty really puts the icing on the cake.

"You sure did," Sarah Frank piped up from the backseat. "I wouldn't be surprised if they gave you your own TV show!"

Daisy returned a dismissive "hmmpf." But she was disappointed when Sarah changed the subject.

"While she was on TV, Cassandra said that somebody named Andrew was dead. I wonder if that might be what the telephone call was about—the one that got Cassandra's sister so upset she left in a big hurry." Sarah's quasi-question hung in the darkness.

After half a mile of slippery road had slipped under them, Moon said, "Beatrice Spencer's husband is Andrew Turner."

The girl's mouth made a silent little O. *Then he must be dead.* Statistically speaking, the teenager was among that

97.1 percent of Cassandra's viewers who never doubted the psychic's deathly declarations.

As the big automobile skimmed over a patch of black ice, the driver sensed just a hint of looseness in the steering. He slowed to thirty-five.

Daisy, who had not witnessed Bea's hasty departure from Cassie's dining room, had other issues on her mind. Such as if you crawl under somebody's coffee table, what kind of surprise you're liable to find. Squinting to see through the veil of falling snow, she frowned at the feathery curtain, mumbled just loud enough for Charlie to hear, "That Cassandra is a smart young woman. But not as smart as she thinks she is." Glowing greenly in the dashboard light, the tribal elder's face suggested that she *knew* something. And might be willing to share it with her nephew, the big-shot tribal investigator.

No response from the driver.

Daisy mumbled again, "Mark my words—there's some bad trouble coming."

Charlie Moon did not ask. Sleeping dogs and all that.

As the silence lingered, the old woman's face slowly turned to stone. *Well, I wouldn't tell you if you got down on your knees and begged me!* It occurred to Daisy Perika that a certain someone *would* be interested in what she had found out tonight. And if she played her cards just right, things might start going her way. She nodded at the glove compartment door. *It's just as well I didn't say a word to Charlie.* Mr. Do-Right would take a dim view of the devious scheme she was beginning to mull over.

• • •

Scott Parris used Beatrice Spencer's telephone to put an emergency call through to dispatch. There was only the slimmest of chances that Andrew Turner might have survived, but slim was better than none. The chief lawman was laying down the law: "I don't care where you've sent those on-duty units or who's beating who over the head with a frying pan—if you have to, get some people out of bed. Bottom line is I want two units with four uniforms, a tow truck, and an ambulance. And I want them on the spot in twenty minutes flat, you got that?"

The dispatcher got it.

All the while, Beatrice paced back and forth across the spacious parlor, shaking her head.

Count a thousand heartbeats.

Far off into the night, a faint wail of sirens.

Parris cocked his ear. "It's one of our units. And an ambulance."

She gave no sign of having heard a word he had said.

And why should she? They both knew Andrew was dead.

• • •

TWENTY-SEVEN
THE CALL

With Aunt Daisy and Sarah Frank snuggled warmly under the covers in their downstairs bedrooms, Charlie Moon switched off the parlor lights, paused for a moment to enjoy the sounds of the night. The snappity-crackle of a dying fire. A persistent pecking of sleet on windowpanes. Icy wind whining in the eaves. Thus fortified, he made his way up the stairs. This had been quite a day. But most of them were.

For the owner of the Columbine Ranch, one day was not much like another. On the contrary. Sundays, which Moon usually spent on the Southern Ute reservation with his aunt and the teenage Ute-Papago girl, were (aside from the tribal elder's verbal acid) generally quiet and placid. Mondays, when he was looking forward to the week ahead and making plans to improve the operation of his adjoining cattle ranches, were hopeful. Tuesdays were almost as good. By Wednesday, Foreman Pete Bushman would be at Moon's elbow with the usual list of complaints and grim premonitions of utter disaster, most of which the cheerful Ute would dismiss with smiles, jokes, and general good humor, which annoyed his scruffy-bearded foreman no end. By Thursday—No. Forget Thursday, which was generally gloomy. Ditto Friday, which was Thursday-squared. Jump right over to Saturday, which was when more than half the hired help would depart from the ranch in Columbine pickups and such personal vehicles as were semiroadworthy, to descend upon Granite Creek's seedy bars and smoky honky-tonks and get riproaring drunk. Almost every week, there would be knock-down-drag-out fights with employees from neighboring ranches, town toughs, and tattooed motorcyclists whose bulging biceps far outsized their brains. On the final evening of the week, it was not unusual for Mr. Moon to hear about a hung-over cowhand who was in jail, and (if the man was a good worker) go his bail. Less frequently, but all too often, he would visit a battered-up employee in the emergency room, and on three occasions during the past six years Moon had ID'd a cowboy's cold body on a slab.

This week had been one of the better ones. Not a single purebred Hereford had dropped dead from a mysterious ailment, all the horses were likewise healthy, and every single piece of equipment on the ranch was in tolerably good working order. On top of all this good fortune, on this Saturday evening, which Moon had spent escorting his aunt to Cassandra Spencer's home and TV studio, not a single employee had been arrested—all were safely back on the Columbine well before midnight. (When the last pickup rolled up to the main bunkhouse, Pete Bushman— whose persistent goal was to find a black cloud lurking inside any silver lining that happened along—grumbled that "Today's cowboys are gettin' soft as girls, Charlie. Why, in my day, any hand who came back from town on Satiddy night still half sober and without his knuckles bloodied up was a A-number-one brass-plated sissy!" The pronouncement was punctuated with a spit of Red Man tobacco juice, which barely missed the polished toe of the Ute's brand-new Tony Lama boot.)

Charlie Moon knelt in his upstairs bedroom, offered up a grateful prayer of thanks. The Catholic finished with an Our Father. Including the hard part: *Thy will be done . . .*

It would be.

As the Seth Thomas clock in his upstairs office began to mark the midnight hour, he pulled a hand-stitched quilt up to his chin, exhaled a satisfied sigh. On the sixth gong, he yawned. On the ninth, he whispered, "Thank you, God." On the twelfth, the consciousness of day was mercifully slipping away. . . .

The telephone rang.

Moon did not open his eyes. *Maybe it was just my imagination. Sometimes, just as I'm going off to sleep, I hear sounds that aren't really there.*

The annoying sound that was not really there made itself heard again.

The sleepy man entertained another hope: *Maybe they'll hang up.*

No such luck. Third ring.

Maybe it's a wrong number.

Maybe twenty-dollar bills will grow on prickly pears. *Brrriiinnng!*

He fumbled around in the dark, found the instrument. "Columbine Ranch."

"Charlie—that you?"

He recognized his best friend's voice. "Nope. This is a recording. When you hear the beep—"

"Don't mess with me, Charlie."

"—You can leave a brief message, one word or less."

"Charlie—"

"If and when I'm of a mind to, I may get back to you. Beep!"

"I ain't got no time to fool around, so quit—"

"Beep."

"What'd you say?"

"Beep-beep."

Parris chuckled. "That reminds me of a cartoon character. That Mexican mouse with the big sombrero—you know the one."

"No I don't. The south-of-the-border rodent, he say *Arriba-Arriba!*"

"You sure about that?"

"Us computerized answering machines never make mistakes."

"Then who was it that said 'beep-beep'?"

"Señor Road Runner."

"That's right. Beep-beep." Parris appended a "Heh-heh."

"Pardner, I know it ain't exactly none of my business, and I'm not one to pry—but during the past hour or two, have you been chugging down alcoholic beverages in sizable quantities?"

"What do you mean by that?"

"Oh, say a fifth or a quart—whichever's more."

"Well, a quart—"

"That's way too much for a man with an ulcer."

"—is more than a than a fifth. Everybody knows that. And who says I got an ulcer?"

"Practically everybody. All over town, it's a subject of conversation and speculation."

"Now listen here—"

"And now you're getting testy—a sure sign of a man who can't hold his liquor."

"Charlie, I'd appreciate it if you'd be quiet for about three seconds so I can tell you what I've got to say."

"Okay, pard. I'll give it my best shot."

"Thank you. The reason I called was to tell you—"

"Andrew Turner's dead in a car wreck."

"How d'you know that?"

"I don't know it for a fact, but I was at his sister-in-law's house, watching her on TV, when she told half the state of Colorado that Andrew Turner was dead. If I recollect correctly, the word *violence* was mentioned. See, I'd gone to Miss Spencer's house to take Aunt Daisy because she was invited to be on the TV program—"

"I saw Daisy on TV. I didn't see the part where Cassie said Andrew Turner was dead—but from what I'm told, she didn't say a word about him wrecking his car—so how'd you know about that?"

"When Mr. Turner's wife got the call from GCPD about a Wye-Star alert, I was sittin' right next to her—close enough to hear every word she said. And most of what Clara Tavishuts was saying on the other end."

"Oh." Parris listened to the slight buzz on the telephone

line. Felt his heart thumping. Wondered when it would stop. Figured the day was not all that far away.

Moon listened to the wind whip a cottonwood limb against the steel roof.

Unable to bear the silence, the white midwesterner cleared his throat.

Taking the hint, Moon restarted the conversation: "So is Mr. Turner dead in a car wreck?"

"That's the way it looks. About halfway down the mountain, there's evidence that a vehicle went off the driveway, hit a tree, bounced off a boulder and into the Devil's Mouth. Which is where I am now, with some other cops, an ambulance, and a tow truck."

"Have you recovered his car?"

"Huh-uh." A cough. "Haven't even spotted it. Snow's still comin' down by the truckload."

"Then you don't know for sure it was Turner's car that—"

"Charlie, please don't make my life more complicated than it already is. If you want to get technical about it, I don't even know for sure there *was* an accident. But the most likely thing is that Andrew Turner's frozen corpse is strapped inside his fine General Motors machine, which is somewhere down there in the Devil's Mouth." *And buried so far under the snow that we'll be lucky if we ever find it.* Parris recalled a Texas citizen who, in accordance with instructions in his will, was interred in his favorite Cadillac.

"How's Turner's wife taking it?"

"Bea's pretty shaken up. But she'll be all right—those Spencer sisters are tough as two-dollar steaks. And speaking of sisters, the one she's got left is here with her now. Cassie drove by in her Caddy just a few minutes ago." He wondered what Charlie would say about that.

"She did, did she?" *Sound's like the lady recovered pretty quick.*

Subtlety having failed, Parris went for the hint. "It was pretty queer, the way Cassie seemed to know about her brother-in-law's death—and within a few minutes of when it happened."

"Mmm-hmm."

The chief of police tried the direct approach: "What do you think about that spooky lady—how does she do it?"

"Pardner, if you want to ask me about something I know a little about, like shoeing a skittish quarter horse or tuning up a pickup truck that's old enough to have points and a carburetor, I'll talk both your ears off. But when it comes to ladies on TV having visions about brothers-in-law kicking buckets, that's not exactly in my line."

"Maybe not, but you've got a close relative who works pretty much the same side of the street Cassie does."

"You want to ask Aunt Daisy what she thinks, be my guest."

"I'll consider that a bona fide invitation to drop by and chat with the elderly lady."

"I'll look forward to your visit. Come for breakfast and stay for supper." Moon wondered why this midnight call could not have waited until the sun rose over the Buckhorns. *I'll bet there's another thing coming.* He waited for it.

"Uh, Charlie—there's another thing."

Moon's smile flashed in the darkness. "What's that, pardner?"

"Right after I got here—close to where Turner's car went over the cliff—I thought I saw something."

"*Something* covers a lot of ground."

"Well, it was hard to see through the snow, which was coming down about an inch a minute, but it looked to me like a *two-legged* something."

"That narrows it down some."

"Well, I can't narrow it much more."

"Any chance it could've been Turner?"

Parris had not considered this possibility. "Uh—no. I don't think so." *Not unless my vision's going bad.* The middle-aged man blinked, rubbed his tired eyes. *Next thing you know, I'll be wearing bifocals. Year after that, trifocals. By the time I'm drawing Social Security, I'll be tapping my way around town with a white cane.*

"Maybe whatever you saw had something to do with Turner running off the road."

"That possibility had crossed my mind." Parris took a moment to scratch at bristly stubble on his chin. "Charlie, don't ask me why, but I got a funny feeling that something awfully peculiar is going on up here—"

Charlie Moon knew what was coming.

"—And I'd like to talk to you about it. I'd sure appreciate it if you'd drop by when you get a chance."

The Ute rolled out of bed, put his feet on the floor. "I'm practically on my way."

"You're a true-blue friend, Charlie."

"And don't you forget it."

• • •

TWENTY-EIGHT
WHERE DID IT GO

Andrew Turner's Corvette? Most likely, under the fluffy white stuff. Most likely.

But there is no doubt about where last night's late-spring storm has gone. After creating havoc on Spencer Mountain, the rip-roaring, sleet-spitting, hell-bent horde of rowdy night riders thundered away to plague tough-as-boot-leather Kansas wheat farmers and hard-eyed we-can-take-your-best-shot Panhandle cattle ranchers. The skirmish isn't quite over, but the outcome is not in doubt. The violent storm will die on the prairie with gasps and whispers and sighs. The plainsmen and their sturdy families will survive. And endure. And thrive.

The Colorado sky that had melted in the rosy glow of sunrise was now frozen anew, annealed into that pale hue of cobalt blue that tints the lips of new corpses. A frolic-some wind rolling down Spencer Mountain had heaped up knee-deep drifts along the long, winding driveway, briskly swept it clean in favored spots in between.

At the tightest curve in the graveled road, a huge, red Ortega's AAA tow truck was backed up to the edge of the Devil's Mouth. This behemoth vehicle was flanked by a boxy white ambulance, the Granite Creek Mountaineers' black Dodge van, Charlie Moon's Columbine Expedition, and three low-slung black-and-white Chevrolets representing the Granite Creek Police Department. In a madcap orchestration of colored lights that produced a mildly hypnotic if not a pretty sight, the Mac wrecker blinked a mellow yellow rotation, the police vehicles accompanied with asynchronous blue-and-red pulsations.

Mr. Ortega, a bewhiskered, fire-breathing enthusiast who could not abide being idle, waved his arms in general exasperation, barked orders at his wooden-faced brother-in-law assistant, paused every few breaths to shout helpful advice down to those half-dozen climbers who had rappelled into the Devil's Mouth. The indolent brother-in-law proved impervious to the assault, and the tow-truck owner's exhortations were ignored by those stalwart volunteers who were risking their lives in an attempt to locate a missing Corvette, which, since it was not on the rocky slope, must be concealed beneath the snow.

A cluster of uniformed GCPD officers and EMTs watched the jolly entertainment and waited.

Standing apart from the gathering, in the downwind shadow of a ninety-nine-year-old gnarly-barked juniper, were two men who happened to be the best of friends. The venerable tree provided scant protection from the wind. The tall, slender fellow and his broad-shouldered, barrel-chested buddy clutched at their hats.

The chief of police said, "I must be stupid." When his Indian comrade did not protest this brutal self-assessment, Scott Parris enlarged on the assertion: "Way I see it, we're *both* stupid."

"Leave me out of it." Charlie Moon grinned into the wind. "My IQ is high enough this morning to suit me." *About the same as the temperature.*

Parris used the hand that was not holding on to his hat to point at Mr. Ortega and his stoic in-law. "If we wasn't stupid, we'd be wearing wool sock-hats that don't blow off—like them wrecker-truck guys." He gazed longingly at the warm, county-issue caps with furry earflaps that his officers had donned for the occasion. "Or we'd have us a couple of those Russian military-style caps." *What do they call them?*

"Ushankas," Moon said.

"Charlie, I'd appreciate it if you wouldn't read my mind."

"Sorry. But what's this sudden obsession with headgear?"

Parris gave the Southern Ute tribal investigator a wry, sideways glance. "The point is—everybody else has hats that cover their ears. You and me, we're wearing lids that don't make any sense for this kind of weather."

"Of course we are."

"But don't that make us stupid?"

"Nope."

"Tell me why."

"It has to do with the Code of the West, which applies to all red-blooded American cowboys."

Though he was eager to believe this, Parris's expression revealed just the slightest hint of doubt.

"You can go look it up in the book. Section six, article four, paragraph two: 'Real six-gun totin', bronco-bustin' cowboys don't give a rooty-toot hoot about comfort or being practical or none of that kind of stuff. All they care about is *looking good.*'"

"You telling me that's actually wrote down?"

"Yes I am." The Indian patted the former Chicago cop on the back. "And you and me, we are sure-enough cowboys, pard." *Even if you are wearing a sixty-year-old Humphrey Bogart hat your daddy gave you.*

"My mother wouldn't like hearing you say that." As a tempestuous gust tossed icy grit into his teeth, the white man cracked a smile. "Momma didn't want me to grow up to be a cowboy."

"Doctor or lawyer, huh?"

Parris shook his fedora. "Investment banker."

"Don't hold it against her. I'm sure she meant well."

"What did your mom want you to be?"

"Indian chief."

"No, Charlie—I'm serious."

"So'm I. Momma wanted me to grow up and get elected tribal chairman."

Parris chuckled. "And you didn't do neither one."

This exchange was interrupted by the appearance of a vehicle coming up the mountain, a snowy cloud boiling in its wake.

The chief of police focused slitted eyes on the blue-and-white Bronco with heavy-tread snow tires. "That'll be Moxon."

All Charlie Moon heard above the wind was a single word, and that one incorrectly. "Moccasin?"

"Moxon," Parris said. Louder this time.

At the mention of the name, the wind fell to a breeze, which quickly diminished to those murmuring whispers that convince imaginative little girls and lonely old men that there are ghosts afoot.

Being unaware of the deeper meanings of these movements of air, Charlie Moon asked, "Who's Moxon?"

Scott Parris's face hardened as the Bronco slowed. "Mr. Nicholas Moxon is Cassandra Spencer's business manager. He also pinch-hits as her publicity agent."

As Moxon braked to a halt and lowered the window, his shiny head reflected a glint of early-morning sunlight. "Good morning."

Moon returned the greeting.

Parris mumbled something about how this particular morning wasn't all that good.

The hairless man cocked his conspicuous cranium to indicate the wrecker truck. "Any late-breaking news about the accident?"

The chief of police assumed his official tone. "I've got some geckos down in the Devil's Mouth. They're trying to locate the Corvette." He shot a glance at the tow truck. "If and when they do, they'll help Mr. Ortega get a cable onto it."

The new arrival glanced over his shoulder, then back at the surly cop. "Any idea what caused Andrew to run off the driveway last night?"

"The fact that the road was slick as snail spit might've

had something to do with it." Parris bared his teeth to grin at Cassandra's muscle-bound friend. "But if you have any interesting notions, I'll be more'n glad to hear about 'em."

Moxon regarded the cop with dead, black-button eyes. "What're the chances of finding him alive?"

"It's a long shot. But stranger things have happened." Parris returned the icy gaze.

Moon made himself a bet. *Three-to-one, my buddy stares him down.*

Indeed, after a few uneasy seconds, during which something unseemly might have happened—a muttered curse, even a thrown punch—it was Moxon who blinked. "I've been out of town for a couple of days. I heard about Andrew's accident and that Cassie was up here with her sister, so I'm on my way to see her." Under the glare of the policeman's unflinching gaze, he blinked again. "And Bea, of course."

Parris put his hands on the Bronco, leaned until the tip of his nose was a finger's length from the driver's face. "I'm sure *they'll* be glad to see you."

Before raising the window and plowing the Bronco through an immaculate white dune, Moxon managed a smile of sorts. The sort of smile that says, *Later, bud.* And means every word of it.

"Well," Moon said.

Parris barked at his friend, "Well, what?"

"I was about to make an observation regarding the relationship between you and Mr. Moccasin." He waited for the inevitable correction.

"It's *Moxon*." Parris spelled it out.

"Thanks, pard. I'll try to remember that."

"So what's this observation you were about to make?"

"Oh, nothing worth writing home about." He watched Parris's face redden, added, "Only that you don't seem overly fond of Mr. Moccasin."

"If Moccasin—*Moxon*—was to run for any elected office you care to mention, I would be happy to vote for his opponent."

"Even if the other politician was a mangy coyote?"

"Even if he was a mangy, yellow-bellied, two-headed coyote. With bad breath from both mouths."

"Well, that's understandable, as far as it goes. But what if this Mr. Two-Headed Coyote wore a pair of green derby hats and two pairs of lady's high-heel shoes and promised to outlaw Coors beer and John Wayne picture shows and raise taxes nineteen-hundred percent?"

Parris jutted the formidable chin. "Wouldn't make no difference. He'd still get my vote."

Moon blinked at a welcome glint of unfiltered sunlight. "There must be some awfully good reason for you to dislike a man as much as that." The expert angler baited his hook: "But it'd probably involve malicious gossip and bald-faced lies and make you look bad, so I'd just as soon not know what it was."

Parris eyed his Indian friend and grinned. "Charlie, I don't necessarily need a reason not to like a man. I'm what you call old-fashioned—if there's even the least little something about a fella that rubs me the wrong way, or something that don't smell just right, then right off the bat, I make up my mind to—" The moral philosopher's remarks were interrupted by a shout from the edge of the Devil's Mouth.

They turned to see the climbers, who were clad in neon-green coveralls and attached to a red-and-white candy-striped nylon rope, appear one by one over the lip of the snow-swept slope. After a brief conversation with the leader of the team, GCPD Officer Alicia Martin approached, flashed the Indian a smile, directed her remarks to the chief of police. "The mountaineers haven't found a trace of Mr. Turner's automobile, so it must be pretty far under the snow. When conditions are better, they're willing to come back and have another go at it."

Parris glared at the climbers. "They are, huh?"

The shapely cop nodded. "But before they do, they recommend that we get a copter with instruments to make a sweep. It'd help if they had a target with coordinates."

Parris watched the EMTs get into their warm ambulance. "We won't find what's left of that Corvette until ten to fifteen feet of snow melts in the Devil's Mouth." *Which might not happen for the next ten summers.* He cast an apprehensive glance in the direction of the Spencer residence. "Guess I'll have to go break the latest bad news to the widow." He fixed a hopeful gaze on the female officer, put on a doomed-martyr expression. "When she finds out there's no hope of finding Andrew alive, Bea'll probably go all to pieces—cry all over me." *Okay, Martin. Time to step up to the plate.*

The pinch-hitter took the hint. "Shall I tell her?"

"Well . . ." He traded in the slightly used doomed-martyr expression for a concerned-supervisor face. "If you're sure you're up to it."

"I think I can manage." As she headed back to her unit, Officer Martin was grinning. *What a big sissy.*

Moon murmured, "That was mighty smooth, pard."

Already bolstered by those heady virtues of selflessness and compassion, Parris had a go at modesty: "Ah, nothin' to it." He watched Martin's black-and-white Chevrolet head up the driveway, taking advantage of the deep tracks Moxon's Bronco had left behind. "Well, I guess we're about done here."

Pleased at the prospect of withdrawing to a lower, warmer altitude, Moon made a proposal: "Tell you what—let's roll on down to town and over to Lulabelle's Dixie Restaurant, have us a king-size helping of hot breakfast."

A stiff breeze was sweeping down the mountain slope, threatening to add frostbite to Scott Parris's other woes. Lifting his jacket collar, he cast his vote for the hungry Ute's proposal. "I can practically taste Lulabelle's scrambled eggs and peppered grits."

"Me too." Moon barely restrained himself from licking his lips. "And waffles soaked in butter and hot maple syrup."

"Let's don't forget a couple dozen strips of crispy bacon."

"I can practically smell it frying in the pan." *I really can.*

The tall, sinewy man sniffed, caught another whiff. He marveled at the remarkable power of suggestion, which was helped along by the thin, chill air and his sharp appetite.

The lawmen were about to depart when a figure in a tattered black overcoat materialized from behind a curtain of blowing snow. The man, who leaned on a spindly aspen staff, was endowed with a bent back and a homely, monkeyish little face that was not enhanced by a toothless mouth. His rheumy, whiskey-smelling breaths came in short, asthmatic gasps. "You guys coppers?"

The chief of police nodded.

"Whacher names?"

Parris introduced himself and Charlie Moon.

"Pleased ta meecha." The shabby personage removed a brown cotton glove that was missing three fingers, offered his hand. "I'm Clevis Parsley. Like the vegetable."

Parris accepted the grimy paw. "Back in Pigeon Creek, my dear old aunt Nell always raised two rows of clevis, right between the butter beans and Big Boy tomatoes."

Mr. Parsley shook his shaggy head. "No, I mean my *last* name—"

"Don't pay my buddy any mind." Charlie Moon tapped a finger on his temple. "He's ain't been quite right since he got kicked in the head by a mule he was tryin' to milk." The Ute leaned to mutter in the startled man's ear, just loud enough that Parris could hear. "He thinks he's the chief of police and I'm his deputy. Whatever he says, you'd best humor him—he's edgy and he's got a .38 tucked under his jacket."

The newcomer glanced uneasily at the presumed madman.

"Clevis Parsley. Sounds like a made-up name to me." Parris conferred with his deputy. "What d'you think, Charlie—is this slicker hidin' behind some kinda patched-up anagram?"

The Ute cocked his head. "Well, now that you mention it, pardner, I see what you mean. Throw away the *C,* swap the *a* for an extra *e,* sort things out some, what you've got is—"

"Elvis Presley." Parris regarded his victim with frank disapproval. "So you ain't dead—all these years, you been pulling a big hoax!"

The unsettled man was backing up. "Uh—I guess you fellas is plenty busy, so I'll be gettin' along home."

"Oh no you won't." Under Parris's left eye, a sinister twitch. "Not till you've told us ever'thing you know."

About to bolt, Clevis Parsley froze at a look from Moon.

Parris spoke in a dangerous monotone: "Start talking."

Words spilled out of the witness's mouth. "Well, I'll get right to the nub of it. Las' night, I seed it."

"Oh you did, did you?" The chief of police produced another twitch. "What was it you seed?"

"Why, I seed that motorcar go down into the Devil's Mouth."

Parris bunched a pair of bushy eyebrows. "You actually witnessed the accident?"

Mr. Parsley shook his head, which was covered by a tight-fitting wool ski cap he had removed from the head of one even less fortunate than himself, who had been dead at the time. "You can call it that if you want to—but it wasn't no ord'nary accident."

Parris asked what he meant by that.

"Them witches caused it."

"Witches, huh?" The lawman vainly tried to revive the twitch.

The odd character lowered his voice, rolled the rheumy eyes upward. "They was up there—above the lane. I didn't notice 'em till that fancy car come 'round the curve, then there they was in the headlights. The both of 'em. Plain as the nose on your face."

Parris and Moon shifted their gaze to the pine-studded mountainside above the Spencer driveway. Then back to Parsley. The chief of police looked down his nose at this unlikely witness. "You saw a couple a women up there?"

"Them wasn't no reg'lar women—they was sure-enough witches!" Clevis Parsley attempted to spit on the snow, didn't notice that he had soiled his shoe.

Parris pressed: "So how do you tell the difference between a reg'lar woman and sure-enough witches?" He thought of a witty response, managed not to grin.

C. Parsley explained. "Well for one thing, reg'lar women wouldn't be a-hoverin' above the lane." He raised a half-gloved hand, wriggled the dirty, naked fingers. "I'm not lyin'—their feets was about a yard off the ground. They was a-floatin' in the *air.*"

"Floatin', huh." *You smell like you've been floatin' in Jim Beam.*

Parsley nodded. "I just wanted you badge toters to know what happened, so you won't waste the taxpayer's dime fiddle-faddlin' around tryin' to figger out why that car ran off the road. But don't think you'll ever put the cuffs on them witches." He coughed up a wheezy "hee-hee," wiped his nose on a coat sleeve. "*Brujos* like those comes and goes as they please, like any ghost you ever saw!" He interrupted the narrative to stick a finger into his ear, twist it, thoughtfully inspect a glob of amber waxlike substance. Smacked his lips.

The Ute grinned. *If he eats it, Scott'll freak out.*

Scott Parris cringed. *Please—don't put it in your mouth.*

The glob was evidently not that appetizing. The odd little man wiped the finger on his coat, addressed the alleged chief of police: "Anythin' else you want to know?"

"Yeah. Just in case we need a signed statement, what's your address?" Parris smiled. *Down at the end of Loony Street—Fruitcake Hotel.*

Parsley aimed a filthy finger. "My place is over yonder on the mesa, 'cross the Devil's Mouth. I got me a nice little lean-to, and a Coleman stove and a previously owned sleepin' bag." He whined, "Now can I go home?"

"All right." Parris shook his finger at the eccentric. "But from now on, don't you be goin' around impersonating the King."

Half convinced that he was guilty of something or other, Clevis Parsley nodded his solemn promise. As the breeze stirred wisps of gray hair protruding from under the woolen cap, he turned, stalked away.

When the unfortunate character was out of earshot, Moon eyed his friend. "Well, imagine that—a reliable eyewitness who walks right up and tells you how it happened. Ain't you the lucky one."

The man who was supposedly suffering from a mule kick on his noggin presented a wounded expression. "I'm glad you're able to have some fun at my expense."

"Me too." Moon looked down at the six-footer. "Pardner, I try to never let a day go by without finding something to enjoy."

Which reminded Scott Parris of a subject Charlie would probably get a big haw-haw out of. In the cold, bright light of day, and particularly after Clevis Parsley's report of witches floating over the Spencer driveway, the mere thought of describing what he *thought* he had seen last night was embarrassing. But it might have something to do with the auto accident. Parris shot a look at the inquisitive uniforms. While straining to catch a word, they were looking anywhere but at the boss and his Ute friend. "Charlie, we need to talk. But not here."

Moon understood. "Tell me about it over scrambled eggs and bacon." Again there was that whiff of bacon frying. *My nose is so good I can smell things that ain't even there.*

The two best friends got into their vehicles, cranked up V-8 engines, shifted to low, headed slowly down the narrow, winding driveway off Spencer Mountain, and through the iron gate, which was—by official order of the Granite Creek chief of police—not to be closed until the investigation of Andrew Turner's auto accident was complete.

• • •

TWENTY-NINE
THE SILVER LINING

While Clevis Parsley regaled Charlie Moon and Scott Parris with his tale about how witches floating above the Spencer driveway had caused Andrew Turner's auto accident, Nicholas Moxon parked his Bronco under a naked, shivering aspen, jammed a classic, custom-made black felt cowboy hat onto his remarkably spherical skull, buttoned a lined gray trench coat from knee to neck, and stalked along the snowy flagstone walkway to the pillared porch of the Spencer residence. While cleaning his boots on a bristly mat that did not have WELCOME printed on it, he removed the spiffy hat with one hand, banged the brass knocker with the other. Cassandra Spencer's business manager was definitely a multitasker; he could simultaneously walk, chew gum, and plot devilishly clever new ways to increase his client's share of the television audience.

Mr. Moxon had memorized a brief but tasteful speech with which to greet the recently bereaved Beatrice Spencer. His remarks would be salted with such phrases as "I was shocked to hear—"; "This must be a terrible time for you"; "I thought I should drop by"; and "If there is anything I can do—anything at all," and so on. But it was not Beatrice Spencer who opened the door.

It was Sister Cassandra's black-clad form and haunted face that confronted him. "Oh, Nicky!"

Though disappointed at not seeing the widow, Nicholas Moxon adapted quickly to unexpected situations. "Cassie, darling." He reached out, engulfed the slender woman in a great, suffocating bear hug.

Once released, she quickly got her breath back. "Oh, Nicky!" The lady tended to repeat herself, which was a source of irritation to her business manager.

But today, Nicholas Moxon was prepared to make allowances. Following the elder of the Spencer sisters inside, he was also prepared to make use of such comforting phrases as were ready in his quiver: "Poor Cassie—this must be a terrible time for you. I thought I should drop by and see if there was anything I could do."

"Dear Nicky—that is so thoughtful of you."

Having dispensed with the necessary formalities, he looked over his shoulder, said from the side of his mouth, "I got word from Gerald Sax that you actually *fainted* during the show!"

"I suppose all of the stress of work finally caught up with me." The pale woman, who was still a bit wobbly at the knees, added, "Fortunately, my plucky little Native American guest was able to carry the rest of the program."

"I wasn't able to watch the show live last evening, but I recorded it on a DVD and reviewed it this morning. That old Apache gal is really a hoot!"

"She's a Ute."

"Okay, so she's a Ute hoot." Moxon frowned at the nitpicker. "Are you feeling better today? I mean you're not likely to—" The muscle-bound man made a face to display his distaste with anything related to swooning. "Uh—you know what I mean."

"Yes, I know." An amused smile. "You needn't worry, Nicky. I promise not to faint on you."

He chuckled, but was greatly relieved.

They held hands; light kisses on cheeks were exchanged. Moxon glanced down the hallway. "Is your poor sister—"

"Bea's upstairs in her studio."

The man who had been dubbed Daddy Warbucks by Daisy Perika raised the gristly subdermal tissue where an eyebrow would have been, had his dysfunctional hair follicles been able to raise a crop. "What's she doing, slapping gobs of paint on a canvas?" Like Andrew Turner, Mr. Moxon did not appreciate Bea's notion of art.

"I have no idea. But I believe she wants to be alone."

Moxon tried not to grin. *I guess a few hours with you goes a long way—even for your sister.* "We need to talk." He took his client by the arm, surveyed the huge parlor, which did not engender a satisfactory sense of privacy. "But not in here."

Without a word, Cassandra led her business manager across the plushly carpeted room, down a narrow, three-step stairway, through a white paneled door into a solarium that was aglow with filtered sunlight. The three outer walls were floor-to-ceiling double-pane glazing. To eyes that had accommodated to the parlor's soft twilight, the effect on dilated pupils of incandescent sunlight reflecting off fresh snow was almost blinding. And despite the sense of being surrounded by an utterly arctic landscape, the twelve-by-twelve space was pleasantly warm.

Cassandra spread her arms to receive the rays. "It is such a glorious day." She added quickly, "Aside from Andrew's tragic accident."

"Yes. Tragic." Mr. Moxon was idly examining a potted plant. Using his thumbnail to sever the stem, he plucked an extremely rare African violet and held the purple blossom close to his eyes, which crossed slightly to focus on the dismembered bit of herbage. "At such a sad time, one hates to mention silver linings."

The final two words got her attention. "Whatever do you mean?"

Moxon assumed that elegantly melancholy expression that is used to such good effect by experienced morticians. "Even though I don't yet have the hard data, I am reliably informed that the numbers for last night's show will go through the roof. Shingles will fly in all directions—tall brick chimneys will tumble."

"Oh." Her face was admirably blank of any sign of pleasure. "Well, that's all very well, I suppose." She found a silk hankie, dabbed at an expertly mascaraed eye that was quite dry. "But with Bea's husband dead, such worldly matters as program ratings seem so...so...unimportant." She dabbed the other eye. "Even if such a development would virtually guarantee an offer from one of the networks."

"Yes." He studied the doomed violet as if it were the most fascinating object he had ever beheld. "Even so."

The TV psychic was trying so hard not to smile. Or, for that matter, not to yell "Wahoo!" and tappity-tap-tap out a lively little jig on the tile floor. "But, Nicky dear, since you have already raised the sordid issue, you might as well tell me. Just for the sake of conversation. How high do you expect the ratings might go?"

He gave her an estimate.

"Oh!" Cassandra's hands went cold, the four-chambered pump thumpity-thumped inside her ribcage. "That much!"

The business manager nodded. "And it's all your doing, Cassie."

She shook her head. "We're a *team,* Nicky."

"Oh, I try to do my part. And I've managed to be helpful from time to time." Pitching the bruised flower aside, the brutish man reached out to take her hand. "But last evening, you really outdid yourself—announcing Andrew Turner's death within minutes of the auto accident."

"As you are well aware, I can hardly take all the credit." Cassandra fluttered the famous eyelashes, flashed the dazzling smile. "After all, it's my *spirit channel* who provides the critical information."

Moxon chuckled. "Which one was it this time—the Cretan galley slave, the Egyptian physician—or the Cherokee basket maker?"

Her smile faded. "Please don't tease me, Nicky."

"Tease you?" The bald-as-a-billiard-ball man cocked the shiny head, made furrows in the brow deep enough to plant black-eyed peas in. "What do you mean?"

The psychic's fingers began to tingle. "Don't *do* this—it isn't funny!"

Moxon's voice went deathly flat: "How did you learn about Andrew's automobile accident?"

If snakes could speak, the psychic thought, *they would sound just like that.* "In the usual way, of course."

"You surely don't mean—"

"Well of course I do!" Cassandra balled her hands into knotty little fists, stamped her foot. "The message about Andrew was from *White Raven.*"

He stared at the woman for a full ten seconds before saying, "Cassie—this is very, very important. Think back to last evening. Try to remember *exactly* what happened that led you to tell your TV audience about Andrew Turner's death."

Cassandra Spencer bowed her head, closed her eyes. For a several-second eternity, she relived that dark experience from the night before. Finally, she blinked, stared at the blunt toes of her business manager's black leather boots. "I can recall it with perfect clarity." Slowly, slowly, she raised her gaze, passing over the bulge of Moxon's knees under his slacks, the pewter bull's-head belt buckle, the silver-veined lump of turquoise dangling on his string tie, stopping just below his comically round face, which suggested a middle-age Charlie Brown—who had lost all his innocence. "It was just like always when I receive a message from White Raven."

"Cassie—look at me."

Their eyes met, exchanging far more in an instant than all the words that had passed between them.

"You're absolutely certain?"

"Yes, Nicky."

"That is very unsettling news."

She searched for some sign of understanding on the blank face. "I had naturally assumed that—"

"Yes. You would, of course."

Cassandra decided that she might as well tell all. "Nicky . . ."

He had heard this tone before. Didn't like it then, didn't like it now. "What?"

She wilted under his icy stare. "I'm afraid I've—uh—misplaced one of my earrings."

"One of the new ones?"

His client nodded. "It must have happened when I fainted. With all that's happened since last night, I've only had a few minutes to look for it. But it *has* to be somewhere in the house."

Nicholas Moxon's reply was soft. "You must find it."

"Yes." Cassandra Spencer gazed through the glass, at a world covered with snow. "I know."

• • •

THIRTY
FINE DINING AT LULABELLE'S
DIXIE RESTAURANT

The lawmen had finished their breakfasts and were enjoying second cups of coffee. Scott Parris looked around the eatery, decided that no one was close enough to hear, leaned across his plate, and said to Charlie Moon, "I expect you're curious about what I saw on Spencer Mountain last night." *What I thought I saw.*

"It's not so much that I'm curious, pard." The full-time Hereford rancher, part-time tribal investigator who had recently been deputized by the Granite Creek chief of police, picked up the sticky plastic bottle of honey, squirted a generous helping into his coffee. "But if memory serves, that's one of the reasons you called me last night." *Just as I was going off to sleep.* Which reminded Moon that he had not had a wink in the past twenty-nine hours. He stifled a yawn.

"I'll tell you, but on one condition—you won't give me the big horse laugh."

"You got my word."

"You double-dog promise?"

The Ute raised the cup of sweet, steaming coffee. "Honest Injun."

"Cross your fingers?"

"Crossed and double-crossed."

Somehow, double-crossed didn't sit quite right. "Swear on your mother's—"

"Let's don't push it too far."

"Right." Gazing at his coffee, Parris was fascinated by the rainbow sheen shimmering on the black liquid. The dazzling iridescence—which would not have been present if the cup had been properly cleaned—was created by a thin film of grease. "What I saw, just as I got near the spot where Andrew Turner's Corvette went off the driveway . . ." His pale face turned a pinkish tint. "Well—it's kinda hard to describe."

"Give it your best shot."

Parris set his jaw. "It was big and hairy."

"Big and hairy's a good start." Moon took a sip of honeyed coffee. *That is good stuff.* He had another helping. Big, mouth-filling gulp.

With an expression of deep, earnest concentration twisting his beefy features, the chief of police continued: "The only way I can get across what it looked like is to compare it to something familiar." He considered several possibilities, then: "It looked to me like a gorilla."

Gorilla? Moon was trying to swallow the coffee. Could not.

"And what really gave me the willies—that big Gomer was totin' something on its shoulder. It was all wrapped up—looked like a big burrito."

The Ute spat the black liquid onto the table.

All over the restaurant, which catered to various sorts of toughs, offended patrons raised bushy brows. Baleful glances were cast, uncomplimentary innuendos muttered. In a few pockets, tattooed hands caressed concealed weapons.

Scott Parris regarded his best friend with a hurt expression. "Charlie, you promised."

"I didn't laugh, pard." Moon coughed. "It was the coffee." He found a paper napkin, wiped at his mouth. "It must've been too hot."

"It was not. You laughed out loud."

"No I didn't." *Had too much coffee in my mouth to laugh.* "But even if I had've, you've got to admit there's something a little bit comical in what you said."

"You can take it from me—it wasn't the least bit amus-

ing at the time." Parris watched his friend use another napkin to mop coffee off the table. "Do you think you could
hold up your end of a serious conversation—maybe for a
whole damn minute?"

"You betchum." The Ute put on a supremely somber expression, not unlike Geronimo's when that Chiricahua
Apache medicine man was captured by the U.S. Army in
1886. The effort made Moon's face ache. "This thing you
saw crossing the road, what do you think it was?"

"Only one single, solitary possibility comes to mind."
Parris lowered his voice. "It must've been one of them—
uh . . ." What was the word? *Abominabubble*? No. That
wasn't quite right. Aha! "One of them abdominal snow-
men."

Abdominal? The Ute put on his best poker face. *God,
please don't let me laugh.* After reconsideration, prayer
resubmitted: *Don't let me belly-laugh.*

Parris took the blank look as a question mark. "You
know—a Sasquatch." Still no indication that this Indian
was getting the drift. "Folks in South Asia call 'em Yetis.
Around here, these who've found their eighteen-inch
tracks call 'em Bigfoots."

Moon pictured his herd decimated by mad cow disease,
an IRS audit covering the past fifteen years, not a drop of
rain for the next ten. That barely did the trick. The rancher
said, "I've heard about Bigfoots."

Parris's expression reflected an inner intensity that his
friend had rarely seen. "Way I see it, Andrew Turner
rounds the curve, picks up this Bigfoot in his headlights,
swerves to miss it, bops the tree, bounces off a boulder, and
over the cliff he goes and down into the Devil's Mouth."
He rapped his knuckles on the table. "It know it sounds
pretty wild, Charlie—but every year, all the way from the
Yukon down to Montana and sometimes even here in Colorado, there are sightings of these creatures." Intake of
breath. "There must be a family of them living up on
Spencer Mountain!" He fixed a steely-eyed glare on the
Ute. "What do you think?"

"Well, until we can come up with a better idea, I guess we've got to consider it a possibility." *Mr. Sasquatch, carrying a huge burrito home to Mrs. Sasquatch and the hairy little kids.* "Especially considering how you saw the critter with your own two eyeballs."

Parris used those same eyeballs to examine his friend. *Is Charlie Moon making sport of me again?*

Charlie Moon was trying oh, so hard to be kind to his buddy. But the merry man could not resist the temptation to have just a little fun. "And like any good theory, the Sasquatch scenario rules out some less likely possibilities for what Turner might've seen when he rounded the curve." The bait had been cast.

Parris was bound to bite. "Like what?"

"Well for one thing—Mr. Parsley's witches."

The theorist nodded. "Right."

"Also King Kong," Moon said with a straight face. "And Godzilla."

It was a rib too far.

The chief of police gave the tribal investigator his stern look. The industrial-strength version, which was capable of turning ordinary men into pillars of chalk—and very nearly able to shame the Ute. But not quite. No matter. Scott Parris had other ammunition and did not mind using it. "Charlie, I hate to say this. But considering the gravity of the matter—and I refer to the fact that Andrew Turner is dead—your flippant attitude is . . . well . . . unseemly." The Ute didn't flinch. Parris fired the second barrel: "And unprofessional."

Ouch.

"Uh—would it help if I said I was sorry?"

"Nope." Granite Creek's top cop leaned back in his chair. "But there is something you could do to make up for it."

"Name it."

"Okay, here it is. Strictly on the q.t., you and me take a hike onto Spencer Mountain."

Uh-oh. "Something tells me this ain't for a picnic."

"I'll take some ham sandwiches and coffee. You'll look for sign."

"What kind of a sign?" *Don't Disturb the Sasquatch?*

"Don't play dumb, Charlie. You're a first-rate tracker and you know what *sign* means. A snapped-off sapling limb. Little tuft of hair caught on a juniper snag. Droppings."

Playing dumb was fun. "Droppings?"

"Scat."

"Oh, that."

"And footprints." Parris put both hands on the damp table, walked them to the napkin holder. Plop. Plop. Plop. "Great *big* footprints."

Charlie Moon wondered how he got himself into these fixes. Probably something to do with ethnicity. *If you're an Indian, everybody who's seen a Western movie believes you can track a deer mouse over a mile of solid sandstone and shoot an arrow into its ear at fifty paces*. He kept the sigh inside. *I hope nobody ever finds out I went out tracking Bigfoots.*

NOSTALGIA IS NOT WHAT IT USED TO BE

That afternoon found Charlie Moon in the Columbine kitchen, smiling. That's right. Smiling. Why? Why, because he was at the kitchen sink, armed with a three-blade Case Stockman pocket knife, an assortment of wrenches, and a formidable ball-peen hammer. What was he up to? Our mechanic was installing a new, hand-crafted leather seal in the hand-operated pitcher pump—and such tasks pleasured him right down to the marrow.

Yes, a hand pump. No, Mr. Moon's home was not what a euphemistically inclined (is there any other kind?) realtor might refer to as rustic. Definitely not. The headquarters was equipped with the essential amenities of modern plumbing, with ice-cold water provided by a pair of deep wells, each served by a 220-volt submersible electric pump that could deliver thirty-five gallons per minute into eighty-gallon pressure tanks, but the antique cast-iron muscle-operated appliance was a reminder of those bygone days when everybody knew how to prime the pump and folks managed to get along just fine without electric bills. Yes sir. Candles and kerosene wick lamps for light. No TV. Great big 1936 Airline Movie-Dial, 32-volt, battery-operated console radio. If you had a crank phone, the thing might ring once in a week, and lonely folks on the party line would listen in to hear the news and pick up gossip. If a neighbor without a phone wanted to say howdy, he'd generally get onto his horse and make a twenty-mile ride, talk for hours, stay for supper, maybe overnight. And not only that, in those days there was no such thing as computers or—Wait a minute. What was that nerve-jangling noise? Well wouldn't you just know it. The telephone.

The wrench slipped, Moon jammed his knuckles on a sharp corner, watched blood ooze from the gash.

Which just goes to prove the point. Whatever the point was.

He stomped to the nearest extension, snatched up the instrument. "Columbine Ranch."

"Uh—Charlie?"

He grinned. "What's up, Sarah?"

"Oh, nothing much." She spent twelve minutes telling him about nothing much. And then: "Oh, by the way—do you still have those DVDs?"

A frown. "What DVDs?"

"The *Cassandra Sees* DVDs. The ones Mr. Sax gave Aunt Daisy as part of her gift for being on the TV show. Aunt Daisy gave them to you."

"She did?"

"Uh-huh. And you put them in your jacket pocket. The gray jacket with black buttons." *That looks so nice on you.*

"Then they must still be there." This was great fun. "Why d'you ask?"

"Um . . . well, I thought maybe the next time you come to see us, you might want to bring the DVDs to Aunt Daisy."

"Mmm-hmm. You think she'd like to watch all those old TV shows again?"

"Oh, sure. Especially the program she was on that night."

"Consider it done." Charlie Moon remembered that Gerald Sax had also given something to Sarah. "You enjoying your big picture of the lady's eyeball?"

"Oh, yes!" Sarah Frank went on to describe every detail of the hugely magnified orb. Including the intriguing fact that there were "strange lights" in the psychic's eye.

WE DON'T KNOW WHY

It might simply have been the girl's mention of "strange lights." Or perhaps the motivator was something entirely *other.* Sometimes operating on autopilot, at other times prompted by a subconscious command, human beings will do things without knowing why. So we don't know why Charlie Moon felt compelled to turn on his little-used high-resolution television, also the DVD player, and, with the aid of an almost incomprehensible manual, stayed up late that night, until he had mastered every function. Including how to freeze a frame, move the little red triangle to identify a region of interest, select MAGNIFY from the menu—and watch the enlarged segment fill the entire screen. Having educated himself almost to the level of an eight-year-old TV viewer, he commenced to watch studio recordings of *Cassandra Sees,* which included scenes that had not been broadcast for viewing by the general public. The tribal investigator was fascinated by a number of items. Count them:

(1) From the most recent program: Daisy Perika with her head and shoulders under Cassandra's coffee table.

(2 through 13) All twelve of these were close-ups of Cassandra's attractive face.

(Back up to 9) This was the *really good one.* During that sensational broadcast where the psychic interrupted an interview to report her vision of a Denver warehouse fire.

For just a fleeting moment, the Ute thought that he saw flames *in her eyes!*

Moon yawned. *I've been staring at this stuff way too long.* It was time to call it a day, hit the hay. *But not before I get a closer look.* The dandy freeze-frame feature came in handy. Not to mention the 4X magnification.

In the neighborhood of 3:00 A.M. (a quiet, peaceful district), Charlie Moon switched off the modern electronic appliances. For quite some time, he stared unseeing at the blank TV screen. Reflected upon what he had seen.

• • •

THIRTY-ONE
THE SICKNESS

The incubation period for Daisy Perika's illness fell somewhere in between that for influenza and chicken pox. While determining the onset of flu and pox can be problematic, there was no uncertainty in this instance—the insidious infection had occurred at the very moment the tribal elder had discovered the stray earring on Cassandra Spencer's carpet—and the TV psychic's most closely held secret.

If stubborn pride had not prevented Daisy from revealing her discovery to Charlie Moon, she would have been inoculated against the sickness. Following that missed opportunity, the progress of the disease was more or less predictable.

During breakfast at the Columbine on day one, the symptoms included a notable lack of appetite and the glaze-eyed expression of one who has *other things* on her mind. Before lunch, the old woman's heart was palpitating with anticipation of how a clever person like herself (always alert for the unexpected opportunity) might use the secret knowledge to personal advantage. That same day, as Charlie Moon drove his silent aunt, a talkative Sarah Frank, and the paw-licking Mr. Zig-Zag to church in Ignacio, thereafter back to Daisy's reservation home at the mouth of *Cañón del Esp'ritu,* her sly old mind was hard at work. Wickedly efficient little ratchets clickety-clicked perversely, crooked little wheels turned and twisted—sometimes in reversely.

By day two, the patient was suffering from a frenetic fever of mental activity. From dawn to dusk, she would hastily contrive a plan, consider it from various angles, discard that flawed design for another that was worse, and so on, *ad infinitum,* deep into *la nightum.*

Days three through six were sufficiently similar to day two to require no further description.

On the afternoon of day seven (a Friday), the acute illness reached its climactic peak (so to speak) when Daisy decided to play the discordant piece by ear. Sadly, when it came to orchestrating an ingeniously clever plot, Mrs. Perika was kindred soul to neither Mr. Bernstein nor Mr. Hitchcock. Indeed, it would not be overly harsh to suggest that the results of her best efforts tended more toward comic opera. As it happened, the Ute elder was not aware of this shortcoming. Another, more admirable aspect of her personality combined with this deficiency to create a truly volatile combination—Daisy was a Woman of Action.

It was time to make the call. She did not need to search her purse for that scrap of paper whereupon she had scribbled the TV celebrity's unlisted number. That critical piece of information was engraved deeply into her memory. Daisy picked up the telephone, mouthed the digits as she pressed the buttons. Waited.

WHAT WE HAVE HERE IS NOT A FAILURE TO COMMUNICATE

One ring.

After she says, "Hello," I'll just say, "This is Daisy Perika."

Two rings.

The tribal elder's mouth twisted into a roguish grin. *I bet Miss Fancy-Pants will be surprised to hear from me.*

Three rings.

Well aware that there was always an "on the other hand," Daisy scowled. *Or maybe she won't even remember my name.*

"Why, hello, Daisy."

The caller very nearly dropped the telephone. *That white woman really* is *a witch!* Another possibility occurred to Daisy: *Or she has caller ID, just like me.*

Cassandra Spencer listened to a few seconds of silence, then: "Daisy?"

"I'm here." About to lie, Daisy crossed her fingers. "I thought I'd call and find out if you was feeling okay."

"How very thoughtful of you. I'm feeling just fine." Cassandra's smile modulated her response: "I've been intending to call and thank you—and your gallant nephew—for tending to me after I fainted. I'm most particularly grateful to you, dear lady, for completing the broadcast. I just don't know what I could ever do to repay you."

You will before we hang up. The old woman's grin had returned from wherever grins slip away to.

"Daisy, please excuse me for just a moment." The psychic was receiving a competing message from an intimidating presence who had just entered her parlor. No, not a spirit. This was a large, flesh-and-blood man, who carried a long-stemmed wineglass in his hand. Nicholas Moxon arched the left, hairless brow ridge—as if to inquire of his client: *With whom are you yakking on the telephone and about what, pray tell?* Of the pair, this was his highly expressive hairless eyebrow.

Cassandra cupped her hand over the mouthpiece, responded to the telepathic query: "It's Daisy Perika—the old Indian woman."

The *right* naked eyebrow arched, as if to say, *Ah.* This was his taciturn brow.

Moxon's client returned her attention to the caller. "Sorry for the interruption. I'm so busy that I hardly have time to breathe."

"Well, I won't keep you long." Daisy told another untruth: "I also wanted to thank you for having me on your TV show."

"You are quite welcome." *Is that all?*

It was not. Not by a long shot. Daisy was getting down

to business. "Oh, I almost forgot." She felt her hands go cold, the thumpity-thump of blood pumping in her neck. "I've got something I need to give to you."

Now it was Cassandra's turn to raise an eyebrow. This one, though plucked and penciled, was—in contrast to Mr. Moxon's poor showing—a well-endowed black crescent. Hair-wise.

Daisy continued: "I think you might be interested in how I come to have it. See, right after you had your fit and—"

Cassandra bit her lip, which made it hard to say, "I beg your pardon—"

"Oh, I'm sorry." Daisy didn't *sound* sorry. "I guess I should've said 'seizure.' " Young people these days were so sensitive.

The epileptic was making a valiant attempt to preserve some semblance of civility. "I fainted."

"Whatever you say. Anyway, after you *fainted,* and Charlie Moon carried you off to your bedroom, that little white man asked me to finish the show for you—"

"Which you did—and very capably, I might add." The star of *Cassandra Sees* shot an exasperated glance at her business manager. "For which I shall be eternally grateful." That particular eternity would terminate in less than a minute.

Though highly disposed to compliments, and able to bask happily in unabashed flattery, Daisy brushed this aside. "And then what's-his-name . . . that little white man—"

"I presume you refer to Gerald Sax, the show's assistant director."

"Right, he said I ought to sit in your chair." Daisy paused to recall the moment. "And I did, but on account of those commercials, I knew I'd have a hard time concentrating."

"Commercials—what do you mean?"

"Advertisements." With admirable patience for one of her cranky disposition, Daisy explained, "You know, when they butt into your favorite TV program and try to get you to buy things—like soda pop and shampoo and automobiles."

The psychic closed her eyes, mentally sighed. "Yes, dear. I know what a commercial is."

"That's good," Daisy said, and frowned at a framed picture of Big Ouray hanging on her parlor wall. B.O. had been Cousin Gorman's prize Hereford bull, long since dead. "What was we talking about?"

Despite the dull, throbbing hint of a headache coming on, Cassandra managed a wan smile. "I believe you were saying something or other about commercials."

"Ah, that's right! The commercials on that little TV under your coffee table was flipping over and over, and that was giving me the flutters. And when I get the flutters, you know what happens?"

The psychic shook her head.

As if she had seen this negative response from afar, the Ute shaman said, "My bladder gets all upset and I can't hold my water. So I have to run to the bathroom."

Cassandra nodded.

"I said to myself, 'I'll have to stop that TV picture from flipping.' So, old and stiff as I am, I got down on the floor and stuck my head under the coffee table and found the right knob and turned it. I got the picture nice and steady and my face was so close to the screen I could read the words on those little ribbons they put on the bottom of the picture sometimes, that say things like 'winter storm warning—expect ten inches of snow above eight thousand feet,' or Mrs. So-and-So has an albino crow that talks to her. Stuff like that."

"Yes. I see." And she did.

"And that was when I saw it."

From someplace far away, Cassie heard her little-girl voice say, "Saw what?"

The tribal elder had shifted gears. "Something round and shiny. It was on the floor, under the table. I thought it might be a button that come off the TV, but then again, it might be something valuable that somebody'd lost, so I picked it up." She added, "For safekeeping, until I could give it back to you." She paused, waited for a few heartbeats. The silence on the line fairly shrieked. "But I expect you know what I'm talking about."

Cassandra: "I'm not certain that I do." This was untrue.

Daisy knew that she knew. "It was your earring."

Cassandra tried to speak, coughed. Her throat was sandpaper dry, and dots of light were appearing in front of her eyes. *I mustn't collapse. Not now, with Nicky watching. I just can't.* She heard the old woman's voice in her ear: "The cameo clip-on."

Cassandra felt her knees about to buckle, reached out to a brass floor lamp to steady herself. "Oh. That one."

"That's right. One of the pair ol' Daddy Warbucks gave you in the restaurant. It's a pretty little thing. Must've cost a lot of money." The Ute woman had not enjoyed a conversation so much in years. "I imagine you'll be happy to get it back."

"Yes. I will." Cassandra struggled to regain her composure. "I suppose it must have fallen off when I had my seiz—" She turned away from Moxon. "My fainting spell."

"I could put it in the mail." Carefully timed pause. "But I'd hate to take any chance of it getting lost. Maybe we'll be seeing each other someday before too long, and I could give it to you then."

"Yes, I suppose—"

"Or I could get Charlie Moon to drop me off at your place some Saturday afternoon. That'd give us time to have a cup of coffee. And maybe I'd get to stay and watch you do your TV show."

"That would be delightful."

Feeling Nicholas Moxon's warm breath on her neck, Cassandra said, "Would you mind holding for just a moment?"

"Okay, but don't take too long. Us folks who have to get by on Social Security don't like to run up big phone bills."

"Tell you what—I'll call you back in a few minutes."

"That'll be fine." Daisy hung up on the psychic, smirked. *I think that went pretty well.*

After putting the torch to Rome, Nero reportedly made more or less the same observation.

• • •

Nicholas Moxon reached out to touch Cassandra's arm. "What is it?"

She recoiled from his caress, avoided the stare. "Daisy Perika has my earring."

He was silent for some time, rolling the possibilities over in his mind. Summarized: "That shouldn't be a problem. But we'll have to get it back."

Cassandra shook her head. "She knows."

"Knows what?"

She could not meet his gaze. "How we do it."

The bald man's painted-on mannequin expression—the frozen-corpse smile, the viper's flat-eyed stare—did not waver. "Just from finding your earring?"

"I doubt it." The woman spoke barely above a whisper. "When I fainted during the broadcast, I had not switched the video monitor off."

"Tell me what she said." He cocked his head. "Word for word."

To the best of her recollection, Cassie did.

At the mention of the albino crow—an obvious reference to White Raven—the man who signed his confidential messages with that moniker lost the smile. "That is unfortunate." Familiar with the dark side of human nature, Moxon posed the essential question: "What does she want?"

"Daisy mentioned how poor she was, so I suppose she's angling for a payoff. She also hinted about making another appearance on the show." Cassandra looked to her partner for guidance.

"Then we'll give her what she wants." Moxon examined the immaculate nails on his right hand. The pinky needed just a touch of the diamond file. "Call the little old lady back. Thank her for finding your expensive earring. But she should definitely not put it in the mail. You will be happy to drive to her home and pick it up."

"I will?"

"Of course you will. And while you're there, you'll offer this clever Indian woman a contract. For a half-dozen weekly appearances as special guest on *Cassandra Sees*. At five hundred dollars a pop."

"And you think that will keep her quiet?"

As the bald head nodded, the smile returned, this time reflecting genuine amusement. "For about six weeks."

"What then?"

"That will be sufficient time to come up with a permanent solution to our problem. But don't worry about the details, Cassie. Leave everything to me."

"Very well." But she was worried. "I'll call Daisy back and make an appointment."

"Tell her you'll show up tomorrow to pick up the earring." He raised the glass to his lips, downed the final sip. "But don't mention the six-week contract on the telephone." *She'd tell all her gabby friends and neighbors.* "Save that for your face-to-face with our spunky old blackmailer." He set the glass aside, reached out to grasp the attractive woman by her shoulders. "Cassie—this is very, very important. Tomorrow, you must bring Daisy back to Granite Creek with you."

"Whatever for?"

He flashed the big, wide smile, exposing three gold-capped molars. "Why, to sign the contract, of course."

Her big eyes grew larger. "Can you have the document ready so soon?"

A dry laugh rattled in his throat. "Cassie, Cassie—has Nicky ever failed you?"

• • •

That evening, Nicholas Moxon dined alone. But not at home. He paid a call on his favorite Mexican restaurant, and on the way in picked up a complimentary copy of *Thrifty Shopper*, which consisted entirely of classified advertisements. After the waiter had taken his order, he began to examine the ads. He was of the opinion that a man could find just about anything he needed in the classifieds. Indeed, the headings covered a multitude of categories. Antiques. Computers. Employment. Guns. Pets. Real Estate. Transportation. And, of course, the lonely-hearts page. Men seeking Women. Women seeking Men. Men seeking . . . But never mind.

Mr. Moxon was seeking something else.

• • •

THIRTY-TWO
SATURDAY MORNING

The Buyer Goes Forth with Enthusiasm

Nicholas Moxon slipped out the back door of his modest home, strode down a graveled path that passed between his tool shed and a thick hedge, crossed the stream on a mossy pine log, and struck off to the south on a little-used National Forest hiking trail. Speaking to no one in particular, he said aloud, "What a glorious day!" And it was. Warm sunshine on the left side of his face, the air scented with a hint of lilac, a sweet promise of rain. And of course, birds sang. He clucked his tongue at frisky jays, warbled whistles at wrens, laughed at startled robins. Whatever his shortcomings, Cassandra's business manager knew how to enjoy life's small blessings. But on this morning, his greatest pleasure was derived from anticipating the whizbang adventure to come.

If he had expressed his philosophy in fewer than seven words, it might have been: Life Is What You Make It.

In due time, our energetic hiker arrived at his destination. After silently mouthing the name on the rusty mailbox, he removed the classified ad from his shirt pocket, read it again. Yes, this was definitely the place. And Hazel, in all her magnificent presence, was here. Waiting for him. He took a moment to admire her attractive form. There could be no question of false advertising; the brief description had not done the lady justice.

Checking his wristwatch, he murmured, "I've got some time to kill." For reasons known only to himself, this struck

Nicholas Moxon as funny. But though the disciplined man allowed himself a smile, he did not laugh out loud.

LET THE SELLER BEWARE

Clad in faded jeans and scuffed cowboy boots, Eddlethorp "Tiger" Pithkin was flat on his back in the sack, reading a tattered Wonder Woman comic book. (The unfortunate Mr. Pithkin was named after his father's favorite uncle—i.e., Uncle Eddlethorp. After years of being addressed as "Ed-dle" or "Pith" by his witty friends, he had assumed the formidable feline nickname.) Upon hearing the knock on the door of his immobile trailer home, Tiger addressed the statuesque Amazon from Paradise Island: "Who d'you suppose that could be?" After cogitating, the reader concluded that he would have to get his carcass off the lumpy mattress, go and see.

Our scholar was mildly startled to encounter a muscular man in crisply creased khaki slacks and a brand-new blue work shirt, both purchased late last evening at Wal-Mart. Though he could not see the eyes behind the wraparound shades, the mouth on the face under the slouch canvas hat was smiling. "Hi," it said.

Tiger grunted, scratched the Betty Boop tattoo on his hairy belly.

"I just happened to be out for a walk and saw your pickup." Nicholas Moxon jerked a thumb to indicate the fire-engine-red monster truck outfitted with five-foot-diameter tractor tires, and bumpers crafted from steel rails that had once supported coal-burning steam engines. HURRICANE HAZEL was painted on the hood. "I thought maybe I'd knock on your door—but if I'm disturbing you or your family, just say the word and—"

"Ain't got no family. Nobody lives here but me."

The grin widened. *That'll make things a lot simpler.* "That big, bad machine with the For Sale sign—what're you asking for it?"

"Hazel?" The owner, who loved to bargain, began the

game by spitting into a dandelion patch. "I don't see how I could let her go for less than six thousand."

Feigning doubt, Moxon hesitated. "I'm not sure I could handle anything that big." The potential buyer pretended to think it over for a moment, then: "But how about taking me for a ride?"

A listless shrug as Tiger tossed his comic book onto a plastic lawn chair. "Awright."

MEANWHILE

The thin blade of a woman (sheathed in a black satin dress) sat primly in Daisy Perika's Early American armchair, warmed her hands on a cup of Lipton tea.

The Ute elder was hunched in her rocker with a mug of black coffee.

The spotted cat was on the floor, just out of Daisy's reach.

The cozy picture suggested a get-together by a couple of good friends—a charming, down-home Norman Rockwell scene. And from the conversation, so it seemed.

Cassandra Spencer and Daisy chatted about the weather, and Sarah Frank's participation today in a church picnic, which led to the subject of the girl's black-and-white spotted feline pet, which led to a discussion of the pros and cons of having cats around the house, which brought up the subject of mice and other pesky rodents.

Neither broached the underlying issue that had prompted Daisy's telephone call, which had brought Cassandra to this arid wilderness of mesas and canyons on the sparsely populated eastern edge of the Southern Ute reservation. Sooner or later, the matter would have to be at least hinted at, but for now the women were engaged in a match of wits, each circling the other, warily bobbing and weaving, waiting for her opponent to make the first move.

Having brought along its mate so that the pretty twins might be united as soon as possible, Cassandra smiled at the matched pair nestled in the palm of her hand. "I am so grateful to you for returning my cameo earring." This sounded a bit awkward, almost as if she were accusing Daisy of theft. She added quickly, "It is so fortunate that you happened to see it on the carpet."

"That was lucky, I guess. If I hadn't spotted the thing, it might've gotten sucked up by the vacuum cleaner and tossed out with the trash." As the Ute elder rocked slowly in her chair, she seemed to be half asleep, but the sly old eyes did not miss a trick. "If I wasn't so old and forgetful, I'd have left it on your coffee table where you'd be sure to find it. But in all the excitement—what with you conking out before your show was over and me about to be on TV all by myself—I must've just dropped it in my pocket. I probably would've never thought about it again, but when I was looking for a thimble yesterday I put my hand in my pocket and there it was."

"Well, all I can say is bless you, Daisy!"

Daisy's lip curled. *No, you could say, "Here's a reward for finding my lost earring—a thousand dollars in cash money."*

Cassandra deftly clipped the antique ornaments onto her ears. "These were a gift from Nicky."

"And the matching pin."

The pale face frowned. "You know about the brooch?"

Daisy reminded the TV psychic: "You was wearing the pin and those earrings that day we met in the Sugar Bowl Restaurant. You told me Daddy Warbucks gave 'em to you."

"Oh, yes—I had quite forgotten about that." Cassandra found a compact in her purse, framed her pretty face in the oval mirror. Liked what she saw. "Daisy, I know you don't mean the least offense, but I suggest that when Nicky is present, you do not refer to him in that manner."

The old woman gave her guest a wide-eyed innocent look. "What manner?"

"As . . . as . . ." She simply could not bring herself to refer to Orphan Annie's well-heeled benefactor. "Nicky may strike you as a rather thick-skinned man. But I can assure you—he is quite sensitive about his baldness."

"Oh." Daisy almost smiled. "You figure he'd get all worked up if I called him Daddy Warbucks?"

A simple yes would have sufficed, but the television personality responded with pursed lips, a curt nod. Also a sniff. A very *superior* sniff.

Daisy shrugged. "Then I'll make sure not to." *If he does something to get my dander up, I'll just call him Cue Ball. Which raised a question:* "When am I likely to see Cue—uh—this Nicky fellow again?"

Taking advantage of this opening, Cassandra caught the elder with a solid left hook: "When you sign the contract." A demure smile. "I'm sorry—I suppose that sounds rather presumptuous. I should have said *if* you sign the contract."

This punch had stopped Daisy's clock. Also her rocking chair. "What contract?"

The elegant white woman let go an uppercut: "To do six consecutive appearances as the special guest on *Cassandra Sees.*"

The elder's teeth clicked together. "Six?"

Now, the blow that would stagger: "At five hundred dollars per appearance."

The frugal Ute woman was down for the count. Which amounted to quite a tidy sum. "That works out to three thousand dollars."

"And you'll be worth every penny." The middleweight from Granite Creek prepared her Sunday punch. "I don't suppose you're aware of it, but your first appearance produced our highest ratings ever."

Knockout. If this had been a cartoon, Daisy would have had Xes for eyes.

Though one does not wish to dwell upon the subject of gratuitous violence, it shall be mentioned that Kid Cassie was not above kicking a defeated opponent in the ribs. "The contract was Nicky's idea. I believe he's quite fond of you."

Daisy groaned. *Then I guess I shouldn't call him Cue Ball.* A significant concession. *Not out loud. But I can still think it.* "Did you bring the legal papers with you?"

"No." The psychic explained, "Nicky's attorney is drawing up the contract today, which stipulates that your first appearance is on tonight's show." Noting a sudden glint of alarm in the Indian woman's eyes, she hurried along before Daisy could protest: "You could stay with me tonight—I have my nicest guest bedroom prepared for you." Cassandra flashed her most charming, disarming smile. "Our viewers certainly wouldn't want to wait another week. I must get you back to Granite Creek no later than six P.M., so that you can sign on the dotted line—and we can go over the details of tonight's broadcast." The star of *Cassandra Sees* glanced at her platinum wristwatch (also a gift from Daddy Warbucks, aka Cue Ball). "So we must be leaving quite soon."

This was all happening too quickly. Daisy began to backpedal. "I don't know if I should leave this afternoon . . . any minute now Sarah'll be showing up in the church van. She'll want to tell me all about the picnic and—"

"Of course, if you're having second thoughts about doing the show, I'll understand." Cassandra snapped the oyster-shaped compact shut, dropped it into her black velvet purse. "The life of a television personality is not all wine and roses. At times, it can be stressful. Telephone calls from the media for interviews, people stopping you on the street, demanding autographs." A roll of the eyes. "Almost every time you look at a newspaper or open a magazine, seeing your photograph and reading stories about yourself that have hardly a word of truth in them." She surveyed the Ute woman's parlor, sighed. "I envy you this private, quiet environment. It must be so *peaceful* for you."

Daisy followed the white woman's gaze. *Peaceful like the grave.* She grunted her way up from the rocking chair. "I'll have to put a few things in my suitcase."

LITTLE ELKHORN PASS

An outraged mountain bluebird trilled a shrill warning at the monster truck. A curious chipmunk scurrying along through the undergrowth halted abruptly to perch on a juniper stump and stare at the alien machine. A collared lizard, only recently emerged from hibernation and unaware of the stealthy approach of a hungry wild turkey, threatened the mammoth vehicle with a bobbing display. Sad to report, Mr. *Crotaphytus Collaris* was promptly beaked and swallowed by said turkey, who, having not the least interest in motor vehicles, trotted away in search of additional victuals, thus leaving reconnaissance of the pickup to the chipmunk, bluebird, and others.

• • •

But enough of local fauna; let us focus our attention upon the truck.

Look. No, not at the weed-choked forest road. Over there—just behind that thicket of blue-black spruce. Right. Almost hidden in the underbrush: Hurricane Hazel.

Listen. One spark plug fouled by a crust of sooty carbon, her big engine idles at an unsteady throbbity-throb.

Peek inside the cab. See Tiger's corpse, knees almost touching his chin, imitating a hideously overgrown fetus. His twice-folded form is on the floor, wedged between the passenger seat, the firewall, and the door.

As befits the alpha male, Nicholas Moxon has taken his rightful place in the driver's seat.

• • •

Oblivious to the human being he had bludgeoned to death only minutes earlier, Moxon was enjoying this quiet time. He was, as nearly as a man of his sort can be, at peace. But do not be misled. Like Mr. Turner as he rolled down the mountain on that snowy night, Moxon's condition was the very opposite of that *peace of God which passeth all understanding.* What he basked in was that temporary, superficial, shadow of peace—the counterfeit version that this world offers, that is, all too often—merely the proverbial calm before the whirlwind cometh.

After reflecting upon his agenda, the TV star's business manager thought perhaps he should place a call to his client and see how things were going on her end. After two rings, he heard her voice murmur a hello. "Hello yourself, Cassie. Can you talk?"

"Yes."

"Everything all set?"

"Miss Daisy is in her bedroom, packing an overnight bag."

"Great. When do you leave for home sweet home in Granite Creek?"

"I really can't say—she's rather slow." A pause. "Will the contract be ready for signing this evening?"

"Even as we speak, I'm at my attorney's office. Mr. Boxman's secretary is printing out six copies."

"So many?"

"Hey, you know how lawyers are, Cassie." He grinned at the chipmunk on the stump. "Uh-oh, here she comes with the contracts. Gotta go." He made a kiss-kiss sound. "Catch you later, kid." Nicholas Moxon stuffed the charcoal Motorola Razr into his pocket, sighed. "Looks like I'll be doing nothing for a while." Which would be extremely tedious. He glanced at the corpse on the floor. "But I guess that won't bother you, pal."

• • •

THIRTY-THREE
THINGS GET DICEY

Charlie Moon had just passed the Welcome to Granite Creek sign when his cell phone warbled. He checked the caller ID. *That's who I thought it'd be.* "This is Mr. Moon's day off and he's gone hunting Bigfoots with Chief of Police Parris. You may leave a message after you listen to Arlo Guthrie sing the twenty-nine-minute version of 'Alice's Restaurant—' "

Scott Parris barked, "Don't mess with me, Charlie. When you get to the station, I'll be at the curb. Slow down just long enough for me to jump in."

The tribal investigator grinned. "You in that big a hurry to go hiking on Spencer Mountain?"

"Forget that."

"What—I don't get to tramp around in the forest looking for broken twigs? And scat? And huge lopsided paw prints?"

"Can it, Charlie. You'll see me on the street."

And Moon did. He slowed to a crawl, backing up traffic as Granite Creek's top cop—in three seconds flat—jerked the Expedition door open, launched his hefty frame into the passenger side of the Columbine flagship, slammed the door, and snapped the seat belt into place. "Drive."

Moon pulled away. "Where to?"

"Aunt Daisy's little house on the prairie."

"What for?"

"I need to have a conference with the lady." The chief of

police pointed an infrared remote-control device at an up-coming stoplight. The traffic signal responded to the stimulus, switching from red to green without pausing for yellow in between. "Put the pedal to the metal." *Hot damn—I always wanted to say that!*

The Ute depressed the accelerator, watched the speedometer needle sweep past forty. Then fifty. "What's this all about?"

"Get outta town—then we'll talk." Another thumbing of the IR remote control, another traffic light shifted from Stop to Go. And go was what they did, doing sixty-plus through a residential section. Bricked homes and shade trees zipped past. As he pondered about what was actually moving—Moon's gas guzzler or the scenery—Parris was reminded that Dr. Professor Einstein was one smart cookie. "Step on it, Charlie—let's break some laws."

Seventy-five. His friend's enthusiasm was infectious but Moon was not sure he wanted to catch this fever. On the long climb up Six Mile Mountain, where the left shoulder dropped off to that rippling, rocky stream for which both the county and the principal community were named, Moon leveled off at eighty. "Okay. We're outta town."

Scott Parris stared straight ahead. "There's been a big break in the case."

"What case?"

He shot his best friend a sour look. "That ain't funny."

Moon passed a Mayflower moving van. "Okay, what's the big break?"

To maintain some semblance of dignity, the chief of police allowed an entire two seconds to elapse before responding. "Remember that truck-stop shooting over on I-25—the one Cassie reported on her TV show *while it was happening*?"

The driver nodded. Such events tended to linger in the memory.

"State police have turned up an eyewitness who claims he saw the shooter. Even though the perp was wearing a hat, and had his coat collar pulled up to his chin, the helpful citizen picked Nicholas Moxon's homely mug out of a dozen other look-alikes."

"That's a nice break, all right." *But not like catching the shooter with a smoking pistol in his hand.* Moon was startled to catch a sudden whiff of gun smoke. He knew what was coming next. And it did—*that haunting sense that all the cartridges in his revolver were spent.* But that simply wasn't so. *I checked my sidearm before I left the Columbine.* As if from somewhere far away, he heard Scott Parris's voice.

". . . But without some supporting evidence, no DA in his right mind'll go for it." He added quickly, "Her or his right mind." Having been lectured by his two female officers, the curmudgeon had been trying mightily to develop a modicum of sensitivity to gender issues. "All we've got is one eyewitness who *says* he saw the shooter outside, at night, in dim light from the restaurant window. It's not half enough to get a conviction on."

The scent of gun smoke had vanished, along with the absurd fantasy that his .357 Magnum was filled with empty shells. In an effort to occupy his mind with something that was real, Moon rolled Parris's remarks over in his mind. Came up muddled. "Pard, can I ask a few questions?"

"Hey, you're a natural-born citizen of the good old US of A, and freedom of speech is your First Amendment right."

The Ute citizen posed query number one: "Seeing as how this lone eyewitness won't be able to make anything stick against Mr. Moxon—why are you so dang cheerful?"

"I am glad as all get-out you asked me that." Parris drew in a breath that threatened to rupture his barrel chest. "I am in good spirits—because I am going to bust this case wide open."

Query number two: "How are you going to do that?"

"By finding out how Moxon's been passing information about his ratings-boosting felonies to Cassandra Spencer— *while* she was on live TV."

Repeat of query number two: "How are you going to do that?"

The passenger shot a sly look at the driver. "Somebody is going to tell me."

The potential *somebody* did his one-hoot-owl imitation. "Who?"

Unaware of what his clever Indian friend had learned from watching DVDs of *Cassandra Sees,* the chief of police told him who. "If I lean on her, Cassie might talk." Parris squinted at a sudden spray of sunlight. "But I wouldn't bet on it."

"Me neither." Moon had put on the poker face. "So who does that leave?"

"Your aunt Daisy, who was sitting knee-to-knee with Cassie when our favorite TV psychic had that 'vision' about her brother-in-law's violent death. And I will lay you ten-to-one odds on this, Charlie—Moxon set up the accident, watched Turner's Corvette go tumbling over the cliff, and relayed the message to Cassie."

"How d'you figure he managed that?"

"Now that's the question, ain't it?"

"But you're hoping Daisy knows something—and that she's going to tell you?" *The Optimists' Club would elect you president. By acclamation.*

"She might've picked up on something, Charlie. As for getting her cooperation, I'll need some help from you."

"My friend, you overestimate my influence with the elderly relative." Now for the fun part. "But I think I might be able tell you a little something."

"About what?"

"How Moxon passes information to his client while she's on a live TV show."

Parris's eyes narrowed. "Has Daisy already told you something?"

"Nope. And don't take this the wrong way, but us real honest-to-goodness professional lawmen don't depend on common gossip for figuring things out."

"Right." Parris snorted. "So what've you 'figured out,' Sherlock Ute."

"Oh, nothing much." Moon paused just long enough to

annoy his passenger. "I had a few minutes to spare, so I watched some old *Cassandra Sees* TV shows."

The Granite Creek chief of police was hanging on every tantalizing word. "And?"

"And right off, I noticed that if you looked at close-ups of that spooky lady's eyes, you could see reflections."

"Reflections of what?"

"Oh, this and that. Anything shiny in her living room." Moon listed several such items that had been visible on Cassandra's corneas. He passed a gravel truck. "And there was this bright little rectangle on her eye. Applying my considerable knowledge of high-tech video recording equipment, I magnified it. Unless I'm mistaken, which I'm not, it was the TV monitor Miss Spencer keeps under her coffee table." The driver smiled at a dark cloud bank off to the south. "Nice day we're having."

"Cut the crap, Charlie. What'd you see on her TV?"

"Oh, lots of stuff." He glanced at his best friend. "Remember that big warehouse fire she reported in Denver?"

"Uh-huh. What about it?"

"Well, while she was talking about it on her show, she was looking at a live video of a fire on her under-the-table TV."

Parris made a long, low whistle. "So that's it. Moxon was transmitting digitized shots from the scene. Had to be by e-mail." *Oh, this is just dandy.* "Her PC video port must be patched into the TV monitor."

"Pictures wasn't all he was sending." The tribal investigator described alphanumeric banners that appeared on the psychic's TV monitor immediately before she had one of her visions. "Like the kind the TV stations use to report severe weather. Election results. Scores on big games."

Parris banged his fist on the car seat. "Charlie, that flat-out *nails* it!"

"So you won't need to talk to my aunt."

The pale face blushed. "Uh—I still need to pay a call on Daisy."

"What's the big hurry?"

"I'll explain later."

"Explain now."

"It's kind of complicated."

"Give me the executive summary."

"You want the dumbed-down version?"

"That'll do nicely."

"Okay." *But you'll get all upset.* "About an hour ago, when I got an alert from the state police about that eyewitness who'd fingered Moxon, me and three officers staked out his house. His car was parked in the driveway, so we figured he was inside. But just to be sure, I knocked on the front door."

"I'm guessing he wasn't home."

"Well if he was, he didn't answer the door. Or the telephone in his house."

Moon opted for a hopeful view: "It's a nice day. Maybe he went for a walk."

"You really believe that, I'll give you six-to-one the rooster's flown the coop."

The Ute did not like the odds. "You figure he got a tip?"

"Wouldn't surprise me. Moxon's got lots of political connections." Parris, who had a few such connections himself, occasionally toyed with the notion of running for public office. "But we'll find him. Cops in nine states are on the lookout."

Charlie Moon was beginning to feel uneasy. "But you figure maybe Moxon's got more on his mind than hiding. Maybe he's up to no good."

"It did cross my mind that if he got tipped about the so-so eyewitness, he might decide to eliminate the one person who could provide hard evidence against him."

"Please tell me you have Cassandra Spencer in protective custody."

"Uh . . . Cassie's not at home."

"Maybe she's with Moxon."

"I don't think so."

"Tell me why."

"For one thing, when Officer Martin spotted her leaving

town a couple of hours ago—this was before I got the call implicating Moxon in the trucker shooting—Cassie was alone in her Cadillac. Heading out of town."

"In which direction?"

"South."

Lots of destinations lay to the south. New Mexico. Old Mexico. Closer still, the Southern Ute reservation. "Pardner, tell me what's on your mind."

The beefy man clenched his hands together, making a fist big enough to KO a full-grown buffalo. "Charlie, an old pro like your aunt could spot a fake psychic a mile away. At midnight, in a heavy fog." A few heartbeats. "And after Cassie passed out during last Saturday's show, Daisy spent the rest of the hour sitting in the star's chair. Maybe the old lady saw something on the TV under the coffee table. And Moxon might've thought of that."

The driver was seeing the road miles ahead, far around the bend. "Which would put my aunt in the number-two spot on his hit list."

"That's about what the worry-stew boils down to."

Under the Ute's heavy foot, the accelerator was against the floor, the Ford V-8 churning out maximum horsepower, the speedometer at eighty-five and climbing.

As the big tires whined around a curve, the passenger clenched his teeth. "I'm in a hurry too. But there's no need to break the sound barrier." *Or my neck.*

"Tell me why."

"A little while before you hit town, I had the dispatcher put in a call to the state police and the Southern Ute PD, request immediate protection for Daisy. By now there'll be cops camped out around her house, thick as fleas on a sickly prairie dog. The old lady's safe as them stacks of gold bricks at Fort Knox."

"Mmm-hmm." *And "The check is in the mail." And "As I insert this hypodermic needle the size of a lead pencil into your spine, you may feel a slight discomfort." And "I'm from the government, and I'm here to help you." And "Trust me—"*

"Trust me on this, Charlie." A sharper curve. Now the tires *screamed*. "She'll be fine."

"Sure she will." Suddenly, like the snap-crack at the tip of a bull whip, it occurred to Charlie Moon that Sarah Frank should be home from the church picnic by now. "But just to ease my mind, call Daisy. Ask her to count those thick-as-fleas cops camped out around her home."

Parris's cell phone materialized in his hand. "Gimme her number."

THIRTY-FOUR
USE YOUR IMAGINATION

As Charlie Moon's Ford Expedition topped Six Mile Mountain, the church van dropped Sarah Frank off at Daisy's home. The skinny little girl was surprised to see the snazzy Cadillac parked in the front yard. *I wonder who's visiting us.* She soon found out. Wow! While receiving a perfunctory pat on the head from Miss Cassandra Spencer, she was brusquely informed by Daisy that "Soon as I get some things together, me and Cassie [first-name basis now] are going up to Granite Creek." Sarah's eyes popped as the psychic's new sidekick explained about the contract she would be signing. "And don't forget to watch us on the TV tonight. I won't be back till Sunday, but there's plenty of food in the house and you know how to take care of yourself."

Though quite grown-up for her age, Sarah had come dangerously close to whining as she pleaded, "Can't me and Mr. Zig-Zag come with you?"

Cassandra, who was fond of neither children nor cats, made no attempt to conceal her apprehension at this suggestion.

Reading Miss Spencer's face, Daisy was characteristically blunt. "No, you can't." And that was that.

More than a little miffed at not being invited along for the overnight trip, Sarah sulked. Neither of the women took any notice of her melancholy effort, so, in search of what small comforts life had to offer, the fifteen-year-old put Mr. Zig-Zag on her lap and a grape Popsicle into her mouth.

It so happened that when Daisy Perika's telephone rang, Sarah was sitting close to the instrument. She picked it up, spoke around the purple Popsicle. "Hebbo."

A gruff, familiar voice spoke into her ear. "Sarah—is that you?"

She removed the frozen obstacle. "Uh-huh."

"This is Charlie's buddy—Scott Parris. Is Aunt Daisy there?"

"Uh-huh."

"Good. Now listen close. I'm going to ask you something really important, but all I want is a yes or no. Don't mention any names. You got that?"

"Sure. I mean yes."

"Okay, now here's the question: Besides yourself and Daisy, is anybody else there?"

She considered the warm fluff of fur in her lap, decided Scott Parris probably did not consider cats as persons. Even so, the answer was: "Yes."

"Cops?"

This struck her as a peculiar question. "Uh—no."

Dammit! Charlie'll blow a gasket. "Okay. Now again, just yes or no." *Please, God—let the answer be no.* "Is Cassandra Spencer there?"

How did he know that? "Uh—yes."

Scott Parris felt a sharp look from Charlie Moon. "Anybody else there besides Cassandra?"

"No."

Thank you, God. He cupped his hand over the phone, said to Moon, "Moxon's not there." Back to the cell phone: "Sarah, can Cassandra hear what you're saying?"

"Yes." She watched the white woman get up from a chair, stride across the parlor. "Not now. She went into the kitchen."

"Good. Now tell me what she's doing there."

"I just got back from a picnic, so I don't know everything they've been talking about. But she's going to take Aunt Daisy to Granite Creek."

The chief of police shouted in her ear, "She's *what*?"

Duly startled, Sarah repeated her previous statement, added, "They'll be leaving in a few minutes. Daisy's going to be on her TV show tonight." *And I have to stay here and do my homework.* Major bummer.

"Is that a fact?"

Sarah watched Cassandra Spencer return with a glass of water. "Yes!"

Parris, who had never had a "way with children," shifted to his pedantic tone: "Sarah, when I say 'Is that a fact,' that's what we call a rhetorical question. Which means you don't need to answer it."

"Yeeessss!"

Realizing that she had reverted to the yes/no mode, he asked: "What is it—Cassandra back where she can hear you?"

"Yes."

"Okay. And if you don't mind me saying so, you're a pretty smart kid."

Sarah smiled. "Yes." *Yes I am.*

"Heh-heh. Now pay attention. Here's what I want you to do—get Daisy on the phone so I can tell her what's happening. But don't say my name out loud, because I don't want Cassandra to know it's me on the line."

The girl yelled. "Aunt Daisy—somebody wants to talk to you."

The old woman emerged from her bedroom with a battered suitcase. "Who?"

Sarah felt the psychic's stare. *I wonder if she can read my mind.* "Uh—he won't say."

"Then it's one of them pesky people who want to sell me something. Or a poll-taker that'll want to talk to me for thirty minutes, asking what I think about this or that." She set the suitcase down, headed for the bathroom. "Hang up on him!"

Sarah murmured into the telephone, "She said hang up on you."

"I heard her. Listen, kid—I don't have time to tell you

the whole story, but here's the bottom line—Cassandra is bad news. You get my drift?"

"Uh—yes." The Ute-Papago teenager dared not look at the white woman, who was sipping from the water glass. *I wonder what she did. Murdered somebody, probably. And cut up the body and burned all the pieces to cinders and buried them in her garden and—*

Parris's voice interrupted Sarah's lurid plotline: "Any minute now, some cops will show up, and me and Charlie will be there in about half an hour." *If he don't run this big car off the highway and wrap it around a telephone pole and kill both of us.* "But whatever happens, you've got to make sure that Charlie's aunt don't leave with Cassandra."

She lowered her voice to little more than a whisper: "How?"

"I don't know, kid—use your imagination!" A crackle of static. "We're going into a canyon, and my phone's losing signal. Do whatever you have to—me and Charlie Moon are counting on you!" This declaration was punctuated by a sizzle in her ear. The kind you hear when the fat is in the frying pan.

• • •

Keeping his eye on the center line, Charlie Moon said, "Fill me in on what I didn't hear."

Scott Parris summarized. Finished with: "Don't sweat it, Charlie. Daisy won't leave the place with Cassandra. Sarah's got the right stuff—she'll get the job done."

"You sure of that, are you?" *Like you were sure the place would be crawling with cops.*

"Sure I'm sure." The chief of police crossed his fingers. "One hundred percent."

• • •

Sarah Frank looked up to see Daisy emerge from the bathroom, watched the Ute elder hurry back to her bedroom muttering, "I'll need to take my blood pressure medicine. And my necklace of turquoise and jet beads."

Cassandra—evidently about to perform that last-minute

preparation for travel that is too delicate to mention—
entered Daisy's bathroom, closed the door.

The teenager stared blankly at the grape Popsicle. *Charlie Moon is counting on me!* How great inspirations come, and where from, one can only speculate. But in an instant, Sarah Frank knew what she had to do, how to do it, and got right to it.

THIRTY-FIVE
WHERE IS A COP WHEN YOU REALLY NEED HIM?

You know how it goes. Let's say it's mid-August. You're in the Audi, tooling along in middle of the Mojave Desert. You slow for that rusty Stop sign at the intersection, look left. Then right. All the way to the far horizon, not a vehicle in sight. You roll *almost* to a stop and then proceed— and who pulls out from behind the Last Chance for Gas for 99 Miles billboard? You know who. John Law, on his shiny black motorcycle. Do not attempt to reason with the no-nonsense officer behind the badge and plastic visor—this will annoy a fellow who's right at the ragged edge of heat-stroke and has an automatic pistol strapped to his hip. Write it off to experience, prepare your mind to pay the fine.

But when the services of a policeman are sorely required—such as at 2:45 A.M. when the three-hundred-pound maniac on crack cocaine is breaking through your bedroom window with a crowbar—you know where the cops will be. Elsewhere, that's where. But to be fair, these are very busy public servants, who—in addition to having to deal with endless paperwork, petty bureaucrats, substandard equipment, low pay, and the list goes on and on— have more than sufficient troubles of their own. Such as spouses who complain of long hours alone.

Consider a Case in Point: On his way to Daisy Perika's remote homestead, SUPD Officer Danny Bignight had blown a bald tire by Capote Lake, run off the highway, wreaked havoc upon an innocent cluster of aspen saplings. Only to discover that his radio was on the fritz and a $#&%$ $#&#% %&%#$! (thoughtless fellow officer!) had removed the spare tire from the trunk. Also the jack. And had not put them back.

Consider a second Case in Point: State policeman Elmer Jackson had been diverted by a DWI who, for obscure reasons known only to herself, had chosen to park her Avis rental car in a ditch just west of Pagosa Springs. The sophisticated lady behind the wheel had flung a one-liter wine bottle at the black cop's head. A *half-full* one-liter wine bottle, which had clipped him on the left ear. And though Officer Jackson may have been tempted, he had not strangled the inebriated citizen, who happened to be a prosperous psychologist from Los Angeles, California, whose PhD thesis title was: "The Breakdown of Civility in Post-Modern Society and Ancillary Effects upon the System of Criminal Justice." *Ancillary?*

After handing the mental-health professional over to a not-overjoyed Archuleta County sheriff's deputy, Officer E. Jackson (this was not his lucky day) happened to be the first to arrive on the scene. At Daisy Perika's residence, that is. The first thing that caught his eye was the sleek, black, 1957 Cadillac Eldorado Brougham sedan. The hood was up. A mismatched pair of women stood by the Detroit City machine, hands on hips, glaring darkly at the motor as if it had committed some despicable offense.

Cassandra inquired of her host what that policeman might be doing here.

"I don't have no idea." Daisy recognized the black lawman as one of her nephew's friends. "You'd be surprised how many oddballs drop by here."

Jackson donned his spiffy state-trooper hat, joined the ladies, peered under the hood. The means of locomotion, which looked much like any other fifty-year-old V-8 engine, provided no obvious clue. "Got some car trouble?"

Daisy Perika said to the state cop, "No, we're just a couple of grease monkeys, talking shop."

"Ha-ha!" Not only did sarcasm roll off Jackson like water off the oily mallard's back—he also enjoyed the experience.

Hoping for some expert help (all men could fix mechanical things, couldn't they?), Cassandra Spencer was more helpful: "It won't start."

"Aha," Jackson said. *Now we are getting somewhere. Probably a loose battery terminal.* "Won't turn over, huh?"

"I don't know." The white woman held up Exhibit One—a key chain with a lucky rabbit's foot and several brass keys affixed to it. "It was just fine on the drive down from Granite Creek. But now I can't get this into the little slot." In case he did not entirely get the picture, she made a jabbing motion with the ignition key and explained, "I push it and it won't go."

His cocked his head. "If your key won't go into the ignition switch, why are you lookin' at the engine?" Silly fellow—to ask such a question.

The wrinkled Ute elder and the pretty young white woman gave him looks that said it all: *When a car won't start, the first thing you do is lift the hood and take a look at the motor, to see if anything looks out of whack. Any dang fool knows that!*

Accepting this silent chastisement with characteristic grace, Elmer Jackson tried to think of a way to deal with the delicate situation. The guiding principle was that a policeman must never let on that he considered a member of the public to be less intelligent than a run-of-the-mill amoeba. While the hopeful diplomat was marshaling his thoughts, other brains were also hard at work. Cassandra Spencer's, for example.

The TV psychic had recently heard a statistic on National Public Radio (or had she read it in the *National Enquirer*?) to the effect that a significant percentage of all automobile failures could be blamed on a particularly troublesome component. Thus armed with authoritative knowledge, she spoke with some confidence: "I think I know why my key won't go into the little slot."

Officer Jackson encouraged the motorist to share her thoughts on the matter.

She did, and with some intensity: "I think it must be the radiator." *Whatever that is.*

After he had recovered from a sudden coughing fit, which was accompanied by copious watering of the eyes and mild abdominal pain, the gentleman regained his composure and admitted that in his time, he had experienced lots of trouble with radiators. He politely asked whether he might borrow the lady's car key and see what he could do.

Though lacking great expectations of help from what was evidently a mechanically challenged member of the hammer-and-wrench gender, Cassandra nevertheless rendered up the object.

Elmer Jackson, who had overhauled more than two dozen internal combustion engines, slipped inside the magnificently restored sedan. *Wow-wee, what a Jim-dandy automobile!* He inserted the ignition key into the "little slot." It went about halfway in, stopped. Now, in addition to being a better-than-average shade-tree mechanic, Mr. Jackson had, once upon a time, been an Eagle Scout, and Be Prepared was practically his middle name. He produced a much-used Swiss Army pocket knife, worked for a while with blade, then the nail file, but as is quite often the case it was the tweezers that did the trick. He extracted several wood splinters from the ignition switch. *Purple* wood splinters. In lieu of talking to himself, the state policeman sometimes preferred to whisper: "Now, how in blue blazes did *that* get in there." He considered a few unlikely possibilities, settled on: "I bet that white woman took something out of her purse, thinking it was her key, and jammed it into the ignition switch. One of them colored wooden toothpicks, maybe." A smile. "But you can bet your bottom dollar I ain't gonna ask her about it. No, sir—*my* momma didn't raise no fools!" By the time he had extracted not quite enough of the broken-off Popsicle stick to render the switch useable, SUPD Officer Danny Bignight had arrived, followed almost immediately by Charlie Moon and his passenger, Granite Creek Police Chief Scott Parris.

Cassandra was quite astonished at the sudden gathering of lawmen, and wondered what might have brought them to this out-of-the-way place. Did the old Indian woman dispense complimentary doughnuts to the local constabulary?

Daisy, who did not waste time in idle speculation, got right to the point: "What are all you cops doing here?"

Having taken note of the disabled Cadillac (the hood still gaped like an alligator's mouth) Charlie Moon tipped his black Stetson: "I don't know for sure, but my best guess is that we must've all picked up the same emergency call: Attractive lady motorist needs help at Daisy Perika's residence." He winked at Cassandra, who blushed rosy pink. "So here we are, to find out what's the matter with the snazzy car."

Officer Jackson laughed. "Well, you're too late—I ain't quite got it fixed yet, but I already got it figured out." He pocketed his pocket knife/tool kit. "There was some splinters of purple wood in the ignition switch."

Cassandra echoed, "Splinters of purple wood?" *How perfectly absurd.* She listened every week to Click and Clack the Tappit Brothers, and those clever *Car Talk* mechanics on NPR had never diagnosed an auto problem as caused by wood splinters. Purple or otherwise.

Scott Parris noticed that Sarah Frank had, at the appearance of Charlie Moon, emerged from Daisy's house. "Wonder how a thing like that could've happened."

The state policeman shook his head. "Beats me, Scott." But having four children and six grandchildren, and knowing what scamps young folks can be, he shot a mildly suspicious look at the teenager.

Ignoring both the black man and the white, the fifteen-year-old Ute-Papago girl smiled shyly at her favorite man on the entire planet. *You can always count on me, Charlie.* She could see that he was very pleased. If she had realized that for the first time ever, the object of her affection wanted to hug her, Sarah might well have fainted.

It was just as well that the orphaned teenager, who had

suffered many bitter disappointments, did not know that Charlie Moon was merely grateful for what she had done to prevent his aunt from being carted off by the TV psychic.

It was just as well that Charlie Moon, who had troubles enough, did not know that Sarah Frank was determined to marry him someday. Or the first chance she got. Whichever came first.

First chance she got, Sarah slipped Moon the broken Popsicle stick.

• • •

THIRTY-SIX
KEEPING SECRETS

Responding to a barely perceptible nod from the Southern Ute tribal investigator—the Granite Creek chief of police, the mechanically inclined state trooper, and SUPD cop Danny Bignight drifted off (casually, they thought) to convene a private conference.

Daisy Perika and Cassandra Spencer watched the withdrawal with justifiable misgivings.

The TV psychic, who was somewhat wrought up over the mysterious failure of her fine automobile, glared at the men through slitted lids, summed up the situation: "I need to go home but my car won't start because it still has purple wood in the little slot. And even if it would start, that state policeman is holding on to my keys. And what are they talking about—football?" A nagging suspicion: *Or does it have something to do with Nicky and me?*

The Ute elder puffed up, huffed a "Hmmpf!" that fell just short of a snort of the derisive sort. "Look at 'em—just like a bunch of half-wit boys huddled up in the school yard, trying to keep their dumb secrets from the girls." But this old girl had a few secrets of her own, which she did not intend to share with the "boys." Nifty secrets. Such as how the TV psychic managed to acquire astonishingly accurate information from her marvelous "visions." If Daisy had realized what her nephew already knew, she would have been too deflated to huff or puff.

Cassandra, of course, had a multitude of misdeeds to conceal.

The one bona fide girl in the female trio had her own delicious secret, which she had been more than happy to share with Charlie Moon. As the grown women glared at the quartet of lawmen, Sarah Frank had eyes only for the tribal investigator.

THE HUDDLE

The first order of business was for Charlie Moon to inform Danny Bignight and Elmer Jackson about Sarah and her Popsicle stick.

After all parties expressed admiration for the girl's on-the-spot innovation, Moon yielded to Scott Parris's urgings and admitted that he had found hard evidence on *Cassandra Sees* DVDs that the TV psychic was receiving detailed information about various felonies *while she was on the air.* These real-time accounts of murder and arson were almost certainly being transmitted to Cassandra by the felon responsible, which was most likely Nicholas Moxon.

After the Ute had had his say, Scott Parris assumed chairmanship of the improvised committee, counted off the essential facts of the matter on his fingers, beginning with the shortest digit (which tough guys such as himself refuse to call a "pinky"): "An eyewitness has tied Nicholas Moxon to the trucker shooting over on I-40." Second finger: "Big question is this—if Moxon has been engineering on-the-spot killings and arsons for his client to use on her TV show, does Cassandra Spencer know her business manager is up to no good, or does she believe he has a gift for being in the right place at the right time?" Parris figured that one might go either way. Third finger: "And whether the psychic's in on it or not, could Miss Spencer be convinced to provide corroborating evidence against her business manager?" The chief of the Granite Creek PD deftly turned down finger number four. "And if she doesn't cooperate, does the Huerfano County district attorney have enough evidence to make a case against Moxon?" He was about to go for the thumb when the black state policeman coughed. With his train of thought derailed, Parris eyed the man responsible for the wreckage. "What's on your mind, Elmer?"

"The witness is a friend of my brother, who tells me his buddy's a sure-enough solid citizen and if this guy says the shooter was Moxon, you can bank on it." His audience sensed that there was a "but" coming. "But the fella wouldn't be able to convince a jury that the earth was round."

Parris prepared to grind his teeth. "This witness has a flaw?"

The black cop looked at the ground. "He's a member of the Flat Earth Society."

Parris and Moon and Bignight stared.

They all entertained more or less the same thought, but it was Parris who said, in a pleading tone, "Elmer, *please* tell us you're joking."

"Wish I could." The state trooper shook his head. "And that ain't all. The trucker that got murdered was pushing dope up and down the interstate. Any defense attorney worth two bits wouldn't have any trouble convincing a jury that he got popped by a shooter working for a competing distributor. So Moxon walks." Elmer Jackson shrugged. "Happens all the time."

Parris glanced at the edgy psychic, who, presumably in a premeditated act of revenge against her cantankerous motor vehicle, was taking a kick at the Cadillac's whitewall tire. "Then the only way to make a case against Moxon is to get Cassandra to play ball." After pursuing this line of thought, he added, "We'd better get her on our team before the eyewitness to the trucker shooting gets interviewed on TV and warns his fellow citizens: 'Be careful, folks—take one step too far, you'll fall right off the edge of the earth.'"

Frowning at this "we" stuff, Officer Jackson reminded his colleagues of a relevant fact: "The trucker shooting happened in Huerfano County. While us state police will grab a piece of the action—you reservation and town cops don't have no jurisdiction."

SUPD Officer Danny Bignight, as was the peculiar habit of Taos Pueblo Indians when they had nothing to say, said nothing.

Which left it to the tribal investigator to speak for the Southern Ute Police Department. Moon grunted.

Knowing it was now up to him alone to deal with the feisty state copper, the Granite Creek chief of police regarded the black man with feigned disappointment. "Elmer, I think it's time we all started acting like brother lawmen and forgot about little details like who has jurisdiction and who gets the credit and all of that nonsense."

"Right." The state trooper allowed himself a lopsided grin. "Just like you did a few years back when that fruitcake Indian shot that little white fella in the antique shop and our boys was there right on the spot and you town cops treated us like we was the North Korean secret police."

Parris responded in a tone meant to soothe, "That unfortunate incident was a minor misunderstanding. And if I— or any of my officers—ruffled any state copper's tail feathers, I hereby apologize on behalf of all of us." Sensing a softening of Officer Jackson's demeanor, he continued, "I'm well aware that GCPD doesn't have any jurisdiction in a killing that happened out of our county. But the prime suspect and his client are citizens of Granite Creek, so I intend to do what I can to assist those who'll be leading the investigation." He swept his glance across their faces. "Fellas, if we don't cooperate on this, a cold-blooded murderer is likely to go free as the breeze."

Moon thought it might be helpful to focus the discussion. "What do you want to do right now?"

Parris offered his best friend a thankful expression. "I want to hitch a ride back to Granite Creek with Miss Spencer."

Elmer Jackson cocked his head as if the former Chicago cop were about to put even money on the Cubs to win the pennant. "You really think you can get that woman to spill her guts about Moxon?"

"I know it's a long shot." Parris glanced at the psychic again, who was having an intense discussion with Daisy Perika. "But, fellas, it's the only shot we got. Anybody here has a better notion, I'm ready to listen to it."

This offer produced a dismissive shrug from the state cop, a half smile on the Southern Ute tribal investigator's face, and nothing whatsoever from the taciturn Taos Pueblo native who was employed by SUPD.

But following his shrug, the doubtful state police officer posed still another question: "How're you gonna convince the lady—who's probably an accomplice to several felonies—to give the local chief of police a ride home?"

Parris's smile flashed across his face. "It'll all depend on you, Elmer."

Uh-oh, I don't like this. "Whatta you want from me?"

"Nothing much. All you have to do is pretend that you can't get those last few splinters of wood out of her ignition switch."

The wary African American had begun to see the light. "And after I fumble around for a while, Mr. Supercop from Granite Creek steps in and shows me how it's done, and bingo!—the engine cranks."

"I couldn't have put it better myself."

"But just getting her car started won't be enough of a deception—you'll hint that the Caddy is likely to conk out again and strand her out there somewhere on a lonely mountain road. Then she'll say, 'Oh my goodness, whatever shall I do?'"

Parris nodded. "That's what I'm counting on."

"Don't I know it." Elmer rolled his eyes. "You'll offer to ride along—just to make sure she gets home safe. And what with being impressed with your thoughtfulness and so-called mechanical skills and worried sick about another breakdown, she'll be relieved to have the likes of you along for the trip north."

Parris fairly beamed on the man. "Elmer, I don't care what your momma says—you are definitely not the dim bulb of the family." A hesitant pause. "Aside from making me a hero in the lady's eyes, there's just one more thing I need from you."

The eyes rolled again. "What?"

"I'll need to get those last few bits of Popsicle stick out of the ignition switch. So would you loan me your Swiss Army pocket knife?"

THE DECEPTION

Scott Parris's plan worked like a charm. Or, as Danny Bignight would say later, "Was slick as snail spit."

While the Granite Creek chief of police was performing the surgical removal of the remaining purple splinters from the wounded Cadillac, Charlie Moon took his aunt aside, informed her that there had been a change of plans. She was not going to Granite Creek with Cassandra. The Ute elder was about to inform her nephew that she was of age, and didn't need some big gourd head like him telling her what she wasn't going to do. But once in a blue moon, Mr. Moon got that granite-hard look in his eye. It was there now. Daisy limited herself to a surly, "Why?"

"A problem has come up."

Surly became outright gruff: "But I'm supposed to be on TV tonight."

The pitiless man shook his head.

Desperate, Daisy fell back on *reason*: "But I've already said I'd sign the contract tonight—at Cassie's home in Granite Creek!"

Aha! "What contract?"

His aunt explained the terms: Six appearances. Five hundred dollars per.

Moon explained the facts of life: Not today. No way.

During this family discussion, Scott Parris was not only granted permission to ride back to Granite Creek in Cassandra Spencer's Cadillac—he would also serve as the lady's chauffeur. When the television personality mentioned that Mrs. Perika would have plenty of room in the backseat, the Granite Creek chief of police informed the psychic (who should have known!) that they would be riding back alone.

When Cassandra opened her mouth to ask why, hesitated, clamped her lips shut—Parris knew he had her in the palm of his hand. Smug was what he was. *This'll be like shooting a fish in a barrel.* Pride goeth before the fall.

ELMER'S HUNCH

State Police Officer Elmer Jackson said his goodbyes to Moon, who was planning to spend some time with his aunt, and Bignight, who was waiting for orders from Moon, then left shortly after the departure of Scott Parris and Cassandra Spencer. Jackson had gotten out of bed before dawn, put in a long, tiring day. Officially, his shift had ended an hour and a half ago. Moreover, his back ached and his feet hurt. For all these excellent reasons, he was planning to head into Pagosa Springs and the heavily mortgaged redbrick ranch-style home where he hung his flat-brim hat. But as he drove away from Daisy's place, along the rutted lane, he got one of those odd *feelings* that experienced lawmen sometimes get. Like something was wrong, and maybe he should trail along behind Scott Parris. *At least for a few miles.* Or even all the way to Granite Creek. *Well that don't make any sense. What I need to do is go home and fix me something to eat and go to bed.*

But he could not shake the *feeling.*

I wouldn't get a wink of sleep for worrying about Scott. Against all common sense, the big-hearted lawman opted to tail the distinctive black 1957 Cadillac sedan. Doing it by the book, Elmer Jackson stayed a mile behind.

• • •

THIRTY-SEVEN
DEALING WITH AUNT DAISY

Like his father, SUPD cop Danny Bignight had a good nose for weather. Sensing the storm that was approaching, he wisely chose to remain outside.

• • •

As Charlie Moon entered his elderly relative's home, he removed his black workaday Stetson, placed it crown-down on a chair. (The sensible Indian did not put any stock in those cowboy sayings—*If you lay your hat brim-down, all your luck will spill out*—but even when it came to absurd *matukach* superstitions, he tended to exercise due prudence.)

Realizing that a lecture was coming, Daisy Perika seated herself on the couch. Folded her hands in her lap. Set her jaw.

Realizing that she was about to witness some entertaining family friction, Sarah Frank seated herself on an armchair that would provide an excellent view of the drama.

Realizing that it was time for his late-afternoon nap, Mr. Zig-Zag curled up on the hearth, enjoyed a toothy yawn, drifted off into a deep, untroubled feline sleep.

Realizing that he would have to handle this delicate situation *just right,* Charlie Moon seated himself across the maple coffee table from his aunt. He began by presenting a conciliatory smile. "I'm sorry you're not going to be on Cassandra's TV program tonight."

"No you're not! And don't show me that silly possum grin." Daisy jutted her chin. "Get on with what you've got to say."

The smile evaporated, his voice took on a flinty edge, cut right to the bone: "You've gotten yourself into some serious trouble."

Daisy face flushed hot. "*What* are you talking about?"

Ignoring her question, the lawman laid down the law: "Until some things get sorted out, you're going steer clear of Cassandra Spencer."

His aunt was angry enough to chew up nails and spit bullets. But once Charlie Moon got his mind set, arguing was a waste of time. On the other hand—*I'm lots smarter than he is.* The sly old woman consulted her vast inventory of Deceitful Ploys. She rejected Intimidation. *Mood he's in, a bolt of lightning wouldn't singe his skin.* She also passed on Heart Attack. *He'd see right through that.* But what about a scaled-down version of the Big Diversion. Yes, that might just do the trick.

Interpreting her thoughtful silence as a sign of remorse, Moon thought perhaps a bare-bones explanation was called for. "Miss Spencer has a business manager—fellow by the name of Nicholas Moxon. And this Moxon—"

Sensing an opportunity, Daisy interrupted, "You talking about Cue Ball?"

Moon's brow had every right to furrow, and did. "Who?"

Pleased that this distraction was showing some promise, Daisy pressed her advantage: "Cassie didn't like me calling that bald white man Daddy Warbucks, so now I call him Cue Ball." Even when people made petty demands, Daisy was always willing to go the extra mile.

"How do you come to know Cue—uh, Moxon?"

Daisy shrugged. "Oh, I ran into him and Cassie at a restaurant in Granite Creek." She frowned. "It was the Sugar Bowl. They have stale doughnuts and a waitress that likes to tell tales." To further confuse her inquisitor, she enlarged on the theme: "That was on the same day I tried out a coffin at the funeral home across the street and scared that money-grubbing little white boy and his uppity momma who come to look at me and thought I was a corpse."

Sarah Frank clamped a hand across her mouth, barely suppressed a giggle.

Oblivious to the comedic effects of her impromptu performance, the seasoned actor was recalling further details. "And while I was in the restaurant, having me a doughnut, I saw those dead people riding by on a motorcycle." With a shudder, she said, "They was dripping with blood."

Charlie Moon stared at the unpredictable woman. *Trying out a coffin—dead people on a motorcycle? Maybe she's getting too old to understand what I'm talking about.* It occurred to him that there was a more likely explanation: *Or maybe that's what she wants me to think. Sure.* The old lady was trying to flummox him. And doing a fair job of it. "You can tell me about your adventures some other time. Right now, you'd best listen to what I've got to say." He commenced to say it: "Nicholas Moxon and Cassandra Spencer are up to their ears in serious crime. First-degree arson for sure. Probably even murder."

Daisy blinked at her nephew.

Now I've got her attention. "There's a good chance they'll both end up behind bars."

Her voice was barely above a whisper. "Even if that's true—what does it have to do with me?"

This was precisely the question Moon wanted to answer. "The hard proof the DA needs revolves around how Moxon transmits information to his client—while she's on live TV." He paused for a few heartbeats. "And I think you know how it's done." He saw the flash of alarm in Daisy's eyes. *Aha!*

To avoiding his penetrating gaze, the tribal elder proceeded to examine the backs of her hands. The familiar surfaces, cross-corded with dark veins, occupied her entire attention.

Moon leaned toward his relative. "Well?"

It seemed that the old woman with the acid tongue had finally lost the power of speech. Not so. Daisy was busy thinking. *I could just tell Charlie what I found out.* For a moment, she seriously considered a full confession. *No, I won't.* Put it down to stubbornness. *I don't have to say a word if I don't want to.* And pride. *Now and then it feels good to know more about something important than Smarty Mr. High Pockets.* And a faint, lingering hope for fame. *If all this stuff about Cue Ball and Cassie doing bad things turns out to be a mistake, I might still get to be on her TV show.*

It was true that her nephew suspected more than he knew, but he knew how to do two plus two and come up with an alarming result. By Charlie Moon's sinister calculation, the summing went something like this: Start with the chicanery between Moxon and the psychic, add to that Daisy's under-Cassandra's-coffee-table image on the DVD, plus the windfall TV contract—the bottom line was blackmail. The even-tempered man was as close as he had ever been to being flat-out angry with his elderly relative. He did not raise his voice, nor did he scowl at Daisy's downcast face. He spoke softly, but the suppressed rage smoldering in the man's dark eyes frightened Sarah Frank.

Moon addressed his recalcitrant aunt: "You found out how Cassandra pulls off her 'vision' stunt. And if you didn't use that information to pressure the shady lady into giving you what you wanted—which was more time on her TV show—then look me straight in the eye and tell me so."

It took considerable courage, but, as the old saying goes, Daisy Perika had plenty of grit in her craw. She raised her face, met his hard gaze. Not a word passed her lips, but Daisy's impertinent glare seemed to say, *So what if I did?*

Moon responded to the unspoken question with hard words that struck Daisy like hammer blows: "Think about this. If Mr. Moxon is the sort of man who'd murder a complete stranger just to promote his client's career, do you think he'd think twice about doing the same to somebody who knows about his scam?" The tribal investigator shot a glance at Sarah. "Or someone who happened to be with you when he showed up?"

Having had just about enough from Gourd Head, Daisy shook a finger in her nephew's face. "You listen to me—I was taking care of myself a long, long time before you was born into this world." She pointed the finger at the Ute-Papago orphan. "And I can take care of Sarah, too."

Realizing that he might as well be talking to a fence post, and afraid he might say something he would regret for the rest of his days, Charlie Moon got up, jammed the black Stetson down to his ears, stalked to the nearest exit.

Expecting a door slam that would rattle windowpanes and shake dust off the rafters, Sarah Frank closed her eyes, clenched her teeth, scrunched up her thin shoulders.

Observing the tensed-up girl, Daisy offered this reassurance: "Charlie Moon don't make noise when he's mad. He gets real quiet."

It was true. As the door closed, they did not even hear a click of the latch.

Outside, Moon paused to cool off, took several deep breaths of the crisp, sage-scented air. He addressed Officer Bignight, who was leaning against his SUPD unit. "I'll talk to Chief of Police Whitehorse and get things set up so my aunt and the girl are guarded around the clock until Moxon's picked up. But in the meantime, *please* don't let either one of 'em out of your sight."

The Taos Pueblo man rested his right hand on the grip of a holstered Glock 9-mm automatic, nodded. "I'll look after 'em, Charlie."

"Thanks, Danny." At this moment, another SUPD unit appeared on the lane. Two officers were inside. The Ute police vehicle was followed by an Archuleta County Sheriff's van. The troops Parris had called for were finally here. Daisy and Sarah's safety was no longer in doubt. Moon removed a cell phone from his inside jacket pocket, pressed the buttons for Scott Parris's programmed number. One ring. *Pick it up.* Three rings. *Answer!* After four more rings, he got his best friend's voice mail. *He must have the thing turned off.*

• • •

THIRTY-EIGHT
DRIVING THE LADY HOME

As the long ribbon of blacktop slipped under the Cadillac, Scott Parris was in the driver's seat. But despite his confidence, the chief of police was not quite in the catbird seat.

Cassandra Spencer was at his elbow, arms folded, looking straight ahead. Since being informed that Daisy Perika was not coming along for the ride to Granite Creek, the professional psychic had not uttered a solitary word.

Now and then, Parris would steal a glance at the attractive woman. *Even a dope would know something's up.* Despite her deficiencies, Cassandra had an IQ of 132. *Well, I might as well get this over with.* Realizing that the conversation might take a while, he slowed to fifty-five. "We need to talk."

"About what?"

"Nicholas Moxon."

"You talk. I'll listen." She brushed a raven lock away from her left ear.

Okay. Here goes. Deep breath. "When's the last time you saw your business manager?"

Her chin rose in a defiant gesture. "I cannot see why that is any of your business"

"Humor me." Parris turned his head long enough to flash a smile. "I'm a curious sort of fellow."

"I was with Nicky yesterday afternoon." She made a fist of her right hand, pretended to inspect her manicure. "We were discussing the fact that Daisy Perika's guest appearance produced a huge spike in the ratings. It was a no-brainer that we should bring her back."

"And you haven't heard from Moxon since?"

"On the contrary. While I was at Daisy's home, Nicky called on my cell phone."

Now we're getting somewhere. "What time was that?"

"I did not look at my watch." A shrug. "An hour or two ago, I suppose."

"Where was Moxon when he called you?"

"Oh." Frowny-eyed pause. "Let me think." Longer frowny-eyed pause, accompanied by a tapping of fingertip against lower lip. "Nicky was with an attorney."

That figures. The bastard's been tipped that the state cops are looking for him on a homicide rap, and he's already hired himself a lawyer! "This attorney—anybody I know?"

"I imagine so. Nicky was at Mr. Boxman's office. He handles all the legal issues for the television show. And if you must know, he and Nicky were working on a contract for Daisy's future appearances, which will involve a fee."

Parris knew Roderick Boxman quite well. The highly respected, semiretired attorney dealt with the occasional will or contract. But not criminal cases. And Boxman's office was in his home, which was only a couple of blocks from Moxon's house. *Maybe Moxon walked over to the lawyer's office to help hammer out the contract. If that's where he's been all day, then he doesn't know we're looking for him.*

Cassandra kicked off her shoes, put her long, silk-stockinged legs onto the seat, hugged her knees. "Why are you asking me all these questions about Nicky?"

"Ahh . . . maybe to pass the time of day."

"Right." Her lips curled in a smirk. "Now tell me what this all about."

Parris had a choice to make. He decided to give it to her straight. "Mr. Moxon is what we refer to as a 'person of interest.' State police would like to have a talk with him."

The smirk slipped off her face. "About what?"

"A homicide." After a suitable pause, he added, "He's the suspect."

She blinked. "You must be joking."

"Not a chance. There's nothing funny about gunning a man down."

"Who?" She shook her head. "I mean who is Nicky supposed to have . . ." She could not get the word out of her mouth.

"You remember that *vision* you had during your TV show—the one where the fella at the truck-stop lunch counter got shot in the back?"

Cassandra felt her head nodding.

"The Huerfano County Sheriff's Office and the state police have interviewed an eyewitness to the shooting." *An eyewitness who doesn't believe the earth is round.* "This citizen is ready to testify in a court of law that he saw Mr. Nicholas Moxon pull the trigger."

"That is totally absurd!" As if she had caught a sudden chill, Cassandra was trembling. "Nicky is not a murderer!"

Parris approached a huge RV with Florida plates. "If Moxon didn't shoot the trucker, he's got nothing to worry about." He passed the motorized behemoth. "And if he's not in serious trouble, neither are you."

Her face blanched. "What do you mean by that?"

As if he had not heard her, the chief of police watched the RV recede in the rearview mirror. Dead silence is potent stuff.

When she posed the next question, the elegant brunette's manner was wary, suggesting a sleek, black cat stepping her way across a rushing stream on slippery, wet stones. "This shooting—what could it possibly have to do with me?"

"Don't bother playing dumb, Cassie." His pale face was like marble. "Your business manager's number one job is to take care of his client. One way Moxon does that is by providing you with information about breaking news while you're on the air."

"If you're daring to suggest that I would—"

"Moxon's been feeding you hot news for months. It's a fact and you know it, and I know it."

"What, precisely, is it that you 'know'?"

Time to lower the boom. "For just one thing—I know about that TV monitor in your parlor." *Thanks to good ol' Charlie Moon.* "The one under your coffee table."

The psychic opened her mouth. Started to say something. Shut it.

"I also know that Moxon was *making* bad things happen."

Cassandra found her voice. "That is an absolutely outrageous charge. I cannot believe Nicky would commit an act of violence."

"Believe whatever you want, but your business partner's responsible for at least one murder, probably three. Plus two counts of felony arson. And he's going down for it." Parris slowed for a half-dozen deer that were crossing the road, chose his next words with particular care: "Which, if you knew what he was up to, makes you an accomplice."

"Well I certainly did not—*do* not know of any such thing!"

Parris watched a six-point buck lead his harem into the underbrush.

She reached over to touch his sleeve. "Scott—I swear on my mother's grave—Nicky never tells me anything about what he's doing." She took a deep breath. "You've got to believe me!"

"What I believe don't matter. You—more likely your lawyer—will have to convince the Huerfano County DA you're not involved in Moxon's felonious activities. My job is to make sure you live long enough to have your say."

"Are you suggesting that my life is in danger?"

"Use your head, Cassie. All the DA needs to put the rope around Moxon's neck—figuratively speaking—is a witness who can testify as to how he was passing information about the trucker shooting to you while you were on the air—*at the same time the victim was shot.*" He waited for that to sink in, then: "If I was in Mr. Moxon's shoes, I'd be awfully worried about Miss Cassandra Spencer telling the authorities what she knows." An Elk Crossing sign flashed by. "And I'd be tempted to make sure she didn't."

There was a taut-as-a-banjo-string silence before she replied, "I know quite well how the police use every means imaginable to intimidate innocent people. But it is quite pointless, attempting to frighten me."

"Well, I gave it my best shot." *And I've pretty much shot my wad.* But then he had a tantalizing thought: "You're bound to have Moxon's cell number. Why don't you give him a call."

Her words lashed out at him: "And tell him what—that you have accused him of murder?"

Parris realized that once again, his big mouth had gotten ahead of his brain. *If Moxon don't know about the eyewitness that's fingered him for the trucker shooting, Cassie spilling the beans could mess things up proper.* But the chief of police had started this dangerous game, and was committed to play it till someone made the final score. "It don't matter a particle to me what you two chat about. The weather. County politics. The price of crystal balls in Rumania." He managed a weak grin. "As long as you find out where he's at."

Cassandra Spencer hesitated, then shot the cop a venomous look. "Very well, I will do just that."

THIRTY-NINE
SUSPICION

As he stared at the caller ID on his cell phone, Nicholas Moxon was mildly surprised. *Cassie should be on the way back to Granite Creek. Why would she be calling me now?* There could be a hundred reasons, ninety-nine of them of no great importance. He was tempted to answer, but thought it best not to. *If and when I want to talk to the silly bitch, I'll do the calling.*

• • •

After ten rings, Cassandra Spencer got Moxon's voice mail. *That's odd. Nicky always answers his cell phone.* She decided against leaving a message.

Scott Parris took another risk. "You could give Rod Boxman a call—maybe Moxon's still there." *But if he is, please don't tell him you're with me.* He crossed his fingers. Mentally, so she could not see.

The well-organized lady also had the attorney's number stored in her telephone.

Mr. Boxman answered on the second ring. "Hello, Cassie—how in the world are you?"

"I'm fine. But I need to get in touch with Nicky. I assume he's not still with you, but do you have any idea where he might have gone after he left your office this afternoon?"

After a momentary silence, the kindly gentleman's voice said in her ear, "I have not seen Nicholas Moxon for almost a month."

Her hands turned cold and clammy. "But surely he called you yesterday or this morning, about preparing a contract."

"No, he did not." A small, sad sigh. "Perhaps he has seen fit to consult with another attorney."

The psychic—who was having an off day—did not pick up on Mr. Boxman's feelings, and provided a reply that was insensitive to his professional self-esteem: "Another attorney? Yes, that must be it." After exchanging a curt goodbye, Cassandra returned the phone to her purse. *What is going on?* Deep, deep down, she knew.

His gambit having paid off big-time, Parris relaxed his white-knuckle grip on the steering wheel. "So Moxon didn't pay a call on his lawyer today?" He feigned a puzzled expression, shook his head. "Now why would a man lie to his client about a little thing like that?" Another brothy question was beginning to simmer in his mind: *If the contract story was bogus, why did he send Cassandra to bring Daisy to Granite Creek?* If Moxon merely intended to drop out of sight, why not drive into Denver, leave his car in one of those umpteen-acre mall parking lots, take a taxi to the airport, a plane to some distant destination. But Moxon had left his wheels at home. Which raised two important questions: (1) *What's he using for transportation?* and (2) *Where is the guy?*

• • •

Proper questions have answers. In this case: (1) humongous big pickup truck; (2) not very far north of the black 1957 Cadillac, approximately a hundred yards off the paved road.

Nicholas Moxon was manning his post behind Hurricane Hazel's steering wheel, the corpse of the truck's owner curled up near his feet. He had removed a fine pair of 1940s-era German military binoculars from his knapsack, focused the precision optics on the highway that snaked along below the wooded ridge where the monster truck was concealed from passing traffic. In the slant of the late-afternoon sun, he saw a small flash of silvery chrome bumper and glistening black tail fins. His smile exposed a display of well-kept teeth, some capped with Mexican gold crowns. He whispered past his precious-metal bicuspids, "Here she comes."

• • •

Hanging out of sight behind the 1957 Cadillac, Officer Elmer Jackson was bone-tired, hungry enough to eat a triple burger and double-size fries, and feeling more than a little foolish. *I don't know why I thought I should ride rear guard for Scott Parris.* He glanced at his wristwatch. *But we'll be in Granite Creek in a few minutes, so I might as well follow him all the way there before I turn around and head for home.* Home. Such a happy word. It seemed so very far away. It was not.

• • •

From his high perch on the east side of the highway, Nicholas Moxon could not see the occupant of the driver's seat; only the passenger side was visible. He had expected to see Daisy Perika seated next to the driver. What he saw instead was his young, attractive client. *What's Cassie doing on the passenger side? Where's the old Indian woman? Who's doing the driving?* Even for a man of Nicholas Moxon's mental capacity, three questions at once were a bit too much to deal with, so he summed them up succinctly: *What the hell is going on?*

As he pondered this conundrum, the venerable Cadillac passed from view.

And then, tagging along a mile behind Cassandra's sleek black automobile, Moxon spotted the state-police unit. *Uh-oh.* What was this—a tail or an escort? Which raised an earlier question: *Why was Cassie calling me on my cell phone?* This turn of events was perplexing. *Okay, I'll start with what I know.*

Number one: *Somebody else is driving Cassie's car. And she never, ever lets anybody drive her daddy's '57 Caddy. Not even me. Which means something is wrong here.*

Number two. *Cassie's got a cop on her tail.*

Adding up one and two, what he got was: *Somehow or*

*other, the cops have got something on me. Could be the fire
in that south-Denver warehouse. Or that fat tourist I
pushed into the river. Or the trucker I shot over on I-25.
And when they couldn't find me, the cops picked up Cassie,
hoping to pump her for information. And that probably
happened after I called her at the Indian woman's house.*
Which brought him back to the psychic's telephone call a
few minutes ago. *And now Cassie calls me from her car,
which somebody is driving for her, and while she's being
escorted by a state copper.* The critical question was *why*
had she called. *Most likely, she's working with the cops.
Trying to find out where I'm at.*

There was another possibility: *Or, Cassie might be trying to warn me that I'm in big trouble.*

Hmmm.

*Either way, I ought to get rolling away from here while
the getting's good.* But not without knowing what his client
was up to. Moxon picked up his cell phone. Dialed Cassandra's number.

• • •

The psychic's slim pink telephone was programmed to
play a few bars of "Jingle Bells" when Moxon called. Yes,
"*Jingle Bells.*" Go figure.

Scott Parris asked his passenger who was calling. *Santa
Claus?*

Cassandra: "It's *him!*"

The cop did not need to ask who "him" was.

Second Jingle Bell.

Cassandra waggled the instrument at her chauffeur.
"What should I do?"

"Answer it."

"What should I say?"

Third Jingle Bell.

Charlie Moon's best friend effected a nonchalant
shrug. "Say 'hello.' Then let him do the talking." After a
hopeful afterthought, he added, "But if you can work it
into the conversation, ask him where he is." *Fat chance
he'll tell you.*

"But if I cross Nicky, he might *kill* me."

Fourth Jingle Bell.

She's admitted he's a killer. This witness was in the bag! "Don't worry about Mr. Moxon. You're under police protection." Parris's smile was all over his face. "And if you help the DA put your business partner away, you'll be in the clear."

Fifth Jingle Bell.

• • •

Nicholas Moxon heard the familiar voice in his ear.

"Hello, Nicky."

"Hello yourself, babe. How's it going?"

"Oh, fine."

You don't sound fine. "You back in town yet?"

"Not quite. I just crossed over Little Elkhorn Pass."

That was perfectly accurate. "How's the old Indian gal doing—excited about being on the show tonight?"

"I hate to tell you this, but she's not coming. Changed her mind at the last minute. Something about an upset stomach."

So far, so good. "Sorry to hear that."

"Yes, it's too bad." Cassie gathered up all her courage. "Especially after you went to the trouble to have Mr. Boxman draw up the contract."

"Ah—that's no big deal. We'll change a couple of lines, specify a new schedule. Granny'll probably be up to doing the show next week." Moxon watched the state-police car disappear from sight. "I hope you're not too lonely, driving back all by yourself."

The was a slight pause before the psychic responded. "Oh, no. I enjoy driving alone. It gives me some quiet time." *You no-good, lying lowlife bastard!*

"Yeah, I know what you mean." *It's a trap. You've sold me out.*

"Will I see you before the show?"

"You can count on it." Moxon's grin split his face. "Drive carefully."

"I will."

"Goodbye, Cassie."

• • •

Scott Parris glanced at his passenger. "Well?"

Cassandra's tone, like her expression, was flat. "He said he'd see me before the show."

"That's great." *I guess.*

"But it was rather strange. . . ."

"How so?"

"I've known Nicky for years. I'm familiar with all of his little habits." A hint of a smile played with her lips. "Like whenever we finish talking on the phone, he always says something like 'Catch you later, kid' or 'See you tomorrow.'"

"So?"

"This time he said 'goodbye.'" She could not suppress a shivery shudder. *Nicky knows.*

So it's goodbye, is it? Parris cursed his bad luck. *Moxon won't keep his appointment with Cassie. The bastard's gonna make a run for it.*

The chief of police was right, and wrong.

Also wrong, and right.

• • •

Nicholas Moxon cranked the V-8 engine to a throaty rumble, put the comically oversized pickup into reverse. As he backed the hijacked vehicle out of the thicket and onto the forest road, the machine flattened a clone of aspens with snow-white trunks as thick as his wrist. Oblivious to the unfortunate fate of a few innocent, teenage trees, the driver glanced down at his inert passenger, grinned. "Hang on, Tiger—you and me are about to go for the ride of our lives—I hope you're game for it."

The mortal residue of Eddlethorp "Tiger" Pithkin voiced no objection. His lifeless face was a dusky blue, the smoky hue of an antique apothecary bottle discarded after all the snake oil was used up. The glassy eyes stared blankly at whatever it may be that dead men see.

• • •

FORTY
A COP'S EPIPHANY

Scott Parris was pursuing a dangerous activity. Thinking. *Cassie's scared of Moxon and scared of ending up behind the walls. Now's the time—I've got to strike while the iron is hot.* The village blacksmith raised his five-pound hammer. *Bam!* "Moxon never showed up at the attorney's office—he *lied* to you, Cassie."

"Yes," Cassandra Spencer murmured. "He certainly did."

Far from being a hot iron, the potential star witness was cool. No, make that cold. Parris's frown deepened. *Cold as a well-digger's butt.* Yes, butt. With a lady present, he watched his thought-language. He was about to make the point that every minute Cassandra hesitated to help the authorities nail her business manager, the guiltier she would look. *Now* was the time to make the righteous choice. But just as the chief of police opened his mouth to speak, the object of his verbal assault posed a question of her own.

"But *why* did Nicky lie to me about being with Mr. Boxman?"

It occurred to Parris that she had raised an interesting point. Which suggested another one: Why had Moxon bothered to call Cassandra when she was at Daisy Perika's home—and again a couple of minutes ago? Under ordinary circumstances, the answer would simply be that he was in the habit of checking on his client when she was on the road, by herself. And since Daisy was supposed to appear on the psychic's TV show tonight, why hadn't Moxon directed Boxman to prepare the contract for the Ute elder's signature?

The answer was suddenly, blindly obvious.

Whatever Moxon's plan is—it doesn't include Daisy being on Cassie's show. Or signing a contract. Or showing up in Granite Creek! His thoughts hurried forward. *How would he prevent that from happening?* Parris imagined himself in Moxon's shoes. *He'd do it on the road. At some lonely spot.* Mentally, so as not to alarm his passenger, Parris dope-slapped himself on the forehead. *Like right here.* The skin on his neck prickled. Which settled the issue. High probability was transformed to dead certainty. His gaze darted left and right. *Moxon could be somewhere up there on the mountain, with a rifle. He might have us in the crosshairs right now.* The policeman knew his duty and was perfectly willing to do whatever was necessary to protect his passenger, but he felt only a slight reassurance from the cold, hard presence of the Smith & Wesson .38 Special snugged into the holster under his left arm. Unaware of the state-police unit a mile behind him, he came to a sensible decision: *I'll call for some backup.* As they entered a steep-walled canyon, the chief of police removed the cell phone from his pocket. Turned it on. Watched the readout. Got the dreaded message: OUT OF RANGE.

THE REAL MCCOY

As Scott Parris fiddled with the useless cell phone, the professional psychic slipped into a genuine *altered state of consciousness.* These inexplicable experiences, which occurred perhaps three or four times in a year, were the basis of her chosen vocation.

Having more than sufficient issues to keep his mind occupied, the lawman took no notice of Cassandra's silence, her glazed, glassy stare. If he had, Parris would have not been alarmed. From his reference point, she was only "away" for a few heartbeats.

Cassandra Spencer blinked twice; her lithe body quivered in a minor spasm. She was back from *wherever. Whenever.* Her face had never been so pale, her soul so filled with fear. But Miss Spencer knew what she had to do. Clenching her hands, she said his name aloud: "Scott . . ."

The driver kept his gaze glued to the road. "What?"

She drew in a deep breath. "I have seen the future."

A hard line to follow, this. The best he could do was: "Is that so?"

The lady pursued her semimonolog. "I am going to die."

Parris set his jaw. "Sure you are. So'm I. But not tonight."

The psychic echoed herself: "I am going to die." *Very soon.*

"Don't worry about Moxon." He shot her a stern look, said with more confidence than he felt, "You're under my protection."

She seemed not to hear. "I wish to make a full confession." *For the sake of my soul.*

Hardly able to believe his good fortune, the chief of police managed to keep from grinning. And understanding the fragility of the moment, said not a word.

Cassandra did the talking. She spoke of many things. But not of cabbages and kings. The TV psychic spun a sordid tale, detailing precisely how Nicholas Moxon had communicated sensational events to the star of *Cassandra Sees* while she was on the air. It was, she explained, really quite straightforward. "For voice communication Nicky would call me on his BlackBerry." Each of her earrings (for redundancy) concealed a microminiaturized receive-only cellular telephone. Twice, as the technology advanced, the resourceful man had provided his client with a new, improved set—most recently, a lovely pair of cameos. But the general operation remained the same. To alert the psychic, the ornaments on both earlobes would vibrate. One buzz indicated that Moxon was about to speak to her. Two buzzes would direct her to video data about to be transmitted. "Nicky used his BlackBerry or laptop to send pictures to my computer, which was routed to the TV monitor under my coffee table." The scam had produced sensational program content. But the occasional report of a plane crash or an assassination that Moxon picked up off the Internet during the show was not enough to sate her audience's increasingly voracious appetite. It became "necessary" for her business manager to generate sensational items by direct action. And once he crossed that line, there was no turning back. Convinced that she had no time to waste, Cassandra passed quickly over the arsons. The repentant TV personality went directly to the killings. The victims, she informed her audience of one, were citizens who would not be missed. Nicky had assured her of this, and subsequent media reports had verified his claims. One of the lowlifes was a car thief, another a known child molester who had moved into a nice south-Denver neighborhood—just across the street from an elementary school! And the so-called trucker Nicky shot dead was a loathsome drug pusher. Surely his removal had been a service to society. Even so, Cassandra admitted that she did feel some guilt in exploiting their deaths to advance her career. It was, she said, gratifying to get this burden off her conscience. With that, her confession ended.

The seasoned, cynical, middle-aged policeman had thought he'd seen it all in his time, heard it all. But this confession took the cake. For a fleeting instant, Scott Parris had the oddest sense that he was caught in an eerie, surreal dream. Any moment now, the classic Cadillac would rise up from the highway ... float away. The alarm clock on his bedside table would ring him back to the light of day.

THE ATTACK

Nicholas Moxon was not an outright fool. Far from it. He was a man who planned. But he was also a stubborn fellow who, once he had made a bold decision, never had a second thought. Now, foot on the accelerator pedal, both hands on the steering wheel, he and the owner's corpse and the big truck were moving resolutely downhill, toward a coupled destiny. Under the hood, eight pistons pumped, *thumpity-thump*. Worn valves clicked, *thrickety-thrick*. Hurricane Hazel was picking up speed. Mass times velocity is not a product to be taken lightly.

• • •

State police officer Elmer Jackson was not a born hero. Far from it. But he was that sort of man who sees his duty and does it, without considering what the consequences for his health and safety might be, much less his longevity. With the speed control set to match the Cadillac Eldorado Brougham sedan's leisurely pace, two fingers resting lightly on the steering wheel, he listened to the new tires underneath his unit hum. And hummed along with them. The words of the familiar hymn sang back to him:

What a friend we have in Jesus . . .

Relaxed? Yes he was. But Officer Jackson was not asleep at the wheel.

He was aware of the big profile behind him.

Coming up fast.

Dummy don't know I'm John Law. Jackson grinned. *Soon as he figures that out, just watch him step on the brake!*

Coming up faster.

The grin turned upside down. *He ought to have spotted me for a cop by now.*

Rolling along like a cannonball!

Maybe the yahoo's drunk. Or worse, high on something or other. *Looks like the moron's gonna pass me. When he does, I'll switch on my emergency lights and siren, and pull him over and put such a big ticket on him that he'll have to hock his overgrown truck just for the down payment.*

AN EXHILARATING NEW EXPERIENCE

It was Nicholas Moxon's intention to pass the cop. But he intended more than this. When he was even with the state-police unit, just as the lights began to flash and the siren emitted its first yelp, he gave the smaller vehicle a nudge.

Not too much—a gentle, experimental prod. And was surprised that was all it took.

ONE DOWN

The state-police cruiser lurched off the highway, over the rocky shoulder, bounced off a two-ton boulder, tumbled end-over-end down the slope, crashed sixty-three feet below in Granite Creek.

Elmer Jackson's final prayer, which never quite made it out of his mouth, was, *Oh, God Almighty!* But these silent words were heard.

The mangled vehicle, the broken body, would not be found until dawn. It was all right. Elmer had no further need of either of them. This good pilgrim's long, difficult journey was over.

INSTANT REPLAY

It is odd, how quickly a notion becomes accepted by the mind as a fact. When Scott Parris glanced at the Cadillac's rearview mirror and saw the profile of the truck, he was still picturing Nicholas Moxon on the mountainside. With a rifle. Crosshairs on Cassandra's classic Cadillac. *That big rig's coming on awfully fast. I'd better pull over onto the shoulder, give the knucklehead plenty of room to pass.*

But as the monster pickup closed, it stayed in the same lane.

What in hell . . . ?

As it happened, Parris had phrased his question well.

• • •

FORTY-ONE
END GAME

Having spent most of the past hour asking himself, *what am I in such a hurry for?* and getting no answer aside from the wordless urgings from his subconscious (to the general effect that this was no time to dawdle), Charlie Moon's boot was heavy on the accelerator, and when he rolled down the north grade of Little Elkhorn Pass, the Expedition's speedometer needle was jittering just below the ninety-mile-per-hour mark. By any sensible measure, this was reckless driving. Officer Jackson would have put a big ticket on him.

The tribal investigator was about a minute too late to witness the deliberate murder-by-truck of brother lawman Elmer Jackson, and the twisted wreckage of the state-police vehicle at the bottom of the rocky embankment was hidden from Moon's view. What he did see was the monster pickup ahead of him, rear-ending the classic 1957 Cadillac.

Without waiting for his mind to consider issues like who or why or what should I do, the Ute's mind instantly switched to instinct mode. While his right hand found the Ruger .357 Magnum revolver, his right foot pressed the accelerator all the way down, his left hand lowered the driver's side window, the Columbine Expedition skidded to a broadside stop between the overturned Caddy and Hurricane Hazel—now about sixty yards down the road. The tribal investigator poked the revolver out the window, took aim, fired. As the monster truck approached a blind curve, the first copper-jacketed lead projectile passed through the cab's rear window, missed the driver's right ear by inches, shattered the windshield into several thousand shards, went on for a half mile to bury itself deep underneath the pinkish bark of a ninety-year-old ponderosa pine.

As an astonished (and now stone-deaf) Nicholas Moxon cursed and raged, another lump of lead passed his head to follow the first projectile through an almost-empty windshield frame, a third slug struck the inch-thick steel rear bumper. These shots were followed by others.

As the huge machine rounded the distant curve and vanished from view, Moon, smoking revolver in hand, sprinted to the wreckage. It took only a heartbeat to take in the scene of the accident. Make that scene of the *crime*. The upside-down Cadillac had flipped over two and a half times. All four doors had sprung open (as had the trunk), leaving a trail of debris along the highway, which included a spare whitewall tire, a stainless steel Thermos bottle, a woman's black purse, a small blue pillow, and Scott Parris's crumpled felt hat. Like Moon's arrival, the site of the attack was fortuitous. If there had not been a wide spot between the road and the stream—if the state highway department had not removed a jumble of basalt boulders to provide a pull-off where tourists could enjoy the view of the towering canyon walls—Cassandra's sedan would have impacted the boulders or rolled down the steep, rocky bank into the chill waters of Granite Creek.

That was the good news. Now for the bad.

Charlie Moon found his best friend on the ground, one foot pinned under the overturned automobile, groaning, bleeding from both nostrils, left arm snapped just above the elbow. The Ute knelt by the sandy-haired white man, pressed a thumb on Parris's right wrist. The pulse was erratic. "Scott—talk to me."

Scott Parris blinked bloody eyes. "Charlie?"

"It's me, pardner."

"What happened?"

"Somebody rammed you."

A puzzled frown. "I . . . heard shots."

"That was me."

Parris's lips parted in a ghastly smile, a chuckle pumped scarlet liquid over his lips. "You *shot* at somebody for reckless driving?"

"Damn right I did." Moon tried to grin. "The rascal tossed a candy-bar wrapper onto the highway."

"Well, that makes it all right." A groan. "Did you nail the miserable litterbug?"

"I put some holes in his truck." Moon blinked away the tears. "But he got away."

A cough. More blood. Parris's head lolled to one side. "Charlie . . . Charlie . . ."

Moon picked up a limp hand. "I'm here, pardner." *Oh, God—please don't let him die!*

"I think I'm . . . finished."

The shouted *"No!"* caught in the Ute's throat, hit the air as a strangled croak.

Parris gripped the Indian's hand. "Don't leave me, buddy."

"I won't." *Hell will freeze over first.*

Hell was determined to have the last word on the matter.

They heard the rumble of an engine. Big engine. The hum of tires. Big tires.

The Ute looked down the highway, barely able to believe it. *He's coming back.*

• • •

He was. Hearing nothing but the awful roaring in his skull, staring through the empty place where Hurricane Hazel's windshield had recently been, Nicholas Moxon addressed his dead passenger in a comradely tone, as if the murdered man were a trusted accomplice. "We can't run, Tiger. The shooter's probably another cop. He'll call in a report and they'll pick us up a few minutes after I ditch our truck." He worked the clutch, shifted down to second gear. "Our only option is to finish this guy off—then, we've got a good chance of getting away." As he came closer, Moxon squinted at the tall, dark form who had—as all men must—taken his position. *There's no turning back now.* But as the sight of the tribal investigator was focused more finely on his retinas, Moxon eased up on the accelerator. *I'm sure I've seen that guy somewhere.* He pondered the prickly situation.

• • •

Charlie Moon was standing by his friend. So close that one of his boot heels touched Scott Parris's arm. So close that he could hear the injured man's rattling breaths. Long arms straight out, the tribal investigator held the heavy six-shooter in both hands, looked down the black barrel at the man behind the wheel, recognized Nicholas Moxon. *I'll wait till he's so close I can put one right between his eyes.* His nostrils picked up the scent of gun smoke. *Actual* gun smoke. An unsettling thought occurred to the lawman, who had not reloaded his revolver. *How many times did I shoot?* Moon counted off. Came up with the number. Which rhymed with "fix," which was what he found himself in. *Well, ain't this one helluva note.* For the best poker player in sixteen counties and for the best friend a man would ever have, there was only one thing to do. *Bluff.* Moon estimated his chance of pulling it off. Recalled the chilling phrase *snowball in hell.* An astute observer would have concluded that the Ute did not have to die. Only yards away, there was a pile of basalt boulders that had been bull-dozed from the scenic stop. A little farther away, the steep riverbank. But taking cover—abandoning his fallen friend—never entered Moon's mind. Here he was. Here he would stay.

• • •

A kindly motorist, heading north toward Granite Creek, gaped as she spotted the overturned Cadillac, was about to stop and offer assistance when she saw the tall, thin, grim-faced man with the big gun in his hand. And the huge pickup. And decided to pass. But not between them. The sensible woman braked, made a tight U-turn, stepped on the gas.

The gray-haired lady and her brand-new Subaru might as well have been invisible; neither Moxon nor Moon took the least notice. This time, this place, belonged entirely to them.

Minutes later, when the tourist from Little Rock, Arkansas, was out of the canyon, she would place a 911 call, report *a bad car accident and there was this man with a gun who looked like he was just itchin' to shoot another fella if he as much as said 'howdy' so I got outta there and called you soon as my cell phone picked up a signal but I'm on Roam so I don't aim to talk too long because last time I did them telephone-company bloodsuckers charged me nine dollars a minute. . . .*

Two GCPD black-and-whites would respond pronto. For all the good it would do.

• • •

Mr. Nicholas Moxon, who was heading up-grade, had been barely twenty yards away when he allowed the monster truck to slow—almost to a stop. The driver frowned at his skinny adversary. *He's waiting for me to get so close he can't miss.* His choices were elegantly simple. *I can make a run at him, duck behind the dashboard, hope he misses. But this guy knows how to shoot.* Deep breath inhaled, the brain's oxygen replenished to consider the sensible alternative. *Or, I could back off, ditch the truck a couple of miles down the road, hike back to town. I'd have at least a slim chance of getting away.*

Hmmm. Double hmmm.

Moxon glared at the man with the pistol.

The Ute glared back. Knew what the bald white man was thinking. Charlie Moon grinned. Cocked the empty pistol.

Moxon was impressed. *This is a sure-enough game customer. It's a wonder he hasn't already taken a pop at me. If I were in his place, I would've*—Like the approaching thunderstorm's first stroke of lightning, the sudden clarity startled him. *If he didn't take time to reload, his pistol may only have a couple of cartridges left in the chamber. Or maybe only one.* His heart raced. *Or none!*

• • •

Charlie Moon watched the bald man's lips split into a triumphant grin. *He knows.*

The truck driver saluted his worthy opponent. With an index finger.

The Ute heard the big engine rumble. Watched the truck surge forward. Hoped against hope. *Maybe I counted wrong.* He tightened his finger on the trigger. Waited until the man's face had filled his narrowed field of vision—pulled the trigger.

Click.

Well, this is it.

It was.

The first hollow-point passed through Moxon's throat, lodged flatly in his spine.

The second entered the driver's left eye socket, liquefied half his brain.

The third missed.

Not to worry. This was one of those occasions where two out of three was good enough.

Nicholas Moxon's corpse slumped forward onto the steering wheel.

Hurricane Hazel veered sharply to the left, caromed off the heap of boulders, rolled down the steep bank, crashed thunderously into the rushing waters, where Moxon's blood mixed with Elmer Jackson's.

• • •

Charlie Moon looked down at his friend.

Parris had raised himself on his good elbow. The .38 Smith & Wesson was in his left hand, his blood-soaked face split in a hideously brutal, marvelously happy grin. "I *got* the bastard!"

"There was no need, I already had him in my sights." Moon stuck the impotent pistol under his belt. "But it's just like you—grabbing all the credit for yourself." The Ute's expression hinted of mild disapproval. "Besides, you was supposed to be cashing in your chips." *Thank you, God. I owe you a big one.*

Reminded of this grim fact, Parris relaxed, rolled over

on to his back. "I was about to cross that River, all right. But I figured if I leave ol' Charlie Moon to take care of business, he's bound to mess things up."

Again, the Ute knelt by his friend. "I was about to take him out."

"Ha!" The small revolver slipped from Parris's grip. "I may be bunged up some—but I can count to six."

Moon let that pass. And now that things had settled down some, he remembered that there was a second passenger.

Nineteen fifty-seven Cadillacs did not come equipped with seat belts. Cassandra Spencer, who had been thrown clear, was several paces from the wreckage, wedged between a black basalt boulder and a sturdy piñon. The psychic's eyes were wide open, staring at the unseen. The tribal investigator put a thumb under her jawbone, felt a weak, intermittent pulse. Cassandra was breathing, but when she exhaled, frothy blood bubbled between her lips.

Moon frowned, shook his head. *She won't last long.*

From somewhere to the north, the hopeful wail of the siren's song. Help was coming. Granite Creek police trained in first aid. Close behind, EMTs with oxygen, bandages, defibrillators, miraculous medications—all the assistance modern technology can provide to pull the dying back from death.

Then, something else. Something altogether *other.* No, do not ask. The how and why are hidden from us mortals. Some will assume that Charlie Moon's perception was colored by symbols of his Catholic upbringing. Again, we do not know. What can be said with certainty is that the Ute felt a definite *presence.* Something infinitely more real than himself. Small, at first. Unobtrusive. But it grew quickly. Soon, all about him, a low rumbling, as if the whole creation trembled. A sudden rush of chill wind took his breath away. Though his body was rigid, his senses were extraordinarily acute. For the duration, he was a witness—and an advocate.

Watch! It cometh upon us—that deepest of Mysteries.
Cosmic accounts to be settled, credits made, debts
paid, justice satisfied.
Her life-book is read. On each side, the weights accu-
mulate.
From the saints, mournful sighs, urgent pleas.
From hellish Darkness, gleeful accusations!
Alas, the scale is fearfully unbalanced.
From the Eternal, cometh judgment.
Exultant shouts from the Black Pit, loud claims of
ownership.
But wait—the accused pleads for mercy.

Silently, the tribal investigator prays.

From the Light, a murmuring of many voices.
Utterly desperate, she calls upon that Name.
Silence.
Then—a small ripping, a sudden unzipping . . .
An ear of corn being pulled from the husk?
Aha! Look—the spirit separates itself from the flesh.
Cassandra is going . . .
Going . . .

Charlie Moon watches her go—

Gone!

The witness watches the hammer fall—hears the thunder
roll!

But where goeth the wretched soul?
Why, to the High Bidder.
The price?
Sangre de Cristo.
The Blood of Christ

• • •

FORTY-TWO
NINE DAYS LATER

Charlie Moon burst through the street-level entrance to the Granite Creek Police Department, gave Senior Dispatcher Clara Tavishuts (a fellow Ute) a salute, bounded up the stairs three steps at a time to the second floor. Grinning from one ear to the other (and back) he strode through the door marked CHIEF OF POLICE, boomed a big laugh at the grumpy-faced fellow seated behind the desk.

Scott Parris's scowl edged up one notch on the Cantankerous Scale, making deep furrows in his brow.

Moon was in a backslapping mood, but restrained himself.

Granite Creek's top cop was not feeling tip-top—only a few hours out of the hospital, he was hurting from a broken left ulna, five fractured ribs, and the corrosive knowledge that he had not been able to protect Cassandra Spencer from the onslaught of her murderous partner. The almost-healed scar that traced an ugly arc from the corner of his left eye down to the hinge of his prominent jaw turned from shocking pink to angry crimson. Unaware of the communicative effect of these colorful visual displays, he grunted and mumbled, "What's so damn funny?"

Counting off fingers, Moon went down the list: "Peanuts comic strips. Dave Barry. And the Department of Agriculture's latest bulletin on how to raise a hundred head of llamas on ten acres of dry-land prairie." He pointed at Parris. "But if you figure I'm laughing on account of a sudden attack of mirth, you are way off the mark."

"I am?"

"Yes you am—I laugh because I'm *happy*."

Parris barely suppressed a snort. "What about?"

"Lots of things."

The injured man grimaced at a sudden pain. "Gimme a f'r instance."

"Well, take today, f'r instance." The rancher spread his arms to encompass the numerous blessings. "A quarter inch of rain on the south thirty sections. How the sun came up over the Buckhorn Range. A fine breakfast of sugar-cured Virginia ham, scrambled eggs, sweet black coffee. The way the air smells like lightning's about to strike—and so crisp you could slice off a piece with your pocket knife." Moon assumed a properly earnest expression. "But most of all, I'm happy to see my buddy forked-end down. And I'm glad I don't have to visit you every day of the week, bringing you chocolate candy imported all the way from Germany and fresh-cut flowers to sniff and fuzzy toys to play with and brand-new magazines to read and other expensive stuff such as even a prosperous rancher like myself can barely afford."

The patient had appreciated the reading material and the hollowed-out giraffe that (what would they think of next!) could be worn as a hat. Which, late one evening, long after lights-out, when the hallway did not pitter-pat with the sound of nurses' rubber-soled shoes, he did. Wear the giraffe as a hat, that is. "You never brought me no candy or flowers."

"Sure I did, pard. But I gave 'em to that pretty little red-headed nurse who took to calling me sweetie and darling and liked to take me by the hand and lead me down the hall to your room like I couldn't remember where it was at."

The older man had also admired that shapely young lady. "Little Red never called *me* sweetie." *Why do the women go for Charlie?* Parris's voice took on a petulant tone: "And don't say you showed up to see me every day, 'cause you sure as hell didn't do no such thing."

"Yes I did."

"Then why was it I didn't happen to notice you being in my room?" He smirked at the seven-foot-tall Ute. "It's not like you'd be easy to miss."

"I'll tell you why—because sometimes when I dropped in you was sound asleep. Snoring like all get-out. And I didn't want to wake you up."

Parris coughed up a "Hmmph," which was his way of saying that he did not believe a word of this Indian blarney. But he was happy to see his best friend. He nodded to indicate a padded armchair. Watched Mr. Moon seat himself. Lean back. The very picture of contentment. Parris eyed the Very P. of C. "While I was in the hospital—did you go to Cassie's funeral?"

The tribal investigator nodded.

"I imagine there was a sizable crowd."

Moon quoted the newspaper account, which he was certain his friend had read. "Seven hundred plus."

"That's a good turnout. Must've pleased Bea." What he wanted to say was, *Charlie, I can't hardly sleep a wink at night without having bad dreams about Cassie's death. I was driving her car—and she was under my protection. Which makes me responsible.* But because a bona fide hairy-chested man does not seek solace, our hero was deprived of the comfort he sorely needed.

Parris had arranged his desk for a view through the window that framed a red maple. A plucky black-crested Steller's jay landed on a spindly branch, cocked its head at him, shrieked a *shack-shack-shack* remark that the cop, who was not a dues-paying member of the Audubon Society, interpreted as a fowl obscenity. *Shack-shack right back at you, birdbrain!* Keeping his glare fixed on the jay, Parris muttered, "State police got a warrant to examine Cassie's computer equipment, but all the memory was wiped clean. Ditto for Moxon's laptop. He must've taken care of that critical piece of business before he stole the big truck and bashed the owner's head in." He was attempting to stare the jay down. "Not that it matters all that much, what with her verbal confession." *And with both of 'em dead.*

"It's finished," Moon said.

Not quite. Parris blinked. The jay made a derisive *eck-eck* chirp that sounded like a bird chuckle. Having been bested by a creature with a brain the size of a piñon nut, the chief of police nodded to indicate the miniature kitchen and pantry at the far end of his office, where a six-quart coffeepot bubbled hot around the clock. "You need a shot of caffeine?"

"Nope, but I've never been known to turn down a free cup of coffee and I don't intend to change my ways this late in life." The perpetually hungry man eyed a grease-spotted cardboard box. "Is that what my nose says it is?"

"Yeah. Those doughnuts are stale as granddaddy's jokes, but stuff your face with as many as you want."

Heading to the source of food and drink, Moon asked whether he could bring his host some refreshment.

Parris was *this close* to asking for a cup of real coffee. Even a sugar-soaked doughnut. He yielded to his conscience, whose voice was identical to his long-dead mother's. "I'll have a cup of decaf—the little pot's full of the stuff." *Nobody drinks that crap but me.* "Put some artificial sweetener in it, and a dash of that powdered, no-calorie, nondairy creamlike substance that tastes almost as good as chalk."

The Indian delivered the chief's beverage first, returned to the canteen. Searched the refrigerator for what he was looking for. Found it.

That java don't smell half bad. Parris took a sip, arched a surprised eyebrow, spoke to Moon's back. "That sure hits the well-known spot."

The cowpuncher punched buttons on the microwave oven.

"If you don't mind, Charlie, bring me one of them rice cakes." *It's like eating cardboard, but a man needs something to chew on.*

Moon returned to place a plastic picnic plate on his

friend's desk. Upon it was a brown recycled-paper napkin. Also a glazed doughnut. Melted butter dripped off the pastry.

Parris's suspicious gaze darted from the doughnut to his coffee cup. Back to the doughnut, tarrying for a long, lustful look. "What's in my cup?"

"Half a tank of high-test java. Other half is half-and-half. And it's sweetened with the real thing."

A halfhearted protest: "I'm on a strict diet."

Dr. Moon offered his prescription: "What you need right now is a stiff dose of caffeine. And a big helping of highly refined white cane sugar."

Parris took another sip of the coffee. *That is sooo good.* Tasted the doughnut. Closed his eyes. *I've died and gone to heaven.* Which reminded him: "This stuff is liable to kill me."

"Not a problem. Bein' your best buddy, I'm bound to be asked to say a few sorrowful words at your funeral." Moon raised his cup to salute the prospective corpse. "I'll tell the two or three folks that show up what a disgusting glutton you was in your former life, and how your untimely passing is a warning to chowhounds who—like yourself—have to keep punching extra holes in their belts."

"Thanks a whole bushel."

"I try to do a good deed every day of the week." Moon returned to his chair with a steaming mug of police-station brew and the box of sugar-encrusted pastries. "Anything new on Andrew Turner's car wreck?"

The weight-watcher watched the tribal investigator get to work on the remaining doughnuts. "Day before yesterday, a state police copter did a few passes over the Devil's Mouth. It was dragging a cable with some high-tech sensors. Magnetic field detectors. Infrared sensors. Ice-penetrating radar. From what I hear, they picked up a dozen 'anomalies'—which is eleven too many." Parris took a long drink of sweet coffee. "It'd cost a truckload of taxpayers' money to dig 'em all out. So until there's a big thaw, whatever's left of

Turner and his fancy car will have to stay right where they are." The chief of police felt his gaze pulled to the window. The bird on the maple branch still had a pair of beady eyes fixed on him. He aimed a scowl at the haughty descendant of dinosaurs. *Go eat a poison bug.* Getting in the last words (*"chook-chook-chook!"*), the impudent *Cyanocitta stelleri* took wing. To celebrate his small victory, Parris took the last bite of buttery pastry, downed the final sip of sugary coffee. *Boy howdy—that was good!* But by his measure, a pleasure must be balanced by a commensurate worry: *I'll gain five pounds and stay awake all night.*

Time passed. Which is another way of saying: One-second segments of the fourth dimension of the space-time continuum were ticktocked away by the electrical innards of a Go Broncos! wall clock.

Parris glanced at the branch where the jay had been. Remorse set in. *I was just kidding about the poison bug.* He addressed the human being in his office: "I'd give a month's pay to turn up Turner's corpse, stuff his bones into a pine box, and nail a lid on this nasty business once and for all." *Which reminds me.* He blinked at the Indian. "Charlie, d'you remember that peculiar old drunk—the guy who claimed he'd seen something or other on the Spencer driveway when Turner had his accident?"

"Clevis Parsley, aka Elvis Presley." The Ute, who was working on the next-to-last of the stale doughnuts, delayed taking a bite so he could say, "That ol' rock-and-roller told us he'd seen a couple of witches."

Parris scratched at the fiberglass cast on his arm. *Charlie has a good memory.* Tempted to have another mug of genuine coffee spiked with half-and-half and genuine sugar, he sighed, pushed the mug aside. "From time to time, I wake up in the middle of the night and wonder." He started to say something, lapsed into an uneasy silence.

"What do you wonder, pard?"

"I wonder did Turner run off the driveway because it was slick with snow and he was going too fast around that curve—or was there something he tried to keep from running into." He also wondered where the jay had gone. *Maybe to heckle the mayor.* "What do you think?"

"I try not to do too much thinking. But if I was to cogitate about it for a minute, I might begin to wonder whether Mr. Moxon was responsible for Mr. Turner's accident."

Parris nodded. "Another spectacular vision for the up-and-coming TV psychic, another big boost in program ratings." He turned to gaze at Moon. "But when Cassie made her final confession, she didn't say a thing about Turner's car wreck." He rapped his arm cast on the desk. "Anyway, why would Moxon want to knock off Cassie's brother-in-law?"

Scott still believes he saw a big hairy Sasquatch on the Spencer driveway that snowy night. Carrying something on its shoulder. What was it? *Oh, right—a king-size burrito. Maybe it was a south-of-the-border Sasquatch, come up from Mexico.* Moon closed one eye, peered through a doughnut hole at his friend. "What you need is a good night's sleep."

"You're right about that." The chief of police stared through the rectangular glass portal into the outer world. The red maple looked downright lonely. He wished the impudent bird would return. Wished his wife hadn't died fifteen years, three months, and six days ago. Wished he could slip backward in time, do a rerun of the confrontation with Nicholas Moxon, get it right this time. *I'd pull off the highway soon as I saw him coming, get Cassie out of the car and down the riverbank, shoot the bastard dead.* . . . He heard the Ute's deep voice.

"Pardner, it's not your fault she died. You did all anyone could have. More."

Parris shook his head. "I don't know, Charlie—"

"Yes you do—you know because *I'm telling you.*" Moon got up, put both hands on his friend's desk, leaned like a cougar about to pounce. An incandescent intensity burned in his dark eyes. "Busted-up and bloody as you was—and with nothin' but that little .38 peashooter—you plugged Mr. Moxon right good. And if you hadn't, he'd have run down a careless deputy whose six-gun was empty as a bucket with no bottom in it."

Scott Parris tried to speak. Could not. He blinked away something that was stinging his eye. A mote of dust, no doubt.

FORTY-THREE
SNIFFING AROUND

Thanks to Charlie Moon and despite the coffee, for the first night since Cassandra Spencer's death, Scott Parris slept soundly, peacefully. Dreamed sweet dreams. Not so, his Indian friend.

• • •

Charlie Moon woke up a dozen times. Whenever he managed to doze off, the Ute would encounter something unpleasant. Like a huge, hairy (big-footed!) creature that lumbered about in the snow, toting a yard-long burrito on each hairy shoulder. Or Clevis Parsley would make an appearance, outfitted in a sequined white tuxedo, a splendid wig of wavy hair, and blue suede shoes, of course. The odd little man would bellow out a few lines of "Heartbreak Hotel," then recite his tale of "witches" that had caused Andrew Turner to drive his Corvette over the cliff, into the Devil's Mouth. The Mouth would burp, belch—vomit Turner up, sports car and all. Lick its lips, swallow him again.

Finally, the dawn came. But not like thunder. Like a cold, gunmetal-gray river that flooded Moon's upstairs bedroom with a current of gloom, and the unhappy realization that he might as well have stayed up all night. The rancher/tribal investigator/deputy sat on the edge of his bed, stared at the floor, then at the door. Thought about it.

Considered alone, the individual pieces of the puzzle were crazy. But looking at the thing as a whole . . . it was still fairly bizarre. But not entirely so. Fitting the warped fragments together in a particular manner, the final picture almost made sense. Enough to justify taking a long, solitary walk in the wilderness? No. But exercise combined with solitude helps a man clear his mind of worrisome thoughts. And build up a healthy appetite. After a long, restless night, Charlie Moon was not hungry.

• • •

After finishing a breakfast that consisted of a cold biscuit (without the help of butter or blackberry jam) and a reheated cup of yesterday's coffee (well sugared), the tribal investigator drove the oldest of the five Columbine F-150s several dozen miles down the road, through the Spencer estate's wrought-iron gate, which, by order of the Granite Creek chief of police, had been left unlocked since that snowy evening when Andrew Turner and his Corvette had vanished. Beatrice Spencer, Moon knew, would not be at home. At Cassandra's funeral, she had confided to the Ute her plans to travel. She planned to go away for a couple of weeks "to get the cobwebs out of my mind." As he shifted down to second gear and eased the valve-tapping pickup up the long, winding driveway, Moon felt the overpowering presence of the grumbling, cloud-capped mountain. It loomed huge, pregnant with ominous possibilities, bulging with sinister energies—all conceived from a tiny spark, a seed concealed deep inside from before the Beginning. *Just the sort of place where Moses received the stone tablets.*

From somewhere up there, a thunderous rumble.

You shall love the Lord your God with all your heart.

A flash of fireworks in the cloud crown, then the drumming—

With-all-your-soul . . .

Another drum-roll—

With-all-your-mind . . .

From below, an echo—

You shall love your neighbor as yourself.

Charlie Moon felt his lips moving. *You shall not murder.*

For perhaps ten heartbeats, the man was totally unaware of his surroundings. And of his *self.* Moon was elsewhere.

No to worry—his mortal body operated the motor vehicle with perfect competence.

A shattering crack of thunder—a white-hot flash of lightning!

The spell is broken. The traveler has returned.

Moon remembered nothing of his brief excursion. Or, for that matter, the last hundred yards up the mountain. A pointless detour? No. For all things, there is a purpose.

His uphill journey continued.

On his left, the heavily forested slope rose steeply at first, presenting a smooth, youthful face. With the Ute's ascent, as if aeons accumulated with altitude, the mountain's skin became deeply wrinkled by a series of ravines where cold water from crystalline springs seeped from beneath flat, mossy rocks, and shy mule deer grazed in shady glens. Separating these shadowy sanctuaries, rugged granite bluffs rose up to vanish in the morning's low-hanging, smoky-blue mists. Off to his right, and before he could see it through the scattering of spruce and aspens, Moon could sense the heavy, brooding silence welling up from the depths of the Devil's Mouth—where Andrew Turner's corpse was presumably entombed. Macabre images of the body floated in the infinite space of his imagination. Bea's husband was suspended in a blue, icy gel—frozen in a lonely eternity. But Mr. Moon was not one to dwell upon grim pictures. By sheer force of will, he banished the grisly scene from his thoughts. The unwelcome guest refused to completely leave the premises. The awful vision retreated from the solarium to the musty cellar, where it would settle in with other rubbish—always ready to creep up the stairway, display its horror in the bright light of day.

As Moon approached the accident site, he pulled off the graveled lane, parked the pickup underneath the windswept branches of a lone pine. As he lowered the tailgate, the Columbine hound looked up at the boss, opened his mouth. . . . "I bet you'd like to go for a walk." No. Dogs cannot talk. This was the human being speaking.

Sidewinder could yawn and sigh, and so he did both.

After which, he rested his graying muzzle between a pair of paws.

Hoping to goad the inert creature into some semblance of animation, Moon assumed a pitying tone: "Poor ol' fella—I guess you've gone a few miles past your prime."

Another canine yawn.

The poker player upped the ante: "Guess it's about time I thought about getting another dog." A thoughtful pause. "A younger mutt, that's still got some fire in his eye."

The hound snorted.

"Maybe I should get me a frisky little puppy."

The dog closed his toothy jaws, then his eyes. Sniffed once. Twice. Slipped off . . . away into the long-ago canine Dreamtime when neither hound nor poodle yet trotted upon the earth. Sidewinder was a lean, gray shadow, running with other wolves.

Charlie Moon gave up the game. It was time to get down to business. He found the spot where he had stood beside Scott Parris on that frigid morning, did his best to recreate the experience. *Sun was a little ways over the horizon, just like now. I was looking down the road. Breeze was coming from my right, down off the mountain. Just like now.* Like the somnolent hound, he closed his eyes. But Moon was not drowsy. He was recalling. *Me and Scott were talking about breakfast. Scrambled eggs. Buttered blueberry pancakes soaked in maple syrup.* And when his best friend had mentioned the meaty subject, Moon's famished imagination had conjured up the scrumptious scent of bacon frying. Or had it?

He turned his back on the Devil's Mouth, gazed up the mountainside.

A bear, so they say, can smell food from miles and miles away. He thought about that folkloric proposition. Considered the pros and cons, came up with a decisive *maybe.* Who knows how well a hungry carnivore can smell—if the wind is right?

The biped carnivore set his sight on the heights, found a convenient ravine, and—one step at a time—began to climb. Before very many minutes had slipped away into the past, he was high above the Spencer driveway and quite out of sight of it—in the depths of the forest. The effect was a familiar one, and thus expected—the farther this son of the People of the Shining Mountains went into the wilderness, the more at home he was. The Ute was in his natural element. At peace with himself. Many happy memories came to call. Like that long-ago time when his father took him into *Cañón del Espíritu* to visit the cave-shelter called Quiet Shade House, where the Old Ones had pecked out sketches of real and imaginary beasts on smoke-encrusted walls. *Dad and me had a picnic. Spam sandwiches with mustard. Black coffee. Ginger Snaps. Those were good times.*

This pleasant walk into the wildwoods was just the sort of refreshment Mr. Moon needed. But perhaps—and this is not meant as a criticism—he should have been paying more attention.

• • •

From within gloomy glades of blackish blue spruce, here and there amidst the clusters of yellowed ferns, and between the knees of those skeleton's legs posing as alabaster aspen trunks, several pairs of eyes watch the man. Most of these forest dwellers are merely curious, a few are alarmed by the brash intruder's invasion. But though quite important in their own right, this multitude of watchers is of no particular concern—they constitute an audience, whom—whether they applaud or hiss—shall have no effect upon the outcome of Act One.

Ah, but what about this toothy fellow who follows?

Look—the brute pauses, sniffs, laps up a quick drink from the brook, lopes along again with that wild, hungry glint in his eye that reveals the unspoken thought: I could eat a bucket of raw liver! Two buckets!

What—this sinister menace chills you—grips the mind with that nameless horror—causes the stomach to churn, the heart to palpitate? Enough is enough, you say—ease up on the grisly stuff?

Very well. Consider it done.

We shall forgo any mention of the far more dangerous creature that stalks Charlie Moon—that massive, hairy, odorous, blood-soaked— Oops. That slipped out.

Pretend you never heard it.

• • •

FORTY-FOUR
CLOSE ENCOUNTER OF THE WORST KIND

Charlie Moon was, as the saying goes, following his nose. Like a bloodhound on a scent, up the forested mountain he went, crossed a gurgling yard-wide stream in a single stride, encountered a deer path that lured him up a rocky slope, around a chocolate-and-vanilla outcropping that was iced between layers with a thick vein of pinkish white quartz. Almost certainly, gold-bearing quartz. After taking note of this interesting finding, the potential prospector continued along a faint trail that meandered pleasantly through a patch of wild roses, then edged more cautiously along the precipitous face of a crumbling granite bluff. The Ute paused to inspect week-old cougar tracks in the dusty shelter of a mossy overhang, then continued along the enticing path through a shadow-streaked thicket of spruce, pines, and bloodberry vines. With an almost startling suddenness, the hiker emerged into the sunshine of a small, saddle-shaped meadow that was populated by a few sturdy ponderosa and dozens of massive, lichen-encrusted boulders. On the far side of this open spot, the broad shoulder of the mountain was split by a narrow box canyon, whose rain-streaked walls soared at least three hundred feet to approach that rarefied altitude where summer was a total stranger, and trees refused to grow. The canyon's triangular floor started out wide at the entrance, gradually narrowed to a blunt point on the far end, where some not-very-expert builder had constructed a crude shack from a clutter of warped, unpainted planks, rough sawmill slabs, undressed pine and aspen logs. Topside, a rusty patchwork of corrugated steel panels was held down with large stones— presumably to prevent gusty west winds from carrying the crude roof away to Kansas. There was no proper door, but hanging limply over a hole in the wall was a drapery that might have been either a tattered blanket or an untanned animal hide. Jutting from a spot where the rough-and-ready roof almost joined the makeshift wall was a long, crooked cylinder, which Moon rightly guessed to be a rusty automobile exhaust pipe. A thin wisp of smoke drifted up from the improvised chimney.

The tribal investigator shoved cold hands into his jacket pockets. *Looks like someone's at home.*

Well . . . yes. And no. Yea and nay at the same time. Confusing? Impossible? Such is the way of physical reality. The question of whether the home was occupied or not was only vaguely similar to what a quantum mechanic would refer to as a "mixed state." And like us all, Moon was closely entangled with his prior assumptions. The issue shall remain undetermined until this conscious entity, who tends to see things with his own particular spin— makes a direct observation.

And speaking of observations—our keenly conscious entity has picked up the scent of strong coffee, also the delectable aroma of sizzling meat. But on this occasion, it was not bacon frying. Charlie Moon's well-trained nostrils took another sniff. *Could be roast pork.* But way up here on the mountain, where would a squatter find a pig? His nose began to have second thoughts. *More likely, it's venison. Or wild turkey.* As his nasal nerve center was attempting to decide, the hopeful gourmet experienced a sudden hunger pang. *In a lonesome place like this, I expect some company might be welcome.*

This assumption, as will become apparent, was somewhat optimistic.

No, that is unwarranted understatement. Wishful thinking is what it was.

In preparation for taking that first step, which would lead him to yon cabin in the far end of the box canyon, Moon had just lifted his foot off the grassy turf—when he smelled something else. Like wild onions. With just a touch of garlic. And fresh blood.

"Hhhnnngh!"

This remark had originated behind him. Having stopped in midair, the Ute's boot settled oh-so-slowly back to earth. The lawman's intuitive antenna was instantly operating at maximum sensitivity. The signal received was DANGER. This headline was followed by: Do Not Turn Around, Do Not Move a Muscle, Do Not Say a Word, Et cetera.

"Hhhnnngh!"

As a chilly prickle jiggered up along his spine and down again, and he considered what this presence might be, Charlie Moon (having limited data) reached these preliminary conclusions:

1. If this is an animal, I can't imagine what kind.
2. If it's human, the fellow's vocabulary is limited.
3. Any fella who lives out in the woods is likely to be armed.
4. I'd better not do anything to make him nervous.

Onto a flat rock—*phhllaaat!* (*Whatever it was had* spat.)

He must have just been clearing his throat. Though his face could not be seen by the spitter, Moon put on his me-not-your-enemy smile, inhaled a breath of crisp, high-country air, exhaled these words: "Good morning."

"Turn yersef aroun'. Slow-like."

He's itching for a fight. Ready to accommodate, the Ute rotated, slow-like, counterclockwise as seen from above, and as he did the Ruger pistol appeared in his hand. Yes, fully loaded with potent ammunition.

Now, Mr. Moon was not a man who startled easily. That last time he'd felt his whole body go cold as ice was several years back, when a mean-spirited cretin had stashed an umpteen-foot long diamondback rattlesnake in the cab of his pickup, and while the Ute was driving along without a care in the world, the thing had slithered under the driver's seat and raised its evil countenance knee-high, to look Moon right in the eye. While wickedly flicking the forked tongue. On that memorable occasion, he had driven the pickup off the highway, and when a well-meaning but certifiably insane GCPD cop showed up and announced his plan to shoot the snake in the head (which was practically resting on Moon's crotch), the Ute had resorted to drastic measures that will not be reported herein; this is now, that was then. Now, what he saw caused Charlie Moon to drop his jaw. *Great Day in the Morning—it's Bigfoot in the flesh!*

In a manner of speaking, yes. The feet were size 16, the mass of flesh amounted to about 340 pounds. The broad face perched atop the immense torso was half obscured by a tangled mat of jet-black hair. This was not what caused the jaw to drop. What unhinged the mandible was the fashion statement. The buffalo-shouldered creature was draped in a skin of a mature grizzly. The bear's snout rested on the top the of the humanoid's head, staring at the Ute through dead eyes. The arms and legs of the bearskin served as "Bigfoot's" sleeves and breeches, the long claws laid over the living fingers and toes. The whole thing was a couple of notches beyond bizarre. But as Moon's mind processed the data, it was beginning to make sense. *This has got to be what Scott saw crossing the Spencer driveway in the snow.* Today, the "big burrito" on its shoulder was a field-dressed deer, dripping still-warm blood. For those who care about such details, the fresh kill was an eight-point buck.

Moon noticed another, more significant element.

The formidable hunter was toting a wicked-looking crossbow. A bolt-filled quiver hung from a cougar-tail belt. More to the point, the bolt mounted in the aforesaid crossbow was aimed at a location approximately three centimeters (1.18 inches) above Moon's six-ounce sterling-silver belt buckle, which he had been awarded for coming in second at the 1992 Ignacio Indian Rodeo bull-riding event. He would, his friends insisted, have come in first if (the week before) he had not gotten into that nasty fight with Carlos "Iron Man" Martinez, and broken a collarbone (his own).

"Hhhnnngh!"

Sounds like he's going to spit again.

Wrong. Swallowed. Yes, this is revolting. There are occasions when even the least detail must be communicated. This is not one of them. This is *gratuitously* disgusting.

The Ute thought it advisable to make another attempt at friendly conversation: "Mr. Bigfoot . . ." *Uh-oh.*

Uh-oh is right.

The homely face scowled. Even the bear's head frowned. "Wattid you say?"

"Well, what I *meant* to say was—"

"You called me *Mister!*" This perfectly correct observation was heavy with indignation. Righteous indignation.

Moon was trying hard to get a handle on this. *Maybe he's got a PhD.* What with pass-fail replacing conventional grading, Internet diploma mills, and who knows what other academic innovations that had been driving the dumbing-down in American education, you couldn't tell who might have a sheepskin tucked away in his hip pocket. "Why don't we introduce ourselves." Having recovered from the drooped-jaw syndrome, the Ute attempted to retrieve the smile. "I'm Charlie Moon."

The little eyes glinted. *I know who you are.*

"Uh—who might you be?"

The hairy person responded gruffly: "Bobbie."

Moon might have offered to shake the big mitt but his right hand was filled with .357 Magnum revolver, which was aimed at the massive person's center of gravity. "Well, sir—I'm glad to meet you." This statement was not entirely factual—but even a scrupulously honest man may occasionally find himself in circumstances where good manners and an instinct for physical survival take priority over strict veracity.

The crossbow had not wavered. As if Moon's pistol did not exist, the banana-size finger twitched on the trigger. "I'm Bobbie *Sue!*"

Moon was familiar with the Johnny Cash song, but from one clue and another concluded that this was not some fellow whose mean daddy had given him a girl's name. "Well, ma'am, it's always a pleasure to meet a lady"—he pointed the pistol barrel at her lethal weapon—"who owns a really fine crossbow. I'm betting you made it yourself."

The big hairy person uttered a guttural sound that might have been evidence of ill temper or acute dyspepsia.

Pride of ownership evidently not being a cleft in her armor, he asked, "Does it have a safety?"

Bobbie Sue's face bottomed off at a tight-lipped mouth, which curled into a thin, half-wit's grin. "Huh-uh." A chuckle gurgled up from somewhere deep inside. "But hit's got a hair trigger." The smile flipped upside down. "An' I got a tetchy trigger finger."

Moon was about to describe the merits of his weapon, when he was interrupted by another—

"Hhhnnngh!"

On this occasion, neither a spit nor a swallow. Do not think about it.

Charlie Moon didn't. The man had more urgent issues to consider. Like the alarming hallucination he was attempting to deal with, and without notable success. What had happened to dull the Ute's characteristic razor-sharp wit? Several possibilities come to mind. Because he had not had a proper breakfast, the cause might have been low blood sugar. Or perhaps this bizarre encounter had unhinged Moon's mind. Whatever the matter was, and it might have been a combination of the above—he was *certain* that he could see a finely drawn, perfectly straight line emanating from the flint tip of the crossbow's feathered bolt. This two-dimensional thread connected dead-center with the third button from the bottom of his shirt, passed through his naval and various indispensable abdominal organs to dissect his spine between the second and third lumbar vertebrae. This causing the potential target some concern, he made this reasonable observation: "That thing might go off."

"Hit might." Bobbie S. cackled another laugh. "So might your pistol."

Fair enough. Deescalation was called for. "Tell you what—you point your crossbow at the ground, I'll do the same with my sidearm."

The long-haired hunter shook her shaggy mane, the deceased griz did the same.

"D'you mind if I ask why not?"

"Hits 'cause you're a . . . a . . ." The ogre face twisted into a painful grimace. What was the word? It came to her. "You're a damn *traspesser*. So I got all the right in the worl' to pull the trigger and pin you to a tree—jus' like you was a . . . a . . ." Came to her again: "Like you was a doodlebug!" She appended this with a cheerful "Heh-heh."

"You telling me this is your land?"

A nod from both heads. "My daddy was a hard-rock miner, and he squatted here for almos' forty years." She jerked a thumb to indicate the ramshackle cabin at the end of the box canyon. "An' now it's all mine. I got me a cookstove and a hand-crank radio."

"Good for you." The trespasser waggled the pistol barrel at the crossbow. "Now lay that thing down on the ground."

This stern command surprised Bobbie Sue. Her "Huhuh" was a tad on the uncertain side.

"If you don't, I'll shoot you right between the eyes." On second thought, that was a small target. The eyes were remarkably close together.

"I been shot before. Bullets don' skeer me none."

Cannons probably don't skeer you none. "Then I'll give you another reason. Sidewinder is about to put the bite on you."

She snorted. "I ain't askeered a no snake that ever lived." The gourmet patted an ample belly. "Whenever I can ketch me a fat one, I eats 'im for breakfast."

Moon did not doubt the claim. "I didn't say sidewinder, I said *Sidewinder.*"

Bobbie Sue's expression suggested that she required further clarification.

Moon provided it: "Sidewinder's my hound, and he's about one jump behind you. I say the word, he'll be all over you like ugly on ape." *I wish I hadn't said it exactly like that.*

Bobbie Sue took no offense. "Is there really a dog behin' me?"

"Take a look."

She looked over the shoulder that was not burdened by an eviscerated deer corpse, saw the beast with hair bristling on his neck, sneered at that *toothy fellow* who had followed Moon up the mountain. "I ain't askeered a no mutt, neither. Roasted dog is almos' as good as fried snake meat." While her head was half turned, and as she licked her lips at the savory memory of past feasts—

Moon grabbed the crossbow around the feathered projectile, snatched it from her hand!

She turned to glare at the brazen man, inhaled to expand the barrel chest, roared, "Hhhnnngh!"

"You spit on me—I'll shoot you dead." He sounded like he meant it.

Behind her, the Columbine hound growled a throaty threat. Sidewinder never bluffed.

The disarmed mountain woman made up her mind. She would not spit. But if the dog attacked, she would kill it with her bare hands. Bobbie Sue watched the tall, thin man throw her crossbow high into a spruce, where it hung on a brushy limb.

Moon fixed his gaze on the apparition Scott Parris had seen crossing the road. "You are in deep trouble."

"No I ain't." She flexed her fingers. "I can take you and that hound dog too."

"I don't think so. But that's not the trouble I'm talking about."

A crafty, deceptive look hung on her face. "What *are* you talkin' about?"

"You know."

The shaggy head rotated on an unseen neck. "No, I don'."

Moon put on a stormy scowl. "That snowy night when

Mr. Turner's car went off the Spencer driveway—you were there. And don't deny it—the chief of police saw you."

"Oh, I don' deny *that.*"

"You don't?"

"Huh-uh."

Very sternly, he said, "Bobbie Sue—look me straight in the eye."

She did.

"Now tell me the honest truth—when Turner came around that curve, were you standing in the driveway?"

"Huh-uh."

Their gazes were locked for a long moment before Moon said, "Do you like strawberries?"

There was no indication that this off-the-wall question surprised her. "Sure do." *An' I likes good-lookin' men.* The mouth curled into a leering grin. *'Specially tall ones.*

The tall man posed another question: "What do you know about that woman who was killed on the far side of the mountain—Astrid Spencer."

"I know the cops figger a bear's to blame."

"What else do you know?"

"A whole lot more'n I'm gonna tell you."

"Maybe all you know is what you hear on your hand-crank radio."

She grunted. "'Twasn't nothin' on the radio about you bein' at Yellow Pines with all them other cops. I spotted you when the sun come up, out lookin' for bear tracks."

Moon had a lot to think about, and some tangles to sort out. But unanswered questions about Astrid Spencer death would have to sit on the back burner. Finding out what had happened to Andrew Turner—that was Job One. He estimated his chances of getting something out of Bobbie Sue at somewhere between slim and none. The player had one card to toss on the table. He stared at the hulk of a woman engulfed in the grizzly bear's full-body embrace. "By late this afternoon, this place is going to be crawling with police officers. And forest rangers. A whole battalion of National Guard. Why, they'll be all over Spencer Mountain, thick as fleas on a coyote." He jabbed a thumb at the clearing sky. "And there'll be helicopters." Seeing a hint of alarm in her eyes, he laid it on thicker yet: "And a dozen bloodhounds."

The mountain woman eyed the Indian. "Whuffor?"

"I'll *tell* you whuffor." The Ute put on his meanest scowl. "They'll be looking for Andrew Turner."

The dark eyes set in the pumpkin face resembled greasy ball bearings. "Whuffor would they think he was aroun' here?"

Moon played his hunch. "Because you carried him up here—on your shoulder." He held his breath.

With the comically hopeless expression of a poorly crafted jack-o'-lantern, she stared.

He stared back. Like a man holding a fistful of aces.

Bobbie Sue blinked. "I din' do nothin' wrong."

An admission! He exhaled the bad air, drew in the good. "You don't think kidnapping is *wrong*?"

The big head hung, the eyelids drooped. From somewhere inside, the close-set eyes gazed at the pointy toes of Moon's cowhide boots. "Since I was jus' a little girl, I allus wanted me a boyfrien'." Slowly, appreciatively, Bobbie Sue's gaze traced a line up his leg, lingered on the slender torso, admired the pearl buttons on his shirt, stopped on his face. "Hit gets awful lonesome up here." The recluse glanced toward her hut. "An' I don' got nobody to talk to." She suddenly shook with a great sob, startling the Columbine hound and Charlie Moon. "So when I saw the car run off'n the road and bump into the tree and that little man get throwed onto the groun' . . . I brung him home with me." Another wrenching sob. "I was hopin' when he got well enough, he'd read to me."

The Indian, as the old saying goes, could have been knocked over with a feather. *A hummingbird* feather. "*Read* to you?"

"Uh-huh." She wiped away a tear with the back of a grimy hand. "I got me lots of magazines with pichurs. An' even some books." Her sigh was like a sudden gust of wind. "I figgered if he stayed long enough, he might even learn me to read some words."

Moon's voice could barely be heard above a breeze that was rattling waxy aspen leaves. "Is Mr. Turner injured?"

A shrug. "A little bit."

"Then he needs to go to the hospital." *Turner's probably in her shack. But she might have him stashed somewhere else. Someplace where I'd never find him.*

Bobbie Sue took the measure of the armed man. Also the dog, who had taken up position beside him. *I could take the both of 'em.* Her expression reflected an intense inner struggle, which the innocent shared with her adversary: "I jus' don' know what to do."

"That's easy—take me to Turner."

But of course it was not easy. She turned her face up, squinted at the bright, midday sky. Watched a pair of red-tailed hawks soar on a thermal. *That's where I want to go when I die. An' fly an' fly an' fly* . . . She heaved a great soul-lifting sigh. "If I do, would you make me a promise—cross your heart and hope to die?"

"Depends on what it is."

"You got to make sure that no cops or sojers comes up here to hunt me down and put me back in that crazy house." Her big hands clenched into formidable fists. "Before I'd let 'em lock me up with all them loonies, I'd hide in a hole in the ground. And if them hounds picked up my smell and cornered me, I'd kill as many dogs and cops and sojers as I could—and then I'd cut my throat an' bleed to death."

Moon knew this was no idle threat. "Bobbie Sue, I give you my word—if you'll take me to Andrew Turner, I won't tell a soul that you're here on the mountain." Fair play demands full disclosure. "But I can't promise that no one will come looking for you." *If he's able, Andrew Turner will talk his head off about you.*

"Then I guess I'll have to go away somewheres where nobody can ever fin' me." From somewhere deep inside, a low moan. "But I been on this mountain mos' of my life."

"There are others places to live. Better ones." He waited three heartbeats. "Now take me to Turner."

The lonely illiterate mumbled, "C'mon."

With the hound tagging along at his heels, Moon followed the enigmatic woman into the box canyon. The hulking figure in the grizzly pelt moved with graceful ease, making no more sound than the grass-scented breeze. When they were within a few paces of the shack snugged up against the base of the vertical canyon wall, Bobbie Sue stopped, pointed at the tattered buckskin flap hanging over the entrance. "He's in the back."

The Ute hesitated. *This seems too easy.*

Following the aim of her finger, the Columbine hound started to go inside.

"No," Moon said.

The dog paused, looked at the Ute.

Moon told Bobbie Sue how it was: "If Mr. Turner isn't in there—or if my dog gets hurt—or if you try to pull any kind of fast one, there'll be ten kinds of hell to pay. And you'll get the entire bill."

She appeared to be genuinely hurt. "He's in the back."

Eager to go exploring and evidently having picked up a scent, the hound whimpered.

Moon exchanged looks with the dog. *Okay, pardner. Go find him.*

Sidewinder slipped into the innards of the shack. After sniffing around, he began to whine. Presently, the gaunt dog stuck his head through the door hole, squinted in the filtered sunlight, looked up imploringly at the human being he had adopted several years ago. In dogeese, his expression said, more or less, *Hey—what are you waiting for, an engraved invitation?*

Charlie Moon was about to suggest that Bobbie Sue lead the way, when he realized that the huge woman had vanished without making a sound. *She's pulled a fast one on me—Turner's probably not within a mile of the place.* He swept his gaze over the forest. Didn't see anything that looked the least bit like an Amazon dressed in a bear suit. *Well, while I'm here, I might as well have a look.* He addressed the dog: "Stay outside, pardner. If she comes back, you let me know."

The noble beast whined, seated himself by the shack's entrance. Like all of his wolfish kind, Sidewinder was ready to do whatever was necessary to protect his friend.

• • •

FORTY-FIVE
INTO DARKNESS

The bearskin-woman's den was surprisingly uncluttered. Bobbie Sue's single room had neither table nor chair; her bed was a pile of hides in a corner. Moon frowned at two of several wall hangings—a pair of uncured German shepherd hides. *She wasn't kidding about eating dog meat.* In another corner there were a few dozen cans and jars of food. A rusty fifty-five gallon oil drum served as her stove. On the crimped-on lid, a battered steel bucket of flesh and onions bubbled. Venison, Moon decided. *That must be what Sidewinder caught a whiff of.* Beside the makeshift kettle, a gallon lard can half filled with black water. *That must be her coffeepot.* A sturdy plank shelf supported an assortment of old, worn magazines: *True Romance. Dangerous Romance. Sweet Romance. Forbidden Romance. Young Romance. Teen Romance.* There were a few paperback books with lurid covers: *My Latin Lover. My Pirate Lover. My Vampire Lover. Lust in Little Havana.* But there was no sign of the man Moon was looking for. Or, for that matter, anyplace where he could be concealed. Even so, Moon called out, "Turner—you here?"

Silence.

Then, at the rear of the shabby room, from behind a tanned elk hide hanging on the stone wall: "Oh, God—is that a human voice?"

Moon lifted the makeshift drape, stared into the inky shadows, smelled the man before he saw him. He found a book of Lulabelle's Dixie Restaurant matches in his pocket, ripped a half-dozen pages from *My Vampire Lover*. The makeshift torch illuminated the entrance to a horizontal mine shaft that swallowed up the puny glow of light. A few yards away, Andrew Turner—half covered in a filthy strip of canvas—was flat on his back on a bed of dead oak leaves and dried grass. The haggard, bearded face might have been that of a man twice as old; the wild eyes stared at the light.

"Who's that?"

Turner heard the Ute's deep voice: "Charlie Moon."

"Oh, thank God—thank *God!*" The captive began to weep. "Please, get me out of here before it comes back!"

"It?"

"That horrible creature that brought me here . . . please hurry!"

"How bad are you hurt?"

"I think my ankle's broken and I'm too weak to crawl. All it feeds me is half-cooked meat and raw pine nuts and roots and—" A gasp for breath. "Oh, please get me out of this stinking place!" His clawlike hand reached out and grabbed Moon's shirt. "If that monster comes back and finds you here, it'll murder both of us!"

"I'll not let any harm come to you." Ignoring the pleading protests, the Ute gently removed the grasping hand from his shirt, placed it on the terrified man's thin chest.

Turner's pleadings did not cease. "Look, I'll do anything, anything. Get me out of here, off the mountain—I'll pay you ten thousand dollars—hell, I'll pay you a *hundred* thousand, and I'll even give you my sixty-thousand-dollar sports car. . . ." For a moment, the face frowned as the mind tried to find a missing piece of a jumbled puzzle. He whispered, "What happened to my Corvette?"

"It hasn't been located yet, but we figure it's at the bottom of the Devil's Mouth. Under the snow."

"Oh, right. The snow. I'd forgotten all about that. It was dark, you know, and I came around that sharp bend in the driveway—" Turner began to shiver and shudder and mutter madly, "They were right there in front of me—so I cut the wheel hard and hit a tree and then I was on the ground, rolling in the snow and—"

"They *who*?"

"What?"

"You said you came around the bend and *they* were in front of you."

"Did I?" A big-eyed stare. A blink. "I guess it must've been some deer." A few raspy breaths. "I don't remember much after that, except being terribly cold—until that hideous, stinking creature picked me up and carried me off and I said to myself, Andrew, you have died and this devil is carrying you straight to hell!"

"You're not dead, Mr. Turner."

"Please . . . please—don't go away and leave me here!"

"I won't. I'm taking you with me." Moon laid the fading torch aside, rolled Turner up in the canvas bedcover. Considered carrying him in both arms. Reconsidered. *I'd better keep my gun hand free.* As Turner grunted and moaned, Moon eased the tightly wrapped man across his left shoulder. As he got to his feet, it occurred to Moon that at night in a snowstorm, a person with a quirky imagination might mistake him for a Sasquatch toting an oversize burrito. Dismissing this comical thought, the Ute ducked through the curtain into the cabin, across the little room, into the bright sunlight.

Sidewinder was at the door, panting happy breaths.

Bobbie Sue was nowhere to be seen. Not necessarily good news.

With the emaciated man folded over his shoulder, Charlie Moon started down the mountain in long, deliberate strides. He never slowed, never looked back. The surreal trip slipped by quickly—it seemed only minutes later when he laid his burden down in the bed of the Columbine pickup. In the bright light of day, he unrolled Andrew Turner from the filthy canvas. *Looks like he's passed out.* Moon checked for a pulse, felt a rhythmic thump under Turner's jaw. The injured man was breathing in intermittent gasps. Moon put in the 911 call, Clara Tavishuts answered on the second ring. He explained the situation, was assured by the GCPD dispatcher that assistance was practically on the way. While the rescuer waited for medical help to arrive, he had a few minutes to turn some interesting details over in his mind, also to look at the big picture this way and that. Before the silent sea of sky was churned up by noisy helicopter rotors, the tribal investigator had pretty much figured things out. *I'll tell Scott what he absolutely needs to know.* But not everything. Charlie Moon had a promise to keep. Moreover, a moral dilemma to deal with.

• • •

Scott Parris arrived in a unit driven by Officer Alicia Martin. With due attention to his recent injuries, the chief of police got out of the low-slung Chevrolet just in time to wave at his Ute friend and watch the arrival of the chopper. The emergency medical technicians had boots on the ground before the rotating-wing aircraft had quite touched down. Tall grasses and spindly young aspens twisted in the machine's self-generated tornado.

Holding on to his Stetson, Charlie Moon pointed at the Columbine pickup.

In the bed, covered by a Columbine horse blanket, the EMTs found a patient who had a decent pulse (54 per minute), pupils that responded to light, edgy blood pressure (88 over 45), a coolish inner-ear temperature (95.1 F), and raspy breaths at the rate of nine per minute. Whether Mr. Turner was merely deeply asleep or unconscious, he did not respond to stock questions like "Can you hear me?" and "What's your name?" Evidently, the talkative part of his brain was at rest. The efficient medics stabilized him with a saline IV spiked with glucose and other restorative ingredients, placed his foul-smelling body onto an ultralightweight gurney, buckled nylon straps across his chest and legs, and inserted him into the Air National Guard rescue helicopter, which lifted off in a swirl of dust and debris.

Parris informed his uniformed chauffeur that she would

return to Granite Creek without him. His plan was to hitch a ride with Charlie Moon, and in the quiet atmosphere of the Columbine, get the whole story. Soon, the sleek GCPD unit was out of sight, the earsplitting sounds of the aircraft were but a memory.

Parris was getting into Moon's pickup—when a terrible wailing was heard from someplace on the mountain.

In response, Sidewinder threw back his head and howled, *Hooo-ooooww . . . Oooow-oooo . . .*

His skin prickling, Parris did not ask, *What was that?* He thought he knew.

Moon was the one who knew. *Poor thing—she's all by herself now.* He headed the old pickup downhill, leaving the lonely woman behind.

As they passed through the open gate, Parris put in a call to the GCPD dispatcher, directed Clara Tavishuts to get in touch with Andrew Turner's wife. Clara was already on top of it. She had contacted the local travel agencies, found out that Beatrice was in San Diego, placed a call to her beachfront hotel. The last of the Spencer sisters would be on the next available flight to Colorado Springs, where she would take a charter flight to Granite Creek Municipal Airport.

• • •

FORTY-SIX

THAT EVENING AT THE COLUMBINE

During a fine supper of slow-roasted prime beef and baked potatoes (the tasty twosome soaked in thick brown mushroom gravy), boiled pinto beans, and made-from-scratch biscuits, Scott Parris and Charlie Moon talked about everything but subject number one. Weather. Politics. Cop gossip. Aunt Daisy. Parris asked how the tribal elder was getting along.

"About the same as usual." Charlie Moon wondered what it would be like to have a normal aunt. Sweet little old white-haired lady who knitted her nephew socks and sweaters. And never got into trouble.

"You two smoked the peace pipe yet?"

The tribal investigator shot his guest a look.

"Hey, Charlie—I'm a professional cop." A smirk. "You can't keep any family secrets from me."

Moon twirled a teaspoon into the honey jar, transferred a big gob of bee-product to his coffee. "Tomorrow morning, I'll pick up Aunt Daisy and Sarah—bring 'em back to the Columbine for a few days."

"That should be fun." Like wrestling alligators.

"Yeah." The Ute stirred the dark liquid. "The kid likes to ride horses."

"And bake rhubarb pies." Parris chuckled.

Moon smiled. "That too."

"Does Sarah like to wash dishes?"

"What?"

Parris waved his hand at the table. "I figured maybe we could leave this pile till she shows up tomorrow."

Nice try. While Moon washed, Parris dried.

Then, to the parlor and fireplace. It was time.

As they warmed their knees, the chief of police said, "Okay. Tell me how you managed to find Andy Turner."

The Ute provided his friend with a truthful but deceptively sparse account of how (with the aid of his hound's highly sensitive nose) he had discovered Bea's missing husband in a long-abandoned mine shaft. But, true to his promise, he made no mention of Bobbie Sue, or the fact that the entrance to the mine was concealed behind a tumbledown shack. The tribal investigator repeated Turner's claim that when he had rounded the curve on that snowy night, he had swerved to avoid a collision.

"With what?"

"Some deer."

"Deer, huh?"

"That's what the man said."

"I guess that makes sense." *More sense that a Bigfoot in the Spencer driveway. Or a couple of witches floating above it.* Parris was half mesmerized by the hypnotically alluring dance of a pair of wavering flames. "Lucky thing for Turner that he got thrown clear. I was sure he was down in the Devil's Mouth with his Corvette, frozen stiff as a post." He experienced a sudden chill. *That fire needs some more wood.*

The Ute got up from his comfortable chair, selected two chunks of split pine, placed them just so.

Sometimes it's like Charlie can read my mind. The town cop cast a sly glance at the Indian. "But there's something a little peculiar about it."

Moon jabbed an iron poker at a cluster of rosy embers. "What's that?"

"How does Turner, after he gets tossed from his Corvette—bunged up and all—crawl across the driveway in a blizzard, clamber up the side of the mountain and into a mine shaft." Parris took a sip of coffee. *This'll keep me awake half the night.* "How do you figure he managed it, Charlie?"

"I don't." Moon leaned the sooty poker beside its fellows—a leather bellows and an iron ash shovel. "Figuring is your department."

"How do you figure that?"

Moon eased himself back into the rocking chair. "Way I see things, I'm just a humble deputized helper. I draw twelve-fifty an hour to do your flunky work—like finding a missing person you figured was stone-cold dead in the Devil's Mouth. 'Figuring' isn't mentioned in my job description."

Scott Parris was certain that his friend was holding a little something back. *But when Charlie ain't ready to share his thoughts, there's no point in pressing him.*

Charlie Moon was holding a lot back. Case in point: Bobbie Sue's recipe for wrapping a man-size burrito. Though honor-bound by his promise not to reveal her presence on the mountain, he had no doubt that Andrew Turner would accuse some vaguely defined "it" of kidnapping, false imprisonment, and providing unfit nourishment. Once the chief of police had heard that alarming testimony, he would be obligated to organize a thorough search of Spencer Mountain. The most likely outcome was that Miss Bigfoot would be captured, nevermore to roam the shadowy forests, slay deer with her homemade crossbow, or dine on succulent snake flesh for breakfast. Properly sedated, Bobbie Sue would while away the rest of her days in a comfortable, barred room, consuming well-balanced meals, drifting from one drugged slumber to the next. Which, Moon thought, was a great pity. But it seemed that her dismal fate was sealed.

Not necessarily.

The future always has a few surprises concealed in its long, voluminous sleeve.

As Scott Parris was debating whether he should finish the potent cup of coffee, the cell phone in his jacket pocket produced a summons and was answered. The caller was the rookie officer on night duty at the hospital.

"Pinkerton reporting, sir."

"What's up, Pink?"

The unseen policeman, who never relied entirely upon his excellent memory, consulted neatly penned entries in his pocket notebook. His report was terse: "Mr. Turner's been moved from the ER to the ICU."

"Well, that sounds hopeful."

"Beatrice Spencer showed up at nineteen hundred hours on the button. She's been at her husband's bedside ever since."

"Has Turner said anything?"

"Not a word."

"Anything else?"

Pinkerton flipped to the next page. "Dr. Jarvis reports that Mr. Turner has lapsed into a coma. Might live. Might not." He observed that this diagnosis had all bases covered.

Parris's voice lowered both in tone and in volume—a danger sign. "Officer Pinkerton, why did you not tell me right up front that the patient had lapsed into a potentially terminal coma?"

Pinkerton's reply, which was stiff, made it clear that the do-it-by-the-book cop was miffed. "I make my notes in chronological order, sir—and that's the way I read 'em."

Rolling his eyes, the chief of police stared at massive pine beams supporting the Columbine headquarters ceiling. *Why me, God.*

A rhetorical prayer-query cannot reasonably be expected to elicit a response. Even so, one should tend toward caution when addressing the Source of all that is.

• • •

FORTY-SEVEN
GRANITE CREEK, COLORADO

Snyder Memorial Hospital Intensive Care Unit

For a slender, elegant, delicately proportioned woman who tipped the scales at 109 pounds, Beatrice Spencer was remarkably effective in throwing her weight around. It helped, of course, that the Spencer clan had been a major contributor to the annual hospital fund-raisers, and that a shiny brass plaque screwed to the wall of the ICU waiting room advised commoners and upper crust alike that Bea was personally responsible for outfitting surgical suites 1 and 2. For these fiscally sound reasons, not to mention her natural butt-heads-with-me-and-die charisma, when Beatrice had sweetly "asked" that Head Nurse Hortense Patten have a full-size couch removed from the visitor's lounge and placed at her husband's bedside, the request was approved without the slightest elevation of the boss nurse's meticulously plucked, finely penciled eyebrow. This victory impressed the foot-soldier nurses, who referred to their superior as "General Patten." Not to her face, of course, which heavy-jowled visage suggested a bulldog with a severe case of distemper.

Juice is what Beatrice had.

And a cold, calculated determination to have her way.

Which, in virtually every instance, she did. Those rare exceptions included Charlie Moon's flat refusal to allow Bea and Cassie to enter Sister Astrid's home, following the presumed bear attack.

The hospital staff, even including General Patten, were

touched by the wealthy woman's devotion to her seriously ill, perhaps dying husband. Beatrice rarely left Andrew's bedside. During the daylight hours, she conducted business on her cell phone, patted his pale, limp hand, bathed his fevered brow with a damp washcloth, whispered in his ear as if the comatose man might hear her endearing words, et cetera. The most astonishing sacrifice was that the gourmet cook consumed the bland hospital fare without the slightest complaint. A case in point being macaroni that never managed to be either hot or cold, but always congealed into a yellowish cheeselike substance. Also, glutinous chicken à la king spilled onto charred Wonder Bread, and little plastic tubs of Jell-O in colors never seen in nature—some bearing small, dark, suspiciously semicrunchy objects that were most probably stale raisins but might just as well have been husks of recently deceased six-legged creatures.

Moxie is what Beatrice had. By the truckload. Plus a focused, passionate resolve to be present when (if?) Andrew opened his eyes, murmured his first coherent words.

Which she was. Present. When he did.

The electrifying event occurred on the third day following his rescue by that strange, taciturn Indian policeman. It happened just after lunch (boiled chicken, cold spaghetti floating in a reddish yellow liquid that suggested the vital body fluid of some lower form of life. Oh, and blue Jell-O).

While Beatrice was manfully (yes, *manfully*) using a three-tined green plastic fork to place the last bite of something or other into her mouth—her husband, almost as if he were being force-fed the writhing spaghetti while blindfolded and being told that he was eating earthworms (an innocent prank played on those young unfortunates who are being initiated into the ranks of certain Greek-letter university fraternities), uttered that first, postcomatose word. Well, not a word one could look up in Webster's or American Heritage. And he did not exactly *say* it. He screeched like a nudist who has seated himself on a bristling cluster of prickly pear cactus. "Heeeaaah!"

Simultaneously, he flung out his right arm, knocked a

lamp off the bedside table, which impact fractured the sixty-watt bulb, which shorted and exploded with a re-sounding flash and *pop!* (thus deserving the descriptor "electrifying event"). As if the first remark might have gone unnoticed, he repeated it, verbatim—"Heeeaaah!"—flung the other arm, sent a sturdy IV stand careening into a corner.

Needless to say, even cool-as-ice Beatrice was startled by this unexpected and energetic display of shrieks, fire-works, and toppled objects. But not enough to drop her fork, or emit a little yelp, or swallow too suddenly. The woman was extremely well bred. But she did look up. Somewhat sharply, and with an expression of frank disap-proval. Putting both plate and fork aside, she leaned close to her roommate, used that tone mothers adopt when piqued with naughty children. "Andrew!"

No response.

"Can you hear me?"

"Mmm-hmmm."

"Does that mean 'yes'?"

"Mmm-hmmm." The left eye opened, the dilated pupil shrunk in the bright light. Then, the right. Both eyes blinked.

The wife reached out to touch her mate's clammy fore-head. "Andrew, I'm so . . . so *pleased* that you are finally able to speak."

"Foog."

She turned her preferred ear (the right one) toward his mouth. "What?"

"Izmell foog."

Almost of their own accord, Bea's perfect lips smiled. "Are you trying to say that you smell food?"

"Mmm-hmmm."

The smile slipped away, the lips pursed to reflect an in-ner worry. *I hope he has not suffered brain damage.*

To avoid unnecessary suspense, it will immediately be revealed that he had not.

Andrew Turner was heavily sedated; "narcoticized," for those who are thrilled to learn a new technical term. His power of speech would return, as good as ever. Indeed, within a few hours, Bea's husband would be counted once again among that glib large-vocabulary clique who are assumed to be highly intelligent. But that popular misconception is neither here nor there. What is of some significance is that the chief of police was not there but here.

Clarification: Scott Parris, who only a half hour earlier had been *there* (in his office, having a lunch of rice cakes and low-cal banana yogurt), was at this very moment *here*, in the ICU. Following Moon's discovery of a still-living Andrew Turner, Parris's recovery from injuries suffered in the Moxon encounter had been remarkable. He had regained his full quota of energy and optimism. Also copish tradecraft. Having heard snippets of the semiconversation between Beatrice and her husband, Parris stepped softly. Entered the room with hardly a sound.

The patient had focused his eyes on the pretty woman at his bedside. "Bea?'

"Yes, dear." She squeezed his limp hand. "How do you feel?"

"Awwfuum." The eyelids drooped.

"Before you . . . ah . . . drift off to sleep again, tell me—do you remember anything about your accident?"

The head on the pillow attempted a nod. "Mmmm-hmmm."

"What happened?"

Turner's eyes blinked, the voice quavered. "Goss!"

Her skills as a translator were improving by the second. "Are you trying to say *ghost*—or possibly *ghosts*?"

"Yesssss," he hissed, and pointed at the apparition that floated in his memory. "Goss-es . . . in fonna my car."

A voice boomed out, "You saw ghosts in front of your car?"

Scott Parris's thunderous query made Bea's heart do a flip-flop, but she neither lurched nor made an audible exclamation. She turned to glare at Granite Creek's top cop, inquired, "Where on earth did you come from?"

The lawman tipped his battered felt hat, gave the question

due thought. "Before I headed west to Colorado, which was five days after I retired, I was with Chicago PD. Back in 1960, I was a mere slip of a lad in East Pigeon Creek, Indiana." There were several notable spots in between that he did not wish to address at the moment.

No great fan of Parris's notion of humor, Ms. Spencer managed a long-suffering smile. She also anticipated the query hanging on the tip of the lawman's tongue. "Andrew regained consciousness about a minute ago."

Parris eyed the broken lamp on the floor, the upended IV stand. "What'd he do, wake up throwing punches?"

"Yes. More or less." She returned her attention to the patient. "Mr. Parris is here." Taking note of Andrew's blank look, she enlarged on the news: "He is, for better or worse, our local chief of police."

Ignoring the jibe, the big, beefy cop knelt by the bedside. "Hey, Andy—what's all this stuff about ghosts?" *You told Charlie Moon you saw deer on the driveway.*

Andrew Turner blinked at the policeman, shot a glance at his wife, dropped his gaze to the blue sheet over his thin form. "Dummo."

Parris scowled. "What'd you say?"

"Andrew has been heavily sedated," the wife explained. "But I believe he was attempting to say 'dunno,' which was intended to convey the message that he 'does not know.' "

Parris was staring holes into the patient. "Anything you might remember about that snowy night when you ran your Corvette off the driveway would be very interesting to me."

Turner licked at dry lips; his fingers played with the hem of the sheet. "Don' meremmer noffin'."

The cop didn't buy a word of it. "You must remember Charlie Moon finding you in a mine shaft."

Fear glinted in Andrew Turner's eyes. "Huh-uh. Don' meremmer noffin'." He heaved a great sigh, closed his eyes. His head rolled sideways on the pillow.

"He's fallen asleep," Beatrice whispered.

"Yeah." *Or he's playing possum.* With a grunt, the big man pushed himself erect. Parris stood with thumbs hitched in his belt, watched Turner's pale face for some in-dication of deception. *I guess he is asleep.* "When he wake ups and starts talking again—try to remember everything he has to say."

"Certainly. I will write it down."

Parris shifted his gaze to her attractive, upturned face. "That night when we were driving up the hill—and you skidded to a stop near where his car had hit the tree . . ."

She waited. "What about it?"

The policeman had a hard time asking the question. "Did you see anything—uh—unusual?"

"Unusual?" Beatrice smiled. "Like what?"

"I just wondered if you might've seen something—" *Like a big ape, carrying something on its shoulder.* He felt his face blush. "Maybe a large animal near the site of the acci-dent."

"If I had, I would have told you." She stared at the police-man with an intense expression. "Did *you* see something?"

"Uh—I thought so."

"I suppose the accident might have been caused by an animal in the road." Bea glanced at her husband. *But poor Andrew believes he saw ghosts. Imagine that.*

"Maybe Andy'll remember something in a day or two. When he's feeling better." Scott Parris scratched at an itchy stubble of beard on his chin. *I forgot to shave again.* "Well, see you later." He took a parting look at the frail figure in the bed, grunted, turned on his heel, and was gone.

Beatrice Spencer watched the door close behind him, lis-tened to the thumping of his boots on the tile hallway floor. *What an extraordinary man.* Coming from a connoisseur of the beard-growing gender, this was no small compliment. One the chief of police—who had a goodly share of male vanity—would have appreciated.

• • •

FORTY-EIGHT
WHAT THE LADY NEEDS IS A SUITABLE
PLACE TO MEDITATE

When Daisy Perika awakened in her Columbine bedroom at dawn, she was agitated. Make that *highly* agitated. What was amiss? This source of her unease was rooted in a recent event. No, not the fracas with Charlie Moon over her shady business deal with the late Cassandra Spencer; Daisy had a rare gift for dismissing all memory of disputes where she was entirely at fault. This particular annoyance, which involved a memory she wished to recall, could be traced to that night when the chilly little *pitukupf* had invaded the Ute elder's cozy home in search of warmth. In exchange for the privilege of sleeping in bed beside Daisy, the dwarf had filled her in on that long-ago event where little Astrid Spencer had gotten so sick that she almost died. No, that is not entirely accurate. The little man, who never quite managed to get the whole job done, had *partially* unlocked Daisy's memory. Thanks to the *pitukupf,* the shaman knew *where* she'd seen the three Spencer sisters and their father—it was at the Durango Arts and Crafts Fair. And Daisy was virtually certain that something the girl had eaten was to blame. *But what was it?* A bite or two of spoiled meat could kill a person. Another possibility occurred to her: *It might've been some perfectly good food that just didn't sit right with the little girl—maybe something she was allergic to.* Daisy held a sigh inside. *It could've been almost anything.* This was terribly frustrating. *At the time, I knew what it was that made her sick—so it's still there in my head, with all those other things I can't recollect.* As the aged woman buttoned her blue-with-white-polka-dots cotton dress, stepped into a pair of soft black slippers, she decided that she needed to get away for a few hours. To someplace that would allow her mind to have some peace. That might enable the memory to come to her.

If she had been at home, Daisy would have taken her oak staff from the corner by the front door and gone on a long, soul-soothing walk in *Cañon del Espíritu.* There were many quiet, out-of-the-way places here on the Columbine to go for a stroll, but if she so much as stepped off the porch, the cowboy assigned to look after Charlie Moon's aged aunt would appear, politely ask if there was "Anything I can do for you, ma'am?"

Daisy hated being "ma'am-ed." And she did not appreciate being "looked after." But what she hated and did not appreciate did not carry much weight on Charlie's ranch. He was the big honcho here.

If she attempted to ignore the hired hand, and went for a walk along the riverbank, Texas Bob or Pink-Eye Pete or Six-Toes would sidle up beside her, offer inane remarks about what a fine day it was for stretchin' the legs and it would sure be nice if we could get some rain and how Charlie Moon was the best boss he'd ever worked for. If Daisy mentioned that she preferred to be by herself, the amiable man under the big, wide-brimmed hat who carried a scent of manure on his big boots (they all looked and talked and smelled the same) would invariably smile and fall a few paces behind. She might not be able to see the cow-pie kicker, or hear his shuffling footsteps, but he was there, all right. And Charlie Moon's faithful employee would dog her until she was back at the ranch headquarters.

It was infuriating.

I need to get away for a little while. If I had some time to relax, what I need to remember might come to me. But how can I slip away from here without Charlie getting suspicious? And if I did, where would I go?

The solution was provided in the fifteen-year-old person of Sarah Frank, who was wearing a happy smile and carrying a grocery list, which she waved at the tribal elder. "I'm going to town to get some cornmeal and sugar and stuff—want to come along?"

"Who's taking you?"

"One of the cowboys."

"Which one?"

"Mr. Kydmann."

Daisy managed to frown with one eye. "That the one they call the Wyomin' Kyd?"

Sarah nodded.

The Wyoming Kyd was Moon's most trusted employee. He was also an uncommonly good-looking young cowboy. Which, in Daisy's mind, made him a particularly unsuitable escort for a semi-pretty Ute-Papago girl who had about as much sense as anyone else her age. Which was barely enough to remember to breathe in and breathe out. Maybe the Kyd could be trusted, but not with this teenager. "I'll come along."

And so Daisy did. With Kydmann's assistance, she got into the mud-splattered pickup truck before Sarah did, so she could sit between the handsome driver and the silly girl.

To the Ute woman's surprise, the ride to Granite Creek turned out to be a pleasant experience. Despite the sound of 1940s' honky-tonk blasting from the dashboard radio, the incessant chatter passing back and forth between Sarah and the driver, the roar of big trucks they met on the two-lane, the old woman managed to relax. Came very near to dozing off.

At the Smith's Supermarket parking lot, Kydmann helped the elderly woman from the pickup, tipped his white cowboy hat, allowed as how he would wait outside.

Inside the cavernous store, Daisy insisted on pushing the cart, which served as a suitable walker for her. Up and down the aisles they went, Sarah picking up a box of this, a carton of that, a bottle or jar of something else, and all went well until they arrived at the display of jams and jellies.

"Oh—there's not any left."

Daisy Perika, who had been musing about something or other, looked up. "Any what?"

The disappointed girl pointed at an empty space. "Honey."

The Ute woman could see a multitude of plastic bottles shaped like cute little bear cubs. "There's plenty of honey."

"Charlie Moon likes the Tule Creek kind." Sarah added a further tidbit of information: "It comes from Texas."

"Texas, huh?" Every man she'd ever met from that state called her "ma'am." Daisy pointed at the shelf. "Honey is honey and my nephew's a big gourd head. Get him some of that Sugar Bear kind—he won't know the difference."

Sarah would not give an inch. "Charlie made out the list himself, and right here it says 'Tule Creek.'" As evidence, she held the piece of paper in front of Daisy's face.

With a rude swipe of her hand, the old woman brushed it away. "If he's too good for Sugar Bear, then let him do without."

The prospect of failing to bring home the proper brand of bee-processed nectar appalled the youthful shopper. "Maybe Mr. Kydmann will take us to another store."

Without a doubt, Mr. Kydmann would have. And if he had, perhaps Sarah would have found those one-and-a-half-pound jars produced by swarms of busy Lone Star bees who reside within the Tule Creek Apiary in Tulia, Texas. But as it turned out, a trip to another food store would not be necessary.

When Daisy turned the cart into aisle 9, she collided with another such vehicle, which was pushed by someone she recognized.

"Beatrice," Daisy said, for that was the white woman's name.

Andrew Turner's wife smiled. "Why, hello." *I should know who she is. Oh, of course . . .* "You're Charlie Moon's aunt!"

"Thanks. But I already knew that."

Bea blushed. "You're his aunt . . . Pansy."

"Daisy."

"Of course. Cassie's Navajo friend."

"I'm a Ute."

"Oh. So sorry."

"Not me. I'd rather be the sorriest Ute that ever lived than Queen of the Navajos."

Beatrice tried small talk: "So—what brings you here?"

"Shopping for food, just like you white people." Daisy's grin was cruel. "When us Utes can't find a deer or turkey to shoot an arrow at, we come to the grocery store and buy us a few pounds of hamburger meat."

To relieve the growing tension, Sarah intervened. "We wanted to buy some honey, but they were all out of the kind Charlie Moon likes."

"That is probably my fault." Beatrice reached into her shopping cart, removed a jar of amber stuff. "Is this brand you were looking for?"

Sarah nodded.

"I have plenty. Please take this one." She placed it into Daisy's cart.

"Oh, thank you so much!" The girl hesitated, then blurted it out: "Actually, we needed two jars."

Though her perfectly trimmed left brow arched by almost a full millimeter, Beatrice transferred another container to the other cart. Breeding will tell.

Daisy, who had been inspecting the contents of the white woman's shopping cart, raised her gaze to the pale, pretty face. "How's your husband getting along?"

So—the mercurial old witch has decided to be civil. "It is so kind of you to ask. I am happy to report that Andrew is much improved. So much so that he will be coming home from the hospital tomorrow." *I must make my escape before she turns nasty again.* Beatrice nodded at the wrinkled woman, smiled at the thin little girl. "If you will excuse me now, I must be off. So much to do, you know—and so little time."

Sarah picked up the jars of honey, held them against her thin chest. "She's a very nice lady."

Daisy barely suppressed a snort. "What's next on your list?"

"Pie mix," Sarah said. "I wonder if they have cherry."

"Charlie likes cherry pies." The old woman was watching Beatrice Spencer head toward the produce section. "But don't buy any of that fancy filling. What you want is some canned cherries and . . ."

The teenager stared at the old woman, who seemed to have drifted off to another place. "Aunt Daisy?"

No response. Charlie's aunt was far away. And so very close to that tantalizing information concealed in her troubled mind. But the coy memory was like one of Charlie Moon's annoying cowboys, who trailed only a few paces behind Daisy—but just barely out of sight. What was it that little Astrid Spencer had eaten that made her so sick—a piece of pie? *No, I don't think so.* It was maddening. Enough to make a person want to throw a rock and break something.

• • •

FORTY-NINE
THE DREAMTIME

After telling Charlie Moon good night and reminding Sarah Frank that she shouldn't stay up too late, Daisy plodded off to her bedroom. The weary woman undressed, pulled on a warm flannel nightgown, took a sip from a glass of cold well-water, seated her shrunken frame in a padded armchair, turned off the lamp by her bed, closed her eyes, sat listening to the night. Little squeaks and creaks as the big log house cooled down. A rushing sound as someone turned on a kitchen-sink faucet. A soft humming as the well pump switched on to fill the tank—a thump as a pressure sensor shut off the pump at forty-eight pounds per square inch. Down at the barn, a restless horse kicked in its stall. In the bunkhouse, a cowboy strummed an off-tune guitar, howled out a Mexican ballad about a vaquero who'd knifed a faithless wife. Up on Pine Knob, a coyote joined in with a mournful chorus. As she enjoyed this peaceful interlude in the darkness, the tribal elder drifted off into her thoughts. *The green chili posole with lamb we had for supper sure was tasty. And that meeting with Beatrice Spencer in the supermarket was interesting.* She frowned at the darkness. *And something Sarah said almost reminded me of something but I can't quite figure out what.*

Feeling the heavy approach of sleep, she got up from the chair, into bed, pulled the quilt up to her chin, began her nightly prayers (mainly a list of names of those who needed healings and other tender mercies), yawned, lost her place, started up again with a mention of Louise-Marie LaForte, her French-Canadian friend in Ignacio, who had been a widow for almost forty years. Daisy reminded God that Louise-Marie was frail and could use some help with her arthritic joints. An afterthought: It would also be nice if some thoughtful neighbor would get Louise-Marie's Oldsmobile up and running again, so she could go places old women need to go to, like the supermarket and the drugstore and the post office and church. The kindhearted petitioner did not bother to mention the fact that it would also be nice if Louise-Marie was able to drive Daisy someplace now and again. God, she suspected, was unlikely to respond to her request if He detected the least hint of a selfish motive.

Another yawn. *Where was I in my prayers? Oh, yes. Now I remem—*

But the memory came too late. Daisy Perika had drifted off to sleep.

And perchance, to dream.

Which she did.

It was probably not a coincidence that the subject of her prayers appeared in her night-vision. Louise-Marie was standing at a long table, ladling out her homemade punch to hordes of squealing, laughing children. What was this— a church picnic? No. Daisy was in a large, freshly mown, grassy field by the river. But which river? Not the rocky Piedra, which flowed through the eastern edge of the Southern Ute reservation. And not the Los Piños, which coursed its way through the central portion of the res, watering Ignacio along the way. This stream (she could tell by the dark-green tint, the telltale scent of curly-leaf mint) was the *Rio de las Ánimas Perdidas*—the River of Lost Souls. And over yonder, maybe a mile away, was the Strater Hotel. This grassy park was in Durango, where they had held the arts-and-crafts fair some thirty years ago.

As Daisy watched the scene unfold, two well-dressed little white girls, one with golden curls, the other with straight-combed, raven-black locks, approached the punch bowl to accept plastic cups of the bloodred concoction from Louise-Marie's ladle. They turned to go and then—as if it were a generous afterthought—requested a third cup. "It's for our sister," Black Hair (Cassandra) said. With an angelic expression, Blondie (Beatrice) added, "She's awfully thirsty."

"I bet you just want the extra punch for yourselves." The good-natured lady with the ladle put on a suspicious expression. "How do I know you've even got another sister?"

This unexpected question produced puzzled looks.

Louise-Marie continued her game: "Does this thirsty sister have a name?"

"Oh, yes," the blond one said. The dark-haired little beauty added, "Astrid." The other sister said, "Astrid is our little sister."

"Well why don't little Astrid come and get her own punch?"

Beatrice: "Astrid never goes anywhere."

Cassandra: "Astrid's a little sissy—she whines and hangs on to Daddy's coattails." The elder sisters glanced at each other, giggled.

Louise-Marie doled out the third cup of punch, and the pretty little *matukach* girls departed.

Daisy Perika watched them go. And after a moment or so, heard a big commotion. Her feet just above the grass, the unseen dreamer glided toward the disturbance. The first thing she saw—and heard—was a familiar figure. Old man Joe Spencer. He was holding a tiny girl in his arms, speaking through clenched teeth to his older daughters. "You foolish, foolish children—what were you trying to do—*kill* your little sister!"

Beatrice and Cassandra were shaking their heads. Both of them said, "No, no, Daddy—we forgot . . . we forgot. . . ."

The visionary understood that now, and for some years to come, all would be well. No one had killed the little girl. Little Astrid was not dead. Not yet. Not here in the Dreamtime.

• • •

Daisy Perika awakened with a start that almost stopped her heart, sat upright in bed, put her feet on the floor. She thought she had things figured out. *But I need to be sure.* Switching the lamp on, she reached for the telephone, dialed the number she knew as well as the one on her Social Security card.

After eight rings, a sleepy voice: "Who's calling?"

The Ute elder snapped at her French-Canadian friend on the other end, "It's me."

"Oh, my—Daisy? You hardly ever call me this late at night—is something wrong?"

Daisy nodded. "Yes. I think so."

The elderly white woman in Ignacio was well acquainted with two kinds of trouble—illness and death. "Are you sick? Has somebody died?"

"I'm not sick." *But somebody has died.* "I need to ask you about something that happened about thirty years ago. It's was at that art show in Durango—where the children brought their watercolor paintings and little things they made out of clay and whatnot."

"Why I recall that. I used to go there almost every year."

Now the Big Question. "Louise-Marie, do you remember what you *did* there?" Daisy held her breath.

"Why I provided the punch—you ought to remember that."

The Ute elder exhaled, took another deep breath. "D'you remember the time when that little white girl passed out?"

A dead silence.

"Louise-Marie—are you still there."

"Yes I am."

"Then why didn't you answer me?"

"Because I don't like to think about bad things. Or talk about them."

Silly old white woman. "So you do remember."

"Of course I do, Daisy. That poor little girl—they said she came very close to *dying.*" A pause, while Louise-Marie found the little-used muscles to assemble a scowl. "Her father blamed her sisters—and my punch!"

Now the Really Big Question. "Louise-Marie—I know it's been an awful long time ago—but do you recall what was in that punch?"

"Well of course I do. I made it the same way every year." Another silence.

"Would you mind telling me?"

A sniff. Then: "It's a *secret* recipe."

Daisy thumped her fist on the bedside table. "Listen to me—this is important. *Really* important."

"Well . . . I don't know if I should. My mother taught me how to make it. And her mother taught her. And all the way back."

Daisy barely suppressed a snort. "I promise not to tell a living soul." *Not unless I absolutely have to.*

"Well, okay then." Not without misgivings, Louise-Marie revealed the top-secret recipe for Glorious Summer Punch to her Ute friend.

• • •

Daisy Perika did not sleep another wink that night. In the darkness, she was beginning to see a little speck of light. As the small hours grew larger, the speck became a candle flame. As a bloodred sunflower bloomed over the Buckhorn Range, the Full Truth dawned upon the tribal elder. But knowing wasn't enough—how could she put her knowledge to work? Especially when the person she needed to manipulate was Charlie Moon, who believed his aged aunt was way over on yonder side of that well-known hill. *The big gourd head!*

• • •

FIFTY

A FINE MORNING AT THE COLUMBINE

By the time Daisy Perika had grunted and groaned her way out of bed, hobbled into the headquarters kitchen, made a pot of brackish coffee, downed half a cup—Charlie Moon was already "up-and-at-'em." Sarah Frank was following the tall, lean man around like a restless puppy, pleading that he let her make the bacon-and-egg, biscuit-and-gravy breakfast, which he did. By the time the day's first meal (watery eggs and half-cooked bacon, excellent biscuits and passable brown gravy) was on the table, foreman Pete Bushman was bam-bamming his fist on the kitchen door, tipping his droopy-brimmed cowboy hat at "the ladies," getting the day's marching orders from the boss, who wanted two men sent to repair a break in the fence north of Pine Knob. While Moon was helping Sarah wash the breakfast dishes, Scott Parris showed up, finished off a cup of leftover coffee, all the while chatting excitedly with his Ute friend about their plans for an all-night fishing cam-pout at Lake Jessie, which was just behind the spruce-forested ridge, set like an emerald in the flowered dress of the rolling high-country prairie.

In Parris's view—and he was an angler who knew how to tie flies and tell fisherman lies—a red woolly-popper would be just the thing. Those twenty-inch rainbows would not be able to resist such a delicacy.

The Ute did not bother to voice his well-known opinion, which was that what sensible fish liked in any season was raw meat. Wriggly red worms. Succulent chunks of beef liver.

Daisy suggested crickets.

When the fisherman turned an ear to listen to the tribal elder's sage counsel, she allowed as how the fat black insects must be tied to the hook. With a hank of brown horsehair if a person had some handy. But don't run a hook through it. Injure a cricket and your gums will bleed, your eyes will cross, and your bowels will—Well, never mind *that.*

Scott Parris assured Daisy that if a cricket happened by he would give it a try. And though he could not assure her that he would use brown horsehair to affix it to the barbed instrument, he promised not to impale the creature.

Pete Bushman returned to inform the boss that four steers were "down in the west pasture with a fever, an' one of 'em's got a big sore on his lip." The animals were not yet dead, but (so the self-educated PhD in cow-ology opined) they would certainly be among the deceased before sundown. "I sure hope it ain't the hoof-and-mouth—that'd wipe us out for sure. But don't worry, I already called the vet'nary doc to come have a look. He said he might get here tomorrow. Or the day after." As if this were not enough, the foreman (noting the presence of the local chief of police) was reminded of what he had disremembered to report during his earlier visit—that three of the cowboys were being detained in cramped quarters at Granite Creek PD.

Scott Parris, who had intended to delay the bad news for at least an hour or two, verified the truth of this report. By eyewitness accounts, apparently after two or three six-packs too many, one of those bowlegged rascals had driven the GMC Columbine flatbed truck through the window of Little Bennie's Bar and Grill. The other two had come along for the joyride. There was no apparent motive, aside from the fact that Little Bennie had, in a fit of pique over an unpaid bar bill and several unwarranted insults, laid a pool cue across the skull of Six-Toes, who happened to be the Columbine employee behind the wheel when the flatbed went through Bennie's plate glass window, which would probably cost at least a thousand dollars to replace. Which, since he ran a rough joint, was well under the deductible on Bennie's insurance policy.

As Moon was attempting to learn more details, Sarah Frank dropped a heavy crockery platter, which did not break. But it did land on her big toe and she let out a terrific yowl.

Sidewinder apparently admired the sound of her wail. The quirky Columbine hound joined in to provide a high-pitched accompaniment. It was, a passing bunkhouse critic would later assert to his comrades, "a memorable piece of disharmony."

It was also a run-of-the-mill morning within the boundaries of Charlie Moon's grassy kingdom.

There was much more during the next few hours, but let us skip over these equally interesting incidents and cut right to the chase. Fast forward to half past four in the afternoon.

On the west side of the two-story log house, on the wraparound porch, we find Scott Parris and Charlie Moon. The men are seated on a redwood bench, watching fuzzy shadows try to pull themselves loose from cottonwood trees, horse barns, and fence posts. Parris, who has already forgotten about crickets, is putting the final touches on a handmade red woolly-popper. The Ute, who appears to be doing nothing at all except staring off into the distance, is thinking about four valuable purebred Herefords that are ailing. *I wonder what's wrong with 'em. Hope it's nothing contagious.* And about three cowboys and a broken window. *I'll go in tomorrow, see what I can work out with Bennie. I'll give the boys a few days to get stone-cold sober and consider the error of their ways, then I'll bail 'em out. But this is the end of the line for Six-Toes. I should've sent that beer-sponge packing years ago.*

Forget Mr. Moon's thoughts—Daisy Perika has appeared on the porch. Toddling along at a sprightly pace for one of her years, she takes a seat on the swing, gives the plank floor a brisk heel-kick. Back and forth she goes. What she's up to, nobody knows.

Scott Parris took his eye off the artificial bait long enough to smile at Charlie Moon's aunt. "Nice afternoon."

She nodded. "Yes it is." *Nice and warm.*

"Hope you're feeling good."

A sly little smile. "I'm doing all right."

"That's good." The witty conversationalist returned his attention to the red woolly-popper, made the final tie. Imagining that he was a famished trout, he took an appraising look at his work. *That looks better'n any worm I ever saw.*

This was one of those pleasant interludes when it seemed that everything worth talking about was in the range of Nice to Good.

Charlie, Scott—enjoy the brief moment while it lasts.

The old woman in the swing is about to do her thing.

DAISY DECIDES TO TRY FINESSE

The operative word is *try*. And add another qualifier: "to the best of her ability." Which was not all that much. Being a damn-the-torpedoes, full-speed-ahead personality, the tribal elder did not have extensive experience with such foreign concepts as finesse. Deception, innuendo, manipulation—these were the principal tools of her trade. And Daisy's shop was open for business.

So, after swinging for nigh unto sixty-four cycles, she addressed the fishermen in this manner: "Looks like a good day for fishing."

Moon and Parris responded with agreeable grunts.

Not the slightest put off by this male conversation, she continued. "Last night, I had an interesting dream."

Even this ominous pronouncement failed to get Moon's attention. Despite the fact that the shaman's dreams had often proved to be a portent of trouble.

Ditto for Scott Parris, who was smiling in a proud, almost fatherly manner at what he had begotten (a handsome red woolly-popper), placed it in a plastic tray, and snapped the transparent container shut.

The determined conversationalist is not discouraged by such minor difficulties as a disinterested audience. Still into the swing of things, the cunning old woman continued her monologue: "That dream helped me to remember something that's been aggravating me for weeks and weeks." She glanced at her favorite relative. "Did you ever have a dream that helped you figure something out?"

"Mmmm," Moon said. *Maybe I should fire all three of those drunk cowboys. That'd teach 'em a good lesson. And send a strong message to the rest of the hired help.*

"My dream was about these three little white girls at an arts-and-crafts fair." The shaman watched a horsefly circle her knee. *Land on me, bloodsucker, you're dead meat.* Mr. Horsefly departed. "There was prizes for the things the kids brought. Like pictures they'd made and sculptures and little clay pots and the like."

The on-the-wagon alcoholic felt a pang of conscience. *No, I guess that's a bit drastic. First, I should invite all three of those cowboys to an AA meeting. And if they don't show up, then I fire their butts.*

"One of these little girls—" Daisy pretended to recall an important detail. "Oh—did I mention they was sisters?"

The word rang a bell with Scott Parris, who was checking his spinning reel. *Sisters?* He looked up. "No, I don't think you did."

"Well, they was. Sisters, that is. All three of 'em. To one another."

"I have an older sister," the chief of police said. "Alice Anne. She went off to school in Bloomington, got trained to be a registered nurse, then married a pipe-fitter and moved to Gary. Gary, Indiana. Like in *The Music Man.*" *Seventy-six trombones—oom-pah-pah!*

Moon had closed the loop in his dismal thoughts. *There ain't been a case of hoof-and-mouth in the United States of America since 1929, and Pete Bushman ought to know better than to be spouting off about something bad as that. All it would take is a rumor or two and the Japanese would put a freeze on importing American beef, which is the best in the world.* But the rancher, who had his gaze fixed on a far horizon, knew that anything could happen and sometimes did. *If one of my beeves was to pick up hoof-and-mouth—I'd be ruined. Finished. Wiped out. Done for.* Lacking a pocket thesaurus, he was obliged to let the matter drop.

Without the least tinge of conscience, Daisy flicked an adorably cute little ladybug off her arm. "A bad thing happened at that arts-and-crafts fair." The porch swing having slowed while she dispatched the beetle, Daisy energized her pendulum seat with a superbly timed kick. "Two of them little girls got some punch from Louise-Marie—the kind she makes from her family recipe. And they got another cup for their sister. But right after the little sister drank some, she passed out—almost died." The Ute elder's voice did not betray her inner tension. "But the punch didn't bother the older sisters, or anybody else at the fair. I think the littlest sister must've had some kind of allergy."

Parris frowned. "Alice Anne couldn't eat peanut butter without getting all green around the gills. And ragweed—all Sis had to do was look at a picture of a plant in a magazine and she'd start sneezing her head off."

Which remark penetrated Charlie Moon's consciousness to provide him with a comforting thought: *I bet them steers got into some locoweed. And the one with the sore on his mouth probably got it from chompin' on a thorn or a strand of barbed wire. Bushman's getting too old to spot toxic weeds. I'll send the Wyoming Kyd and some sharp-eyed young men over to check that pasture from one end to the other.*

Daisy closed her eyes. "I thought I remembered what was in that punch. But just to be sure, I called Louise-Marie last night—and I found out that I was right. It was nothing but crushed-up ice and white cane sugar and . . ." She paused for dramatic effect and got it. *"Strawberries."*

Moon looked at his aunt. "Strawberries?"

Daisy nodded. "In the punch. That was what almost killed little Astrid. She must've been about five or six years old."

Now she had their attention. One hundred percent.

Parris: "Did you say 'Astrid'?"

Daisy repeated the nod. "Astrid Spencer." The aged woman's lips went thin. "It was her sisters—Beatrice and Cassandra—who gave her the fruit punch." She frowned at the memory. "The way old Joe Spencer yelled at them girls, I guess they must have knowed that their little sister couldn't have anything with strawberries in it. But they were just dumb kids, and wasn't paying attention." She put her feet firmly on the floor, stopped the swing. "But you'd think that after a bad experience like that, no matter how much older she got, Astrid wouldn't have ever put a strawberry in her mouth again." She smiled at her nephew, pushed herself up from the swing. "Well, I shouldn't be bothering you young men with stories about my dreams, and old-time memories. I expect you've got more important things to think about." She turned, headed for the parlor door. "Like fishing for trout." After a few steps, she stopped, turned to smile at Scott Parris. "Best bait for rainbows is *black* crickets. And don't forget to tie 'em on the hook."

He nodded, heard himself mumble, "Horsehair."

"Brown horsehair." She took two more steps, paused again, turned again, addressed the chief of police again: "Did you know Andrew Turner was getting out of the hospital today?"

Parris shook his head. *I thought he'd be in Snyder Memorial for at least another week.*

Moon presented a poker face. Kept his thoughts to himself.

Not so Daisy. Moon's aunt was happy to share the product of her cogitations. "I think his sweet little wife got tired of her man being in the hospital, and made up her mind to take care of him at home." With this parting shot, she departed. The screen door, which was held shut by a long, coiled spring, slammed behind her: *Bang!*

This awakened Sidewinder, who had been napping in

the slanting sunlight. The rangy old hound got up, gaped his mouth in a toothy yawn, sauntered by the lawmen without taking any notice of their presence.

Parris watched the big dog lope off the porch, disappear under it.

The Ute was gazing wistfully in the general direction of Lake Jesse.

The hopeful angler made a polite inquiry: "What are you thinking, Charlie?"

"Pard, I'm thinking we ought to go fishing."

• • •

FIFTY-ONE
A FAMILY OUTING

The man in the wheelchair looked up at his cheerful wife, blinked as if full comprehension of her proposal was just dawning on him. Andrew Turner repeated, word for word, what she had said, turned Bea's enthusiastic statement into an apprehensive question: "We're going on a picnic?"

"Right-o. A good stiff dose of the out-of-doors is precisely what you need." Beatrice offered up a bright, encouraging smile. "It will do you a world of good."

"But I just got home from the hosp—"

"Hold on to this while I push." She plopped a wicker basket onto his lap. The lid was closed. "And no peeking inside."

His curiosity aroused, the patient sniffed. "Fried chicken?"

She laughed. "It would appear that your nose is not working."

Thus challenged, he sniffed again. "Baked ham?"

Bea pushed him toward the open door. "Wrong again. And you'll never guess what's for dessert."

Turner gave it a try: "Apple pie."

"Afraid not."

As they passed the garage, he glanced over his shoulder. "We're not going somewhere in the car—like to the park in Granite Creek?"

"Certainly not. I know of a much better spot."

As they crossed over the driveway, approached a sturdy

redwood picnic table that was sensibly placed in a sunny, hedge-edged oval of lawn, the weak fellow smiled, and felt the initial twang of a manly appetite. When his wife passed this opportunity by, he frowned. "Where are you taking me, Bea?"

"Into yon quiet forest glen, where goat's-beard moss grows pearly moist and emerald green, where sprightly fairies dance and lithesome elves do pipe and sing."

The snobby wife was always quoting some dead person. "Who said that?"

"I blush to admit—'tis mine own." The handsome woman tossed her head in a gesture that could only be described as haughty.

They passed through a cluster of youthful aspens where a thousand-thousand waxy leaves glittered and chattered in the mild breeze and freckles of filtered sunlight sparkled on the forest floor. It was a delightful little grove, which terminated abruptly as they entered the old-growth forest, where a thick stand of blue-black spruce blocked the sunshine, producing a diffuse, eternal twilight from morning to night. As they proceeded, the silence thickened, burdened the atmosphere with a chill, gray heaviness. Moreover, the path narrowed.

This was not that Narrow Path recommended by the Teacher from Nazareth.

As their way became slightly steep, Beatrice's exertion in pushing the wheelchair was replaced by a struggle to hold it back. She began to sing. "It's a long way down . . . to old Chinatown . . . a long, long way to go."

Feeling better by the minute, her husband began to grin. After the long, dreary stay in the hospital it was good to be home again. *Maybe I should think about settling down for a while—behaving myself. At least until I can walk again. And while I recuperate, I'll have ample opportunity to make plans for the future.* The grin became a broad smile, exposing his perfect teeth. *Like what I should do with you, my healthy, wealthy wife.*

Down, down they went. A long way down. But not toward old Chinatown. The footpath intersected a long-abandoned logging road, and Bea, just as if she had been there many times before, did not hesitate. Decisively, she took a turn to the left.

Andrew Spencer did not know when he had lost the grin, but it no longer curled the slit between his nose and chin. "Ah . . . we've come quite a distance."

"Yes." His wife was absolutely—No, "cheerful" does not adequately describe her frame of mind. And the dignified, cultured woman could certainly not be portrayed as "chirpy," which suggests a frivolous, birdlike gaiety. There is no other word for her hale and hearty good humor—"chipper" is what she was.

It is not going too far to assert that even on his best day, Andrew Turner did not appreciate chipper women. It is, in fact, not going far enough. He detested them. Her jollity put him off. To put the thing bluntly, it *rankled*.

"Bea, I think we've gone quite far enough. Let's stop here and have a bite—"

"Oh, don't be such an old party-pooper." She removed one hand from the wheelchair, used it to pat his head. "We're just about there."

"We are?"

"Certainly."

And they were. Only a few yards down the logging road, the trail abruptly ended in what folks in Kentucky and Tennessee refer to as a "holler." She brought the wheelchair to a halt in a lovely little meadow that might have amounted to an acre. It was known, to those very few who had been there, as The Bottom. And indeed it was. From this place, every pathway, be it for quadruped or biped, was uphill.

Andrew Turner blinked at his surroundings and was pleasantly surprised. A small willow-bordered stream rippled along a bed of smooth, shiny rocks, terminated in a mirroring pool encased by clusters of cattails. "It's very nice."

"When we were little girls—Astrid and Cassie and me—we used to come here with our father. We would pick flowers and play hide-and-seek, and in the summertime Daddy would let us wade in the water." Beatrice took the picnic basket from his lap, began to remove the contents.

Terrifically innervated by the flower-scented air, the sweet chirping of innumerable unseen feathered friends, and his delightful imaginings of whatever delicacies his wife had prepared—especially the mystery dessert(!), the invalid was beginning to salivate. He watched his wife unfold a navy-blue cotton bedsheet, which would presumably serve as a tablecloth. But instead of stretching it out on the moist grass, she set it aside on a flat-topped granite boulder.

As she reached into the basket again, Turner leaned to see what she would produce.

Bea smiled at her famished husband and said, "Honey." No, she was not addressing her spouse. What the lady had removed was a pound-and-a-half jar of—that is correct. Honey. Tule Creek brand, of course.

Assuming (correctly) that this had something to do with the mystery dessert, Andrew smiled back. Sweets were fine at the proper time, but what he wanted up front was meat. Potatoes. Deviled eggs. Bread. Cheese. "Where's the stick-to-your-ribs grub?"

"Patience." The wife twisted the lid from the jar. While her astonished husband watched, she began to pour it out—onto a fungus-encrusted pine stump.

Turner detested waste, also puzzling behavior—and he was not one of those timid persons who prefer ignorance to asking straight-out. "What are you doing that for?"

She ignored this perfectly reasonable question.

Which struck him as bordering on rudeness. "I don't see why you're dumping perfectly good honey onto a—"

"I've been doing this every day since Charlie Moon found you alive."

His pleasant hunger was suddenly replaced by a cold, clammy unease that began to curdle in his gut. The acre of meadow had shrank to a tiny cell. The tall spruce,

seemingly loose from their roots, were closing in on him.
"Uh—Bea?"

She was screwing the lid onto the almost-empty jar.
"Yes, dear?"

Assaulted by a sudden rush of claustrophobic fear, Mr.
Turner attempted to clear the sawdust from his throat. "I
don't know what's the matter . . . but all of a sudden, I'm
not feeling so good."

"Really?"

"Yes. I think we should go home now."

She turned wide eyes on her husband. "What about our
lovely picnic?"

"I'm sorry, precious. I seem to have lost my appetite."

Her tone was mildly scolding: "After all the trouble I've
gone to?"

He patted his flat tummy. "I'm feeling kind of . . .
well . . . queasy."

"Poor thing." She had switched to a cooing, motherly
sympathy. "You really don't want anything to eat?"

Thinking that perhaps he ought to humor this strange
creature, Turner forced a faint smile. "Well, maybe just a
little dessert."

"Dear me—haven't you guessed?" She removed a second jar of honey from the basket.

"Guessed *what*?"

"I am disappointed in you, Andrew." Beatrice was now
behind him. "You should have figured it out by now." Un-
screwing the lid from the second jar of Charlie Moon's favorite brand of honey, she said, "*You* are dessert." She
tilted the jar. A long, amber stream of honey dribbled
down. Onto his head. Over his forehead. Along the back of
his neck.

His voice cracked: "Bea . . . what on earth are you
doing?"

"In your natural state, you are hardly sweet enough to
be considered tasty." She watched gravity pull at the
viscous liquid. "If you were not such a self-centered

oaf—*Andrew*—you might have realized that I was onto you. Ever since that last day of our honeymoon—when you told me that Astrid snacked on strawberries—I have not once addressed you as 'Andy.'"

"I don't understand." This was half true. Under the circumstances, the wife's reference to Astrid and strawberries was downright alarming. As to her abandonment of the familiar "Andy," he had thought that odd, almost too formal—even for Bea. But, like many husbands, Andrew Turner had given up trying to understand his wife. This was to be his downfall. "Listen to me, precious—whatever is bothering you, I'm sure we can talk it out." He took a lick at honey dribbling down his nose, dripping over his lips.

Beatrice was putting the empty jars into the picnic basket. "As delightful as it would be to chat for a while, I must be leaving." She glanced at the darkening sky. "Bears are very punctual creatures. They will be coming soon—looking for their nightly snack on the stump." She offered a rhetorical question: "Won't they be pleasantly surprised to find what's new on the menu."

Turner's white-knuckled hands gripped the wheelchair arms. He searched for a suitable protest, came up with the timeworn "You'll never get away with it!"

"You don't think so?" The lady's brow furrowed with concentration, as she reviewed her plot. "I do not wish to be argumentative, but I am inclined to disagree—having worked this out with considerable care, I believe my chances are rather good. I have prepared and rehearsed so many plausible explanations for this terrible tragedy that I can hardly decide which one suits me best. I do admit this—when your remains are discovered and the grisly similarity between your fate and Astrid's becomes apparent, it is probable that suspicions will be raised. But there will be no evidence whatever of my involvement in your untimely passing." She smiled at her wild-eyed husband. "You, on the other hand, do not have—what is the quaint expression? Oh yes, 'a snowball's chance in hell.' You will be ripped to shreds well before the sun comes up again."

Bea heard a twig break in the forest. "Perhaps even before it goes down." She patted his hand. "Well, I must be off now—talley-ho." She started to go, paused, leaned close to her wedded mate. "When the beasts come, and start licking the honey off your face—" she licked a drop off his ear, "I hope you will remember poor Astrid, and the strawberries you used to lure the bears into her bedroom." She stood up straight. "If you had taken proper interest in my sister, you might have learned that your lovely wife was extremely allergic to strawberries."

So that's it. But how was I supposed to know. . . . "Bea, please listen to me—"

"Andrew, I am not the least bit interested in anything you have to say." She bit her lower lip. "Unless you wish to make a full confession of your misdeeds."

The drowning man grabbed at this sliver of driftwood. "If I did admit to doing some things that I very much regret, would you—"

"Would I reconsider my plan to leave you to the mercy of the wild animals?" She seemed to mull it over. "Yes. Yes, I suppose there's a small chance that I might."

"Okay, then." He took a deep breath. "I hardly know where to start."

She made a suggestion: "Begin with your first wife."

This was like a slap in the face. "Why—whatever do you mean?"

"You know very well that I refer to April Valentine."

"Oh—*that* first wife." Never a quitter, the desperate fellow gave it his best shot: "I can explain why I thought it unwise to mention poor April—"

"Oh, shut up, Andrew." *Perhaps I should have just pushed his wheelchair into the Devil's Mouth.* "On the day when Cassie saw us off on our honeymoon, April's mother showed up at the airport. Mrs. Florence Valentine gave my sister a bag of newspaper clippings. Most were about the horrid death of her daughter. But not all. Some were of happier times. One of them had your picture, with April. The ecstatic bride and her smiling groom. If the poor woman had only known that she was marrying a cold-blooded—"

"Bea, April's mother is certifiably insane." He pointed a trembling finger at his accuser. "There was not a *shred* of evidence to support her preposterous suspicions that I was responsible for her daughter's tragic death. April must have fainted when she was feeding the pigs, and fallen into the pen." Seeing just a hint of doubt on Beatrice's face, he pressed the point: "Ask any insurance company actuary— they'll tell you farmwork is among the most dangerous occupations."

"Your first wife's death could have accidental." *Not that I believe it for a minute.* "It is entirely possible that you had nothing to do with it."

"Your sister must have realized that." He trembled with inner rage. "But Cassandra was determined to create a scandal—publicly humiliate me."

Beatrice nodded. "Cassie was always terribly impetuous. I tried to talk her out of her absurd scheme. Imagine, pretending that she was communing with your first wife's vengeful spirit. But she thought that if she managed to unsettle you, you might do something foolish—something that would provide evidence of your guilt." She closed the lid on the picnic basket. "But you didn't react as Cassie had hoped. Rather than panic, you decided to discredit our family psychic. You sent Cassie that phony e-mail— announcing your death by violence. What did you have in mind? No, don't tell me. Let me guess. You planned to wait until Sis had received the phony 'message'—which she would assume had been forwarded by Nicky Moxon. I'm guessing you would have been across the street from her home, in the Corner Bar, watching your victim on TV— waiting for her to make the dramatic announcement of your death. No doubt, you and some of your boozy friends would have a good laugh at my sister's expense. And then, you would have crossed the street, entered Cassie's home to announce that reports of your demise were 'greatly exaggerated.'" When he opened his mouth to protest, she said, "Don't bother to deny that you sent the e-mail, Andrew. That devious little plot had your grubby fingerprints all over it." Her eyes were orbs of blue ice. "It was quite a coincidence that, on that particular evening, your prophecy came so close to being fulfilled." *And should have been.* "By the way, if you don't mind satisfying my curiosity—how did you discover that Cassie was receiving clandestine messages from Nicky Moxon?"

He was too proud of that accomplishment to be coy about it. "I hacked into her computer. Found copies of Moxon's encoded e-mails—and passwords."

"Ah—I should have guessed."

Turner continued in a repentant tone: "I don't know why I did such an absurd thing, Bea. I must have been out of my mind. Crazy."

She arched both eyebrows. "The accused chooses to plead insanity?"

"Yes. Yes I do." He added quickly, "Not for April's death—I had nothing whatever to do with that. But sending your sister the e-mail while she was on TV—it was a lunatic thing to do."

"I quite agree. And it was also very mean-spirited. But considering Cassie's alleged communion with April Valentine's spirit, I suppose you had a right to retaliate." She patted him on the cheek. "So don't give it another thought. Consider yourself forgiven."

Relief flooding over him, he said, "Thank you, Bea. Thank you for being so understand—"

"There is, however, the matter of Astrid's death."

"But—"

"But me no buts, Andrew. You have used up your allowable quota of lies. I simply cannot tolerate another one." The judge, jury, and executioner cocked her pretty head. "But if you come clean—and I mean *squeaky clean,* I might find it in my heart to forgive all. And even, as time passes, to forget." She pointed a finger at his nose. "But do not cut any corners. I assure you—aside from a few minor details, I know precisely what you have done. I merely want to hear it from your own mouth. Clear the air between us, so that perhaps . . . we can go on from here."

Turner was grateful for this one last chance. "Very well."

"Defendant shall have three minutes." She consulted an exquisite diamond-studded wristwatch. "You may begin."

He cleared his throat for the recitation. "There were things about your younger sister that you didn't know. Astrid was making my life miserable. She was insanely jealous. Listened in on my telephone calls, checked to verify where I'd been. And I'm sure you never had a hint of this—Astrid even thought she was hiding it from me. She had become an alcoholic. Poor thing was sipping martinis before breakfast."

"Really?"

A glum nod. "She kept a half pint of Jack Daniels concealed in the drawer of her antique sewing machine. Finally, it became more than I could stand. I tried to reason with your sister, convince her to submit herself to therapy, but it was no use. Once, in desperation—and I'm ashamed to admit this—I even brought up the subject of divorce. Astrid went wild with rage, and threw a wine bottle at me!" He paused, as if to rid himself of the bitter memory. "I felt hopeless, trapped in a failed marriage. In an attempt to regain some level of sanity, I started going on long walks into the forest." Turner frowned. "I suppose the seed must've been planted on one of my strolls. I found a deer carcass—a cougar kill, I imagine. But there was evidence that a bear had been feeding on it. I remember thinking . . . 'If that unfortunate deer had been my alcoholic wife, we would both be better off.' From that moment on, I began to bait the forest nearer and nearer to our home with fruit." A wistful sigh. "At first, it was merely a game—therapy for my troubled mind. But day by day, as the bears got closer to the house . . . I began to think of the exercise as something real. Something I could actually accomplish . . ."

"And on the day of her death, before you left for Denver, you left strawberries in her bedroom."

"Yes," he said. "On a paper napkin, under her bed." *But if you're thinking of telling the DA about this forced confession, it won't do you a bit of good.*

"And you jammed her bedroom window, so it wouldn't shut."

He gazed at Beatrice's face for some sign of pity. "I was under unimaginable stress. I'm so terribly sorry—please believe me."

"Oh, I do."

This was too good to be true. "You do?"

"I believe you're a terribly sorry *liar,* concocting all that nonsense about Astrid. My little sister and I had a telephone conversation almost every day. There were no secrets between us." Her look could have frozen bubbling lava. "You fed your first wife to the pigs to acquire her five-hundred-acre farm, and used the proceeds to set yourself up in business in Granite Creek." She shushed his protest with a wag of the finger. "You arranged my sister's death with the expectation that you would inherit Yellow Pines. Poor Andrew—that must've been quite a bitter disappointment for you."

• • •

It shall be mentioned that this small drama had an audience of several dozen creatures. Including some who qualified as *Homo sapiens.* For example, those ardent anglers who—at Daisy Perika's prodding—had denied themselves a few cherished hours of night fishing to do their duty. Which compelled them to shadow Beatrice Spencer and her husband.

Some forty yards away, Charlie Moon and Scott Parris were belly-down on the ground, concealed in a thicket of chokecherry, bitterbrush, and fairy-comb ferns. The chief of police shook his head. "Charlie—can you *believe* this?"

The Ute nodded. Appreciatively. *What a woman!*

• • •

Beatrice hooked the picnic basket handle onto her arm, looked beyond the clearing, deep into the inky shadows. "It is beginning to get dark, and that's when the hungry bears come out, so I really must say goodbye." She raised a hand, wriggled fingers to simulate a wave.

"But—you said if I would confess that you'd reconsider . . . you promised."

"Au contraire; I said that I *might* reconsider."

His shrill shriek was filled to the brim with unabated hatred: "You filthy, lying bitch!"

"Ah, now the real Andrew Turner appears." She turned away. "Give the famished bruins my bon appétit. Ta-ta."

"Wait . . . I'm sorry, Bea." He banged his fists on the wheelchair armrests. "Please don't leave me here all alone!"

Like his life, Turner's words were wasted.

His wife had departed, leaving a cold, cruel emptiness in her wake. The response to his pleading was a chill twilight breeze—a melancholy sigh in the spruce, a sorrowful whine in the pines.

• • •

Scott Parris whispered to his Ute friend, "Well what do you make of that?"

"Pard, ask anybody who knows yours truly, and they'll tell you Charlie Moon may be a lot of things—but he's not a fella who leaps to conclusions." A thoughtful pause. "But it looks to me like the honeymoon is over."

• • •

FIFTY-TWO
CLOSE COMBAT

Scott Parris made this observation: "Bea figures she's pulled off what them hack mystery writers call a 'perfect crime.' "

The Ute nodded. "Way the lady tells it, she took her invalid husband on a stroll in the forest, intending to treat him to a nice little picnic. Only when they got there, she remembered that she forgot something essential. Like maybe—"

"Pickles," Parris said.

"Okay. Let's say sweet baby gherkins. So she says, 'Tarry here a few minutes, sweetie-pie, whilst I return to our cozy twenty-room bungalow and glom onto a fresh jar of Mrs. Vlasic's finest.' And he says—"

"Wait a minute."

"What?"

The chief of police pointed out a flaw in Moon's plot: "That won't explain how he got the honey poured all over his head."

"Yes it will, if you won't interrupt me for about sixteen microseconds."

"Sorry."

"Apology accepted." Moon gathered his thoughts, commenced to splice the broken storyline. "So she says: 'Tarry here a few minutes, sweetie-pie, whilst I return to our cozy twenty-room bungalow and get a fresh jar of Mrs. Vlasic's finest.' And he says, 'But I'm a poor, sickly cripple in a wheelchair—if you leave me here all alone, I might get et by a bear.' And she says, 'Don't be such a scaredy-cat, Andrew—there ain't been no scumball-eatin' bears in these woods for years and years.' And off she goes, skippin' back home like the darlin' little wife she is, to get the cucumber condiments. But her husband gets despondiment and decides to prove her wrong even if it kills him. So, to up his chances of being a bear's supper, he twists the lid off the honey jar, pours it right on his head and—"

"Charlie, that's downright silly."

"Yes it is. And so's your objection to the lady's devious plot. See, after the bears get finished with Turner, there won't be enough left of the fella to find any hide or hair on, much less honey."

Parris recalled the grisly remains of Astrid Spencer. "Good point."

"And even if his corpse was found soaked in honey, no-body could prove it was his wife that put it on him."

"But, Charlie—both of us watched her do it!"

"That's a fact. But beside the point."

"Please tell me why."

"Because you and me won't be telling a solitary soul what we saw or heard here."

"Please tell me why again."

"Because if we did, the lady would very likely be charged with a serious crime."

"Excuse me, Charlie—but I kinda figured that was the whole idea."

"Scott, you got to look deeper into the matter. If all we had here was a ticked-off woman setting up her innocent husband to be a carnivore's supper, a murder charge would be just the thing that was called for." The Ute paused to lis-ten to a noise in the forest. "But this particular husband fed his first wife to the pigs and his second one to the bears— just so he could get title to some real estate. And if Beatrice doesn't see that justice is done, Turner'll get away with *both* of those killings—clean as a whistle."

Parris was beginning to get the gist of it. "Because even

though we heard him admit to Bea how he lured the bears to her sister's bedroom, that so-called confession was what the DA will define as 'under duress.' "

"Which it dang well was."

"But you and me, we know Andrew Turner's guilty as a fat man with his hand in the cookie jar and—"

"Sure we do. Which leaves us with only two options. Neither of 'em much fun to think about."

Parris blinked. "You suggesting we walk away, leave Turner for the bears?"

"Nasty as it is, that plan gets *my* vote."

"Well I say we get him out of here before the—"

"Shhh." Moon touched his companion on the shoulder. "Listen."

Scott Parris strained both ears. "I don't hear nothing." And then he did. Something coming through the woods. Something that did not bother to keep quiet. Something big and bad and unafraid. This was top of the food chain. He muttered under his breath. "Jeepers—it must be a bear come for the honey."

The Ute was listening carefully to the creature's approach. *That's a bear, all right.*

The chief of police reached for his shoulder holster. "I don't care what Turner's done—I'll have to shoot it."

Moon caught his first glimpse of the hairy, four-legged forager, shook his head. "You take a pop at it with that little .38, you'll just make it mad."

"But we can't just do *nothing*."

"Pard, have you ever tangled with a hungry bear?"

"No, I haven't, but—"

From the man in the wheelchair came a pitiful, lost-soul wail that made the lawmen's skin crawl and prickle.

"Charlie, we have to do something—beat it off with a stick—anything!"

"We are doing something." *Letting nature take its course.*

The bear, trotting along on all fours, was a big-shouldered black with a cinnamon stripe running the length of its bristled back.

His thin arms raised in a futile attempt at defense, Turner was whimpering.

Parris remembered his friend's big horse-pistol. "Charlie, you can stop it with your .357."

Within a few yards of the source of the sweet scent, the beast saw the creature in the wheeled chair. Puzzled by such a novel spectacle, the animal raised its long snout, sniffed.

Charlie Moon had a hard decision to make. He reached for the Ruger revolver, cocked it, closed his left eye, laid a bead dead-center on the animal's chest, all his thoughts coming during the intake of a breath. *If I fire a shot over the bear's head, maybe that'd scare it off.* Or a sudden, loud noise might make it charge. He tightened his finger on the trigger. *God, I wish I didn't have to do this—*

Prayer answered.

The Ute's one-eyed field of view was blocked by the backside of another hairy something. Big one. Twice the size of its opponent. And the slugger in the near corner meant business. Legs firmly planted on the moss, it crouched slightly forward as if ready to pounce. The newcomer had taken a stand—between the bear and the defenseless man.

The black bear was surprised at this development. Perhaps even startled. But not greatly impressed.

Scott Parris was impressed. Greatly. His jaw had dropped to his collar. He managed to get it back in the hinge, and in a croaky whisper urged, "Shoot, Charlie—kill 'em both!"

But his friend, who recognized the new player, had lowered the pistol. The game was out of his hands.

• • •

On his hind legs, standing straight as a lodgepole pine, the bear eyed this aggravating barrier betwixt him and supper, rumbled a guttural growl.

The response was immediate and unequivocal: "Hhhnnngh!"

Mr. Bear displayed a magnificently clawed paw, made a warning swipe.

Bobbie Sue raised a ham-size fist, in which was clenched a club large enough to stun a three-ton mammoth.

The preliminary gestures were over. The main event was about to begin.

Mr. Bear made a lunge, the huge woman in the grizzly skin made a swing.

What followed was something the likes of which this forest had never seen. Howls, yowls, claws a-slashing, bludgeon a-bashing, bodies a-rolling, teeth a-snapping, bones and saplings fracturing, blood and spittle spraying, then—the opponents parted.

Armistice.

The formidable warriors circled the small battlefield, clockwise. Eyed each other. Mumbled. Muttered. Grumbled. Gurgled. Reverse circled.

The bear bared his teeth, showed her the extended paw with bloodied claws. Growled.

Bobbie Sue reached inside her hairy garment. Showed him the shiny blade of a Bowie knife. Unbloodied, but thirsty.

Upon a telepathic exchange of signals, the circling stopped.

The black bear, who had somewhat lost his appetite, snarled.

Bobbie Sue, who had never been in such a scrap, coughed up a "Hhhnnngh!"

The animal eyed the woman. *I can take you.*

Her beady black eyes stared back. *C'mon then. Show me whatcha got.*

Not a creature-sound in the forest.

Charlie Moon, who had never witnessed such a wonder, was transfixed.

Scott Parris was not entirely there. His consciousness had slipped away elsewhere. All he could see was a self-induced hallucination orchestrated to match his superstitious expectations. But he could hear his wristwatch. *Tick-tick.* And feel his heart pump. *Thump-thump.*

The bear glared.

Tickety-tick. Thumpity-thump.

The mountain woman glared back.

Tickety-clickit.

Hairy bear snarled.

Clickety-clickit! Thumbumpity BUMP!

Hairy Woman snarled louder.

Something just *had* to happen to put an end to this. . . .

It did.

Bobbie Sue slowly raised the Bowie knife to her face, drew the razor-edged blade under her nose, licked up the ooze of blood, smacked her lips. "Hhhnnngh!" She spat a crimson stream at the bear's right eye! Hit it, too. Dead-center.

Enough was enough.

Señor bear blinked. Cocked his head.

Bobbie Sue grinned. Blood dripped off her chin.

Deciding to call it a draw, her worthy opponent dropped to all fours, and—like a chunk of black chocolate pitched into a boiling, bubbling candy pot—melted away into the night.

The bloodied victor turned to gaze upon her prize.

What she saw was Andrew Turner, in the wheelchair—gazing back at her. With bland expression, blind eyes. Bobbie Sue turned, vanished like a shadow into midnight.

• • •

Parris's heart was knocking against his ribs. "Charlie—that was the damnedest thing I ever did see!"

"It was some scrap, all right." Moon holstered his pistol.

The white man was waving his arms. "At first, I thought the big one was another bear."

The Ute cocked his head. "And now you don't?"

He glared at the Ute. "Don't mess with me, Charlie."

Moon had put on a puzzled expression.

Parris pointed toward the field of battle. "Tell me this—did you ever see a bear whip out a hunting knife?"

"No." *Puzzled* was replaced by *concerned*. "Did you?"

The chief of police wagged the pointing finger at his deputy. "You know damn well I did." The finger froze as he tried to organize his jumbled thoughts. "Uh—what I mean is I *didn't*. That's the whole point—*bears don't use knives.*"

Moon smiled at a fond memory: "Few years ago in Kansas City, I saw a little chimpanzee in a sailor suit eat a peeled banana."

"So what?"

"He used knife and fork."

"Dammit, I don't care if he—"

"After lunch, he rode a blue tricycle and tooted on a brass trumpet."

"Charlie—read my lips. I don't want to hear about some silly ape in KC. You're changing the subject because you know that big one wasn't no bear!"

"Then what was it?" Moon grinned. "The big Doo-Dah you thought you saw in the snowstorm—totin' a burrito big enough to choke a buffalo?"

"Make fun of me if you want to." Parris jutted his chin. "But it *was* that big Doo-Dah that fought the bear!"

"Hey—if that's your story, stick to it." Moon brushed a dead leaf off his sleeve. "But don't mention me being here with you."

"Charlie, I saw a sure-enough Bigfoot and you're my best friend and you've got to back me up!"

"Even if you're hallucinating?"

"Damn right!" Parris tapped a finger on his best friend's chest. "Code of the West."

"Okay, then. Write it all down in your official report. I'll say you must've gotten a better look at that big bear than I did." The Ute set his jaw like steel. "And when all those beer-soaked barflies and pool-hall louts start poking fun at you, they'll have me to answer to."

Parris blinked. *I'd be laughed out of town.* His eyes narrowed. *I'll come back with my deer rifle, hunt it down.*

Charlie Moon knew what his friend was thinking.

• • •

During all the commotion and excitement, the lawmen had forgotten about the prize Mr. Bear and Miss Bigfoot had been fighting over. No matter. They would soon discover that the man in the wheelchair was no longer with them. Only the husk remained. From a purely physiological perspective, Beatrice Spencer's husband had expired on account of a heart that refused to pump. But Andrew Turner's life had been whisked away by claws that slash, teeth that bite, that nameless terror that comes by night.

• • •

FIFTY-THREE
AFTERMATH

Upon returning on the following morning to find out what had happened to her husband, Beatrice Spencer was gratified to find him dead, but the lady was surprised and also dismayed to find the corpse without a mark of tooth or claw. A lady who lays careful plans for a picnic hates to see them go awry. It may have been because she was miffed that she spoke so unkindly to her silent spouse: "It just goes to show, Andrew—what a distasteful man you are. Even with honey on your head, hungry bears pass you by." The mention of the honey raised a sticky issue: *This is going to be such a bother.* But there was no other way. Beatrice Spencer hiked back home for the necessities. Upon her second return, she gave the corpse's head and shoulders a thorough cleaning, paying particular attention to his matted hair.

Please forgive an aside. By mere chance, she happened to have just the item, purchased at a small import shop in Colorado Springs that specializes in fragrant candles and soaps. Also shampoos of every fruity, flowered scent— from Apricot Nectar to Zinnia Sunrise. Including Strawberry Surprise.

• • •

Six days later, Andrew Turner's death would be officially listed as stress-induced cardiac arrest.

The infinitesimal traces of honey on his scalp had gone unnoticed by the medical examiner. But Doc Simpson did catch a whiff of that other scent. Leaned closer. Got a stronger whiff. *Eeew! What kind of a man would wash his head with sissy stuff like that.* Not one to give the dead any slack, the crotchety old physician scowled at the offending cadaver. *If I was to run out of Old Leather or .45 Caliber, I'd let my hair go dirty as a toilet-bowl brush before I used a ladies' shampoo.*

• • •

FIFTY-FOUR
THE WIDOW

Surprised at how lonely she was without a man in the house—even a mate with such serious shortcomings as Andrew Turner—Beatrice Spencer was soon hankering for a suitable replacement. It was not necessary for the widow to compile a list of eligible bachelors and consider them one by one. She already had a certain *someone* in her sights. Yes, that's right.

Beatrice spent days on end thinking about her quarry. She was, as she had demonstrated, a calculating woman. As she excused the man's minor minuses, added up his substantial pluses, she arrived at a nice round sum. Charlie Moon was first-rate husband material. A man a woman could depend on. On top of that, the Ute cowboy could not be described by the cruel epithet that authentic stockmen reserve for a certain class of city-bred hobby ranchers, i.e.: "All Hat, No Cows." Moon owned the two largest ranches in ten counties, and word had it that both the Columbine and the Big Hat turned a modest profit. *And he's rather good-looking.* Her pretty smile glowed. *And I do believe Mr. Moon is interested in me.* The woman did not know *how* she knew. But know she did. It might have been how attentive Charlie Moon had been at Andrew's funeral, the intense look in his dark eyes when he took her hand in his, expressed his sorrow over the recent loss of both her sisters. *Odd, though, how he didn't even mention my husband's death. It's almost like he senses that I'm better off without Andrew.* One speculation tends to lead to another. *Perhaps Charlie Moon and I are kindred souls, linked by Fate's invisible chain to meet in life after life, again and again.* The artist was a definitely a romantic. But as she had demonstrated in dealing with Andrew, Bea also had her let's-get-down-to-business side.

The business at hand was this: *One way or another, I must finagle an encounter with Mr. Moon.* One way was to pick up the modern version of that marvelous nineteenth-century invention, punch in the bachelor's telephone number. Another was to invite him to dinner. She decided to do both.

• • •

Eyeing the caller ID, Charlie Moon picked up on the third ring. "Good morning, Miss Spencer."

Miss Spencer. Beatrice liked that. "And a good morning to you, Mr. Moon." An embarrassing moment followed. The lady had forgotten what she had intended to say. "Uh . . ." This was a start. But not a good one.

Moon to the rescue: "I'm glad you called."

"You are?"

"Sure."

"Why?"

He had no intention of revealing his number one reason. Went straight to reason number two. "Well, I was kinda hoping you might invite me over for a meal."

"Consider yourself invited to dinner. Tomorrow evening. Show up at six."

"Sorry. No can do."

"You can't?"

"I'm planning on having supper here at the Columbine. With a very special lady friend of mine."

"Oh." (This was a twenty-below-zero *Oh.*) "Then you already have a date." Ouch. *Why did I have so say* date?

"I sure hope so." Moon explained the complication: "It depends on whether or not she says yes to my invitation."

"Let me get this straight, Mr. Tact. I've just asked you to my home for dinner, and you've turned me down flat—just on the *off chance* that this 'special lady'—kindly consents to dine at the Columbine?"

"Couldn't have said it better myself. So what do you say?"

"I say you certainly have a lot of nerve—" Full stop. Dead silence, while the lady thinketh. *Hmmm.* Little brain wheels turneth, grindeth fine the gristy gist of Moon's remarks. *Did he just*—"Charlie, did you just invite me to dinner at your place?"

"No."

"Oh." (Forty below) *I could strangle him with my bare hands.*

"Dinner's too fancy for the Columbine. I invited you to *supper.*"

With the sunshine smile cometh the heart thaw. "Mr. Moon—you are a most exasperating man."

"So I've been told. Pick you up about six?"

"It's a date." Forehead slap. *Date—I went and said it again!*

• • •

FIFTY-FIVE
AGENDAS (HIS AND HERS)

The setup was perfect.

In the parlor, Strauss was spinning on the CD player. Barely audible strains of the "Wine, Women and Song" waltz drifted into the dining room, which would have been dark had it not been for thin flames perched upon a pair of ivory candles, whose soft glow flickered on the white linen tablecloth. The grilled almond-crusted trout served with lightly buttered wild rice and thinly sliced marbled rye toast—was absolutely first-rate. And the peach cobbler with hand-cranked vanilla ice cream (both desserts courtesy of the foreman's wife)—what can be said. Sufficient praise would exhaust all superlatives.

During the meal, they chatted about this and that. Charlie Moon's time with the Southern Ute Police Department. What he'd done—and hoped to do—with his beef-cattle business. Beatrice Spencer shared stories of childhood. Her formidable parents. And her sisters, of course—when they were young and death seemed a million years away. Though unmentioned, the recent calamities in her life hung like a dismal fog over the conversation.

Though Beatrice had not had a bite since a breakfast of green tea and a blueberry muffin, she barely picked at the delicacies. Since receiving Charlie Moon's invitation to an evening meal at the Columbine, the recently bereaved widow had quite lost her appetite. For food. But from time to time, she would eye the lean man across the table. Lick her lips.

Armed with fork, knife, and spoon, Mr. Moon had cleaned his plate. He was thinking about a tasty dessert. No, not the pie and ice cream. He wondered how Sweet Thing was getting along. *When's the last time me and Lila Mae talked?* Sometime last month. *It's about time I gave her a call.*

Bea shot the cook another look. *He's gotten quiet all of a sudden. Like there's something he wants to say, but can't quite decide just how.* She was a very perceptive woman. Up to a point. "It was very thoughtful of you to attend Andrew's funeral."

Her host was about to speak, substituted a shrug.

She tried again: "It's very lonely, up on the mountain—all by myself. But of course you would understand." She took a dainty sip of coffee. "You live alone in this big house."

Moon nodded. *And for way too long.* "I'm glad you could come for supper."

His words fluttered the candle flames. Also her heart. She held her breath. Then: "May I call you Charlie?"

"Only if I can call you Bea."

Her laugh was like little bells. Little *silver* bells. *I might as well ask him outright.* "Charlie, why did you invite me to dinner?" She corrected herself: "I mean supper."

"Why?" He offered her a bowl of mints, was politely declined, chose his words with care. "Why, for the pleasure of your company."

"How kind of you to say so."

"But that's not the only reason."

She set her cup aside. "Oh, do tell me more!"

"Well, it's like this." Moon looked her straight in the eye. "You're the kind of woman I like. A real go-getter."

Go-getter? "I like you too, Charlie."

"I'm glad to hear it." *But before the evening's over, you're likely to change your mind.* "Bea—there's a matter we need to talk about."

"Involving you and me?"

"Well, yes." *And my buddy Scott. And your dead husband.* "Way I see it, we need to clear the air. Get some things sorted out."

Both her eyebrows arched. "Gracious—that sounds rather ominous."

It was. And he intended to ease into it. "I'd like to make you a proposition."

Oh, my—and I thought he was shy! She placed both hands in her lap, crossed two sets of fingers. Lied: "I hope your intentions are honorable."

A brief smile passed over Moon's face. "It has to do with Mr. Turner."

"Yes. I see." *He's concerned that I am still in love with Andrew—that my husband's cherished memory would be a barrier between us. What a lot of rot!* She cleared her throat, began: "I want to assure you that any lingering affection for my lately deceased spouse will not be an issue." Eager to assure the startled man, Bea hurried on: "Though Andrew did have his positive attributes, we were basically incompatible." Raising a hand to prevent Moon from interrupting, she provided a for-instance: "If I had known how little he cared for art—how brutally he would criticize my best efforts—I would have never consented to the marriage. Believe me, Charlie—"

"I do believe you, Bea. And I like your pictures."

Wide-eyed: "You do?"

He helped himself to a mint. "During the past couple of weeks, I've lost count of how many art galleries I've visited. I've looked at dozens of your paintings." *Now I could spot one at thirty yards.*

This revelation was almost too much. "You actually sought out examples of my work?"

"You bet. And I bought some watercolors you did when you were a kid."

Each eye was wetted by a single tear. "That is so sweet of you!"

Moon felt his face blush. "Well—I wouldn't say that."

"Well of course it was!"

It was time to face the unpleasant task head-on. The lanky man unfolded his angular frame from the chair. "How about I give you a tour of the house."

"I can hardly wait." She dabbed a napkin at immaculate lips. "Where shall we begin?"

He helped Beatrice from her chair. "Upstairs."

"What's on the upper level?"

"My office. Three bathrooms. Six bedrooms."

"Ah." She took his arm. "Do you sleep upstairs?"

"Every night of the week. Would you like to see where?"

"Yes. I would."

Down the twilight hallway they go. Into the huge parlor, where piñon flames flicker in a sooty fireplace. Two big boots and a pair of lady's slippers pad across the thick wool carpet. At the foot of the stairway, they pause. The gentleman waits for the lady to precede him to a higher altitude. She is rooted to the floor.

Uh-oh. She's got an inkling I'm up to something.

"Charlie, I must ask you a question."

"Go right ahead."

"When we go upstairs, is something very important going to happen?"

Yep. The smart lady's onto me. "Well, you can never tell." This was truer than he knew.

Bea took a deep breath. Spent it on a sigh. "Will what happens upstairs change my life—forever and ever?"

He gazed at the upturned face. *She's pretty as a peck of peaches. And she's afraid something bad is going to happen.* "Tell you what—let's skip the tour of the house. We can go sit in front of the fire. Or if you want to go home, I'll take you right now."

"No." She took his big hand in hers. Squeezed it. "We will go upstairs." *To your bedroom.* "But on one condition."

"What's that?"

"I shall go like Scarlett."

"Who?"

"Scarlett O'Hara."

He was an old-movie buff. "Ah—*Gone with the Wind.*"

"The very same." Tapping her finger on his chest, Beatrice Spencer expanded upon the condition: "You shall play the part of Rhett Butler."

Moon's brow furrowed. "Before we go upstairs I got to kill off a whole platoon of Damnyankees?"

Miss Scarlett put on the cutest little-girl frown. "That can wait till later." Her voice had taken on a lilting down-south drawl: "What I crave right now, Rhett, is romance." Addressing Clark Gable's reluctant stand-in, she laid down the law: "Before you take me to your bedroom, you must sweep me off my feet."

Mr. Moon was beginning to get the picture. "Bea, I don't think you un—"

"Hush your mouth." She pointed at the stairway.

"You sure you want to do this?"

Her head bobbed in a perky nod.

This is crazy. But, caught up in the moment, he snatched her up, cradled the lady like a week-old baby.

"Oh—oh!" Bea wrapped her arms around Moon's neck. Laid her pretty head on his shoulder. "Whatever are you doing, Rhett—put me down *this very instant!*" (She did not remember the lines.)

There was no figuring women. "Okay." *Down you go.*

"Don't you dare, you hateful man!" Her little fist banged his chest.

He rolled his eyes. *How do I get myself into these situations?* How, indeed. Volumes could be written.

"Hurry, darlin'—before I change my mind."

Charlie Moon was a man with limited options. Count them: one.

So up the stairs they went. Down the long hallway. Moon kneed his bedroom door open, stepped into the darkness, used an elbow to flick a light switch. The table lamp by his bed cast a yellowish glow.

"Oh!" What the lady saw, on the wall over the head of his bed, quite took her breath away. But what really caught her attention was on the night table beside Moon's bed—a framed-in-walnut photograph of a drop-dead gorgeous, dark-haired woman. Bea was fast on her feet. And off. Instantly understanding her error, stunned by what she saw, Bea's fingers gripped Moon's arm like a falcon's claw.

Those sharp fingernails biting into his flesh did not escape the man's notice. *I bet she's wondering who that is.* "That" was FBI Special Agent Lila Mae McTeague—Moon's absent sweetheart. He directed Bea's attention to the three watercolors over the head of the bed. "You do nice work."

"So do you." Scarlett was gone. With the wind, perhaps. Beatrice was back, her body stiff in his arms.

Moon steeled himself for the finale. Ever since Miss Spencer had called him about a dinner date, he had rehearsed for this moment. And so far—aside from the dubbed-in carry-me-up-the-stairs scene—things had gone pretty much to script. Now it was time to turn her around, so she could see the opposite wall where he had strung up the canvas that was two yards high, eight feet wide. His first line to the stunned artist would be: "Here's what you were looking for when you hurried back home on that snowy night when your husband had his 'accident'—and blocked your driveway so Scott wouldn't see you taking it down." What Bea would see was her unsigned masterpiece—the photo-realistic, life-size images of Andrew Turner's murdered wives, standing side by side. Astrid Spencer and April Valentine's vengeful expressions were chilling enough for Nightmare of the Week. But those two pairs of outstretched arms—inviting their murderer to come hither and *be with us where we are*—well, it was no wonder Turner ran his Corvette off the road. Moon's line two would go something like this: "When I found your husband in the mine shaft, he was wrapped in it." The widow didn't need to know that Bobbie Sue had done the wrapping; she would assume that her injured spouse had found the painting—probably ripped by the Corvette from where she had tied it across the driveway—and used it to protect himself from the cold. While she was still off balance, the Ute would reveal that he and Scott Parris had witnessed her attempt to honey up her husband for bear bait. Whether or not to arrest her had been a close call. Considering what sort of man Andrew Turner had been, she got a pass this time—but only by a whisker. From now on, she would walk the line—or suffer the full consequences of law and justice. This was about 99 percent bluff, but Bea didn't know what the lawmen had on her or what they might do with what they knew. The best poker player in umpteen counties was certain that he'd play out his hand, walk away with the pot. Which would be a solemn promise from the lady to cease and desist from plotting violent felonies.

But wait. The star of Gone with the Wind *has returned. The lovely armful relaxes, her whisper fills his ear:*

"Oh—you are so sweet!" Her arms tightened around his neck. "After poor Astrid was mauled to death by a bear, I thought I'd never get through the gloom. During my darkest days, I fell into that unfortunate marriage with Andrew." Her sigh was a fragrant, springtime breeze. Scented with cherry blossoms. Really. "Then, poor Cassie was murdered by that horrible Moxon person." Bea's voice cracked. "Now my husband is dead and I'm all alone in the world." Warm, salty tears dripped onto Moon's shirt. "It has been almost more than I can take. But just when I thought I couldn't make it through another day, you invite me to the Columbine, carry me up the stairs to show me these silly little paintings you've gone to so much effort and expense to collect—" Miss Spencer smiled through the tears. "This is the first truly happy moment I've had in ages." She planted a prim little kiss on the side of his face, fired the heavy artillery: "Charlie Moon—you are the most wonderful man in the whole world." Another kiss. "I think I love you."

Well.

What could the man do?

Tell his number one admirer that he had the goods on her—if she so much as spat on the sidewalk she'd be looking at ten years behind bars? Hardly. That shot was not on the table.

Could he reconsider? Cut his losses? Surrender? Yes indeed. Moon did all three.

The victor nibbled at his earlobe. "Do you love me—even just a little bit?"

Under the best of circumstances, that question is hard for a man to deal with. When his earlobe is being nibbled, forget it.

She noticed that her victim was having some difficulty. Thoughtfully ceased nibbling. Ruthlessly repeated the question.

Mrs. Moon's little boy Charlie could not tell a lie. "Well . . . I *like* you."

Bea closed the blue eyes again. Rested her head on his shoulder again. Sighed again. "I suppose that will have to do." *For a start.* "Now, you may take me home."

"D'you want to walk?"

"No, silly. Spencer Mountain is much too far."

"I mean . . . downstairs."

He is so *cute.* "If your arms are tired."

Evidently, they were not. He carried Bea down to the parlor. Helped her put on her coat. Escorted her to the Expedition. Drove her home. Walked her to the front door. Got a good-night kiss that would have felled a lesser man. And without a thought of the lady whose picture was next to his bed, smiled all the way back to the Columbine. The cad.

Let us leave it there. Call it a night to remember, and close the book on the Three Spencer Sisters. The End.

• • •

Footnote: For those few who care about such minutiae, a few additional details may be of interest. Or not. In any case, here they are.

Mr. Moon was not the only person who experienced a revelation upon encountering an unexpected image on a shiny surface. (We refer to his sighting of flames in the TV psychic's eyes.)

The other, more recent event occurred in this manner: When Moon carried Beatrice Spencer into his bedroom, switched on the floor lamp so that she could see the watercolors hung over the head of his bed, the startled lady fastened her fingers into his arm, and her gaze upon the framed photograph of Lila Mae McTeague. You remember this, of course.

Now think about it. Nothing comes to mind? Think again.

It still does not compute?

Then *reflect* upon it.

Aha! Quite right.

On the glass over Miss McTeague's pretty face, Bea had seen a reflected image of her murderous masterpiece—knew in a flash that the crafty tribal investigator was about to confront her with evidence of an unseemly application of fine art—and immediately launched the ruthless "You are so sweet" counterattack.

Charlie Moon (bless his honest soul) never had a chance. But his earlier appraisal had been right on the mark.

What a woman!

• • •

EPILOGUE

Whatever happened to Bobbie Sue?

We do not know. But every now and then there is an un-substantiated rumor, an unlikely anecdote. Of the latter class, the following is the unlikeliest.

Oscar "Bud" Yirty, an easygoing, hard-drinking, Columbine fence-rider known for his tale tales, *swore* to three of his bunkhouse confidants that last November, whilst he was looking to poach one of Charlie Moon's big bull elk that graze up yonder where the north pasture butts up against the Buckhorns, he had encountered "the dingety-damnedest thing I've ever seen, boys, and I'll tell you whut—if I'm a-lyin', I'm a-dyin'. I saw it all from up on Bent-Nose Crag. Now I'm not claimin' I could hear ever'thing that was said, but I sure heard enough, and I saw both of 'em through my brand-spankin'-new adjustable-power Leopold rifle scope, and I'm talkin' *in broad daylight.* There in a little clearin' in the pines, hunkered down by a campfire like they was ol' friends, was the boss with a book in his hand, readin' out loud. And sittin' on the cold ground was the biggest damn bear I ever saw. And it was leanin' for'ard—listenin' to ever single word Charlie Moon said."

After the rude laughter and vulgar abuse had died down, the patient storyteller continued without taking umbrage: "Now boys, I know for a absolute *fact* that Charlie was a-learnin' that animal from the book 'cause ever' now and then, why that ol' bear'd nod, or shake his head, an' once he even raised his paw, like he had a question to ast!" Bud paused for a sip of Bud.

His audience was won over; the utter extravagance of this appalling lie was met with the respectful silence that occurs when spectators realize they are present at a historic, once-in-a-lifetime, stem-winder performance. "And here's the real corker, boys. After I laid my rifle barrel on a rock and got me a good, steady look through the scope, I could see the cover a that book Charlie Moon was readin' from as good as I can see the hairy holes in your noses." The storyteller jutted his bristly chin, glared with bile-yellow eyes. "You know what the name a that book was?"

The mystified cowboys shook their heads.

Bud Yirty told them, "*I Learn My A-B-C's—that's* what it was!"

Well. Who would believe such an improbable tale.

NIGHTMARE

Yours? Not tonight.

This particular horror is reserved for two souls already deep in sleep—and a third who burns with a perverse appetite.

You have nothing to fear from this nasty business.

Unless . . .

Unless you should assume too intimate an interest, allow yourself to become unduly absorbed—irretrievably *entangled.*

Not a chance?

Very well.

But there are invariably some who do. A few. Perhaps one or two.

For those reckless souls, the following cautions are hereby provided.

First, a suggestion: Refrain from focusing too closely on the stark desert dreamscape—such intense concentration is likely to unduly excite the fertile imagination, which will conjure up all manner of poisonous viper, rabid rodent, and other vile nocturnal characters that slither and scuttle about in the darkness.

Second, a recommendation: Do not incline your ear to the unwary pair's sighs and groans and snores and moans, and firmly refuse to hear the lurid murmurings of the third wretched creature, who—in frantic anticipation of the atrocity—*giggles.*

Last, this warning: Remain where you are. Resist any temptation to drift off into the shadowlands, and beware any glib stranger who might invite you to witness the unsavory event. Yielding to such an enticement could prove dangerous.

• • •

While no guarantee of absolute safety is made or implied, paying close heed to the aforementioned counsel should keep you reasonably—

What—you have already crossed that beckoning boundary, are even now entering into the dismal regions?

Then it is too late.

You have purchased your share of the nightmare.

Be advised that all such transactions are final.

There are no refunds.

And no *returns*.

WHEN AND WHERE

All these big brouhahas have to get started sometime and someplace and this one commenced two summers back, about midway between Pecos and El Paso.

It was a few owl-hoots past sundown when a brand-new moon floated up to shine a fine, silvery sheen on the favored side of the mountains. Very nice. And it should've stopped right then and there, but no—like some folks you know, that two-faced satellite has a dark side, and just as it was brightening up the eastern slopes, it flooded that big dusty trough between the Delaware peaks and the Sierra Diablos with shadows, and we're not talking about a widow's veil of night shade that wouldn't keep you from seeing what o'clock it was on your granddaddy's dollar pocket watch. Nosiree, this was sure-enough mucky stuff, black as Texas Tea, too thick to churn and firm enough to slice with Mr. Bowie's knife.

If we were to wait around until that pockmarked face gets about four hours high, the murky lake would start to drain and dry and any poor soul who happened to happen by and got blinded and drowned in it would be able to see and breathe again. But this is right now and that'll be then and it's not night-meandering pilgrims we're interested in, so let's mosey on over to where the trouble's about to begin.

Watch your step, now. Don't put your foot on them prickly pears. Or that feisty little sidewinder.

See that tattered old tent over yonder?

Aim your eyeball a tad more to the left.

They're camped right beside the rusted-out pickup that's hitched to the horse trailer that's empty because just this morning the rider swapped his piebald pony for a shiny Mexican trumpet and three bottles of Patrón Reposado tequila. The feller still has the brass horn, but he's too high to toot on it and too far under to have the least notion of the serious Bad News that's about to bite him in the neck.

• • •

The forty-four-year-old woman (married, mother of one) is entwined in the arms of a broken-down old rodeo cowboy who never asked her name. Oblivious to his indifferent embrace, Chiquita Yazzi has drifted away into a twilight place. While she watches a splendid black swan glide upon a mirrored pond, a bright-eyed little girl runs along the grassy bank to hug Momma's neck. How do mother and daughter while away these blissful hours? They laugh at fluttering butterflies, sing happy songs, pick pretty flowers. In even this feeble facsimile of paradise, only the sublime should be called to mind—ugly memories should not be permitted entry. Sadly, it is not to be. The bright vision takes a dark turn into a vermin-infested alley. The mother—as only mothers can—senses danger close at hand. She instinctively reaches out to pull her child close. The little girl, a moment ago so warm—is cold to Momma's embrace.

An unhappy turn of events. But it is merely a dream, which will quickly fade from memory. What we desire is a change of scenery, so let us return to the world of flesh and blood and see what is afoot there.

For the most part, ordinary events common to the nighttime desert.

In a shallow arroyo, a scaly something glides silently by.

A melancholy breeze heaves a wistful sigh.

Inside the tent?

Already stinking of beer and sweat, the has-been bull

rider adds urine to the pungent brew. Thus relieved, he sinks ever deeper in his drunken stupor.

And the woman is . . . But what is this?

No. Don't look.

A tarantula strides oh-so-deliberately along the lady's forehead. Before moving on to explore other parts of her anatomy, the fascinated arachnid pauses—extends a bristly foreleg . . . strokes her dark eyebrow.

Altogether too dreadful? Then let us depart from the canvas shelter.

On the way out, we shall encounter the third member of this ill-fated trio.

SNAKE DREAMS

But do they, really?

This is a highly controversial subject, hotly debated among distinguished zoologists and eminent herpetologists—which shall be settled here and now. The answer is:

Yes.

They most certainly do.

The more fascinating, and not quite settled, issue is—*what* do slithery-slimy serpents dream about?

We are about to find out.

THE SERPENT'S NIGHTMARE

Underneath a shadowy sea, unseen by the rusty red moon face hanging high in the dusty West Texas sky, the night crawler watches. Waits.

Is this entity a human being? By the most generous definition—yes.

A he or a she? Moonlight has not yet illuminated the subject sufficiently. We must wait and see. What do we know with certainty?

That the assassin is cold sober, wide awake, recently bathed—and near enough to hear the woman's raspy breaths, the boyfriend's intermittent snores.

The time has come to settle scores.

Inching along on its belly, the sinister pseudoviper wriggles into the tent, rises above the intended victims. A crooked grin splits the hate-twisted face—a silvery straight razor glistens in a pale hand.

Flickity-flash!

Snickety-slash!

CENTRAL COLORADO

When the high prairie stretched between the Misery and Buckhorn Ranges transforms from snowy white to bright green, and wildflowers start sprouting up like this was a sweet little girl's happy dream, you know for sure it's springtime in the Rockies.

But is it time to start picking a bouquet of posies for the favorite lady, perhaps making plans for an alpine picnic? Let's put it this way: Don't put your long underwear in the cedar chest just yet. The weather at these altitudes doesn't care a whit about hardware-store calendars or showy spring blossoms. And genuine, gold-plated summer (if it doesn't pass by altogether) might tarry for a week or two.

At this very minute, huge, rumbling thunderheads are boiling up over the blue granite peaks and you can hear that icy wind come a-roaring down the mountain like ten thousand runaway freight trains. It's been huffing and puffing all night, whipping spruce and cottonwoods left and right.

Pete Bushman, a crusty stockman who's been with the outfit since way back then when men were men and women were mighty glad of it, has seen all kinds of weather, so when he chomps down on a big chaw of Red Man and spits and declares, "That wasn't nothin' but a cool little breeze," not one of the hired hands will argue with him. Not to his face. That might be partly because the old-timer's the foreman of the Columbine Ranch.

As might be expected, your regular cowboy who rides the wide-open spaces and mends fences tends to experience Pete's "little breezes" from a different perspective. Here's a f'r instance: "When that there wind came a-whistlin' over Pine Knob, it had a edge like a brand-new butcher knife and it was a-whacking off stalks of buffalo grass and when it took a slice at the bunkhouse, it shaved the frost right offa the winda glass!" Now that's what Six-Toes claims, and ol' Six never tells a bare-faced lie unless he has his mouth open. And even if he is touching the weather report up just a mite, that norther did rip a few shingles off the bunkhouse roof and almost shook the door off its hinges. The cold winds also kept most of the day-shift cowboys hunkered down in their bunks with the blankets pulled up to their bloodshot eyeballs.

Shameful behavior for fellows who pack six-guns, strut around like bowlegged peacocks, and generally act like they're just itching to strap a saddle on the worst Texas tornado you ever saw, and spur Mr. Twister all the way from here to Laredo.

Pete Bushman has something to say on any subject and will be glad to inform you that "today's cowhands ain't what they used to be." To hear the foreman tell it, there's only two sure-enough cowboys in this outfit—himself (naturally) and that Ute Indian by the name of Charlie Moon, who happens to be the owner of the Columbine Ranch, which makes him the big chief hereabouts.

Fact is, there are at least a dozen top hands on the Columbine who can perform any chore from shoeing a fractious quarter horse to overhauling a sixty-year-old Farmall tractor. But there is a reason for the foreman's confidence in the boss: Charlie Moon can outwork and outfight the best of his employees. And there is also this: The hardy fellow is not bothered by any kind of weather. He likes mornings that're brisk, don't you know—and *brisk* for Mr. Moon is ten below.

Which is most likely why the Ute came out onto the ranch-headquarters porch while the wind was still whipping up a fuss, sat down on a redwood bench with an old banjo, and began to pluck all five strings. Is he good? Honest reporting compels one to admit that Charlie Moon is no Earl Scruggs, but he has been working at it for months, and if practice does not always make one perfect, it generally leads to marked improvement. And as Grandpa Jones or Stringbean (bless their souls) might have observed: *That long tall drink a water sure does make that banjer ring!*

Moon could also sing. Loudly.

Which did not please everyone.

The porch where he picks taut banjo strings and croons lively bluegrass tunes is only about two stone throws from the bunkhouse down by the river, which is where a bunkhouse should be, because water rolling over rocks has a fine way of lullabying a tired man off to sleep. On the contrary, Moon's instrumental and vocal efforts have a way of waking that same fellow up. Him and all his bunkhouse buddies did not appreciate it.

Didn't matter. The sun was about to explode over the Buckhorns and it was by-gosh time to be up and at 'em.

Among those residents who did not share the Indian cowboy's brand of sunrise enthusiasm, the twanging and singing particularly annoyed Sidewinder, who, in case you two have not been properly introduced, is the official Columbine hound. At the beginning of the impromptu recital, the long-eared, sad-eyed canine was stretched out under the porch, dreaming about a mighty fine lady hound who was following him around, licking at his face. Now the dog was awake, and mightily ticked off. The Ute's booming baritone also startled a skittish little mare, who kicked a board loose in her stall.

Even way out here in the wide-open spaces, there is no shortage of critics.

The performer accepted it all in good humor. Mr. Moon was feeling good.

You want to know why?

We will tell you.

This final frigid blast of winter, which drifts down from

the Never Summer Mountains every year about this time, is potent stuff for a fellow who enjoys invigorating weather—especially on top of a breakfast of three fried eggs, a slab of Virginia ham thick as a boot sole, a heap of crispy home-fried potatoes and a quart of steaming black coffee fortified with a generous helping of Tule Creek honey. The potent combination is sufficient to persuade a pessimist that good times are just around the corner and convince a man like Charlie Moon that he is alive on one of those golden days when life is fine and dandy and that he can accomplish anything. *Anything.*

Such as persuade Lila Mae McTeague (aka Sweet Thing) to accept a diamond engagement ring.

And why not? Here on the high plains stretched between two snow-capped mountain ranges, where a rolling river rollicks and chuckles its uproarious way to the western sea, anything is possible.

Almost anything.

One hates to be heard saying a discouraging word at Moon's home on the range, but despite a hardworking fellow's best efforts, his plans will occasionally go awry. Putting it another way, the Ute has plenty of the right stuff but sometimes his best effort is not quite up to snuff.

The full-time rancher and part-time tribal investigator knows how to handle hardcase cowboys, high-spirited horses, cranky internal-combustion engines, leaky plumbing, and—when absolutely necessary—deadly weapons. Sadly, Moon's expertise does not extend to an understanding of the daughters of Eve.

Case in point—the diamond engagement ring. It is not brand new. On the other hand, the ornament has never encircled a lady's finger and so cannot be categorized as used merchandise.

It happened like this. Quite some time ago, and at considerable expense for a man of his means, Charlie Moon purchased the ornament for another charming lady. It is a melancholy story that he would just as soon forget. He particularly prefers to disremember the stunning finale, where (after refusing the ring) the potential fiancée roared away in a shiny Mercedes-Benz—spraying dust and grit in his face.

Why bring up such an disagreeable event? Surely, Charlie Moon does well to forget the bitter disappointment and move on. But, unless we are badly mistaken, the residue of that unhappy romance will come back to haunt him.

And we are not.